Additional Praise for *The*

"Mayo's novel not only offers a close look at health care at the turn of the 20th century, but also addresses the racial, class, and sexual tensions that existed alongside strict, bigoted Victorian-era standards of morality. Mayo brings her characters and settings to life with deft prose and careful research. Her descriptions of the crowded streets of New York are visceral and authentic...A compelling and diverse historical novel."
—*Kirkus Reviews*

"*The Sharp Edge of Mercy* is a stunning tale of a woman caught between the ethics of the day and the truth of the human heart. Mayo writes with enormous eloquence, transporting the reader into the distant past in a manner that feels familiar and immersive. An absolutely riveting book!"
—Crystal King, author of *The Chef's Secret* and *Feast of Sorrow*

"Connie Hertzberg Mayo's *The Sharp Edge of Mercy* tells the compelling tale of Lillian Dolan, whose aspiration to become a nurse finds her working as an assistant at the New York Cancer Hospital in turn-of-the-twentieth-century Manhattan. With Mayo's previously demonstrated skills (*The Island of Worthy Boys*) at portraying poor, disadvantaged characters rising to adversity with resilience and grace, and her thorough research, the reader is immersed and enchanted by *The Sharp Edge of Mercy*. Mayo deftly weaves Lillian's story of ambition, love, loyalty, and friendship set against challenges of race, class, disability, sexual preferences, and questions of medical ethics. This is historical fiction that anticipates many of the weightiest issues of today through an engaging read."
—Barbara Stark-Nemon, author of *Even in Darkness* and *Hard Cider*

"*The Sharp Edge of Mercy* is a powerful and gripping story of inner strength, determination, and the imbalance of power. It deals head on with weighty and relevant issues like end of life care, bigotry, medical ethics, and the uneasy bargains people make in an attempt to survive. As Lillian doggedly pursues her dream of becoming a nurse while struggling to support her sister, she perseveres despite the numerous obstacles she encounters along the way. With sharp dialogue and a rich setting, this work of historical fiction had me rooting for Lillian from the first pages."

—Emily Cavanagh, author of *Her Guilty Secret*
and *Everybody Lies*

"In her second and aptly named novel, *The Sharp Edge of Mercy,* Connie Mayo takes little-known nuggets of old New York history and weaves them into a smart and thought-provoking page-turner. As young nursing assistant Lillian Dolan discovers the scandalous secrets of the New York Cancer Hospital and its staff, she is caught between controversy and conscience in a compelling tale that will captivate lovers of historical fiction."

—Kristen Harnisch, international bestselling author of
The Vintner's Daughter series

"Rich in period detail, *The Sharp Edge of Mercy* is a deeply immersive look at a New York City hospital at the end of the 19th century. With her well-drawn characters and crisp prose, Hertzberg Mayo's novel is a treat to read. I look forward to whatever she does next."

—Stacie Murphy, author of the *Amelia Matthew Mysteries*

"In *The Sharp Edge of Mercy*, Connie Hertzberg Mayo captures the sometimes visceral realities of hospital life in 1890s New York, where friendships grow in unlikely places. Hertzberg Mayo takes readers behind closed doors, from crematoria, hidden bars, and Hell's Kitchen walk-ups to glowing upper-class firesides…. The story tackles medicine and ethics, race and class, love and identity, all embedded in a story of loyalties, trust and misunderstandings."
—Dr. Julie Collins, University of South Australia, author of *The Architecture and Landscape of Health*

"Readers who loved Addison Armstrong's *The Light of Luna Park*, and Susan Meissner's *The Nature of Fragile Things* will enjoy author Connie Mayo's story of shattering secrets, of perseverance, and of love of family above all else."
—Tracey Enerson Wood, author of *International and USA Today Best Seller The Engineer's Wife* and *The War Nurse*

The
SHARP
EDGE
of
MERCY

The
SHARP
EDGE
of
MERCY

Connie Hertzberg Mayo

 Heliotrope Books

NEW YORK

Heliotrope Books LLC
heliotropebooks@gmail.com

ISBN 978-1-942762-87-4
ISBN 978-1-942762-88-1 eBook

Cover design by Lindy Martin
Typeset by Malcolm Fisher, Naomi Rosenblatt, and Jonny Warschauer

To my mother,
who was awarded her PhD in Anatomy back in the 1970s,
demonstrating that a woman can do anything.

Other books by Connie Hertzberg Mayo

The Island of Worthy Boys

O, let him pass! He hates him much
That would upon the rack of this tough world
Stretch him out longer.

—William Shakespeare
'*King Lear*', Act 5, Scene 3

Our nurse is not like others, she is one of the elect,
Her smile and bedside manner are perfectly correct;

She never finds the day too long, nor any time to waste,
And in her leisure cultivates a literary taste;

Of humouring her patient she has a perfect knack,
And tells her when she takes a walk, "My dear, I'll soon be back."

When the doctor pays his visits, she beguiles him into chat,
And if she tries to make him smile, well, what's the harm of that?

—From *"The Exceptional Nurse"*
promotional postcards
produced in London, c1910

New York, 1890

❧ Chapter 1 ❧

Lillian jiggled her foot so impatiently that it worked its way out from under her skirts. She stilled her foot to observe it. Even without drawing it closer, she could see the sorry condition of her boot. The crease near the big toe had cracked, and the blacking she had applied last night did little to reverse a year of daily wear. On rainy days, she lined the interior with squares of newspaper to absorb the water that seeped in, but this morning the September sun beat down with a vengeance as if it were summer, which she took as a good omen. She would just have to hope that no one noticed her feet today.

That is, if she could ever leave the apartment. *Where was Mrs. Oberman?* Lillian checked the mantel clock again, which showed that it was one minute after she had last checked it. It's not as if the woman had far to travel—her rooms were on the first floor of this very building. Lillian had seen her occasionally on the stoop in the weeks since they moved here, and when this job opportunity fell into Lillian's lap, she cornered Mrs. Oberman and asked her to watch Marie this morning. But Lillian realized now she hadn't really described the nature of the job in any detail. She had planned to outline everything when Mrs. Oberman arrived and couldn't easily back out, but now it was getting late. Had she forgotten?

Lillian's stomach knotted as she imagined how crowded the El would be at this time of day, and how long her trip would be to the 103rd Street station. She had only ever been as far as 59th Street, just the southernmost part of Central Park, for Marie's birthday every year. Their mother, Helen, would pack a picnic lunch and Marie would want to touch all the trees, roll around on the grass, joyful as a pup. Helen often remarked that it was a shame Marie was born a city girl.

But Lillian forced herself to stop thinking of Helen. As far as Lillian was concerned, she and Marie had no mother.

She rose from her seat and went to check on Marie in the bedroom. *No, not the petticoat!* She rushed over to where Marie sat crosslegged on the floor, happily cutting her petticoat into ragged squares with Lillian's sewing scissors. Lillian grabbed the scissors from Marie, accidentally scraping the pointed blades across Marie's palm.

"So you got bored of the buttons, I see." When Lillian had left Marie minutes ago, she had been lining up buttons by size, a daily activity that usually occupied her for the better part of an hour. "You know I can't afford another petticoat for you. So you'll be wearing that one with these square holes. Just so you know." After they had moved to this tenement and it was just the two of them, Lillian started ed talking more to Marie, even though she knew Marie wouldn't answer. It was too quiet otherwise. And she could say anything to Marie. After all, Marie could hear perfectly well. She just didn't speak. Any secret was safe; it was like shouting your troubles down a well.

Lillian looked around for a place to hide the sewing scissors. With her back turned, she didn't hear Marie creep up behind her, and startled when Marie hugged her around the waist in her clumsy and exuberant way. Prying the arms from around her waist, she turned around and looked at Marie. When they were younger, Lillian had been wildly jealous of her sister's looks, even cutting Marie's hair while she slept one night. Lillian had taken the locks, shiny mahogany, and held them to her temple, covering her own mousy strands, pretending she sported this beautiful mane. When Helen found out the next morning, Lillian had extra chores for a week and Marie snubbed her for two, but Lillian hid the hair, tied with a ribbon, and sometimes took it out to stroke it like a cat.

At 14, Marie was now far more beautiful than she had been then, but Lillian felt no envy ever since the scarlatina took Marie's sight and part of her mind.

A knock at the door pulled Lillian out of her reverie, and she rushed to answer it. Mrs. Oberman shuffled in with a curt nod of her head and lowered herself down in a chair, easing her humped back into a comfortable position. Lillian thought she might have detected a whiff of alcohol but decided it was instead the lingering smell of some fermented food.

"Mrs. Oberman, we had agreed to half past eight this morning."

"Ach, at my age, not all the parts of the body want to cooperate so early in the morning. You're too young to understand."

Lillian had no time to explain that Mrs. Oberman's body parts should not be Lillian's problem. "Marie needs to be watched closely. You must be in the same room with her at all times." She put on her coat and checked that her keys were in the deep pockets of her skirts while she talked. "I should be back by midday. Marie likes bread and cheese for lunch, and she's already had breakfast."

There were ten other things she should tell Mrs. Oberman but she ran out the door without saying goodbye to either of them. She hoped to get down the stairs before Marie realized she was gone and started crying. She didn't need that echoing in her ears during her interview.

The bench outside the Head Nurse's office was uncomfortable, and Lillian shifted when she felt pins and needles in one leg. She had been five minutes late, a miracle that it hadn't been more; the El had arrived just as she approached the station, an omen even better than the sunny weather. But now she had been waiting on this bench for fifteen minutes. Was she being punished for being late? Or was the Head Nurse running late herself, and Lillian needn't have rushed at all? Would her interviewer be irritated with her, or apologetic?

Before she could decide which was more likely, the door opened and the Head Nurse waved her in without comment.

"I am Nurse Holt," she said as they sat down. "I am in charge of all nurses and nursing activity at the hospital." She paused and eyed Lillian carefully, looking her up and down. Lillian was thankful that the desk between them hid her shoes.

Nurse Holt finished her examination of Lillian with a barely audible "Hmm," and then looked down at a sheet of paper in front of her. "It says here you are eighteen and have an aspiration to matriculate over at the Bellevue Training School."

"Yes ma'am, but I've been told I'm not old enough."

"Certainly not, and there may be other obstacles." Nurse Holt rested her forearms on her desk. "They prefer to take girls with college experience. Many are from families of means."

Lillian wasn't sure if this was an insult or a test—had Nurse Holt spied her shoes as she had walked in? "But if I worked here as a nursing assistant, that would help to balance the scales when I go to apply." Lillian started to tremble. She didn't want to seem desperate, but in truth, this job was the only way she could see to make progress toward her goal of becoming a nurse. Her previous plan—applying to the live-in Bellevue program next year with a glowing letter of recommendation from their family physician, Dr. Pratt that would mitigate her young age—had not worked out.

"Well, that is a fine articulation of why our nursing assistant job would benefit you. But tell me, how would you benefit the New York Cancer Hospital?"

Lillian felt perspiration surface under her collar, but she hadn't traveled so far uptown to give up without a fight. "I'm a hard worker. I have a strong stomach. I'm not given to gossip with other women. I'm neat in my person and punctual." She inwardly winced at that last word, remembering her lateness this morning. But that was Mrs. Oberman's fault. Lillian had been ready to go with time to spare. Quickly, to draw attention from her comment about punctuality, she added, "And I don't mind menial work."

"You think the work we do here is menial?" Nurse Holt asked with an unreadable expression.

"No! I didn't mean to imply..." Lillian thought frantically. What was the right answer here? She could feel the sweat dampening her collar now.

Nurse Holt sat back in her chair which creaked in the silence. "As it turns out, you are correct. The tasks assigned to the nursing assistant are quite menial. Rolling bandages, changing sheets, cleaning bedpans. So I need to be clear here. You will likely not have much contact with patients. Girls that come here because they are driven to help people can be frustrated that they are not soothing fevered brows. You need to be satisfied that you are a small cog in an important wheel, and not aspire to be more than your station dictates."

"Yes, ma'am."

"You should also know that the hospital has had some minor financial hardships of late. This is merely a temporary situation, but we communicate this to the staff because we expect everyone to police for waste and inefficiency. And as you may know, the position of nursing assistant is a relatively new one, one that not every hospital has."

Lillian was all too aware of this. Hospital nursing was generally an 80-hour-a-week job that required living at the hospital. This was highly appealing to many girls, who wanted a safe and respectable way to live on their own. But even if she were old enough, Lillian could not do that and also take care of Marie.

"Our beautiful new building has lodging for our nurses, of course, but when our nursing need started to exceed our lodging capacity, it made more financial sense to hire nonresident assistants than it did to expand our facility."

"Most sensible, ma'am."

"Yes," said Nurse Holt as she straightened the piece of paper on her desk. There were several heartbeats of silence during which the only sound Lillian heard was the rustle of a nurse's skirts rushing past the office door. *Was the interview over?* As she opened her mouth to express her thanks, Nurse Holt looked up and said, "51st Street. That's quite a distance to travel."

"Yes, but quite direct on the El."

"You must keep in mind that our nurses lodge in this building, and thus are never late. They don't say, 'The El was slow today', and so neither must you. There is no excuse for tardiness."

"Yes, ma'am."

"You have no children, correct?"

"That is correct."

"Good. This job is incompatible with the unpredictable needs of caring for dependents."

Lillian said nothing, curling her toes inside her boots with the effort of maintaining a neutral expression on her face.

"Well, I must say that your taciturn demeanor is refreshing. Many girls have sat in your seat, blathering on about their desire to help mankind and gushing about how they get on with everyone. That sort doesn't last here." Nurse Holt placed the piece of paper on the left side of the desk. "Congratulations, Miss Dolan, you've got the job. Report tomorrow at 8am to the nurses' station on the second floor." She held out her hand.

Lillian stood and shook her hand as she began to wonder how she would find a regular someone to look after Marie on such short notice.

As she put her key in the door, Lillian's stomach gurgled with hunger and her thoughts were split between Marie and the hard-boiled eggs she had left in a bowl on the kitchen sideboard. When she entered the kitchen, it seemed her dual thoughts had merged in reality, because on the floor sat Marie with the hard-boiled eggs, the empty bowl beside her. She was rolling the eggs on the floor with the flat of her palm, over and over again, the shells fragmented into a mosaic of pieces, now gray with grime. Marie's face was a picture of content-ment as she enjoyed the sensation of the fractured shell bits upon her hands.

Lillian whisked past her to find Mrs. Oberman fast asleep with mouth open in the very chair where Lillian had left her three hours ago. The smell of whiskey was undeniable now.

"Mrs. Oberman!" When she received no response, she kicked Mrs. Oberman's boot, which elicited a snort and a minor effort to wake. As Lillian waited for Mrs. Oberman to become fully conscious, she walked from room to room to assess the damage. Marie's fabric and notions covered the bedroom floor, chamber pot used but not over-flowing, silverware scattered across the bed, tarts Lillian had been saving for dessert tonight gone, one crock broken. Lillian breathed a sigh of relief that nothing bad had happened. She strode over to Mrs. Oberman and gave her foot another rough nudge to bring her around. Mrs. Oberman blinked a few times and looked up.

Lillian held out a coin and said, "Can you come tomorrow for the whole day?"

❧ Chapter 2 ❧

Just as Lillian and Marie had finished supper that night, they heard a knock at the door. When Lillian answered and saw it was Michael, her pleasure was marred by the sight of her neighbor behind him, leaning against the frame of the opposite door with arms crossed.

"Good evening, Mrs. Sweeney." Lillian wondered when Mrs. Sweeney would stop coming into the hallway when she heard someone at Lillian's door.

"Mrs. Sweeney," said Michael with a slight bow and a touch of the brogue Lillian knew he had labored to vanquish from his speech. "It's as lovely to see you this week as last." Sounds of children fighting and screaming drifted out from the rooms behind her. "Family," added Michael with a somewhat beatific expression arranged on his face. "It's a blessing, I'm sure you agree."

"Always the wiseacre, Michael Dolan," said Mrs. Sweeney, lips pursed as she retreated back into her apartment.

Lillian pushed Michael's shoulder. "You are beastly," she admonished as she dragged him through her front door. "You know this will get back to your mother."

"That is the cross I'll have to bear for you living here." Michael's mother and Mrs. Sweeney had met on the boat over from Ireland

and had stayed in touch throughout the years. If it weren't for these two tiny rooms opposite Mrs. Sweeney's, Lillian wasn't sure where she and Marie would be living now.

"Or instead of bearing that cross you could just not say rude things."

Before Michael could respond, Marie ran into the room and wrapped her arms around him. "Magpie!" he exclaimed. "It's been entirely too long since I have experienced one of your bear hugs. Do not tell your sister but you are my favorite cousin." He kissed the top of her head.

Lillian looked at the two of them and felt better than she had all day. *Why couldn't family always be like this?* It had always been easy for her to think of her cousin as more of a brother, not only because they had always been close but also because he and Marie looked so much alike—more like siblings than she and Marie. Michael and Marie shared the Dolan Black Irish glossy dark hair that shone in the sun and a thin, delicate nose flanked by high porcelain cheekbones. Lillian had her mother's French peasant coloring and sturdy features, with hazel eyes so closely matching the color of her hair as to make her look like a sepia-toned photograph. It was a disappointment Lillian had grown to accept.

Marie started rummaging through Michael's coat. While she dug through his left pocket, Michael reached into the pocket on the other side. "Looking for this?" He put a length of lace trim into her hands. She immediately ran into the bedroom with it.

"What happens when we run out of room for your notions and fabrics?" asked Lillian as she went to put the kettle on.

"Can you get rid of some of the older ones?"

"Oh certainly, if I want to start a war." Michael had been giving Marie leftover bits from his job as a tailor's assistant since he started almost a year ago. At first she was just interested in organizing them using some system known only to her, but one day Lillian gave her a napkin along with a needle and thread to see if she remembered any of her sewing skills from before the fever. Without hesitation, Marie selected a button and began sewing it to the napkin. In a few weeks, the napkin was entirely covered with buttons, the back dotted with spots of blood from where Marie had poked her fingers with the needle. She was on her third napkin now. Though the other two were filled, they were still among Marie's most beloved possessions, and she often shook them to hear the buttons clack together. Lillian had enjoyed the sound until Marie started using it to wake Lillian up in the morning, and now she regretted the whole idea.

Michael sat down on a kitchen chair and planted one elbow on the table. "You know, much as I love to chat about our Magpie, I would really like to hear about your interview."

"Interview?" Lillian feigned confusion. "Was that today? I believe it slipped my mind."

"Wipe that smirk off your mug and tell me how it went."

Lillian brought the steaming teacups to the table and sat down. "I got the job."

Michael popped out of his chair and gave her a hug. "Well done, Lilypad! You'll be perfect."

"I feel so indebted. I'll never be able to make it up to you," she lamented. The list of debts she owed Michael went on and on. The night she and Marie left Helen and showed up on Michael's door-step, Aunt Fiona was confused, but after Lillian's tearful private conversation with Michael, he convinced his mother to take them in without asking questions. The next day, he told Fiona a summarized and sanitized version of why her nieces had to leave their mother and that they wouldn't be going back. But after a hellish week of the two of them sleeping on the kitchen floor and trying to keep Marie from breaking things and driving everyone crazy in their four small rooms, everyone could see that the arrangement could not continue for long.

Casting about for a solution, it was Michael who remembered his mother's old friend Mrs. Sweeney and her landlord husband on the edge of Hell's Kitchen. As luck would have it, there were two mildly dilapidated rooms right across from Mrs. Sweeney and her family that were being vacated. Michael lent Lillian money to supplement her meager savings (and what she swiped from Helen when they left) so that she and Marie could move in and have a bit left over as a cushion while Lillian figured the rest out. While Aunt Fiona still did not approve of Lillian moving out on her own despite her friend's assurances that she would keep an eye on her nieces, no one had a better idea. And Mrs. Sweeney insisted that although the building was on the edge of Hell's Kitchen, decent families lived there and the gangs didn't look for trouble on this street.

And last week, Michael had alerted her to the opportunity at the hospital when his sister's friend was fired from that position.

"No one is asking you to return any favors, Cousin," Michael assured her, "but when the situation arises, yours is the first door I will knock on."

"With this job I can start to pay you back."

"I have told you that the money was a gift, not a loan. And you will barely be able to cover this palace." He referenced the dingy kitchen with a careless wave of his hand.

"Yes, but you had been saving so that *you* could move out, and now you're still there."

"Things have calmed down a bit at home." Battles between Michael and his father had ebbed and flowed over the past year or two, and Lillian wanted to believe that things were getting better between the two, but she wasn't so sure.

"Besides," Michael added after a sip of tea, "I get to come here for a bit of escape. My home away from home. And I'd be here more often if you weren't so damned far. It's a hell of a trip to get over to the West Side."

"I know. But it turned out to be good fortune for me. At least it's a straight shot on the Ninth Avenue El to get up to the hospital. I couldn't have even considered this job if I were still on the East Side."

"Well, then I suppose it was meant to be."

Lillian hesitated briefly before asking, "How are things with Uncle Martin, really?"

"Well, you know him," said Michael softly as he looked down at his cup and rubbed his thumb back and forth over a chip. "Happy when I hand over a piece of my wages from Abraham's shop. And by happy I mean he grunts his happy grunt. But he still works himself into a lather when I come home in the small hours. Waking up Ma and Kate with his bellowing."

"Maybe if you just came home a little earlier—"

"Lilypad, I'm twenty years old. I work hard at my job and I help out with the rent when I would much prefer to be saving that money so that I can leave. So when I have an opportunity to go out, I'm going to do it. And I'll accept the consequences. Besides, I find it quite ironic that you, of all people, would be preaching the don't-make-waves-with-the-family sermon."

"You cannot possibly be comparing our situations. Would you have me leave Marie living there after what my... after what Helen did?" Lillian bristled.

"Hackles down, cousin. I'm on your side. Always. All I'm saying is, sometimes you need to stand up for what is important to you, and you know that can get a little ugly."

After a heartbeat, she asked, "And going out at night, it's that important?"

"Yes, it is." He looked at her with a smile that didn't include his eyes. "I don't expect you to understand."

"I don't need to understand. If you tell me it's important, it's important."

In the past few years, Michael had become somewhat of an enigma to her. Growing up, he had been the responsible oldest child, affectionate with his younger sister and cousins, the apple of his mother's eye. His father had never been warm to him, but that did not stop Michael from trying to please him. Until he did stop, more than a year ago. Michael was still respectful at home, still caring, but he no longer strove to be in his father's good graces, around the same time he started venturing out late into the night. The regular extended-family dinners were often tense affairs, although no one spoke about what was bothering them. When Lillian asked him about it, he mentioned something about how his father didn't approve of his job at the tailor's. Lillian didn't believe him but she let it go.

Michael took a deep breath as was his habit when he was about to change the subject. "And who is taking care of our Magpie when you are off curing cancer?"

"Well," said Lillian as she ran her finger around the rim of her cup. "As it turns out, there is a woman who lives in this building who is willing for a small sum. She's very... relaxed. Unlikely to let Marie upset her." All true, she told herself.

"So it's all worked out. That's grand! An auspicious beginning."

Lillian pushed thoughts of Mrs. Oberman aside. *Yes, auspicious.*

As the train pulled into the 103rd Street station, Lillian looked over the shoulder of a man checking his pocket watch and saw that it was two minutes of eight. She started pushing people aside before the doors even opened, and flew down the cast iron stairs so quickly that she didn't see the rain puddle at the bottom until her shoe was in it. She felt the shock of cold water seeping into her stocking as she ran the two blocks as fast as her corset would allow, her skirts brushing against people on the sidewalk. When she reached the doors of the hospital, she took a deep breath and smoothed her hair.

Once inside, she was unsure where exactly to go. When Nurse Holt had given her instructions yesterday, Lillian had been so focused on the 8am piece and what she would do with Marie that she hadn't listened very carefully to the rest of it. Ahead of her was a wide corridor devoid of people, but when she glanced to her left she saw an open door and a small sign that said "Waiting Room."

"Pardon me," she started, addressing a young woman behind the desk. "I'm the new…, that is, I was hired as a nursing assistant? Yesterday? By Nurse Holt?" She realized all her phrases were questions. "I'm to start today."

The woman consulted a paper on her desk. "Lillian…?"

"Dolan. Yes."

"You're to report to the nurses' station. Two minutes ago." She looked behind her and then leaned forward conspiratorially. "Don't give an excuse." She leaned back, the private communiqué evidently over. "Stairs are all the way down the corridor, second floor, front of the building, ask for Nurse Collins, she takes all the new girls."

Lillian started to run down the hallway but adjusted to a brisk walk when a man with muttonchops emerged from an office and frowned a look of disapproval that needed no clarifying words. At her reduced pace she was able to take in a dining room on her right where a handful of people were having breakfast, and a well-appointed parlor on the left with large windows facing Central Park.

When Lillian reached the nurses' station and announced herself, Nurse Collins wordlessly handed her a tidy pile of clothing and pointed to a room where Lillian could change. Emerging from the room in starchy white pinafore topped with a frilly pillbox cap, she found herself alone. She peered down the hallway and saw nothing, only hearing what sounded like a patient complaining bitterly between bouts of a hacking cough.

Eventually, Nurse Collins reappeared. "Nursing assistant," she said a little sourly. "You are our third since the position was imagined earlier this year. The first received a sudden proposal of marriage. The second misjudged the type of constitution required for this job."

This must have been cousin Kate's friend. Michael had told her that the girl was let go when she vomited while assisting a particularly nasty dressing change. It was this piece of information, in fact, that made Michael sure Lillian would be great for this job. The whole family had become aware of Lillian's strong stomach years ago when a neighborhood boy had tumbled from the rooftop on a blistering hot night when all the tenement families had brought their bedding to the roof to escape the heat. Michael and Lillian had been on the stoop across the street, and when they both rushed over, Michael fell back in horror and struggled to keep his dinner down. But Lillian knelt by the boy, gently cradling his fractured skull in her skirts, careful not to bump the arm with the bone poking through the skin, looking into his eyes until the light in them went out. The boy's mother burst forth from the building a moment later; they had heard her screaming like a freight train as she barreled down all the flights of stairs. There was so much blood on Lillian's skirt that they had to throw it out. She was twelve years old.

"I'm unlikely to have those problems," said Lillian to Nurse Collins.

"No question was asked, Miss Dolan. If Nurse Holt hired you, I trust you will be an improvement on those who came before you." She looked down the hallway and called out "Nurse Weatherbee!"

A plump woman several years older than Lillian turned around and headed their way, a tray of small china cups in her hands. Nurse Collins looked relieved at her arrival. "Nurse Weatherbee, meet Miss Dolan, our new nursing assistant. She will be shadowing you today. Please inform her of her responsibilities in detail. I'm sure you remember them from the last one we had scurrying around here."

"Certainly, Nurse Collins." Nurse Weatherbee's face was a mask of neutrality.

"Excellent," murmured Nurse Collins as she whisked away.

Nurse Weatherbee's face relaxed. "You can call me Janey, but not in front of the others. Collins is supposed to be showing you the ropes today, but she can't stand the new ones. How old are you anyway?" They started walking down the hall.

"Eighteen."

"Hmm, hiring them younger and younger. Well, at least I'm not the youngest around here anymore. Have you been to the wards yet?"

"I haven't been anywhere."

"All right, clean slate, here we go." Janey looked straight ahead as they walked, the tray perfectly level, the white cups as still as if they were glued down. "All the patients are women. They've been working on a men's wing but they don't quite have the coin to open it. A bit of a cashflow problem, so goes the chatter. We've got the paying patients on the higher floor, swank rooms, champagne and carriage rides in the park, etcetera etcetera, and then there are the ones that pay less or not at all on the lower floors."

Lillian hesitated before she spoke. "You wouldn't be pulling my leg about the champagne and the carriages, would you?"

"That I am not. Did you think we were in the business of curing cancers? Well, I suppose the doctors would tell you so, and plenty have a chart marked 'cured' when they leave. But who knows where they are in a year unless they come back to us?"

Lillian wondered what 'cured' actually meant, but decided not to ask. Instead, she said, "So the champagne and carriage rides are for the purpose of…"

"Morale! And the champagne isn't bad for the pain, either." They stopped in front of a door. "But for more serious pain relief, this tray of doses is more effective."

"Morphine?" inquired Lillian.

"Only for the worst of it. Expensive, you know. Everyday pain is managed by the considerable power of plain old whiskey." And with that, Janey opened the door to the ward.

Lillian had been struck by the unusual architecture of the building from the outside – the large round castle turrets like some strange mushrooms that sprouted among the rectilinear brownstones – but now she could see the purpose behind the design. Beds were arranged in the room like spokes of a wheel with a station for the nurses at the center. Large windows admitted streams of sunlight in a way that would have been cheery had it not been for the presence of the patients in their various states of discomfort.

By the time Lillian had taken it all in, Janey had already checked in at the central desk and was proceeding to the beds and Lillian had to double-step to catch up.

"Quite a room, eh?" said Janey softly as they approached an emaciated woman lying rigid, her face damp with perspiration. "Mrs. Mancini, looks like you could use a cuppa comfort this morning," she said as she gently propped the woman up far enough to drink the whiskey. "Has the doctor seen you today?" The woman shook her head as Janey straightened her sheets. "He'll be by in a little while." Janey patted the woman's veiny hand, deep valleys of skin between the knuckles.

Around the room they went, doling out their cups with occasional editorial asides from Janey. "That one never takes her whiskey—her husband is a violent drunk and she won't have a drop touch her lips, as if she doesn't have a tough enough row to hoe." One groaning woman with long flowing black hair shot through with silver could not be woken up for her dose. "Not long now," whispered Janey, which gave Lillian a chill. Although what did she expect at a cancer hospital?

All morning Lillian and Janey walked hallways, visited rooms, checked in at stations. After the first hour Lillian was glad she did not have new shoes as she had originally wished—her feet ached but at least she did not have blisters. She noticed that there was a particular pace at which all the nurses walked that might best be described as "brisk." One could hear an approaching nurse even with eyes closed, based on the steady quick tempo of swishing skirts and starched petticoats.

Finally they stopped into the linens room on the first floor and sat, and Lillian's legs sang with relief. Janey tucked a curl under her cap. "You might think I'm riding you hard, but truth is the others will be looking for reasons to report you. This position you have, it's not popular with a lot of the nurses."

"But why?" According to the hiring nurse, she was only to do menial jobs—wouldn't this benefit the nurses? Right after they had whiskey-dosed the patients in the ward, Janey had made it clear that everything she did was off limits to Lillian, even though Lillian had to understand those things completely.

"This has always been a 'round-the-clock job. Not a one of us has escaped the call in the dead of night—spike of post-operative fever, emergency surgery, what-have-you. The price we pay for this respectable job. Heck, part of it being respectable is the fact that we live here. The Dormitory of Virtue," Janey said with a smirk as she got up to get a bin of cloth strips. "But along comes a young bit like yourself, living God knows where, doing God knows what with your spare time, and yet you wear the cupcake like the rest of us."

"With no ribbon," Lillian hastened to add. While waiting at one of the stations this morning, Janey had explained how the navy ribbon around her own cap signified that she was a certified nurse, and Lillian had taken hers off to see that indeed she had no ribbon.

"We all know that, but the patients may not, and just the fact that you're buzzing around here, well, some feel that you haven't earned your cap." Janey plunked the bin of cloth strips down in front of Lillian. "Me, I like that it will be you who rolls these two hundred bandages." After brief instruction, Janey told her to come find her when she was done and whisked away.

A dozen bandages in, the steps became automatic and Lillian's mind roamed. Who washed these bandages? Evidently there was someone with a more menial job than hers in this building. Every place has its pecking order, and this seemed no exception. Earlier, she observed Janey stop mid-sentence when a doctor crossed their path. Janey may have even tucked her chin ever so slightly. What were the rules for nurses interacting with doctors, and would they be the same for her? Because there were no other nursing assistants, who would determine what was appropriate for Lillian's behavior?

She looked up to see Nurse Collins standing in the doorway. "Good morning, Ma'am," Lillian ventured. Nurse Collins strode over to her pile of rolled bandages and selected one for inspection. "Adequate," she ruled, though Lillian thought she looked slightly disappointed as she left.

Finally, fingers tender from the rub of the rough cotton, Lillian was done. She realized she would have to figure out where in this building Janey might now be. The third nurse she asked thought Janey had gone to the kitchen to tell them to "try again" with the lunch for one of the top-floor patients. Lunch! In her rush, Lillian had forgotten to bring anything to eat. Perhaps she could procure a bit of food while she was in the kitchen.

As was true of all the floors in the hospital, there were scant signs on the basement level to tell people where to go—evidently, one was just supposed to know. As she turned down one hallway, she could feel the air becoming warmer, and took this as a sign that she was nearing the kitchen ovens. Her stomach growled as she neared the big door at the end of the hall—surely there would be something she could quickly eat.

With enthusiasm for the snack she envisioned, she yanked open the heavy door and froze. A fire roaring in the background framed a Negro boy covered in ash and bent over a corpse, pliers in hand, evidently having just successfully extracted a tooth.

🀅 Chapter 3 🀅

Lillian slammed the door and her mind immediately began doubting what she had seen, even as her body trembled. What was that tableau from Hades doing in this hospital? Her breath came in little puffs and she blinked a few times, and then she saw the words painted in thin block letters on the door: "CREMATORIUM." An element of this building that no one had mentioned to her.

She put her hand flat against the door in front of her. Warm to the touch. What did it mean that a hospital this small had its own crematorium? She thought of Janey's comment about patients being marked as cured. But those were the ones who were discharged. Here in the basement, this was another way your struggle with your illness could end.

She turned this over in her mind as her breathing slowed. She was vaguely aware that she was edging toward the very thing that her mother—Helen, that is, the woman she would not think about—always said would be Lillian's downfall. Looking at things too closely. Forming opinions about things that were none of her business. Questioning the decisions of her superiors who clearly knew more than Lillian ever would on the subject at hand. When Lillian was younger, she tried to tame her thoughts as Helen suggested by repeating silently, "I must stick to my knitting," but soon she would be back to wondering how clean the butcher could get his knife by wiping it on his bloody apron before he cleaved their chops, or why the police didn't just close down the opium dens when everyone knew where they were in the city. She learned not to ask these questions of her mother.

The door under her hand moved and she pulled away, startled. The boy she had seen poked his head out. "Ma'am? Help you wi' sumthin?"

"Oh, uh, no thank you... I was looking for..." She lost her train of thought as she got a closer look at the boy, who under the film of ash was really more of a man. Shorter than her but older, certainly.

"Been here long enough to give you directions, if you wanna tell me where you tryin' to get to, Miz..?.." He opened the door a little more. Lillian could hear the purr of the fire.

"Dolan. And it's the kitchen. That I'm looking for."

"Well, you couldn't be much farther. Kitchen's up the top floor, Miz Dolan. Somebody tell you it's down here?"

"Well, no, I just assumed... For food deliveries and such, kitchens are usually... I should have asked. Thank you for your help." As the door started to close, she grabbed the handle. "And you are...?"

"Jupiter," he said, and with a nod he gently pulled the door closed until it clicked.

Up four flights of stairs she found Janey, arguing with one of the cooks. "I'm not saying it's too salty. I'm sure you have salted it to absolute perfection. I'm saying that *Mrs. Van Alstead* thinks it's too salty. And since she's paying full freight, she's the only opinion that matters on this plate."

The cook frowned and muttered under her breath but took the plate away. Janey caught sight of Lillian.

"Good timing," Janey said. "Once Greta concocts something that will satisfy Mrs. Van Alstead, I can show you the rooms on the third floor. Would be a charming place if it weren't for the cancer." Lillian realized she would have to get used to Janey's occasional gallows humor. Outside of this building, Lillian had never heard a joke about cancer; indeed, she had rarely heard the word uttered. Everyone she knew believed cancer to be contagious and incurable. In the neighborhood where she grew up, no one spoke of cancer until someone was laid low by it, months after that person first knew something was wrong and proceeded to ignore it. Lillian was surprised to discover in a medical journal lent to her by Dr. Pratt a study that showed cancer was not contagious, although most hospitals did not agree with this new way of thinking and regularly turned the afflicted away at their doors.

"I thought the kitchen would be in the basement and found the crematorium." Lillian was slightly embarrassed to admit she had been lost but wanted information from Janey.

"So you met Jupiter."

"He was removing a tooth from a corpse."

Janey ushered Lillian over to corner. "That's the sort of observation you might want to keep to yourself."

"Well, I didn't bring it up with Jupiter, if that's what you mean."

"I'm sure he appreciated that. Look, very few people even talk with Jupiter. You as a nursing assistant will have more reason to be down there than most."

Lillian thought about this. "Because I bring him…"

"Yes, you will ferry the unclaimed deceased to him. A part of the job they may not have mentioned. But one where you can't do too much harm to the patient, so a good fit for you. My point is, although few people deal with Jupiter, they all know he's down there, and we need him. They can't afford to pay much for the job and many wouldn't consider it. I'm not even sure why Jupiter does it—even a Negro could do better in this city, and their lot is generally a superstitious bunch. But the point is, no one is served by Jupiter getting in trouble with the higher-ups."

"But why was he removing the teeth from a corpse?"

"I suspect it was one very special tooth."

Lillian understood now. "A gold filling."

Janey looked across the kitchen. "Well, I wasn't there so I don't know. But here comes Greta with what I hope is not the same meal for Mrs. Van Alstead."

On the top floor, it was easy to forget—or pretend— that this wasn't a hospital at all, which Lillian supposed was the point. The carpeted hallway displayed paintings in gilt frames, and glass-knobbed doors left ajar revealed decor befitting the boudoirs of respectable women. In the last room on the left, Janey and Lillian found Mrs. Van Alstead propped up in her bed wearing a brocade bed jacket and a look of impatience.

"Our apologies, Ma'am," stated Janey neutrally. "The cook will pay more attention to seasoning in the future." Lillian had heard no such thing from the cook.

"Perhaps," Mrs. Van Alstead said as she patted her lap to indicate where Janey should place the tray, "it is the staff who should pay more attention when they are hiring the cook."

"Of course, Ma'am." Janey stood waiting for Mrs. Van Alstead to arrange her linen napkin and taste her food, giving Lillian time to look around and see a small Pekingese snoozing on a chair in the corner. She realized that she could hear it snoring gently.

Mrs. Van Alstead took a second bite of her meat and nodded, which inspired Janey to say, "Best of luck tomorrow, although I may see you before then," and turn to leave.

"I should hope luck has nothing to do with it!" she proclaimed as she tucked into her roast.

As they walked down the hallway, Lillian asked Janey, "Is it surgery she's having tomorrow?"

"Indeed."

"You were both rather cavalier about it."

"Oh, it's not cancer for her. Hemorrhoids. Eating scones all day in a tight corset will do that."

"But surely we are not the New York Hemorrhoid Hospital," Lillian said before she could stop herself.

"Well, the new little lamb has a sense of humor. That could get yourself thrown out of here on your ear. Your job is not to crack wise." They started down the stairs as Janey returned to the subject of Mrs. Van Alstead. "The bottom line is that cancer isn't the money maker this place needs it to be. So they bend the rules for the ladies who can pay $20 a week for a private room. You'd be surprised how many conditions are 'pre-cancerous' according to the charts. But don't go chatting about that."

"Why? What's wrong with—"

"Because the money for this place from the high-falutin Astors and their like was for cancer, and anyone we can convince now to throw money our way gets the hard sell on how we are battling this scourge. They won't be too pleased to know their donation is helping to ease Mrs. Van Alstead's rump." Janey flicked Lillian's cap, knocking it off center. "And you'd do best to ease off on the 'why'. Curiosity is for the doctors."

The afternoon wore on, made all the more tiring because Lillian decided not to ask for anything to eat for lunch. Janey took pity on her and gave her half her apple, which Lillian insisted was plenty since she was not terribly hungry. In one of the empty top floor rooms, Janey showed her how to make a bed properly and how to identify the finer soft linens for these beds, not to be confused with those that belonged on the ward beds downstairs. Mostly Lillian watched —she watched Janey change a reeking dressing soaked with pus on a woman's breast, swap out bloody padding under a woman who had just had uterine surgery, feel any number of foreheads for fever, hold a pan while a woman vomited up the water she had just downed. Occasionally Janey seemed to be observing Lillian's reactions.

At the end of Lillian's shift in the late afternoon, Janey gave her verdict. "You've got a stomach built for nursing. Can't fake that. We'll have to see if you can fall in line."

"But I did everything you asked."

"You did. But you're thinking too much. This is a doing job, not a thinking job." Just then a nurse summoned Janey to the wards, and with a quick word of goodbye she rushed off. Lillian was left to ponder Janey's words. On the face of it, she understood—she was to follow orders, nothing more. But she wanted this job, and not another job she could get nearer to where she lived and more compatible with caring for Marie, because she found it all so interesting. She supposed she had Dr. Pratt to thank—or to blame—for that.

Several years ago, not long after Marie's scarlet fever, Lillian had come down with a different fever. A first, they thought it was the scarlatina making a second ghastly appearance in their home, but there was no rash. Still, Lillian could not rise from her bed for weeks, fading in and out of consciousness. She came to suspect that she was hallucinating in some of her waking moments. Once she woke with a raging thirst and, peeking over this side of the bed, saw the floorboards rippling under a foot of water. She tried to scoop some up in her hand and would have fallen from the bed if Helen had not been there to catch her.

Off and on throughout those weeks, she remembered Dr. Pratt coming to care for her, checking for rash, making her stick out her tongue, consulting with Helen on the administration of beef tea. He was an imposing man with a wild mane of hair and a bushy beard. One evening he appeared by Lillian's bedside as a lion and placed an enormous paw on her forehead. Another time he wore a jeweled crown. On a more lucid day she recalled him bleeding her, hanging her arm over the side of the bed with a china bowl on the floor to catch the blood. She had heard Dr. Pratt and Helen in the other room talking about this procedure, an old-fashioned treatment but a last ditch effort. Lillian heard fear in her mother's voice but was too weak to think about what it meant.

When Lillian recovered, she went to Dr. Pratt's office to thank him, although what really drove her there was the beehive of questions in her head about her illness and treatment. She had never met him before she took ill, and when she found his upscale office, she regretted not wearing her best dress for the visit. He was delighted to see such a robust recovery and didn't seem to mind her peppering him with questions about fevers and rashes. To the contrary, he seemed happy to indulge her inquisitive mind. Why did Marie lose her sight but Lillian did not? What was the purpose of the bleeding? Why did her fever rise and fall? What finally made it go away? He answered all with confidence, and when his secretary informed him that his next appointment had arrived, he plucked a book from his bookcase and handed it to Lillian, the first of several loans that Lillian would read at a steady clip.

But Dr. Pratt's encouragement was perhaps the worst preparation for working at this hospital, where there was so much she wanted to learn and nothing she was supposed to ask about. A dullard would do better here, she thought. But she wouldn't give up. She still believed this would lead to better things.

As she walked down the hall to the main entrance, a group of well-heeled ladies were being served their second round of champagne in the parlor, chatting as if they were in the home of a good friend and not sitting below a ward of women praying to overcome their illness and above a furnace for those who could not.

At the hospital Lillian had not once thought of Marie, but as soon as she got on the El she became anxious and impatient to get home. At each stop the crowds shuffled from the platform into the car at a lethargic pace, and the train crawled lackadaisically down 9th Avenue from station to station. She realized that she would be doing this every day and gritted her teeth at the thought.

When she put her key in the door, she paused to take a breath, preparing for whatever chaos had been brought on by Mrs. Oberman's neglect. Instead, she found Marie and Mrs. Oberman eating an early supper at the kitchen table. Lillian brushed aside the facts that Marie was eating the stew with her hands and that Mrs. Oberman was eating the last of the stew that Lillian had been counting on for herself. Her relief made her slightly weak in the knees and she leaned up against the wall as there was not a third chair in the kitchen.

Once Mrs. Oberman had collected her coin and hobbled out the door, Marie tackled her sister with a bear hug. Lillian saw it coming and grabbed her wrists before Marie could plaster her greasy hands all over the back of Lillian's skirts. After rinsing hands at the sink, Lillian allowed Marie her hug. "Not such a bad day, right? You had your supper at least." This was working out, she told herself. Mrs. Oberman was sober enough to heat up some stew, in a pot that Lillian would now have to clean. She peered inside, hoping in vain that there might be a little left. She ran her finger along the bottom and licked it. Her stomach growled.

As Lillian sat down with some bread and a block of cheese, carving a few furry spots off with a paring knife, Marie took the contents of the silverware drawer and dumped them on the table. Lillian was used to this and didn't startle at the noise; Marie made silverware sculptures at least once a week. Knowing that Marie would be occupied with this for a least a half hour, Lillian took this opportunity to pretend that they were having a normal dinner together. "How was it? Well, it was my first day after all, so it was all I could do to try to remember everything. Janey seems nice enough. Fond of telling me all the things I shouldn't talk about. Might be simpler to just tell me the few things I am allowed to talk about." She watched Marie arrange the spoons like the spokes of a wheel. Or maybe it was supposed to be the petals of a flower? Lillian would never know.

All of a sudden loneliness hit her like a gust of wind. She wished Michael were here, but this wasn't one of the days he regularly visited. She was sure that with minimal prompting, he would be able to do an absolutely wicked impression of Mrs. Van Alstead. Despite her melancholy, she smiled at that thought.

Later that night, as she and Marie were dressing for bed, Marie took off her blouse, revealing an ugly burn on her upper forearm. Lillian grabbed her wrist and took a closer look. It was weeping. "When did this happen?" she asked Marie, angrily, uselessly. But Lillian knew. It must have been not too long before Lillian came home, but with enough time for Mrs. Oberman to dry Marie's tears and distract her with an early supper.

Lillian dragged Marie to the sink and rinsed the burn off as best she could, and smeared on a bit of butter from the icebox. She tied a clean rag around Marie's arm with a tug of anger directed at Mrs. Oberman and heard Marie whimper. Lillian loosened the knot a bit, wishing she could just focus on her anger and push the other thoughts away, the ones telling her that no, it was not really working out with Mrs. Oberman.

🦚 Chapter 4 🦚

The next day, Lillian sprinted from the El station but was still ten minutes late when she crossed the threshold of the hospital. As soon as she had heard Mrs. Oberman heaving herself up the stairs, she realized she did not have time to discuss Marie's burn in the stern and authoritative manner she had planned. As Lillian made her exit, she passed Mrs. Oberman on the stairs and lamely shouted a few instructions over her shoulder, including to keep Marie away from the stove. She boarded the El with what should have been just enough time, but the train halted inexplicably only a few blocks before her stop and sat there for fifteen minutes. She could have easily walked the distance had there been a way to get off. To make matters worse, there had been no available seats and the man jammed next to her reeked of beer, although whether it was last night's or this morning's was hard to tell. When the train finally lurched forward, he stumbled and fell against her, grabbing on to her waist and arm for what was clearly a little longer than was necessary. His grin belied his apology, and Lillian wondered if she could refrain from screaming in frustration before they reached her station.

She cleared the hospital front door without attracting any attention and snuck up to the second floor to don her uniform. Janey walked in just as Lillian was tying her pinafore strings. Janey frowned and crossed her arms. "It just as easily could have been Collins who walked in here. If you want to keep this job, you have to be on time."

"But the El just stopped at 101st Street for no reason—", began Lillian.

Janey held up her hand. "Nobody cares if Jesus himself stopped the train to let the lambs cross. Find a way to get here on time, or find another job. This is the last time I will refrain from reporting your tardiness." With a quick about-face, Janey was off traveling down the hallway and it took Lillian a beat to realize she was supposed to follow. In her haste Lillian tripped on her skirts before she caught up.

"A little grace wouldn't hurt your prospects either," murmured Janey as they took the stairs.

They entered the circular ward and made a beeline for the bed on the far side. Lillian recognized the woman in it by her black and silver hair: Not Long Now, as Janey had proclaimed her. The woman's head was tilted back on the pillow and her mouth was slightly open, framed by colorless lips.

"The doctor has already pronounced her earlier this morning. She has no next of kin, so she will proceed directly to Jupiter." Although Janey spoke quietly, Lillian could understand the reason for euphemism when speaking of the crematorium within earshot of the other patients. Janey handed Lillian some paperwork. "Go to the basement and wait by the dumbwaiter. It's not too far from where you need to end up."

As Lillian descended the stairs, she realized she had not thought to wonder about the logistics of the crematorium. Certainly patients die in this building, but how would the bodies get from the upper floors to the basement? Beyond navigating the curving staircases, there was also the unpleasant sight of a corpse being carted past patients who would not appreciate a reminder that cancer is often the victor.

A dumbwaiter, of course, was the perfect solution.

Lillian found it in the corridor leading to the crematorium. A gurney was parked in front of the two wide doors. She opened them and saw four dusty ropes as thick as her wrist, reaching into the velvet darkness above and below. She marveled at the thought that went into the design: how the opening was right at the level for the gurney, how its width would accommodate a six-foot person. She reached in to feel the roughness of the rope just as it sprang into action with a mighty creak from above.

In fits and starts, the ropes moved in opposite directions until the platform came into view and then stopped at just the right level. How did Janey, or whomever was up there, know exactly when to stop? Perhaps there was a mark on the ropes.

Lillian tugged on the sheet underneath the body, shuffling the body inch by inch from the dumbwaiter to the gurney. One of the feet caught within the dumbwaiter cavity and Lillian had to free it and tuck it back under the sheet; the ankle was smooth and cool to the touch. For a moment, she was overcome by the ghastliness of what she was doing and stepped back, tucking her hands under her arms. Two deep breaths later, she stepped forward again and reminded herself that this was just the shell of a soul who had departed this earth. And beyond that, this was part of the job, and she would do this, and anything else that was asked of her.

With one more jerk of the bottom sheet, she centered the body on the gurney. She was glad that Janey wasn't here to comment on her lack of grace in these maneuvers. As she started to wheel the gurney toward the crematorium, the long salt-and-pepper hair tumbled from beneath the sheet and hung down. Lillian stopped to wind it around her hand like yarn and tuck it under the sheet. A memory of her mother knitting washed over her, unwanted. Lillian with yarn looped between her small hands as she listened to Helen's stories about her parents' life in France, their dramatic escape during the February Revolution, their arrival in New York with jewelry sewn in the hem of their coats, Lillian rapt as she unlooped the yarn at just the right rate to accommodate Helen's rapidly clicking needles… Lillian stamped her foot to chase those memories away. She would not think of Helen, especially good things that Helen had tainted, had negated by what came later. She grabbed the gurney and shoved off with a vengeance.

Jupiter answered her knock on the crematorium door promptly. "Miz Dolan," he acknowledged as he helped her roll the gurney inside. She noticed that he was not dusted with ash this time, perhaps because this would be the first cremation of the day. Nor was the fire going yet. Obviously Not Long Now would be waiting on the gurney for a while.

"Looks like your shift has just started, same as mine," Lillian ventured.

Jupiter looked guarded, as if he were not used to chit-chat here. After a pause, he said, "Yes, ma'am, just about to build that fire. I ain't behind, I'm right on schedule, same as always."

"Oh no, that's not what I meant." Already it felt like she had gotten off on the wrong foot. "I'm new here."

"I did sense that when you was down here lookin' for the kitchen."

"Oh, yes, that's right. But I, well I don't know many people except Janey, Nurse Weatherbee, that is, she's rather nice but putting me through my paces, of course, and the other nurses don't seem to like me, Janey says it's something about nursing assistants not having to pay their dues in school or some such nonsense, which isn't my fault, but they won't talk to me, although this is only my second day..." Too late she realized she was babbling, a train run off the tracks. She blushed.

Jupiter pushed the gurney over to the side of the room. "Last assistant looked like she seen a ghost every time she had to come down here. Said it weren't natural to be burnin' people up, ain't the good Christian thing to do. Looks like you made of stronger stuff."

"Well, when they opened the crematory in Queens County a few years ago, it was all the talk. I actually thought it was the only one in New York State."

"Was at the time. This one come afterwards."

"Most people in my neighborhood, they thought it was savage, likened it to the Hottentots dancing around bodies in a bonfire."

"And you?" Jupiter appeared to be studying her.

Lillian felt a little rush of pleasure at someone asking her opinion. Certainly none of the nurses, even Janey, seemed likely to do so. "Well, it seems to me that it's very... clean."

"Yes, ma'am. Fire sure do purify."

She found herself focusing on the sound of Jupiter's words, the twang and elongation of syllables that was anything but native New York. "You're from down South, yes?"

"Alabama, ma'am."

"That's quite a distance. What brought you—" Just then, the door opened to admit a disgruntled Janey. "Did I suggest you have tea with Jupiter and ask after his family? We have living patients with bedpans that are not emptying themselves. Your job is to deliver and return. Nurse Collins will have both of our heads!" She grabbed the paperwork from Lillian's hands and thrust it toward Jupiter.

"It actually took me quite a while to get Not Lon—, I mean, the body, off the dumbwaiter—"

"Look," said Janey more quietly, and she took Lillian gently by the wrists. Lillian was aware of Jupiter watching her, though Janey clearly didn't care about his presence. "I think you could do well here, but you need to understand that your job is to do what you are told. Not to make excuses, not to offer opinions, not to get to know people. If you are fired, it will reflect poorly on me, so you need to decide if you are ready to follow the rules here. If not, save us all some trouble and leave now."

"I can do better. I will do better." And she had to, Lillian knew, or her one chance to eventually become a nurse would dry up and blow away.

Janey turned to Jupiter. "Why is there no fire?"

"Yes ma'am, right away." He walked quickly to the furnace and pulled a handle, and the resulting din of coal rumbling down the metal chute made any goodbyes impossible as Janey and Lillian left the room.

When they reached the ward, they paused in front of the doors. "Bedpans. It's very simple," Janey stated patiently and perhaps a little sarcastically. She explained the process — stack two, front facing away from you, carry carefully, *carefully*, to the slops room off the hallway... At the end of the litany, she added, "This doesn't require any interaction with the patients. If you have any questions *about the bedpans*, ask any nurse in the ward."

Lillian resolved that she would be the best bedpan cleaner the ward had ever seen. She would show Janey that she could do this job like an automaton.

When she finished the ward, Lillian congratulated herself on her machine-like focus and efficiency. No chatting, no squeamishness about the surprisingly varied contents of the pans, and, importantly, no spilling. She could clean one hundred bedpans without flagging.

Looking around for Janey, she saw two nurses across the ward in close conversation. One glanced at Lillian and when she looked back, they both smiled. Or perhaps smirked.

Lillian pursed her lips and forced herself to think of what the automaton would do. The automaton would spin on her heel and leave the ward to find Janey with no memory of this scene of petty behavior. Lillian had seen this behavior among the girls at school, mostly directed at others but occasionally aimed at Lillian, and she knew that it did no good to confront them.

But in school, that knowledge had not stopped her from confrontation.

She walked over to the nurses. "I've finished the bedpans on this ward. Is there anything else I can do before I report to Jane— er, Nurse Weatherbee?"

"Has she lost her pet again?" said the shorter one, and the other giggled.

"I'm just trying to do my job."

"Well, you can go do it in another ward," said the giggler.

"Oh, let's leave her alone," said the other, "at least she's on bedpan duty. It's not like she's a real nurse." They walked back to the nurses' station.

Lillian's face burned as she left the ward to find Janey, but their words only galvanized her resolve. She could be a better nurse than those two, and someday she would be.

❦ Chapter 5 ❦

Despite her resolve, Lillian felt deflated for the rest of the day. Even when Janey complimented her on her nimble assistance in sponge bathing a fragile post-operative patient, Lillian took little joy from it. As much as she wanted to brush aside the nurses' prediction that she would never become a nurse, she felt it keenly. And in the monotony of folding bed linens in the afternoon, her doubts cascaded and she began to think about Mrs. Oberman and Marie. Until now she had been able to convince herself that this was a viable solution for the foreseeable future, but the truth was now seeping in through her melancholic state. Hadn't she moved out with Marie to keep her safe? And could it be said that she was in fact doing that? But there was no going back.

Most times when she thought about her decision to take Marie away from Helen, she felt a jolt of righteous pride. After all, if Lillian were not going to protect Marie, who would? But in Lillian's moments of weakness, she recalled how Michael had always told her that her only flaw was that she was too quick to judge, and judge harshly. The truth was, she had not thought through how difficult it would be to care for Marie by herself. But although she had always talked through all the ups and downs of her life with Michael, she could not bring herself to confess this self-doubt to him. It felt like she would be pulling on a thread that would unravel everything, that would shine a light on something she would rather Michael not see, and didn't want to see herself.

That evening when she got home, Mrs. Oberman was in the toilet down the hall, just for a moment or so she claimed when she came back, and Marie was rolling around in a pile of clothing that included every garment she and Lillian owned, topped with all the linens ripped from the bed. The icebox door was ajar and all the ice that was to last them another day had melted. As soon as Mrs. Oberman made her lumbering exit, Lillian leaned against the front door. Her stomach hurt, a familiar and unwelcome companion whenever things weren't going well.

As she pinched the bridge of her nose, there was a knock on the door that she could feel through her shoulder blades.

"Michael!" She threw herself at him and hugged him tightly. "I didn't expect you tonight."

"Well, it appears I'm welcome nonetheless. Where's my Magpie?" He pulled back and saw the tears standing in Lillian's eyes. "Hey, hey, Lilypad, what's all the fuss?"

Lillian pushed the tears from her eyes with the heel of her palm. "Sorry."

Michael led her to the kitchen table. "Let me guess. Your boss is an ogre. And very windy. Smells like a chamber pot on a warm day."

Lillian laughed as tears spilled. "If that were only it. It's Mrs. Oberman. You must have passed her on the stairs."

"You mean the drunken crone who knocked into me? *That's* who is taking care of our Magpie?"

"Don't look at me that way! What was I to do? The interview and the job came up so suddenly and—"

"I'm sorry. I'm sorry. Look, Marie is fine, nothing has happened." They both looked into the other room where Marie was rolling around on the floor, wrapped in a quilt.

Lillian thought of the burn on Marie's arm. "It's not fine, Michael, I have no one to replace Mrs. Oberman. And I don't know anyone in this neighborhood yet. And I can't pay a lot. So I keep giving Mrs. Oberman her coin and hoping when I come home that I don't find…" She trailed off. There were many things she hoped not to find when she came home.

Michael stood up and walked around the small kitchen. "So I can assume that you are very open-minded about solving the Oberman Situation, yes?"

"Very." All of Lillian's senses were tuned to Michael. She was familiar with this tone of voice. Michael had a plan, or was formulating one.

"I have a friend," Michael began.

"I like this friend."

"Cork it, Lilypad, and let me continue. This friend is kind and loves children, but circumstances do not permit her to have a child of her own. I believe she may have had a brother or cousin who was simple."

"Oh Michael, how perfect! Why did you not tell me about her before?"

"Well, you told me you had already found care for Marie."

Lillian stood to hug Michael but then stopped short. "You said I had to be open-minded. What else is there to know about your friend?"

Michael motioned for them to sit at the kitchen table. He knit his hands together and took a breath. "I met Josephine down on the Bowery."

"But why would you have been there?" Lillian measured the silence between them and decided to ask a different question. "What was Josephine doing down on the Bowery?"

"She was working there, until recently."

"She was a barkeep?"

"She was an… adventuress."

"Michael! You expect me to trust Marie to a woman who has sold herself to men?" Lillian had another thought and blurted out, "Were you her… customer?"

Michael laughed so hard that Marie heard him underneath all her blankets and came running out to see him. Michael gave her a kiss and strip of ruby sateen ribbon from his pocket, and she trotted back to the bedroom to add it to her collection.

"Lillian, Josephine's preferred clients were… of the gentler sex."

"Tell me you are pulling my leg and that you are not suggesting your cousin be cared for by a… by a sapphist whore."

"No, I'm suggesting that your sister continue to be watched by an inebriated hunchback." Lillian could see the angry gleam in Michael's eyes and regretted her words. She couldn't understand his sudden change of mood.

"I'm sorry, I didn't mean to insult your friend."

"What you should be sorry about, cousin," said Michael as he stood and headed for the door, "is that you are so very judgmental and have been since we played knucklebones in the dirt together." He grabbed the doorknob but then spun around again. "Tell me. What offends your sensibilities more: that she was a whore or that she is a lesbian?"

Lillian could not remember seeing him this furious in recent memory. It was as if she hit some tripwire that ignited his outrage. "That seems a trick question," she said tentatively.

"All right, here's an alternate question: Is it inconceivable to you that this woman, a woman I have told you is *my friend*, that I have *recommended* to come into your home, could be a good person? Could be a good caretaker for my beloved Magpie?"

Lillian opened her mouth but an answer did not emerge.

After some tense moments, Michael agreed to stay for a cup of tea and talk it over. In exchange, Lillian agreed to withhold judgment and only ask questions. Over their mismatched steaming mugs, a more detailed picture of Josephine emerged. True, she was well known on the Bowery for hiring out to women, but she had attracted the attention of a man who liked his companions petite. He would not be dissuaded no matter how many times the diminutive Josephine declined his offers, and so one night he took what he wanted in an alley and beat her as a parting gift. Just now she was recovered, vowing not to return to her old vocation.

"She wants a safe place and a fresh start," Michael explained. "No one starts out as a little girl with the ambition of working the Bowery."

"I suppose I hadn't thought of it that way." But in truth, she felt that anyone who ended up working on the Bowery must have had it in them from the beginning. What Michael was implying was that, well, even Lillian herself could end up there if the circumstances of her life took an unexpected turn, which was clearly not true.

"Are you sure she would be interested in the job?" Lillian asked.

"Pretty sure. She lives not too far from here. I'll visit her on my way home. If she is interested, I could have her stop by here tomorrow night so you can meet her."

Lillian didn't see how she could say no to Michael without starting a fight. "All right. 8pm." She couldn't fathom how this could be a better solution than Mrs. Oberman, but just the fact that she might have a choice eased her mind. And unburdening herself to Michael was a relief. Even as a child, Lillian could not tolerate something coming between her and Michael. The few times they had been at odds, Lillian had trouble falling asleep at night and her appetite was off. When one of them finally offered an olive branch and it was over as quickly as it had begun, Lillian's heart soared.

As she hugged Michael goodbye, she assured him she would give Josephine a fair shake. And she would. She would simply look at the two choices and choose the better one. That couldn't be too hard.

Chapter 6

Lillian wished for nothing more than to have an uneventful day at work the next day, and her wish was granted. With each hour of work devoid of criticism or drama or mistakes, she felt the despair of yesterday ebbing farther and farther away. Collecting her wages for her first week of work boosted her mood further, and she found herself humming as she mounted the stairs of her building.

As she dismissed Mrs. Oberman, Lillian tried and failed to ignore the strong smell of whiskey as the old woman squeezed by her in the narrow kitchen. But everything in the house seemed in order, perhaps more so than on previous days. Nothing appeared to be broken, the contents of drawers were not strewn across the floor. Marie was lying on the bed, absently petting her button napkin. It was a bit unusual that Marie didn't come charging at Lillian the minute she turned the key in the lock, but she guessed Marie was just having a lazy day. God knew Lillian was planning on having one of those tomorrow, since she didn't have to work at the hospital. Although of course there were all the chores she couldn't get done in the evenings after work—the food shopping, preparing food to eat during the week, the laundry. But maybe she wouldn't get started with all that until after lunch. If the weather held, she would take Marie to the park in the morning.

As she was preparing supper, Lillian remembered that Michael's friend Josephine was likely to stop by this evening. Why had she agreed to that? In fact, now she couldn't even believe that Michael proposed it. He knew full well the situation from which Marie had been extracted, and so how could he imagine Lillian would want to expose Marie to the seedy side of this city through the likes of this Josephine? Certainly Mrs. Oberman wasn't perfect, but things were getting better, judging by today. She would talk to Mrs. Oberman tomorrow about a few ground rules, and she would dispatch the odious Josephine tonight as quickly as possible.

"Marie! Supper!" Such as it was. They were down to the last of what Lillian had prepared and purchased last weekend. A pot of beans and some stale bread, but she had bought two squares of caramel earlier in the week which had miraculously not been discovered and devoured. Helen had started this tradition after Marie recovered from the scarlatina — a special sweet after Friday night dinner — and Lillian had continued it so that not everything in Marie's life would be different after the move. Which was why it was odd that Marie was not racing to the dinner table. She somehow had a rather accurate sense of what day of the week it was and usually sped through Friday night dinner in anticipation of her treat. Lillian called out again but then started in on dinner alone. After a full day on her feet at the hospital, she was famished and didn't feel like waiting for Miss Lazybones.

Lillian glanced at the clock while washing the dishes. Josephine would be here soon. *Well, the sooner she comes, the sooner she'll be gone*, Lillian told herself. She tossed the wash rag to the back of the sink and knocked something to the floor in the process. As she picked up the unfamiliar object, she went numb. She held the little glass bottle with its cork stopper in her trembling hand, the writing too tiny to read at this distance, but she didn't need to read it. She ran into the bedroom and grabbed Marie by the face. Marie's empty eyes opened to half-mast. Lillian leaned down to hear her breath, slapped her cheeks, placed her palm over Marie's heart. "She's fine, she's just groggy, she's fine," Lillian chanted through gritted teeth. She placed her hand over her own heart, which was beating fiercely in her chest. Mrs. Oberman had probably given Marie just a small dose, to start out. But how much laudanum would it take to accidentally kill her? And would an old woman in her cups be all that careful with the dosing?

Tears burning like acid pooled in Lillian's eyes just as there was a knock at the door.

"You all right? You look like you've seen Lincoln's ghost," said Josephine as they sat down in the kitchen.

"I'm fine, I, I've had a fright," said Lillian, blotting tears with her apron before slipping the laudanum bottle into the pocket. "A mouse, in the cupboard."

"Hell's Kitchen has been known to have a few," she offered with a smile. She sat back in her chair with her hands in her lap. After a moment, she said, "Ya wanna look me over a bit, it's all right. Respectable folk will do that."

In fact, Lillian had already been looking her over. She wasn't sure what she expected, but Josephine wasn't it. Only a few years older than Lillian, Josephine was petite and her dress modest. Her gloves, when removed, revealed small pale hands, and her face was passably pretty with a delicate pointed chin, marred only by the red ropy scar across her left cheekbone. It did appear that she was not wearing a corset, but beyond that, she looked remarkably normal.

"And there's this," Josephine added, and she unpinned her trilby hat, a modest felt with small spotted feathers, to reveal dark copper curls cropped to her jaw. "You might as well know," she intoned with a mock seriousness, "I have *cut my hair.*"

"Oh, ah, of course," replied Lillian, caught off guard and unsure what to say. "How very, ah, practical."

"You bet. Dries in a trice on washday." She bounced her curls gently with the palm of her hand.

Lillian felt herself liking Josephine, which was unnerving. And then she realized what was most unexpected. She thought Josephine would be embarrassed, or at least try to hide the evidence of her depraved lifestyle. Instead, she seemed at ease with Lillian and unafraid to acknowledge what she was. It was as if Josephine didn't agree with the rules of civilized society which prescribed norms of behavior and therefore ignored them. To break those rules with shame, Lillian could at least understand, but to break them without concern was beyond her ken.

She decided she needed to take control of the conversation. "Miss Josephine—"

"Oh, it's just Josephine. And can I call you Lillian?"

Well, now Lillian would sound like a prig if she said no. "Certainly. So Josephine, you are here about a position looking after my sister. Michael likely told you, but the scarlatina blinded her and made her simple years ago."

"I'm very sorry."

"Sorry is not what we need," said Lillian, finally feeling like she was back on solid ground. "We need someone who understands what it means to care for her. It's not easy." Surely it would not be hard to dissuade Josephine once she understood how difficult Marie could be. But was that really what Lillian wanted? She could not allow Mrs. Oberman to be alone with Marie again, and she had two days before she needed to be back at the hospital. How would she find anyone else in that time? And here was someone interested enough to come here—on time, Lillian noted, unlike Mrs. Oberman—to inquire about the job.

"My nephew was kicked in the head by a cart horse when he was five," Josephine said. "He's not right, needs to be fed and cleaned and such. I've cared for him now and then."

"Well, Marie can feed herself." If Lillian were being honest with herself, she would admit that she put Mrs. Oberman to no such test regarding her abilities and temperament. She might as well tell Josephine the real sticking point. "I'm sure you could do the job. Forgive me, but my hesitation is that you.... is the fact that... is because...."

Josephine set her jaw. "I know Michael already told ya, so I'll say it. I like women. And I been paid for it."

"Yes!" exclaimed Lillian in relief. She almost thanked Josephine for articulating it so she didn't have to.

"So let's take them two things separately. Of the first, well, that's really only my concern."

"But it's unnatural." Lillian felt cruel saying this, but it had to be said.

Josephine did not seem offended. "It is entirely natural to me. I never been another way."

Lillian frowned. "Did nothing happen to you that caused you to... turn?" This was certainly the conventional wisdom about these kind of preferences, for both men and women. An event at a young age with a monstrous adult, or an abuse with the opposite gender so terrible it ruined normal relations for life.

"There weren't no turning, you can be sure."

Lillian could not unwind a lifetime of conviction in one conversation, but she was no longer sure of what she had always believed. It would be easier for Josephine to say she was a victim, that it wasn't her fault. Yet she did not. Could she be the exception to the rule?

"As for the second part," Josephine continued, "I'm not proud of my days on the Bowery. My Pa kicked me to the curb when they figured out that my friend was more than my friend. Our family weren't living the high life, but we always had a roof over our head and food to eat. On my own, I had no idea how to live without money. Maybe I shoulda learned to make do with less, but what's done is done. Now I'm done with earnin' my scratch that way and I want to stay done." She looked down at the table and gently ran a finger over her scar. "I just want a normal life," she added.

"So you are saying you want to throw over both your job and your... preferences. To live normally." Lillian felt a glimmer of hope. If Josephine really wanted to turn her life around and Lillian could help her—while having Marie taken care of—maybe all interests could be served. Lillian could even play a supporting role in Josephine's redemption.

Josephine looked up. "I want a normal job. A respectable job. But who I am, who I like—that's just a fact. Might as well try to stop the rain from fallin'." After a beat, Josephine continued. "There's something else we gotta get out on the table. I got no interest in young girls, if you take my meaning. You had to have been thinking on that. But that's not me. Still, you'd be a low person indeed if you didn't have concerns."

Lillian took a deep breath of relief at finally having this out in the open. "So you understand why this won't work."

"What I understand is that I been honest with you about everything. I spent too much time lying to everyone around me, it about ate me up inside. I tell it true now," said Josephine, and her delicate chin thrust forward slightly. "And that's what I'd want in someone looking after my sister."

Throughout the next half hour, Lillian felt her resolve fraying. Marie stumbled out of the bedroom in search of her supper but perked up when she smelled a new person in the room. Initially cautious, Marie skirted Josephine and dug into her beans—Lillian gently insisting on the use of a spoon, so as to show Josephine that they did have standards—but when she was done, she went over to feel the fabric of Josephine's clothing. When Marie had brushed the feathers on the trilby to her satisfaction, Josephine gently brought Marie's hands to her cropped curls, bringing a look of surprise to Marie's face. She slowly finger-combed the short tresses while Josephine and Lillian talked about mealtimes, getting dressed, Marie's amusements both allowed and discouraged.

When Josephine went with Marie to look at the collections of notions from Michael's shop, Lillian planted her elbows on the table and held her chin in her hands. Josephine could have lied about several things to make herself a more attractive candidate for the job, but she did not. Did that mean she was being honest about everything? Lillian could not defend the choice of Josephine to a stranger, but she could see that Marie was safer with Josephine as compared to Mrs. Oberman. Perhaps if she had more time she could find a proper alternative, but time was one thing she did not have. At least in the short term, she could think of no other solution than to hire Josephine.

Chapter 7

Toward the end of her next week of work, Lillian started to experience the unending nature of her job's repetitive tasks, but the monotony freed her mind to observe. As she rotated through the wards, she could see what a patient's time here was all about. Many were here for months, some being kept comfortable while they waited for the end, but most in long periods of recovery from surgery. In fact, it seemed that for every surgery to excise a tumor, there was at least one other to reopen a surgical wound and clean it out. Lillian had become adept at scanning charts in a way that did not attract the attention of the nurses, and she found that most patients went through weeks if not months of battling post-surgical infection. In the more extreme cases, she could smell the infection while standing beside the bed, and wondered if the patient could smell it too.

As she settled into her job, she also settled into Josephine's presence in her life. Her days with Marie seemed to go smoothly, as much as Lillian looked for evidence to the contrary when she returned home. Nothing broken, nothing in disarray, supper dishes clean and drying on the sideboard. On her first day, Josephine had brought with her a length of twine and taught Marie Cat's Cradle, which Marie had rushed to show to Lillian before she was barely through the door that evening. One side of Josephine's hair had been braided despite its short length and pinned in a jumble, no doubt the work of Marie. Josephine hadn't bothered to unpin it before she donned her trilby and said goodnight.

As Lillian worked through the bedpans in the third floor ward, she contemplated how easy it was to forget Josephine's previous job. There was nothing bawdy or masculine, or… well, Lillian wasn't quite sure what the characteristics were of such a person, but much as she looked she could find nothing out of the ordinary about Josephine beyond her short hair, which could not even be said to be masculine because it was so curly. Last night when she let Josephine go after a brief chat about Marie's day, Lillian realized that she hadn't thought about all her objections to Josephine since the day before. In fact, it was hard to remember all that unpleasantness when Josephine was around.

As she mulled this over, she rose from retrieving a nearly-empty pan beneath a bed to hear the bed's occupant say in a labored whisper, "You're Lillian."

Lillian startled but luckily held on to the pan. "Yes ma'am, do I know you?" The woman's apple cheeks told Lillian that she was not at the end of a cancer battle. She saw red streaks reaching up the woman's neck and recalled one of Dr. Pratt's books describing this as the telltale sign of infection. Post-surgical, then.

"Your mother," she said wheezing through gritted teeth. "Building on 37th Street."

"Nice to meet you, ma'am." Lillian turned to go. Not only was she determined not to talk to patients as per Janey's instructions, but she certainly had nothing to say to a neighbor of her mother's.

"You moved," the woman stated, right before she was gripped with pain that crumpled her face.

"Do you want me to get a nurse?" This seemed like an acceptable interaction with a patient, and one likely to curtail this conversation.

After a beat, the woman's face relaxed a bit. "Because of what your mother did."

Lillian froze. She knew that a few neighbors were aware of her mother's transgression, but had hoped never to talk with them about it.

"Took your sister. Good girl." The woman closed her eyes.

Yes, Lillian thought, I am a good girl. At least she could be sure of that.

As Lillian started to walk away, the woman grabbed Lillian's arm with surprising strength. Lillian would have thought she could barely raise her arm. "A favor," she hissed.

"Ma'am, I should get a nurse—"

"No!" The exclamation used up a reserve of energy. After a few wheezy breaths she continued. "Not them. You. Good girl."

Lillian looked over at the nurses' station. The two ward nurses were deep in conversation and mostly obscured by the central ventilation shaft. "I'm new here, I don't even know where they keep most things."

"Morphine."

"Ma'am, a nurse can certainly—"

"A lot. Double. Triple. Ten times." She was panting now. "Please."

Lillian went numb with the realization of what the woman was asking. What would a nurse say? "That's not God's plan." She blushed at her own hypocrisy; God's will was the last thing she saw in illness. But she could think of nothing better to add.

"The hell with God." She drew in a ragged breath. "Gonna help me?"

Lillian looked over at the nurses' station. The two nurses had stopped talking. One was coming around the front of the desk.

"I can't," she whispered and walked away from the bed, bedpan sloshing, but not fast enough to avoid hearing the woman say, "The hell with you, too."

When she got to the slop room, she dropped the pan in the sink and leaned up against the wall. Clearly she did the right thing. She waited for the feeling of virtue, but it did not come.

The woman with apple cheeks took all day to die.

Lillian was able to peek at the woman's chart over Janey's shoulder later in the day. It confirmed that she was dying of infection; her radical mastectomy three days prior had gone well but a fever set in that evening, and the irrigations and dustings of iodoform powder had no effect. Lillian had hoped it would happen during the night shift, that she would come in tomorrow and the woman's bed would be empty with a pile of fresh sheets for Lillian to deploy, but the doctor verified her death not long before Lillian's shift ended.

"I'll take her to Jupiter," Lillian quietly volunteered to Janey after the doctor had finished completing the forms, which confirmed there was no one to claim her.

"All right," said Janey as she handed the paperwork to Lillian. "I like your gumption." She paused. "But don't mistake Jupiter for a friend. The nursing staff is separate from the understaff. You need to stick with your kind."

This struck Lillian as patently unfair, since the rest of the nursing staff shunned her, but she held her tongue.

Wrestling this body off the dumbwaiter was both more difficult than the last (because the body was heavier) and also easier (because Lillian had done this once before). While tucking the woman's arms firmly under the sheet, Lillian realized the woman's skin was not yet cold. Was this because she had died of infection? Had the fever heated her blood so much that she would take longer to cool than one who died with no fever? She wished she could ask Dr. Pratt. Certainly Janey would not welcome the inquiry.

She glanced down the hallway to make sure she was alone, and then gently pulled the sheet back from the woman's face. Her cheeks were still prominent but now devoid of their rosiness. Lillian still did not recognize her from their old neighborhood. She lifted the woman's hand and saw the calluses on her palm. Hardworking, then, but poor and alone; Lillian had seen the words "Charity" and "No Next of Kin" on her chart, so it was no surprise that she ended up here in the basement. Had she been destitute before the lump in her breast could no longer be ignored, or did her illness propel her into poverty? Lillian placed the woman's hand back on her chest. She thought of the woman's awful request and tried to imagine the kind of pain that you wouldn't mind trading for an early and intentional death.

If Jupiter remembered their prior friendly conversation, he gave no indication. "Miz Dolan," he said neutrally as he wheeled the gurney over to the side of the room.

"I hope I didn't get you in a fix when I last saw you, with the fire. And Nurse Weatherbee."

"No problem at all, ma'am." He accepted the paperwork that Lillian handed him.

"She can have a sharp tongue," Lillian said, but this elicited no response from Jupiter. He stood patiently, holding the paperwork in both hands in front of him, seeming neither impatient for her to leave nor encouraging her to stay. She thought of the long El ride home, the silent evening with Marie, the improbability of a visit from Michael. "This patient...." She knew she should stop now. "She asked me for morphine. Quite a bit. Way too much."

Jupiter's eyes widened, the whites vivid against his mahogany skin. "Ma'am, I can't be hearing about nothin' you done—"

"No, no!" All at once Lillian saw that he thought she was confessing. "I didn't! She asked, but I said I couldn't! I would never!"

Jupiter closed his eyes in relief. "Lord have mercy."

Taking his statement as evidence of a religious take on the subject, she offered, "I told her that it wasn't God's plan, for me to... help her."

"Hope that gave her some comfort."

"It didn't. But do you think it's true?"

"Don't much matter what I think."

She could see he was trying to slip out of taking a stand, but she wasn't willing to let him of that easily. "It matters to me. Tell me."

He rubbed the back of his neck as he thought. "I guess I seen some things that are mighty hard to explain as God's will."

"In Alabama?"

"Don't have to look that far to see suffering." He walked back to the furnace and checked the dials. Lillian could see she had pushed a little too far, but she admired his answer—true, diplomatic, unrevealing. He would have made a fine nursing assistant.

"Well, I'm off shift so I'll see you 'round."

"You ain't goin' to night class?" Jupiter was still facing away from her, fiddling with the furnace.

"What night class?" Lillian had not heard of any classes.

"Oh that's right," he said, "You just an assistant." He turned around. Was that a smile on his face?

She stepped toward him. "Please explain."

"Well, the nurses, they go to these lectures by the doctors. Learn about all nature of things. In the evening, on their own time, but they live here and I s'pose they got the time. They all go. But I guess they ain't mention that to you, must not be for assistants."

Lectures! Happening in this very building, for free. She had to go.

Janey would never allow it. And if the other nurses didn't already hate her, this would seal the deal.

And then there was Marie and Josephine. Lillian glanced up at the clock on the wall.

"I've got to get home. When are the classes?"

"Tuesdays and Thursdays, 6pm." There was no doubt now that Jupiter was smiling.

🎔 Chapter 8 🎔

The next day, as soon as Lillian and Janey walked through the ward doors, Janey stopped short and gestured toward one of the beds where a doctor and nurse stood. "That is Dr. Metcalfe, the house surgeon. I will trust you can be seen and not heard." Lillian wondered why, if Janey didn't want her interacting with the doctors, they were headed over at all. It did not appear that Janey had been requested for this patient. But after they arrived at the foot of the patient's bed, Lillian could see how Janey was straining to hear the soft-spoken doctor. It seemed that Janey wanted to learn every bit as much as Lillian did. Most of the cases Janey saw were probably hum-drum to her by now. But the presence of a surgeon on the ward must signal something unusual. And if Janey found it interesting, Lillian was sure she would too.

Dr. Metcalfe was dictating to a senior nurse, who was somewhat frantically making notes on a clipboard. "Upon admission patient was semi-conscious. Distended abdomen indicates advanced tumor in the upper left quadrant." Through the sheet that covered the woman in the bed Lillian could see the asymmetric bulge. The doctor pressed gently on it with four fingers flattened. The woman moaned without opening her eyes. "Tumor is tender. Pallor is gray." He plucked at the skin on her forearm. "Patient is slightly dehydrated. Course of treatment is fluids and pain relief with morphine hypodermics. Nurse, come find me if her condition changes." He spun on his heel and left the ward while the senior nurse made her final notes.

"Nurse Matheson," began Janey respectfully, "may I assume this patient will continue on a palliative care course?"

"You may assume that, as do I." She lifted the patient's limp wrist to take her pulse.

"I thought that it was hospital policy that we don't take the incurables."

"Generally that has been the case." Nurse Matheson noted the pulse on her clipboard. She leaned in ever so slightly and took her voice down a notch. "There has been some difference of opinion among the doctors on this issue. Some feel that there is much to learn post mortem, enough that it warrants admissions which will harm our statistics." She suddenly looked over at Lillian and seemed to realize that the circle of this conversation was a bit too wide. The nurse looked at Janey and tipped her head toward the central desk, and the two of them walked a few yards away to consult the clipboard and continue the conversation quietly.

Lillian was left at the side of the bed, where she looked at the patient's face and saw that she was now awake, and likely had been during that conversation judging by the two tears running from the corners of her eyes down to the thin pillow.

An hour later Lillian was eating lunch with Janey and two other nurses. Or, more accurately, Janey was having lunch with two nurses and Lillian was also there. The brother of one of the nurses had evidently recently shown some interest in Janey and there was much conversation on that subject, which seemed to please Janey greatly. The two nurses finished their lunch early and left, and Lillian realized that this was the ideal time to talk to Janey in words she had rehearsed last night.

"Janey, may I speak with you about a matter?"

Janey still had a little smile on her face as she popped the last of a biscuit in her mouth. "This would not be a bad time to speak of a matter. Your timing is improving."

Lillian cleared her throat. "The patient that Dr. Metcalfe saw. The, er, bad statistic. You were very interested in her chart."

"Yes, the majority of patients have female cancers here, which that probably was not. And a lot of abdominal cancers don't present outwardly."

"So there was something new to learn with this patient."

"Potentially."

"I don't mean to put myself above my station here, but I would like to suggest that I am not terribly different from you in this respect. I also want to learn."

"You've made that clear," Janey said, but not unkindly.

"I have tried not to ask pesky questions while we are on the ward or at other inopportune times. I will keep trying to remember my position here. But I'm sure you can understand that I do not want to still be a nursing assistant in five years' time."

"So what are you asking me?" Janey rotated in her seat to fully face Lillian.

Here was the part that Lillian had been dreading, but there was no turning back now. "I would like to attend the night classes."

"Ah," said Janey as she leaned back in her chair. "Of course. I should have anticipated that. Assistants do not attend the classes."

"If I'm not mistaken, there have only been two other assistants before me, and perhaps they never asked." This was a gamble but it seemed a safe one.

"All right, I'll give you that. But tell me: if you begin to learn all the wonders of the human body, how will this not inspire you to have even more questions? Won't this make it even harder for you to hold your tongue?" Janey looked like she might know the answer to that question already.

Lillian had not thought of this when rehearsing this conversation in her mind, so she racked her brain for a satisfactory reply. "I can… I can write down all my questions and ask you at lunch!"

"That sounds like a dreadful lunchtime for me."

"I can look them up in books! Please, Janey, I would not say a word in the classes, I would be as quiet as a church mouse."

"Goodness, I hadn't even considered you piping up in the class. I was just thinking about the wards." She closed her eyes for a moment. "You know this will not make you any friends among the other nurses."

"I am not here to make friends." Not that it seemed possible, even without attending the classes.

"Well, that's sensible, at least." Janey stood up and balled the newspaper in which her lunch had been wrapped and threw it in the trash pail. "You do have one thing pulling in your favor, as it turns out. Dr. Metcalfe would have to approve this, and as it happens next week is his last week. He is retiring and will be replaced by a Dr. Bauer. So I doubt Dr. Metcalfe much cares about this decision, and he is also kindly. I will ask Nurse Holt to bring this up with him."

Nurse Holt! Lillian had assumed it would be Janey asking for permission. Her hope withered like a plucked flower.

"Don't crumple up, now, I'll put in a good word. Surprised, eh? I can see you trying here. And I do think you could be a good nurse someday. Besides, if you start letting your curiosity get the best of you, we'll just yank you out of the classes, and believe me, there will be no going back. Should keep you on the straight and narrow."

Later in the day, Lillian had just finished putting fresh sheets on a recently-vacated ward bed (removal of a tumor on the neck with only mild post-surgical infection, discharged "cured," according to the chart she surreptitiously read) when a nurse informed her that she was wanted in Dr. Metcalfe's office. Lillian's heart leaped with hope and then clenched with worry as she rustled off in the direction indicated by the nurse.

Both Janey and Nurse Holt were standing in front of Dr. Metcalfe who was seated at his desk, attempting to light his pipe. When Lillian positioned herself next to Janey, Nurse Holt said, "Doctor, this is the assistant, Miss Dolan."

Three puffs later, his pipe now aglow, he looked up. "Miss Dolan. New here, how long?"

Lillian took a breath to answer but Nurse Holt got there first. "Nearly two weeks, Doctor."

"How are you liking our little hospital thus far?"

Curls of pipe smoke wafted from his mouth and obscured his face. She waited a beat to see if Nurse Holt would answer this question too, but Nurse Holt was silent. "I'm very happy here, sir. Doctor."

"And yet here you stand before me with a special request. You would like to attend the evening lectures."

"Yessir, I would. I—" She looked over at Janey as she started to explain, but Janey's furrowed brow dissuaded her. "I would."

Dr. Metcalfe swiveled in his chair and sucked on his pipe. "The question and answer period at the end of each lecture is brief, so as to maximize the time for the doctors to impart their knowledge. I ask all attendees to think whether their question is well thought out and also of interest to the broader group."

Janey interjected, "Miss Dolan wouldn't be asking any questions, Doctor. That is our agreement."

"Well then," said Dr. Metcalfe, "Do either of you see any reason Miss Dolan should not attend?"

There was a pause. "Seating is limited," said Nurse Holt in a nasal tone.

"Surely we can find another chair in this building! If that's the best reason you can come up with, she is approved."

Lillian wanted to jump up and down but forced herself to stay stock still, so still that Janey had to grab her arm as the two nurses exited. "Thank you, Dr. Metcalfe," Lillian remembered to say as she nearly tripped on the door sill. Dr. Metcalfe raised a hand briefly but then busied himself knocking the ash out of his pipe into a saucer.

The remaining hour of the afternoon found Lillian filing charts, filling in for a secretary who had been out sick for several days. "You won't normally be on paperwork," Janey had said when showing her the filing system, "but we're a bit light on patients and backed up on charts." Lillian had noticed that the upper floor for paying patients —"Posh Row" as she overheard one nurse say to another—was particularly empty. Mrs. Van Alstead and her dog had evidently been discharged, presumably hemorrhoid-free, and when Lillian was up there this morning to make a bed, it appeared that no room on the floor was occupied.

With Lillian's anticipation of all that she would soon be learning in the night classes, it didn't take long for her to start wondering about the contents of the charts she was filing. The first one she opened described a cervical cancer surgery. "*Cervix and anterior wall were thoroughly scraped with a Volkmann scoop and some small tumors cut away with a scissors. Usual Antiseptic Precautions taken.*" She didn't know what a Volkmann scoop was, but she guessed those precautions were the dreaded Lister Spray Janey had mentioned. The nurses hated it due to its caustic effect on any skin it touched. Some of the more senior nurses who assisted the most in surgeries displayed their red and cracked fingers like a badge of honor.

The next file was more confusing. "*Extirpation and cleaning out of Axilla.*" She tried to remember from Dr. Pratt's books what the axilla was. Something to do with the shoulder? If so, was this breast cancer? Janey had said they mostly saw cancers of the female anatomy. But why would they be cleaning out her shoulder? She read on: "*Patient went bad on the table and was given hypodermics of whiskey and ether.*" Lillian hadn't known that either whiskey or ether were things to be injected, she guessed as stimulants to revive the patient. "*Wound could not be closed entirely. Severe post-operative course.*" She read to the end of the notes, where the patient was discharged seven weeks after the initial surgery after dozens of skin grafts. She tried to imagine what that would look like. Who were the donors of the grafts? How did they take skin grafts? Wasn't there a risk of infection to the donor? And then she had a startling thought: what if they took skin grafts from the recently deceased? She made a mental note to check the next cadaver she had to haul off the dumbwaiter.

Lillian could feel her heart beating in her chest. For her, these post-operative notes were more exciting than any penny dreadful. Dr. Pratt's books were interesting but dry; reading this report was like being present in the operating theater as life-or-death drama unfolded. She imagined the perspiration beading on the surgeon's brow, blotted delicately by a nurse who could someday be Lillian. She could almost feel the tension in the room as the surgery took an unexpected turn, the clatter of instruments tossed in haste upon the tray, the metallic smell of blood rising in the air.

In a panic she looked over at the tiny clock on the desk behind her. Twenty minutes, and she had only filed one report! Janey would never let her do this again if she discovered how slowly Lillian was working. She worked through the towering stack diligently without opening any more files, until she picked up the last one. A glance at the desk clock showed that Lillian was officially off duty now, and she didn't hear anyone approaching in the hallway. She opened the file and started from the top.

🎆 Chapter 9 🎆

The next Tuesday, Lillian was the first to show up for night class. She chose a seat on a bench in the middle, a compromise between the front row where she wanted to be and the back row where the nurses would undoubtedly want her. She looked at the pendulum clock on the wall and tried to contain her excitement. Tonight's class entitled "Antisepsis in the Operating Theater" would, she hoped, answer the many questions that had been forming in her mind. The subject was also of special interest since she guessed she had little chance of ever being invited to witness a surgery.

The door to the lecture room opened and nurses started to trickle in. Two that sat behind her started to whisper. Perhaps they were not talking about her, but she told herself it didn't matter either way. She was here with the blessing of Dr. Metcalfe and no number of whispering nurses could remove her.

As the clock gonged, the last few nurses rushed to take their seats, including Janey who sat next to Lillian. "Never start an enema a half hour before class," she muttered as she settled, writing today's date in a journal of lined paper. Lillian realized she had brought nothing to take notes, the very thing she promised Janey she would do in order to defer the asking of questions. She hoped Janey would not notice.

A few minutes later, Dr. Metcalfe entered the room and the

murmurs of conversation died down. "Good evening, ladies," he said as he walked to a small podium and arranged his notes. "Tonight I speak to you on a subject of great importance. When you stand at the side of a surgeon as he pierces the protective layer of a patient's skin with his scalpel, that patient is instantly rendered vulnerable by that very act. Your job in the operating theater, beyond the tireless support of your doctor, is to make sure you are not inadvertently the agent of that patient's demise."

A chill went through Lillian. What responsibility every soul in that theater had! She leaned forward, waiting for Dr. Metcalfe's next words as he stroked his beard and cleared his throat.

"When my father first became a surgeon, the prevailing theory on infection as well as disease was Miasma Theory. Foul, poisonous air, invisible but deadly. Today we now embrace Germ Theory and know its truth through the work of Dr. Louis Pasteur. We have weapons in the war against the germs that cause infection from the work of Dr. Joseph Lister: carbolic acid, iodoform, bichloride. It is your duty to understand these solutions and our procedures."

Lillian saw that many nurses were starting to write in notebooks and on pieces of paper, and she itched to do the same. Dr. Metcalfe started with patient preparation (shaving and a rub of carbolized Vaseline the day prior), room preparation (the hefting of the five-kilogram carbolic steam sprayer around the room, the covering of the instruments with towels soaked in bichloride solution), and the dressing of the wound (iodoform powder and layers of bichloride gauzes). As Janey had predicted, there was hardly a statement Dr. Metcalfe made that did not spawn a question within Lillian. Wouldn't dirt stick to the Vaseline? Was the procedure prescribed for nurses washing their hands identical to that of the doctors? How did they figure out how many layers of gauze were ideal for a dressing? And most of all, with all these procedures and solutions, why was there still so much infection on the wards?

Too soon for Lillian, Dr. Metcalfe was done. "I have time for two thoughtful questions," he stated after consulting his pocket watch. A senior nurse inquired about antiseptic suture preparation and another about hot carbolic dressings, and when both were answered Dr. Metcalfe announced "Very well, then," and strode out of the room.

Lillian turned to Janey as the nurses stood and shuffled out of the room. "You had no questions?"

"Of course I did, but I'm not yet senior enough to ask, especially when the doctor has only called for two. I can ask the other nurses if need be."

But, Lillian thought, what if they don't know? Or what if they provide an answer but it isn't correct—because they were not senior enough to ask the doctor?

She kept those questions to herself as well.

Two days later, Lillian was prepared for the night lecture. She had bought a cheap notebook and positioned herself one bench closer to the podium, remembering that Dr. Metcalfe's voice had been hard to hear when he looked down to consult his notes. "Suppuration," Dr. Metcalfe's final lecture before his retirement the next day, reviewed the four types of pus—Aqueous, Sanguineous, Inchorous and Healthy—and appropriate treatments, including poultices of flaxseed and balsam of pine. Lillian wrote quickly and neatly amid the scratching of other pencils on paper surrounding her, and she felt, if not equal, at least great satisfaction in sharing the same experience as the other nurses.

The next day there was an admission to Posh Row. Lillian had not been to these rooms recently and the contrast between them and the wards hit her anew as she delivered an early supper to the new patient. All the features of the wards that were promoted as infection-inhibiting—the round room, the iron beds, the hard cleanable surfaces—were not employed in these rooms, with their carpets and upholstered chairs. Was the austerity of the wards not important for preventing infection, or would the rich simply not tolerate that austerity? Based on Dr. Metcalfe's first lecture, she guessed it was the latter, but how could the hospital in good conscience provide accommodations for the rich that were more likely to cause infection than those given to the poor?

As Lillian set the tray down, she calculated the risk in trying to read the woman's chart hanging discreetly at the foot of the bed. On one hand, no other nurses were around, but on the other hand, the woman was fully awake. Some patients felt the frilly nurse cap endowed the right to read the chart but others balked, especially the modest ones whose charts detailed highly personal details. This one didn't look like the overly modest type, so Lillian plucked the chart off the hook with feigned confidence.

This did not escape the attention of the patient. "Say there, girl, what business do you have looking at my doctor's notes?" She waggled a plump finger bedecked with an amethyst ring in Lillian's direction.

"Yes, Mrs...." Lillian scanned the chart. "Mrs. Tremont. I was just checking the doctor's direction on your meals. I see right here you are on the House Diet, but you can't be too sure. Always pays to check." Lillian had thought of this excuse earlier in the week, which could work when delivering meals. It had only one drawback: the patient's diet plan was actually not recorded on the chart, so if the patient asked to see what the doctor had written, Lillian wasn't sure what she would do. "May I help you with your napkin, ma'am?" she said, in an effort to distract.

"No, no, I'm not hungry. But leave the tray for later. And the girl checking me in mentioned that there is champagne this afternoon in the first floor parlor, but I am far too fatigued to walk those stairs and make chit-chat. I will take my champagne in my room."

"Yes, ma'am, I'll have it brought right away."

"And bring some sweets. They will revive me. The trip here in the brougham was exhausting—no one mentioned that 8th Avenue is not paved this far north! So sweets—anything will do: pralines, fondant, Turkish Delight." She waived her hand lazily in the air, as if to brush away the drudgery of sorting through the many choices.

Lillian paused, but then replied, "I will see what the kitchen has today, ma'am." Janey had instructed her to never say no to a patient. Although Lillian knew they did not stock such exotic sweets in the kitchen, she knew Janey would figure out what to do. In fact, with Janey's famous sweet tooth she was the perfect nurse to resolve Mrs. Tremont's demands.

And that was when Lillian figured out how to get some of her questions answered.

The sweet shop where she bought Marie's caramels every week was just about to close when she got there that evening. In addition to her usual weekly purchase for Marie, she bought a small box of two marzipan shaped like fruit. That night in bed, while staring at the flaking ceiling and listening to the whistle of Marie's breathing, she reviewed over and over how she would use the little box tomorrow.

She had hoped that Janey would linger over her lunch as she sometimes did, occasionally even reading a story or two from the newspaper that had wrapped her food, but Janey rose with the other nurses after their eating and chatting was done. "Janey?" Lillian ventured. "Might this be a good time for a word?"

"All right, certainly better than on the wards." She plopped herself back down in the chair.

"A kindly man runs a sweet shop near me which closes as I pass by each night. He is… a friend, really, knew my father." This was untrue. "He offers me the sweets that have not sold." Also untrue. "So I thought I would perhaps offer you a, well, a trade of sorts."

Janey frowned. "Trade?"

Lillian brought out the box from her apron and removed the top. The sugar crystals twinkled pleasantly. "A sweet for a question." She smiled at Janey.

"The cheek of you!" Janey exclaimed, and Lillian felt the horror of a mistake wash over her. Perhaps this was considered bribery? Was this against hospital rules? But before she could respond, Janey began to laugh. "Oh, you are a panic, I'll tell you that. A sweet for a question!" When her laughter died down, she took a long look at Lillian. "So you've been quiet as a church mouse during night lectures, and on the wards you've kept to your work, so I see no reason I can't answer a question or two for a spot of dessert." She selected the candy shaped like a red apple from the box and held it up. "The fruit of the tree of knowledge—how appropriate." She took a bite and pointed at Lillian. "Ask away."

"If a patient has cancer of the breast, why does the surgery venture into her shoulder?" This had been bothering her since she read that chart while filing.

Janey's eyes narrowed. "How do you know about that?"

"Well… I've overheard some of the nurses talking." This was partially true, in that she had heard nurses talking about how recent mastectomies actually seemed less extensive, but it had only registered with Lillian because of the chart she had read.

"So, once the surgeon opens up the breast, it's generally a lot worse than one could tell from the outside. And if so, they remove the lymph nodes in the shoulder as well. But Dr. Metcalfe told us in one of the recent night classes that this doesn't do much long term, and he favors a more moderate surgery with a quicker recovery." Janey eyed the remaining candy. "And since many of our mastectomies are not paying customers, quicker is better."

Lillian wasted no time in launching into her next question. "Why do the women on Posh Row generally not come to us with cancer? Do the wealthy not get it?"

Janey plucked the pear from the box, green with a blush of yellow on one side. "You might think that. All sorts of advantages to being rich, right? But no, they get it just as much as the poor folk. They can just afford to get treated at home. Dr. Metcalfe performs about one surgery a week on the fine dining room tables of New York. And who wouldn't prefer that?" Janey popped the entire pear in her mouth and stood up, closing her eyes as she chewed. "Mmmm. Completely worth the questions. And if you're that desperate for answers, I can throw a few your way without a delicious bribe, as long as you choose your time wisely." She stood up and brushed the sugar crystals from her hands. "But we both need to get back. Beds to be made on the third floor."

Lillian followed Janey back to the wards, ready for anything and relieved that part of her salary would not have to be spent at the sweet shop every week.

By some sort of miracle, the El arrived at the 103rd Street station just as Lillian was mounting the stairs to the platform, and then went express through a few stops, much to the annoyance of people on those platforms who were also trying to get home from work on a Friday evening. Even standing in the crowded car with all its attendant smells and sounds could not dampen Lillian's mood. The marzipan had worked as well as she had hoped, perhaps better. She had thought long and hard about Janey, who could be friendly in the morning and yelling at Lillian in the afternoon, and she realized that it was, as Janey herself said, all about timing. While Janey didn't approve of Lillian's endless curiosity, she would tolerate it in the right setting—when others were not around and work was not being put off. In fact, Lillian suspected that Janey enjoyed the role of instructor, certainly not a role that the most junior nurse on staff could play with anyone but Lillian.

She was a good fifteen minutes early getting home, affording her the opportunity to see what might be going on at home when she was not yet expected. She crept quietly into the kitchen and saw Josephine and Marie washing the supper dishes, something in which Lillian was never able to make Marie participate. Although upon closer examination, it seemed that Marie was just playing, slapping the stopped-up water in the sink with the flat of her hands to hear the sound. But still, Lillian knew from her experience that just keeping Marie occupied nearby was better than suddenly realizing you hadn't seen her in a while.

"Oh, hello there, didn't hear ya come in," said Josephine as she brushed her curls out of her face. Lillian was finally used to seeing a woman with short hair. Hats these days were much smaller than in previous years, and she wondered if Josephine received looks from passers-by, and if so, if she cared.

Marie ran over and gave Lillian a hug, leaving wet patches from her soaked dress on Lillian's coat, and then ran back to the sink. Josephine hung up the dishrag and said, "Left a bit of supper for you in the icebox. Marie was a bit off her food, I think she's got a tooth hurtin'."

The thought of needing to get Marie's tooth pulled was a sobering one. Helen had once taken Marie to have this done and would only say to Lillian afterward that the dentist came out worse for wear and that they could never go back there. She hung up her coat and hat on the nail by the door and decided not to think of the dentist. If Marie's tooth became worse, there would be plenty of time to do something about it.

As Lillian fished in her purse for Josephine's payment, Josephine sat at the table and asked, "How was your day at work?"

Lillian sat down in the other kitchen chair. "My day was... well, actually, it was quite good." Josephine just looked at her, waiting for more, though Lillian thought that would have sufficed. "I… I was able to get some questions answered."

"That hard to do there?"

"Oh yes, it's not my place to ask questions as a nursing assistant."

Josephine looked amused. "Not your place, but there ya are, askin' away."

"Is it so wrong to want to know more?" Lillian huffed.

"Seems like you got yourself a cogitatin' mind. Bet you were one of those that liked school."

Lillian looked for any sign that Josephine thought her snobbish or superior, but saw none. "I did at that," she admitted. Helen had instructed both girls from an early age that education was the way to better themselves, for free in this country, and they would be fools not to drink up every drop of learning the school had to offer. Lillian had hardly needed persuading; she loved all the subjects and was sad when she became too old to attend.

"Well, then," Josephine concluded, "You can't help it. It's too deep in ya now. Might as well give yourself over to it."

Lillian turned this over in her mind: the idea that her desire to know all the workings of the medical world was some sort of unstoppable force, not her fault, pointless to resist. That the grooves of learning had been carved by years of schooling, like wagon wheels digging ruts in the packed dirt making it impossible for carts to deviate from the path. Not a defense she could use at the hospital, but an idea she could keep in her pocket for comfort.

Chapter 10

Lillian and Janey were helping a post-surgical patient back from the toilet when Nurse Holt swept through the ward announcing an immediate and mandatory meeting in the lecture room, leaving behind only one senior nurse per ward. Janey seemed to be expecting this. "New doctor, new rules," she whispered to Lillian as they settled the patient back in her bed and filed out.

Once the staff was seated, Dr. Bauer strode through the door at a clip brisk enough to leave the tails of his cutaway coat streaming behind him. Tall and wiry, he was otherwise unremarkable to Lillian in his appearance until he turned his gaze in her general direction. Even in the dim gaslight, his eyes were so pale in color, if such a pale blue could be said to have color, that they seemed to generate their own light. Everywhere he looked out in the audience conversation froze, as if his gaze were the lamp of the constable in your eyes when you had the stolen goods in your hands.

"I am Dr. Bauer, your new house surgeon as of this morning. I am Chief Physician at Presbyterian Hospital and will continue in that capacity but have been persuaded to become your visiting surgeon upon the retirement of the esteemed Dr. Metcalfe." His voice rolled out over the rows of benches, sonorous tones effortlessly slapping the back walls of the room. He gripped the podium with both hands. "I have only had the briefest of time to review the procedures of this hospital, so what I have to say is only the beginning, but as much as Dr. Metcalfe has achieved here, this morning I must tell you that certain things will change."

Lillian looked over at Janey who gave her the smirk of someone proved right.

"First, I will start with news that should be welcomed by the nursing staff. There will be no more use of carbolic spray in surgeries."

A murmur of approval went through the rows of nurses. Dr. Bauer continued as if there were no disruption. "The latest research proves that the bacilli that cause infection are not airborne, so there is no need for doctors and nurses to be blanketed with caustic mist. In my recent previous post at Johns Hopkins, I witnessed doctors focusing on the sterilization of instruments and surfaces with great success— success we will replicate here." He took a breath and surveyed the room. "Secondly, I have read the charts of recent surgeries and was dismayed to find a less-than-aggressive approach in the vanquishing of our common enemy. It then struck me that perhaps not everyone understands why we are here. So let me make this plain: We are here to eradicate cancer from every patient. And how do we do this? There is no medicine one can swallow, no injection one can take." Here, Dr. Bauer became more animated, his voice rising and falling with new energy. "We must *cut*. We must cut and cut until there is simply no place remaining in which cancer can hide. Timidity will kill our patients, and that will not occur on my watch."

Lillian felt equal parts thrilled and frightened by these words, though she was not sure why.

Later, Lillian was queued up behind two nurses in the kitchen as the staff scrambled to assemble dinner trays. Minutes before, the cook had tripped on a rolling pin that had rolled off the counter and the pot of stew she was carrying spewed its contents all over the floor, a brown blanket dotted with carrots and potatoes. Half the kitchen staff was still cleaning up the viscous mess while the rest were constructing an alternate meal, leaving the nurses to tap their toes while they waited.

Lillian was not surprised to overhear the nurses talking about Dr. Bauer's pronouncements, since it was all Lillian could think about. "No more Lister spray!" the taller one said. "Some say the worst part was what it did to your hands, but for me it was how it made your eyes sting."

"Or your lungs ache. Good riddance. But what do you make of all that 'cut and cut'?"

"Makes sense. Why do half a job once you've opened them up?"

"Well, you weren't around a year or two ago. We had one, Hattie McGregor, I'll never forget her. Washerwoman, cheerful as the day was long, had it in the breast. It wasn't Metcalfe that cut her, some visiting surgeon. Went all the way up to her neck and her armpit, cut her collarbone, removed the pectoral, you name it. Surgery took hours. I assisted," she added with some pride.

Lillian inched closer, holding her breath.

"By some miracle, there was very little infection. Strong as an ox, those Irish washerwomen. But the recovery—Lord have mercy, it was bad and it was long. And when she was ready for discharge, well, that arm was of no use. All swelled up and not going down. The whole shoulder caving forward, already starting to give her back pain she was so twisted."

"But her cancer was gone?"

"Haven't seen her back here. Who knows? But let's say it was gone. She couldn't wash clothes anymore. How does she live?"

Just then, the staff started plunking down trays onto the counter. "Finally!" said the taller nurse. "Now I'll have to cut my own lunch short if I'm to finish morning rounds of whiskey." The nurses each took a tray and walked off, but Lillian was still contemplating that last unanswered question. *How does she live?* Based on Lillian's weeks at the hospital, she was sure that no one told Hattie what might happen to her body, and to be fair, perhaps the surgeon did not know it would be that drastic before he began. But even if he had known, would it have been a cruelty to tell Hattie? After all, as Dr. Bauer said, there is nothing but the knife that can solve this problem. Hattie's only other choice would have been to decline the surgery entirely, which given the extent of her breast cancer, would probably have killed her fairly quickly.

Lillian became entranced by a stream of thoughts that begat

other thoughts, but they all seemed to lead back to Hattie and what happened to her after she left the hospital. If we only knew how she fared. In fact, the more Lillian thought about it, the more she wondered why there was no attempt to track...

"I hate to interrupt your daydreaming but there is the matter of these *trays piling up*," said the cook as she put her hands on her hips. Lillian's thoughts scattered as she grabbed a tray and left the kitchen.

As Lillian was removing her cap and apron at the end of her shift, Janey approached. "I've been instructed to inform you of some staffing changes," she said neutrally.

Lillian went numb. "Janey, no no no, please, I've been trying so hard—"

"Oh no, not you!" Janey exclaimed. "Although I see how I could have made that clearer from the outset. No, it's Nurse Cahill and Nurse Drake."

Lillian knew of these two, thick as thieves. She squashed her impulse to ask what had happened, given that Janey was clearly here to tell her.

"They've been dismissed, and Nurse Holt feels that the other nurses should understand why, so know that I am not gossiping here."

Lillian nodded, feeling only a little guilty at the pleasure of these two nurses being dismissed while she remained.

"Evidently, they have been covering for each other for some time. They share a room, of course, and have been sneaking out at night upon occasion, one staying back to make excuses for the other. In fact, they were caught only because they had decided to sneak out together, showing bad judgment atop bad judgment. It was nearly midnight when they returned. And not surprisingly, their reason for these jaunts involved young men—two brothers they met on their afternoon off. I'm told one was quite handsome." Janey turned the beginnings of a smile into a frown. "Regardless, those nurses have been escorted from the hospital and we are down two, so our burden will become greater. And Nurse Holt asked me to make sure you understood that the same standards of morality apply to nurses and assistants equally."

"Of course," said Lillian. "You needn't worry about me."

"At least in that regard," added Janey with a wry look.

As the nurses filed into the lecture room that evening, there was a tension to the air as conversation buzzed. Lillian could hear snippets of soft conversation, mostly speculating about the dynamic ways of Dr. Bauer, and his lecture did not disappoint. No one in the room could accuse him of a lack of passion for his subject, "The Four Elements of Hospitalism—Septicemia, Gangrene, Pyemia and Erysipelas". Lillian had thought that infection was infection, but she now quickly jotted down these four evils in her notebook, taking her best guess at spelling, and Dr. Bauer's methods for detection on the wards at the earliest possible moment. "Nurses are the front line in this battle," Dr. Bauer proclaimed, and Lillian contrasted this nurses-can-save-lives message to Dr. Metcalfe's message about operating theater hygiene which was more nurses-can-kill-patients. Although they were not mutually exclusive.

"Now," said Dr Bauer after a half hour of energetic discourse, "who can tell me the first warning sign of erysipelas?"

Lillian felt Janey stiffen beside her, and in the ensuing silence she heard a nurse whisper behind her, "What is he doing?" Several nurses turned to look at the one beside them.

"Am I to believe," said Dr. Bauer, "that despite all those pencils scratching away, no one has written down or remembered what I said?"

The whispers mounted. Lillian was sure that nearly every nurse had written down that red, shiny skin was the hallmark of erysipelas, also known as St. Elmo's Fire for that reason. It was perhaps one of the more memorable images in Dr. Bauer's lecture, and although Lillian had not seen it on the ward, she doubted she would ever forget it. And yet the whispers continued and not one nurse raised her hand.

"Ah," said Dr. Bauer, "I can only conclude that Dr. Metcalfe did not take a similar approach to his lectures. You there, in the front." He gestured to a stout nurse on the end of the bench. "In what way were nurses encouraged to participate in Dr. Metcalfe's lectures?"

"Participate, sir?" She gripped her pencil with both hands.

"Verbally. To vocalize. To operate their vocal cords and allow sound to pour forth. And stand when you address me."

She stood with a slight wobble. "Two questions at the end, sir."

"Huh," said Dr. Bauer as he started to pace. "So no matter how complex or simple the subject matter, there were two nurses that could venture forth, only at the end, and the rest of you allowed to sit in your ignorance. I put it to you that this is not the way to instruct our nurses. I expect, no, I *demand* participation. I could give this lecture to the fireplace in my own parlor if I wanted dead silence as a response." He strode back to the podium and banged the flat of his palm upon it. "Warning sign of erysipelas!"

Half the hands in the audience shot up, quickly followed by most of the rest. Panic rose in Lillian's chest. What should she do? She looked over at Janey who was raising her hand and looking straight ahead, as terrified as the rest. Dr. Bauer peered out into the room and pointed to a nurse in the back, one of the few whose hand was not raised, perhaps believing she was obscured from his view. "Your answer," he said quietly.

She got to her feet. "Red…" Her voice broke, and she cleared her throat. "Red skin. Shiny, red skin."

Every nurse was frozen in place and there was no sound anywhere in the room.

"*Red. Shiny. Skin.*" Dr. Bauer slapped the podium with each word. "Yes." With that last word, a collective breath was released among the sea of nurses. "What is the treatment for gangrene?"

Lillian saw every hand shoot up, and then raised hers as well. If Janey would not advise, Lillian would do what she thought best to avoid attention.

"Aha," said Dr. Bauer with evident satisfaction. "Now we all seem to know." He walked to the left and pointed a finger behind him into the crowd. "You," he said without turning his head.

With quick consultation it was decided among the nurses in that general area who had been Dr. Bauer's intended target. "Bromine injections," said a nurse with some confidence as she stood.

Dr. Bauer spun around, as if he would pounce. "And?"

"And…" The nurse faltered. Lillian found herself trying to send the answer to her through telepathy—*topical application!*—even though, for all Lillian knew, that nurse could have been one that had spoken poorly of her behind her back. But she was swept up in the moment that Dr. Bauer had created, a contest where the goal posts were constantly moving and they all wanted the nursing staff to measure up, or at least get out alive.

"Half an answer is no answer. You, what is the other half?" He gestured to the left.

A nurse from the second row stood and answered in a timid voice, "Topical application of Bromine."

"Correct. Now if we add you and the other respondent together, we shall get one passable nurse."

The lecture continued, interspersed with questions at unexpected moments that prompted every hand to rise. Lillian scrambled to write it all down, her handwriting devolving as the tension of the class took its toll. Tendrils of hair escaped her cap but she had no time to tuck them back in. The point of her pencil snapped but she continued to write, the wood digging into the paper—*Pyemia symptoms: intermittent fever, putrid breath...* Dr. Bauer took no pause between pronouncing his last fact-laden sentence and asking, "Who has a question?" Lillian's right hand automatically rose, as she had trained it to do in the last half hour, while her left struggled to finish her notes, her eyes still glued to the notebook.

"You," Dr. Bauer announced, and Lillian looked up to see his index finger pointing her way.

"Lillian!" hissed Janey, but it was too late. Lillian could see that only a few others had raised a hand, now lowering quickly, and none were near her, so there could be no mistaking who was expected to speak now. What happened to him calling on people that *didn't* raise their hand?

Her knees shook as she rose from her seat. Her mind went blank.

"We await your question." Dr. Bauer crossed his arms.

She said the first thing that came to her mind, something that had been rattling around in her brain since one of Dr. Metcalfe's lectures. "If we know how to address the four types of infection, why do so many patients still die of infection?" As soon as the words were out of her mouth, words that came out at a louder volume than she had intended, she heard an intake of breath from Janey and realized that this was not a good question to ask, that it was in fact quite a bad question. It challenged whether all the treatments their brand new doctor had taken pains to describe were actually effective.

In the ensuing silence she thought of three questions that would have been intelligent, respectful and would have shown she was paying attention. She braced for whatever was about to come.

Dr. Bauer uncrossed his arms and slipped his hands into his trouser pockets with an almost casual posture. "And your name is…?"

Out of the corner of her eye, Lillian could see Janey put her hand to her forehead. "Lillian Dolan, sir," she replied. Her stomach started to hurt.

"You will come see me tomorrow morning, 9am. You are all dismissed."

As the nurses around her stood, they all turned and looked at her as they filed out. Lillian took her seat on the bench, and she and Janey sat side by side until Dr. Bauer and all the nurses had left the room.

"Janey, I thought if I didn't raise my hand that he would call on me, like the other questions! It wasn't my intention to ask a question. And it took me by surprise, I didn't have a clever one prepared. I'm sorry."

Janey looked up at her, not angry, not agitated, as if Lillian were already a thing of the past, the third assistant to come and go. "Fix your hair," she said wearily, and left the room.

Chapter 11

Until she crawled into bed that night, Lillian was able to force herself to think of other things—the rent due tomorrow, the shoes that barely fit on Marie's feet—but when her head was resting on her pillow, she could no longer stop the scene with Dr. Bauer from playing out over and over again in her mind, and with each iteration her stomach hurt a little more. Soon, she began to imagine her meeting with Dr. Bauer in the morning. In one version, he fired her and Lillian pleaded for her job; in another, he fired her and she challenged him as to why, which enraged him; in a third, he demoted her to…what was lower than she was now? The house laundress? Could she go on some kind of probation? But why would he bother? Already he will be irritated at having to spend his time in this meeting dealing with an upstart girl. It could be a great opportunity for him to show the staff what happens to nurses that don't know their place.

Lillian's stomach cramped enough to double her over, and she pulled the chamber pot from beneath the bed while trying not to wake Marie.

The next morning Josephine was a few minutes early, as usual. Over the weeks, they had taken to chatting before Lillian left, mostly about Marie and what the day might hold for her, occasionally about the hospital or Josephine's family or a new storefront opening in the neighborhood. But today Lillian sprinted out the door, determined to be early and beyond reproach in what might be her last hour on the job.

She stood with her best posture outside Dr. Bauer's office at five minutes before the hour, and as she heard the grandfather clock on the first floor chime nine, she knocked on the door. "Enter," he bellowed, clearly audible even through two inches of oak. She turned the brass knob with a sweaty palm.

Dr. Bauer carefully placed his pen in the ink pot and leaned back in his chair, hands knit together over his vest, and studied Lillian as she stood in front of his desk. Lillian focused on the ink pot and waited to be addressed. As much as she endeavored to be humble and submissive, she could not help but become slightly irritated with the wait. Was it not cruel to stretch this out, and what was the point of this cruelty?

Finally, Dr. Bauer began. "Nurse Dolan."

Lillian's heart sunk a little lower. "Begging your pardon, sir, but it is Assistant Dolan."

"*Assistant* Dolan. I see. We do not have assistant nurses at Presbyterian, so perhaps you can tell me your responsibilities here."

"I roll bandages, serve meals, clean bedpans." Lillian fought against her growing feelings of irritation. Why was it so important that he humiliate her? She raised her eyes and looked at him directly.

"And you were in the night lecture for nurses because....?" His eyebrows rose a fraction.

"Because I asked to be." Lillian felt the dog of her emotions start to slip the chain. *Respectful*, she told herself, and took a breath.

"These classes will somehow help you clean bedpans?"

"No sir, but it is not my life's ambition to clean bedpans. I aspire to be a nurse."

"Have you not been informed that a good nurse knows her place in a hospital?" He looked almost amused. Lillian's irritation blossomed into anger.

"Yes sir, I have been informed, and I do know my place. It is at the bottom. I am reminded of that every day. But I choose to clean bedpans here, happily and without complaint, because I hope to also learn here. And to learn, I need to ask questions."

Dr. Bauer shot back at her, "Such as why we cannot always eradicate infection."

"Yes."

"And why do you think we cannot do this?"

Lillian faltered. "Pardon?"

"I believe you heard me. What do you believe is the answer to your own question?" Dr. Bauer leaned forward in his chair, intently staring her down with his glacier-hued eyes.

Off balance, Lillian hesitated. "Surely the proper order of things is that the doctors answer the questions."

"It seems to me, Assistant Dolan, that you are not such a stickler for the proper order of things. Your answer, please."

Lillian thought about this. "With the understanding that I don't presume to know the true answer, I would venture that sometimes we do not identify early enough that infection has begun."

"And other times?"

"And perhaps our procedures on the ward are not always as antiseptic as they should be, and reintroduce infection accidentally."

"Anything else?"

"That is all I can think of." Despite her neck currently being on the chopping block, she couldn't help but hope that Dr. Bauer would tell her the real answer.

"I don't think either one of your answers is correct," he said as he leaned back.

She looked down at the ink pot again. *But honestly, did you think this meeting would go well?*

"The truth is," he continued, "that we actually don't know why our methods are effective sometimes and less so at other times. Only through experimentation will we progress. And despite the inaccuracy of your answers, they were well reasoned."

She looked up in confusion. Was she not to be reprimanded?

"Note that you ought to have said 'aseptic'. Antiseptic is the property of a substance that kills bacteria, whereas aseptic means sterile. Antiseptic is curative, aseptic is preventive. Now sit."

She sat in the chair before him, with only a small part of her mind making a note to later write down what he had just said.

"You will refrain from asking questions of the other nurses that are remotely provocative. You will carry a small notebook in your apron and write your questions down when you are not in view of the other nurses."

"Yes sir." Her heart began to beat faster. She was not to be fired!

"Your behavior here will be impeccable. I will never hear a complaint about you. And on Thursdays, you will meet me here in this office at 6pm, and you will tell no one about it. You may go."

"Pardon me, sir, but isn't that during lecture time?"

"I am limiting lectures to Tuesdays only. Lectures that you will not be attending anymore. Anything you need to know you can get from me. Now off you go."

Lillian rose and left before he could change his mind. She tried not to feel the bite of being banished from the lectures and instead focused on the joy of being able to keep her job.

"Michael!" Lillian had hoped Michael would stop by that evening but he usually arrived after dinner. Today he was sitting with Josephine at the kitchen table when Lillian came home from work.

"Abraham closed the shop early today, some family thing, so I thought I would come straight away," he said as he gave up his chair to Lillian and leaned up against the wall. "One day I will get you another chair," he added, looking around, although where it would fit was not clear.

Lillian happily plopped down on the chair, causing an alarming creak. "Well, I have avoided disaster today."

"I knew you weren't right this morning," said Josephine, and turned to Michael. "Weren't I just telling you that she was stern as a sea captain leaving for work?"

"You were," said Michael. "Since the most interesting thing at the shop today was when we ran out of blue thread, I must hear this story front to end."

Lillian recounted Tuesday's lecture where she invited the focus of Dr. Bauer while intending just the opposite, and this morning's meeting with its unexpected turns. "I was certain this was the end, perhaps so bad that it would follow me if I could ever apply to nursing school and it might nix my chances there. But it all went the other way!" She looked from Michael's face to Josephine's, expecting a reflection of her happiness but instead finding… was it concern? Perhaps they didn't quite understand. "I'm in the clear. Do you see?"

After a silent moment, Michael said, "Tell again about the Thursday nights."

"He wants me to meet with him. Because I can't ask questions, but I write them down. Did I mention he wants me to write down my questions? So you see, he will answer them then!" Though he hadn't specifically said he would, she now recalled.

Josephine wore a tiny frown. "But why would he do that?"

"Because he… is kind?" A sliver of doubt crept into her understanding of what had happened. Dr. Bauer had seemed anything but kind, both in the lectures and in his office.

"Will there be other nurses in these meetings?" asked Michael.

"Perhaps." She thought about it. "Well, I suppose not. He instructed me not to tell the other nurses."

"Lilypad." Michael traded glances with Josephine and then looked back at Lillian. "I think you should consider whether these meetings are a good idea."

"What would you have me do, say, 'Thank you, esteemed surgeon who has taken an interest in my ambition and curiosity, but I don't need your instruction?'" She got up and attempted to pace, but there was nowhere to walk in the small kitchen, so she sat back down. "You can't understand what an honor this is. I am no one. I do housemaid work within the walls of a hospital. And this is my chance to learn —not from a nurse, but from a doctor!"

Josephine placed her hand over Lillian's. "But ya gotta ask yourself *why* he's doing this."

Lillian removed her hand. "What does it matter? If you find a silver dollar on the street, do you wonder, why did the owner drop it? But all right, let's have it your way. What could he possibly see in me? I am plain. I do not dress like…" She stopped herself from mentioning the Bowery. "I am modest. A man like him could have whoever he wants."

"Yes, whoever he wants," said Josephine, although it didn't sound like she was agreeing with Lillian.

"It's not about your irresistible charms," said Michael. "It's about… it's about the fact that he can do it."

"You don't understand," insisted Lillian. "To use his position to compromise me, the lowest rung on the ladder, would be no achievement at all. He was completely professional with me." She turned to Michael. "You have always celebrated the good things that happen to me. Why can't you be happy for me? I thought I was to be fired, and instead I've kept my job. Isn't that a good thing?"

"Yes, of course," said Michael. "The job, it suits you. I'm happy you've kept it, absolutely. I just think there is a way that you can bow out gracefully from these meetings that seem... odd. Tell him the person who takes care of Marie cannot stay that late."

Lillian looked away. "The hospital does not know about Marie."

Josephine look startled. "But what will you do if I can't come some day? What if I'm sick?" she asked.

"I hadn't thought about that." Another thing to worry about. Josephine had been so reliable it hadn't crossed her mind. "But this is all beside the point because I will not tell Dr. Bauer any such thing. He has done me a great favor just by allowing me to keep my job, and I will not disrespect him by doing other than he says." She sat up a little straighter in her chair. "If you knew the way it works at the hospital, you would understand."

"If you knew the way it works in the world," said Josephine sadly, "you might understand somethin' different."

❦ Chapter 12 ❦

When Lillian delivered breakfast trays to the bedridden on the ward the next morning, she was saddened to see the stomach cancer patient's bed vacant, but then noticed her chart still hanging at the foot of the bed. She approached the central desk. "Is the patient in Bed 9... still with us?"

The nurse behind the desk didn't look up from her paperwork. "Well, she's with Dr. Bauer in the operating theater, so I suppose the answer is yes."

"But I thought she was inoperable..." The nurse's peeved expression halted Lillian's line of inquiry. "Thank you," she said.

Lillian went to the toilets and took from her apron the notebook she had used for the night lectures. *Stomach patient—purpose of surgery?* she wrote. If the nurse was not interested in answering her question, Lillian thought with a touch of smugness, so much the better to get the answer from a doctor.

Later that afternoon, she was handed new linens for Bed 9, now devoid of a hanging chart, and could therefore conclude that the surgery had not gone well. Janey had said yesterday that she didn't expect the woman to last through the weekend, so perhaps it was not surprising that she hadn't survived the surgery. But this only deepened her curiosity at why it had been attempted at all.

At the appointed time, she made her way to Dr. Bauer's office and knocked after making sure no one was in the hallway. There was no answer. Surely he must be in there? She knocked again.

"Yes, fine, enter," she heard. *Once he sees it is someone he asked to see, he will not be so irritated*, she told herself as she opened the door.

He was writing with an intensity that evidently prevented him from greeting her, but the click of the door closing caused him to look up with a quizzical expression. "Yes?"

"Dr. Bauer, I am here as requested."

He frowned. "I have no time for whatever it is that ails you, Nurse...?"

"Assistant Dolan, sir." The cushion of happiness on which Lillian had been riding all day abruptly deflated. Had she imagined the whole meeting yesterday morning? No, it must be that this meant so little to him that his offer—well, his command—to come here had not even stuck in his memory. Not even her name was worthy of remembering. She felt tears starting to well and blinked hard.

"It is very important that I complete these surgical notes before I retire this evening, and I can't be distracted by other topics." He checked the pocket watch in his vest.

"But that is the subject of my question. The surgery today, on the patient with stomach cancer."

"And what about that patient?" he asked, with a look of minimal tolerance.

"She was admitted two weeks ago by Dr. Metcalfe, put on a course of... comfort. Palliative care." She hoped she had pronounced that word correctly. When Dr. Bauer didn't correct her, she proceeded. "The nurses felt that she only had a few days left."

Dr. Bauer considered her for a moment, then leaned back in his chair. "Are the nurses usually accurate in their predictions?"

"Yes, sir, I find them quite accurate." She had only seen a handful of deaths in the month she had been at the hospital, but at least with those it did seem that the nurses had a sense of a patient's last day on earth.

"It is less so at Presbyterian," he remarked, although it appeared he was talking more to himself than to her. "Perhaps because the causes of death here are so few in number—really just the disease itself or post-surgical infection..." He trailed off, staring at the transom window above the door, lost in thought.

"But Mrs. Feinman."

"Who?"

"Your surgical patient today." Lillian had managed to look up her name, as well as verify that she had next of kin, explaining why Lillian did not get the call to bring her to Jupiter. "She was beyond hope?"

"Of course. She came to us far too late."

"So my question is… why did you operate on her?"

Dr. Bauer slid his gaze to the chair in front of his desk, which Lillian took as an invitation to sit. He regarded her for a moment in her seat before answering. "You tended to her on the ward. Was she comfortable?"

"Well, she was one of the few patients that was given morphine rather than whiskey, as per Dr. Metcalfe's orders on admission, so I would assume she was comfortable."

"What are the side effects of morphine?"

A tremor of fear ran through her as if she were back in the lecture hall with Dr. Bauer commanding the stage, but she pressed on. "Drowsiness. Disorientation. Constipation. Dry mouth." She was sure there were others, but these were the ones she had heard of.

"She was in and out of consciousness, as per the head nurse in the ward. Dead in two days' time, according to the fortune tellers you work with. But she had something very valuable to give to this hospital. What do you think that was?"

Lillian only had to think for a moment. "Information."

The look of mild annoyance that had dominated Dr. Bauer's face melted away. "Exactly right. The abdomen that had betrayed her was a gift to us, and to future patients with the same ailment."

"But did she give that gift freely?" She cringed inwardly as soon as this was out of her mouth. Was this disrespectful? But what good was learning only half of a subject?

Rather than angering Dr. Bauer, her question seemed to entertain him. "Imagine a scale." He held up his hands as if presenting her with two apples. "On one side is the patient dying on Saturday in an increasing narcotic fog, of no help to anyone. On the other is the patient dying on Thursday in a deep ether sleep and providing insight that ultimately helps a father of four small children recover from his stomach cancer surgery. Which is the better course?"

"Why, I suppose the latter. On balance."

"Precisely." His imaginary scale collapsed and his hands fell into his lap.

"But if she was going to die within a few days, why could you not wait until after her death for your information?"

"Tumors construct a blood supply of their own. There is much to be learned in studying a tumor, especially a large one, while the blood is still circulating." He took his feet off the desk and planted them on the floor. "And I don't work on the weekend."

"I see." Lillian chose to imagine that his last sentence was a sort of joke.

"And now, I must return to my notes. Off you go." Already he was dipping his pen in the ink pot.

She rose from her chair. "Dr. Bauer, I can't thank you enough for taking time—"

"Close the door on the way out, please," he said absently in a sing-song voice as he began to write.

In bed that night, Marie curled up next to her like a pup, Lillian felt sleep slowly reaching for her while she reflected happily on her evening. Beyond the enormous satisfaction of being able to get an answer to her most pressing question of the day—and from a surgeon, no less!—she felt great optimism for their future meetings. Dr. Bauer seemed to relish the difficult questions that would be seen as the most impertinent if she had asked any of the nurses. The trick was that she was asking these questions without other staff present, so he did not have to contend with the appearance of having his authority challenged. She couldn't wait to tell Michael how wrong he had been about Dr. Bauer's supposed dark motives.

As she faded in and out of a wakeful state while going over the entire meeting in her mind, green shoots of doubt crept into her garden of happiness. *"Did she give that gift freely?"* Well, he had not actually answered that question. Or perhaps he had—she had not given that gift freely. But the greater good had outweighed that consideration, right? So was her question, in a sense, the wrong question to ask?

And what if the surgery was not ultimately informative, and therefore did not save the father with four children? Was the surgery still the best course?

And was he actually joking about the timing of the surgery being influenced by his not working on the weekend?

She turned toward Marie and pulled the quilt up over her shoulder. Dr. Bauer was a respected surgeon and physician with years of education and experience that Lillian could not even begin to imagine. If he was not correct on questions of medicine, who would be? Certainly not a bedpan cleaner. It was merely her habit of questioning everything that led her to question the words of such an authority. She resolved going forward to accept his words as truth and was eased by the balm of that simplification as she drifted off to sleep.

🎴 Chapter 13 🎴

On the bed were all the objects Lillian would need: the button napkin, the string for Cat's Cradle, the box of the newest notions, and a small pile of turkey feathers she was able to get from the butcher. She shook the button napkin and the clacking brought Marie running from the kitchen. Once Marie sat down in front of Lillian on the bed, she took a big breath and started, ever so gently, to brush Marie's hair.

Marie sprang off the bed but Lillian was ready for her. "*Beautiful dreamer, wake unto me...*" she sang as she grabbed Marie's hand and brought her back to the bed. Soon they were both singing: "*Starlight and dewdrops are waiting for thee...*" Helen had sung this song to them at night, and although Lillian had tried to find a song that didn't remind her of Helen, she could never find one as calming for Marie. Neither sister had a very good voice, but Lillian would have listened to cats in heat if it meant she could brush out Marie's hair without a fight. Plus it was the only time she got to hear Marie's voice; while speaking was a thing of the past, singing had never abandoned her sister. Lillian placed Marie's hand on the pile of feathers, and Marie brought one to her face and gently brushed it against her cheeks as they sang on. Lillian picked up the hairbrush and started on the ends of Marie's hair, and soon Marie stopped noticing.

By the time they reached the second verse—back in the Helen days, the girls agreed this verse was their favorite because of the mermaids—Lillian was able to drop out of the singing and focus on the difficult task at hand. How long had it been since she had brushed Marie's hair? She couldn't remember. And she wouldn't be doing it now if they weren't going to their aunt and uncle's for Sunday supper. Earlier in the week, Michael had extended the invitation from his parents. At first Lillian had declined.

"I don't know," she said, "I haven't even talked with them after moving here. Marie was like a tornado while we were there. When she put all those fork holes in your granny's linen tablecloth, I thought your mother was going to cry."

"So shall we wait longer and make it even more awkward?" asked Michael. "All has been forgiven. And I never liked that tablecloth anyway."

"What about if they want to talk about...you know?"

"They know the basics of why you left, and believe me, they won't want to bring any of that up. Or anything about your mother. Aunt Helen is not discussed in our house. With my family there is nothing a little denial can't take care of." Michael's smile was more of a grimace. "Anyway, I think they didn't invite you before this because they were just getting used to how things had changed. Now it's enough in the past that they can totally ignore it and pretend it was always this way!"

"I don't know, Michael."

"Well, I thought you might resist, so when my mother stated her intentions to make her bread pudding—"

Lillian made a face; she and Michael agreed Fiona's bread pudding was like lead.

"—I convinced her to spring for her gooseberry tart."

"Oh, that's her best one. I'll have to leave room for dessert, although you know there is no way to say no to her when it comes to food."

"Too full?" Michael had long ago mastered imitating his mother to make Lillian laugh. "Surely not! Just a wee bit more roast on yer plate now. Yer as thin as a twig in the kindling bin!"

"It's really Marie that's the twig. She doesn't love what I put on the table but she really lights into your mother's meals."

"And when we do the dishes, I've got bags on washing." He placed his hands on her shoulders. "So may I report back two yeses for supper?"

She pretended to think about it. "Fine. But I've got washing."

By the time they got to Martin and Fiona's apartment, Lillian had long since realized that she had misjudged the distance. It was a balmy fall afternoon and Lillian decided to save the cab fare and have the two of them walk it. Marie had started out a bit nervous when they first set out, clinging to Lillian's arm as she acclimated to the sounds and smells of outdoors, but once they turned east onto 42nd Street and began walking the long blocks between the avenues, Marie began to enjoy herself. By the time they passed Grand Central Terminal, however — *a shame Marie can't see such a beautiful building*, thought Lillian—Marie slowed down and Lillian had to pull her along. Without warning, Marie plunked herself down on the sidewalk and started tugging at her boots. An ember of panic started to catch and glow inside Lillian. She had known for a while that Marie's boots were too small but had forgotten to take her out for new ones, something she easily could have done yesterday had she remembered. And now she would have to persuade Marie to walk the remaining distance. A glance at the street signs told Lillian they were only four short blocks north of her aunt and uncle's apartment, but that was probably too long to walk in just stockings.

Lillian had double-tied Marie's boot laces, and consequently Marie grew more and more frustrated that she could not remove her boots, now kicking her heels against the sidewalk. A few passers-by raised eyebrows at the scene but most just flowed around her, giving her a wide berth. Lillian, however, could see the situation was about to escalate, and her glowing ember of panic flared. Helen had been an expert at distracting and maneuvering Marie in times like these, and the pragmatic side of Lillian put aside her feelings about her mother and thought hard about what Helen would do.

"Gooseberry tart!" she whispered enthusiastically as she bent down next to Marie. "Aunt Fiona has a gooseberry tart sitting on her kitchen table, and she wants to give you a piece right now!" Aunt Fiona would not be pleased to have Marie spoiling her supper but Lillian would explain. Surely Marie could have just a little piece.

Lillian tried not to look too closely at what was on the back of Marie's dress when she rose from the sidewalk, but at least the rest of the trip was without incident.

"You look exhausted," commented Michael as they sat down with Martin in the parlor, minus Fiona and Michael's sister Kate who were in the kitchen finishing supper preparations and doling out a sliver of tart for Marie.

"It was a longer walk than I thought, and Marie was ready for it to be done about four blocks too early."

"Walking!" exclaimed Martin. "It's almost two bleddy miles! Why the devil didn't ya take a hansom?"

"It was such beautiful weather. And Marie doesn't get out all that often." Not to mention Lillian was trying to economize, all the more important with a looming purchase of new boots.

"Well, you'll be taking one back on your uncle, especially in the dark. Hell's Kitchen is no place for the likes of you to be wandering around at night."

"Thank you, Uncle. Although we are right on the edge of that neighborhood, it's really not so bad." When she and Marie had first moved in, Mrs. Sweeney across the hall had told her never to go west of 9th Avenue, and so far she'd heeded that advice and had no problems.

Kate walked into the parlor and plunked herself down on the floor. "It's not at all dangerous?" she asked.

"I heard that Negros live cheek to jowl with whites over there." Martin took a sip of his beer while Lillian tried to decide how to answer. Michael had often told Lillian that Martin disparaged Negros at every opportunity, something to do with elevating the status of the Irish by positioning them on the white side of the gulf between white and black. This had only served to make Michael take the opposite stance, inspiring many conversations with Lillian in recent years convincing her on the equality of all men. But now she didn't want to get into a discussion that would put Michael's teeth on edge and potentially ruin the evening.

"My block is mostly Irish and German." That was true at least of Lillian's building. She didn't know who lived in the other buildings, although she'd seen Negros as she walked home from the El at night, coming out of a groggery that seemed to have an exclusively Negro clientele.

"Well then," said Martin just as Fiona came in from the kitchen. "Supper's on!" she called out, drying her hands on her apron.

Most of the conversation during the meal was dominated by Fiona's questions about Lillian's job. "What are the other nurses like?"

"Very... professional," said Lillian. She thought about Janey. "One took me under her wing to show me the ropes, but I've learned the basics by now."

"And the cancer. Are ya being careful?"

"Aunt Fiona, it's not contagious."

"Still, it couldn't hurt to be a wee bit careful," she commented as she heaped a few more boiled potatoes on Lillian's plate. "Any winsome lads there?"

"Well, the patients are all women."

"Just as well. Sure an' you don't want to fall in with a lad that's got the cancer!"

"Good thing that can't happen then." Lillian smiled. Aunt Fiona was relentless in her pursuit to marry off anyone over the age of 16.

"The doctors, then. Any that have caught your eye?"

Lillian exchanged a glance at Michael and then looked back at Fiona. "I think they're all married."

Michael raised his eyebrows. "Even your Dr. Bauer?"

"Ooh," said Fiona. "Who's this?" She rubbed her hands together.

"He's the house surgeon," said Lillian as she kicked Michael's foot under the table.

"He's taken a shine to our Lillian," said Michael as he poured water from the pitcher to his glass. "Isn't that right, Lilypad?"

"House surgeon!" marveled Fiona. "That sounds grand!"

"Is he handsome?" asked Kate, wiggling her eyebrows.

Lillian laughed. "He is as plain as muslin. You would forget him the moment you passed him on the street." *Unless he looked at you with those eyes like chipped ice.* "But he's quite a talented surgeon, and it's an honor that he wants to speak to me about anything."

"I knew you would be better than that silly old Annabelle who couldn't keep her dinner down after seeing a few little bandages," said Kate. "You always were the tough one that way. But is it really awful? The smells? The blood? Do you see a lot of dead bodies?"

"All right, that's enough!" yelled Martin. "I'll not have all this revolting manner of things talked about at my table!" Fiona crossed herself.

After a pause, Lillian said, "A lot of it is very workaday. Bandages. Bed linens."

"Dead bodies," Kate added under her breath, just loud enough for her father to hear and pound the table. "What the bleddy hell did I just *say?*" Lillian had to look away from Kate and Michael grinning into their napkins so she would not burst out laughing.

Kate volunteered to help with the dishes in exchange for the more repulsive details of Lillian's job. "What about the surgeries? Is it very bloody?" she asked as she jammed a cloth inside a glass to dry it.

"I haven't assisted in one, but I've walked by the theater afterward and once there was a lake of blood on the floor. Something must have gone wrong."

"Did it smell?"

"Like copper and warm milk," she whispered loudly, and Kate squealed in disgust and delight.

"You are certainly making this up," said Michael as he gathered dirty silverware.

"Not a bit." Perhaps the lake had been more like a large puddle, and she hadn't smelled anything from the hallway walking by that day, but she'd changed enough bloody linens to know what it was like.

"What about dead people?" asked Kate.

"One of my jobs is to ferry them around. Well, to the crematorium."

Kate's eyes widened like saucers. "What? Do they have to burn you if you die of cancer?"

"No! It's just those who have no one to claim them."

"How can you do it? Aren't you scared?"

Lillian thought about this as she watched the water fill the plugged sink. "I was a little nervous the first time. But really, if you think about it, the body is just a machine. A broken machine, by the time they come to the hospital. There are people inside the machines, but when they pass, they just leave this shell behind. It's not them anymore. They're just leaving their broken machine behind." She hadn't really thought this through until this moment, and it came out in such a somber way that it cast a pall over the kitchen.

Michael broke the silence by clearing his throat dramatically. "This conversation has become entirely too maudlin. Kate, go relieve our poor mother from that endless game of patty cake with Marie."

Michael handed Lillian the big platter to dry as Kate trotted off to the parlor. "They're happy to see you," he said.

"You were right, it's like nothing happened."

"You know Aunt Helen never quite fit in. Not just because her people were French. She didn't exactly make an effort with this family."

Lillian nodded; she and Michael had discussed this before. "Wouldn't give her daughters good Irish names. Insisted we speak the King's English." According to Helen, her own parents were never able to overcome their French accents here in America, and this held them back in all sorts of ways; Helen vowed that her children would speak well and forbid them to use slang. Michael bought into his aunt's reasoning and elevated his own language in recent years. Lillian suspected it was to annoy Martin.

Michael continued the litany. "Moved you across town after your father died. To a less Irish neighborhood she couldn't afford. Putting on airs. And then—"

"Yes, well, no need to go over any more of that." Lillian took a breath. "But I take your point. They didn't mind removing her from the family portrait. It's just nice to know that they didn't feel like they had to remove Marie and me too."

Lillian carried a stack of plates from the counter and submerged them in the soapy water. She felt the familiar anger about her mother sneaking into her brain and quickly changed the subject. "You know, I had my first meeting with Dr. Bauer on Thursday, and he's not the deviant you suspected. We discussed the reasons for a surgery he performed that day. It was very professional. I could never learn these things from a nurse."

"I have no doubt he knows many things that would interest you." Michael thought for a moment. "What do you mean, reasons for surgery? Isn't it always to remove cancer? Why else would you have surgery in a cancer hospital?"

"Well, this was a far-gone case. There was no hope, she only had days to live." She was pleased at how professional that sounded, hoping Michael noticed how much she knew about what was going on with the patients.

"So why did they operate on her?" Michael frowned.

"Evidently there were important things that could be learned from seeing...er, what was going on. Inside." This sounded much less convincing than when she was talking with Dr. Bauer.

"But wouldn't recovering from surgery be pretty awful for someone who was about to die?"

"She didn't survive the surgery." Lillian handed Michael a wet plate but he didn't reach for it.

"What are you saying? They killed her because they thought they might learn something?"

"No! Well.... No. It wasn't like that. They didn't mean to... they didn't mean for her to die." That was true, right? The walls in the kitchen felt as if they were just slightly closing in on her. "She was in pain. She was about to die anyway. She had something that could help people in the future with her kind of cancer." Lillian was still holding the wet plate that Michael wouldn't take, now dripping on the floor.

"Lillian." Michael leaned against the counter and stared at her. "Did this really happen? What did her family think?"

Lillian hadn't thought about the woman's family, though she did know from the chart that she had next of kin. "I don't think they knew." She slid the clean plate back into the dirty water and saw it quickly swallowed.

"So they had no chance to say their goodbyes? And the woman agreed to this?"

Lillian was now quite sorry she had brought this up with Michael. Dr. Bauer had been so compelling as to why this surgery was justified, but here in her aunt's kitchen it all seemed different. Instead of convincing Michael to think favorably of Dr. Bauer, it seemed she had done the opposite.

"We can't know all of Dr. Bauer's reasoning," she stated, but she could not look at Michael as she said it. She looked down into the sink, the dishes under a thin film of suds, the washrag floating limply in the corner.

Michael gently pulled her over to the kitchen table and they both sat down. "You did nothing wrong. Maybe your fancy doctor did something wrong and maybe he didn't. But this sounds dodgy to me, and what worries me is that it seemed pretty easy for him to convince you not to think about the dodgy parts."

"Michael, he is house surgeon and I roll bandages."

"That's exactly what I am talking about! Stop saying that! Who cares what he does and you do? You have a mind that can think, and you don't have to turn it off because you roll bandages."

Just then, Fiona walked into the kitchen with Marie. "This one is getting a wee bit restless. I've got your fare." She folded coins into Lillian's hand.

Outside, Lillian and Michael walked to Third Avenue to find a cab, Marie between them swinging their hands back and forth. "Michael, please don't be angry."

"I'm not, Lilypad. I'm worried. Just promise me that you won't let your guard down."

"What am I guarding against?"

He turned to her. "Anything. Everything."

🕸 Chapter 14 🕸

Despite their uncomfortable discussion of the surgery, Lillian felt the lingering warmth of being with Michael, the one person in the world who would always look out for her. When Lillian was young, she believed Michael had magical qualities that warded off bad things. She imagined her cousin had an aura of protection around him, a silvery cloud in which he was centered, and she tried to stay physically close to him to be in it. She leaned back in the hansom now, thinking about what he had said. She had done nothing wrong. Everything would be fine.

But as the cab traveled away from Michael, the power of the silvery cloud faded.

She had noticed as she entered the cab that its horse looked off. Though the night was cool, a sheen of sweat on its neck gleamed in the lamplight, and she saw a bit of froth around its mouth. She quickly forgot about this as they started out, but soon their pace slowed and the driver began to apply the reins more vigorously. Just as she began to consider whether this would be a problem for their trip, Marie began to fuss with her boots again, trying to untie the double knots. Lillian reached into her coat pocket for the button napkin and realized she had forgotten to bring it. She started to run through her list of distractions: tickling the end of Marie's nose with the tips of her own hair, chanting nursery rhymes— *"Lucy Locket lost her pocket, Kitty Fisher found it..."* —jingling the few coins from her purse inside her balled-up fist. Marie ignored her and started trying to toe off her boots while they were still laced. Lillian gave up. She looked out the window and realized they had already entered Hell's Kitchen and were now west of 9th Avenue. Michael must have given the driver the wrong address and they were now traveling the very streets that she had was told to avoid.

Lillian twisted in her seat and opened the trap door behind them. "Driver! This is the wrong street!"

The driver brought the cab to a stop, peering down into the cabin from his perch. "He told me 11th Avenue. Almost didn't take the fare. This here is one sketchy neighborhood, missy. If it ain't the Irish gangs it's the Nigras."

"I don't live here, I'm two blocks east."

"Well that ain't Buckingham Palace but at least it's better than—"

"Can you just go?" said Lillian. Marie started to stamp her feet on the floor of the cab and pound her fists on the seat.

"What's wrong with her?" asked the driver, frowning.

"Just please *go!*" Lillian shut the trap door. *We'll be there in five minutes and I will take off Marie's boots and I will make us warm milk.* She took a deep breath and felt just a little bit better.

The driver called to the horse and brought the reins down, but the cab did not move.

No, no, no.

As the minutes wore on, the driver's application of the reins and level of profanity increased but to no avail. Marie seemed oblivious to the situation until the cab jolted precipitously forward. Lillian saw with alarm that the horse had gone down on its front knees. *What will happen to the cab if he falls over on his side?* But before she could consider this further, Marie bolted from the cab.

Lillian chased after her, ignoring the shouts from the driver, and reached Marie just seconds after she had tripped on the curb. "Where in God's name did you think you could run given that you can't see?" she said uselessly to Marie. Blood was starting to drip from Marie's elbow where she had skinned it by bracing her fall. Marie started to cry. "It's fine, it's fine," she soothed Marie. "We're only a few blocks from home."

Lillian looked around and tried to figure out exactly where they were and in what direction they needed to go. "Well, let's pick a way and when we get to the corner, the signs will tell us." She grabbed Marie's uninjured arm and they started to walk.

As they progressed, Lillian became aware of other people out on the street—men noisily exiting a saloon across the street, a man and woman slouching in a doorway. Under the corner streetlight up ahead two men faced off against each other, drunken fists raised and wobbling as a few others cheered them on. A woman's shrill laugh came from an upstairs window, and a bottle broke somewhere.

Lillian just wanted to get near enough to the corner to see the street signs but without attracting the attention of the fist-fight crowd. The sounds all around them caused Marie to cling tightly to Lillian, her skinned elbow now forgotten. Just as Lillian was wondering if they should turn around — although there were no assurances that the opposite direction would be any safer — she felt a presence by her side and jumped in fear.

"I sure didn't think I'd be runnin' into you tonight," said a familiar voice.

She spun around. "Jupiter, what are you doing here?" Lillian couldn't believe he was really beside them.

"Well, Miz Dolan, it ain't so surprising because I live here. On 10th, a little further south."

"I didn't know you lived in Hell's Kitchen."

"You gonna tell me what you doing here?"

"Doing here? We live here." She remembered that Jupiter knew nothing about her outside of the hospital.

Jupiter frowned. "Y'all live here? Just the two of y'all?"

"Yes. This is my sister Marie."

He looked at her and cocked his head. "She all right?"

"She's blind and simple. Scarlatina a few years back."

"We should get movin'," said Jupiter, looking over his shoulder. As they started walking away from the escalating fight, he resumed their conversation. "So you tellin' me you and your blind sister live alone together down here."

"Well, we're on 9th Avenue, right on the edge of the Kitchen, but yes."

"Lord in Heaven, you got some courage on you." Jupiter shook his head and smiled. "I thought you was a brave one wheeling that corpse in when you first started at the hospital, but I didn't know the half of it."

"The nurses act as if it's just another job I have to do, like it's the same as pushing the bed linen cart."

Jupiter chuckled. "I been runnin' that oven for near on two years, and I seen plenty of nurses wheelin' in their first body. Some o' them about to wet their drawers. Their faces be all ashy, hands a-tremblin'. *Jupiter'*, they say." He imitated the nurses in a high voice. "*'Take this dead body before it done snatches my soul!'*"

"Nobody ever said that," said Lillian, but she laughed anyway.

"You right, nobody said that," he admitted. 'But they sure did beat feet outta there like they was late to the dance. Later on when they done it a bunch they act all casual like it ain't nothin', but I remember who was shakin' their first time. And it weren't you."

They arrived in front of Lillian's apartment. Marie broke off from Lillian and stumbled up the stoop through the front door. "I better get in there," said Lillian, holding up a key. "She won't like that our door upstairs is locked."

"I'm just glad to see that you lock it."

"Jupiter, I don't know how to thank you. If you hadn't been there tonight—"

He took a step backwards, hands in pockets. "But I was." He smiled and stepped out of the lamplight, disappearing into the inky night.

On Wednesday it had been a full week since Nurses Cahill and Drake were let go, but their positions still had not been filled. The chatter Lillian heard in the changing room was that the applicants were few and those that showed were too young, too old or too inexperienced. One was said to have worn rouge to her meeting with Nurse Holt. "Can you imagine?" Lillian overheard one nurse say to another as they were checking the level of each other's caps. "The common sense of a pigeon!"

The dearth of nursing staff was of particular concern because a patient had been admitted yesterday with a tumor on her tibia, and a surgery was anticipated for today. The wards were full and Posh Row even had two patients, so nurses were already stretched to their limit. Yesterday and today, Lillian had been told to do morning whiskey rounds— "a very temporary responsibility" she was admonished, but one that she took on with enthusiasm, eager to prove she could perform the duties of a full-fledged nurse.

As she carried her carefully-balanced tray past the bed of the tibia tumor patient, the woman buttonholed her. "You have cup for me?" she asked in broken English. She looked up at Lillian with a pudgy face that telegraphed low expectations.

"I'm sorry, Miss…." Lillian looked at the chart hanging from the bed. "Mrs. Sokolova. You are scheduled for surgery in a few hours, so they would prefer you not have whiskey."

"But I have pain. You have nothing for pain?"

"I'm afraid not." She started to walk away.

"One more question." Mrs. Sokolova waved Lillian closer. Lillian could see a sheen of perspiration on the woman's face and knew she was not lying about her pain, as some occasionally did. "My leg. What will they do to my leg?"

"Ma'am, I'm only a nursing assistant, so I'm not—"

"Will they take out bump, or will they take off leg?"

Lillian gave the pat answer she had heard other nurses employ. "The doctor will look at the problem once he starts the surgery and make the determination then." For a moment, guilt fluttered since she did not know her statement to be true in Mrs. Sokolova's case, but she pushed that feeling aside. This is what she was supposed to say, and to say otherwise would put her job at risk.

"You have nice words. Good at job. You know what I do for job?"

Lillian shook her head, sensing this conversation was not going in a good direction.

"I scrub floor in theater. Every morning. Beer. Cigarette. Little beads from dresses. Sometimes feather. I clean up from all that fun the night before. You think I can do that without leg?"

Lillian knew she should describe how the nursing staff would help her learn to walk with crutches and eventually there would be the possibility of a prosthesis, but she knew this would only get her to even more complicated questions, such as how long the recovery would be (likely months), and whether Lillian thought that the theater manager would hold her job during that time (of course not) and how well she could compete with other women for another floor-scrubbing job without both of her legs (not well) and what she was supposed to live on during all this time (unclear).

The tray Lillian was holding wobbled, nearly spilling the cups that were still full. "I need to get more whiskey for the other patients," she said in a strained voice and quickly walked out of the ward, pretending not to hear Mrs. Sokolova calling out to her, "What job is good for woman without leg?"

It occurred to Lillian as she was changing bed linens in the afternoon that despite the fact that few nurses spoke to her, she usually had a good idea of what was going on in the hospital. It was probably because she was always listening, she reasoned as she stuffed a pillow into a case and fluffed it back into shape. When you are talking, you can't listen, but Lillian was mostly silent at work as she went about her business. And the nurses did love to chatter and gossip. In her first weeks at the hospital, the nurses took care to have their conversations outside of Lillian's earshot, but after a while they became complacent, or perhaps just lazy, and discussed all manner of things that Lillian found interesting.

For example, she had heard that Mrs. Sokolova went into surgery that afternoon one shy of the usual complement of two nurses, and that Dr. Bauer was definitely planning an amputation. Hearing this, she thought about Mrs. Sokolova's job, the beads and feathers on the dance hall floor, and a wave of sadness washed over her. Was there really no alternative to amputation? How long could the woman live without the surgery? Lillian made a note in her notebook to ask Dr. Bauer about these things in his office tomorrow night.

Though Mrs. Sokolova had only been here a day, Lillian had been told to change her linen while she was in surgery, and as Lillian approached the bed, she could see why: it was soaked in perspiration. She was just bundling the sour sheets into a ball when Nurse Paterson approached.

"They want you in the operating theater," she said, with a hand on her hip in a stance that seemed to imply wrongdoing on Lillian's part.

"Me? Specifically?"

"No, they wanted me but I thought I would give you the opportunity." Nurse Paterson pursed her lips to underscore her sarcasm.

"Sorry," said Lillian as she stuffed the ball of dirty sheets under the
bed so no one would trip on them. "I'll make this bed right after."

"It will be waiting right here for you," said Nurse Paterson.

Lillian's stomach twinged with excitement at the prospect of her
first time crossing the threshold of the operating theater. Dr. Bauer must have requested her, perhaps to see something unusual revealed in the surgery that they would discuss tomorrow night. Or
perhaps they needed another pair of hands to stanch the bleeding
and Dr. Bauer thought she would most benefit from the experience.
Of course, such favoritism would work against any headway she was
making with the nurses, but what could she do? She could only
follow orders, she thought to herself as she smiled and pushed open
the door to the theater.

She was on the verge of asking if she should wash her hands when
the nurse assisting Dr. Bauer turned to Lillian and tapped a metal
tub on the floor with her foot. "Take this to the dumbwaiter and
down to Jupiter," she said and turned back to the operating table
where she was receiving tiny clamps Dr. Bauer was removing from
Mrs. Sokolova's stump. "Put a towel over it first," said the nurse without looking back again. Dr. Bauer did not look up.

Lillian looked down into the tub and saw Mrs. Sokolova's leg, amputated above the knee, in a bed of sawdust.

❧ Chapter 15 ❧

Lillian had supposed that using the dumbwaiter for an amputated limb was just for discretion, but she soon discovered that the surprising weight of the limb would have made carrying the tub down flights of stairs awkward. Once she made it to the dumbwaiter and hoisted the tub onto the platform, she pulled one of the ropes hand over hand until she felt the platform hit bottom, then closed the doors and proceeded to the basement.

"Miz Dolan!" said Jupiter as he opened his door for her and the gurney. "I see they got you back on the fancy jobs."

"Yes, although a hopeful prognosis is possible this time, unlike my other trips down here."

Jupiter lifted the towel. "Above the knee," he murmured before replacing it.

"Why do you mention that?"

"As I hear it, tougher to get one of them fake legs that way. The bend in the knee, that ain't so easy."

Lillian thought about this. "But the surgeon must have thought it was necessary to amputate at that level in order to prevent the cancer from coming back."

"I suppose." Jupiter lifted the tub from the gurney and put it on a table near the ovens. "So how long you been living there on 9th Avenue?"

"Just a few months. We moved there right before I started at the hospital. How about you?"

"Oh, I been living there since I come to New York from the South. 'Bout two years."

"What made you come to New York?"

Jupiter braced himself on the table and leaned back. "That's a long story. Maybe as long as why you and your sister living in the Kitchen."

Lillian thought back to her initial impression of Jupiter as a diplomat, and how this comment was equally deft. He was not asking her to tell her story, which would have been impertinent, but leaving the door open to her telling it if she were inclined. For all his lack of proper grammar, he was gifted in language nevertheless.

"You're quite clever," she said, leaning against the wall and crossing her arms as she contemplated him.

"Aw, Miz Dolan, I just run these here ovens." He smiled.

"But you could get a better job. Why are you here?"

"You know, you the first person that asked me that. Even when they interviewed me, nobody asked me, 'Jupiter, why you want this job?' I guess they was just happy enough that I wanted it and they could pay me black wages."

"Which doesn't answer my question."

"No, it don't." He walked back and pulled the coal chute lever, and the coal clattered down into the oven. Lillian suspected this was more to end her line of questioning than it was to fill the oven. Once the noise stopped, he asked, "Them nurses upstairs, they gonna be mad you been away so long? I ain't pushin' you out, I just don't want to catch it with them."

"Nurse Paterson told me I was wanted in the surgery, so she probably can't predict how long I'd be." Lillian realized that this was one of the rare times she was at the crematorium where someone wasn't tapping their toes upstairs, waiting for her to get back. "Jupiter, do you know Dr. Bauer?"

Jupiter brought over two rickety chairs. Lillian sat down gingerly, afraid the chair might collapse, though Jupiter evidently did not share her fear given the way he plunked himself down. "He the new surgeon. Hands touched by God."

She laughed. "Perhaps he thinks so."

"Wouldn't be the first sawbones to think that."

"So Dr. Bauer has…" She almost said 'taken a shine to me'—Michael's phrase he used at dinner Sunday, but it sounded wrong coming out of her mouth. "He has asked to meet with me. As a sort of mentor, I suppose."

"Like he do with other nurses?" Jupiter tilted back a few inches and the chair complained with a drawn-out creak.

"Why does everyone ask that? Maybe it's because I am the only assistant here, and I need more training!"

"Who is 'everyone'?"

"Oh, my cousin Michael and the woman that takes care of Marie. They both think the situation is dodgy. But that's ridiculous."

"So why you bringing it up with me?" He tilted back another inch, regarding her curiously as the chair groaned.

"Because I thought maybe you would understand!" Lillian got up and started to pace the room. "You work here. You know what it is like to be nobody here." She stopped, embarrassed. "I didn't mean—"

"Oh, naw, you go right ahead. Ain't nobody more nobody than me around these parts." Jupiter seemed to be enjoying this.

"OK, so they see me as a glorified housekeeper, so how am I supposed to rise up? I want to be a nurse but I'm the only one who seems to want that here. Except maybe Dr. Bauer."

"You think that's what that man wants?"

"I don't know what he wants. But I know what I want. I want to learn from him."

"So you know how you usin' him."

"Yes." She stopped again. "That sounds odd, but yes, I suppose that's true."

"You just don't know how he usin' you."

Lillian sat down, this time without as much caution, and the chair complained but held together. "Yes. Michael says to be on guard, but I don't even know what I'm supposed to guard against."

"It ain't a bad thing to be on guard. Folks ain't usually sorry that they was careful."

"You don't seem to be trying to persuade me to… to…"

"To what?" Jupiter made a steeple with his hands. "What you gonna do, say no? He even give you that choice?"

Lillian looked down at her lap. "He did not. He just told me to come to his office on Thursday nights."

"Well, where I'm from, when the white man tells you to do something, maybe there's danger in doin' it but there's also danger in not doin' it. But besides, even if he gave you a choice, ain't no way you gonna pass this up. You got that ambition, and Lord knows you got courage. So seems like the best you can do is learn what you can and keep your eyes open."

Lillian stood, and Jupiter followed suit. She took a deep breath. "Thank you, Jupiter. I feel better just being able to talk about it. But you can't tell anyone."

"I just the Negro that run these here ovens. I don't know nothin'." He grinned.

The following evening Lillian was late to Dr. Bauer's office because two nurses were chatting conspiratorially in the hallway nearby. By the time she could enter the office undetected, she saw by the wall clock that she was ten minutes late, but Dr. Bauer didn't seem to notice. "Assistant Dolan," he said as she entered, and in contrast to their last meeting, he seemed glad to see her. "Please sit."

She arranged her skirts around the chair and took care that her posture was beyond reproach, although her corset did most of the work. "Sir," she nodded, but then she was unsure what to say next. *I have a question? How was your day? Why are we meeting?*

"The nurse called you into the theater yesterday after the amputation. It appears we are short staffed for nurses. I was told a pair were found to be morally lax."

"Yes, sir."

"What was it that they did, exactly?"

Lillian was confused. Were they going to talk about the nurses' code of conduct? "They were keeping company with young men. Sneaking out at night."

"Hardly the sort we want around here, wouldn't you say?"

Was that a question she should answer? "Well, the nurses are supposed to be available all night for emergencies, so yes, sneaking out at night should not be acceptable."

"But what if they had only seen their young men on their afternoon off? I believe they are allowed one afternoon to themselves per week, as it is at Presbyterian?"

"As I understand it, that would still be grounds for dismissal." Janey had made Lillian read the Code of Conduct her first week here, although it was unclear which parts would apply to an assistant nurse.

Dr. Bauer wrinkled his brow and crossed his arms, clearly peeved. "Of course, but do you think that is just?"

"No, sir, I do not." Lillian had thought about this when she had read the manual, and if Dr. Bauer wanted to know what she thought, she would tell him. "I believe what you do on your own time should not be relevant to your job."

He picked up a pencil from his desk and suspended it horizontally between the pads of his index fingers. He peered at her over the pencil with his glacial eyes. "What if you are a drunkard on your own time?"

"As long as you are sober and clear-headed at work, you should be able to drink on your own time."

"What if you are a whore on your own time?"

The impropriety of this question was like a slap in the face, although a moment later Lillian reasoned that this was just a theoretical conversation, just an abstraction, not as inappropriate as it had first seemed. "The hospital should not employ people who break the law."

"All right, not a whore, per se, not of the fee-collecting type, but a woman of easy virtue."

She shifted uncomfortably in her seat and thought of her conversation with Jupiter. *You know how you usin' him.* "That is her own business. But I should like to talk to you about yesterday's amputation."

He considered her over the pencil for a heartbeat, and then placed it carefully back on the desk and took an audible breath. "Osteosarcoma of the proximal tibia, amputation at mid-thigh. As you know."

"Was there no hope of saving her leg?"

"Not if she wanted me to save her life."

"Did you? Save her life?" Lillian leaned forward slightly in her chair.

As if in response, Dr. Bauer leaned back slightly and knit his fingers together behind his neck. "Time will tell, will it not?"

"So you don't know."

"Do you think doctors know everything?"

A trick question if ever there was one, she thought. "Do they?"

After a second of tension, Dr. Bauer laughed. "I was right about you. At least I knew that much." Lillian waited for him to elaborate but instead he stood. "You were late today."

She rose from her chair. "There were nurses in the hallway. You asked me to keep our meetings…." *Secret*, she thought. "Private."

"I do not wish to make your life difficult, skulking about. I think it would be easier on you to meet at this address on Thursdays." He wrote quickly on a piece of paper and held it out to her. "Half six should give you time enough."

A little warning bell chimed in a far corner of her mind, but then Dr. Bauer took a step closer and said, "You are quite clever. I have not been impressed by the nursing staff here as compared to Presbyterian, but you are proving an exception to the rule. Something the other nurses wouldn't understand. A mind worth nurturing." A small smile spread beneath his mustache, and Lillian took the slip of paper with a blush rising in her cheeks.

🏵 Chapter 16 🏵

When Lillian arrived home that evening, Marie was already asleep and Josephine was reading the afternoon edition of the Post. "How's her cough?" asked Lillian as she hung up her coat.

"She's worn out, poor thing. I thought she'd have kicked it by now." Josephine folded the *New York World* neatly and brought her mug of tea to the sink. "She seemed spunky enough when we went out for the paper but she was draggin' by the time we came back up the stairs."

Several weeks ago Josephine had lobbied for taking Marie out of the house on a regular basis. After some negotiation, they decided on a walk to the corner of 9th and 57th where the newsie sold a variety of papers, Lillian trying not to show her surprise that Josephine was a newspaper reader. Once Lillian got used to the idea of Josephine taking Marie out of the building, she was thrilled that Marie was getting out more without Lillian having to dress her. Josephine seemed to have endless patience for wrestling Marie into her clothing.

"She's not giving you any trouble with the boots?" A few days ago, Lillian had stopped by a shoe store on her way home from work armed with a piece of string she'd cut to the length of Marie's current boots, and bought a pair a half inch longer. This had been Helen's solution to the intractable problem of getting Marie to try on shoes in a store.

"They seem to fit. She ain't sayin' otherwise." Josephine took her coat off the nail in the wall. Lillian found herself wishing that Josephine did not have to go.

"Anything exciting in the *World* today?" she asked casually as she unfolded the paper on the table.

"Some killer sentenced to the chair up in Ossining," said Josephine as she worked the hatpin through the velvet of her trilby. "Don't they just love to tart up the story, the pretty wife sobbing in court and all that." Lillian saw the story in the "Extra" column: *To Be Shocked to Death at Sing Sing Prison. The Young Murderer Unmoved by Judge Moore's Terrible Words.* Josephine cocked her head slightly. "Everything all right at work?"

Lillian opened the icebox and took out the remains of the chicken she had boiled two nights ago. As she carved a slice and put it on a plate, she thought of her meeting with Dr. Bauer this evening and knew she shouldn't bring it up with Josephine if she didn't want to hear what she knew Josephine would say. But she couldn't help it. "Today I met with the doctor."

"All on the up and up?"

Lillian thought of their conversation about the code of conduct. "Basically, yes."

"Basically?" Josephine looked dubious.

"He wants to meet outside the hospital." Put that way, it sounded even worse than she thought it would. She looked at Josephine and got the impression that Josephine was trying very hard to keep her face neutral.

"Where?" Josephine asked.

"I have an address. I suppose it is some sort of restaurant. Perhaps I'll get a free meal out of it," she added, but she could see her attempt at humor fell flat with Josephine.

Josephine held out her hand, and Lillian rummaged around in her pockets until she found the slip of paper with the address.

"Hmmm," said Josephine as she looked at it. "If I recollect, this neighborhood is more brownstones than saloons."

Lillian blushed at her own ignorant assumption, or, if she were being honest, her willful ignoring of the more likely reality. "Please don't tell Michael. I'm afraid he wouldn't understand."

"I'm not sure I understand. But all right. You might be tougher than Michael thinks you are. But don't be stupid."

Despite understanding Josephine's concern, she bristled a bit. "According to Dr. Bauer, it's because I am clever that he is interested in mentoring me."

Josephine rose and slowly put on her coat. "So I been around a few men that tend to get what they want. One thing they got in common is they size up the other person. Figure out what that person wants to hear. Then they tell 'em that. Works like a charm with most folks. Mostly I seen it when a girl hasn't felt pretty enough her whole life. Man comes along and tells her she's beautiful, she'll do just about anything."

"But it's not like I haven't been told that I'm clever before. I did well in school. Michael tells me. My mother told me."

"But you ain't been told by the likes of that high-falutin' doctor."

After Lillian had finished her chicken, she pushed the bones around on her plate with her fork and thought about what Josephine said. What did it say about her plans with Dr. Bauer that a girl who had whored down on the Bowery was concerned about Lillian meeting with a doctor? She almost laughed out loud. And yet, she still felt that she could handle Dr. Bauer. Hadn't she cleverly redirected their conversation toward the amputation?

Her exchange with Jupiter on this subject spun around in her mind. *You know how you usin' him. You just don't know how he usin' you.* She had told Jupiter that she wanted to learn from Dr. Bauer, and that was true—but to what end? She wanted to be a nurse, but was her goal to get Dr. Bauer to promote her at the hospital? If the other nurses didn't hate her now, they certainly would then. And as she had seen over the last month, there were any number of ways that the nurses could make her life miserable.

So therefore, she wanted to be a nurse somewhere else. And to do that, she needed to attend one of the nursing schools in the city. Live-in programs where the minimum age was years older than she was. And what would she do with Marie?

Lillian took her plate to the garbage bucket and scraped the chicken bones with her fork, watching them fall, listening to them hit the wooden bottom. Maybe she didn't know all the possible options.

Maybe that was the greatest value that Dr. Bauer could provide— maybe he could see a solution that she could not.

But why would he help her? *You just don't know how he usin' you.* Meeting outside the hospital would probably reveal that more quickly. So be it. Either his intentions were acceptable or they were not. She knew right from wrong, and she would pursue this until she knew which it was.

On Sunday morning, Lillian had just gotten dressed and was about to heat up the kettle when she heard a knock on the door.

"Josephine!" she said as she opened the door wide. "I suppose you haven't mistaken the day for Monday?"

Josephine forced a smile. "Let's sit."

As they sat down opposite each other at the kitchen table, a cold stone dropped in Lillian's stomach. "Please don't tell me you can't take care of Marie anymore. She loves you and I'm sorry I ever judged you—"

"Lillian. It's about Michael." Lillian's eyes opened wide in horror, and Josephine quickly continued. "No, he's fine. Well, not entirely up to snuff, but he's alive. Jesus, that sounds bad, I'm mucking this all up. He's been beat up pretty good."

"What?" Though the news was a shock, Lillian recalled a day months ago when Michael showed up to Fiona's dinner table with a black eye and a split lip. He'd made light of it, a barroom argument gone bad, but even then it had not had the ring of truth. She knew Michael wasn't much of a drinker and it didn't make him surly. And now this sounded much more serious.

"He's OK, he's at home, his Ma is tending to him, she wants to call the doctor, he's having none of it."

"How did this happen?" After the words left her mouth, she wasn't sure she wanted to know the answer. Things were moving too fast for her to think through it all, but instinctively she felt there was something behind a curtain, a curtain that was about to be pulled back. "How did you know about it?"

"Street urchin brought me a note from Michael. The one thing he and his Ma agree on right now is that they could use you. Michael knew you couldn't leave Marie and it would be hard to bring her. I can stay with Marie till you get back."

"Josephine, thank you so much." Lillian grabbed her boots and laced them up quickly, then smoothed down her hair. She stopped to take a breath. "Why did this happen?"

Josephine unpinned her trilby and held it under her chin with her elbows on the table. She looked up at Lillian. "I think you need to talk to Michael."

The hansom cab made good time in the empty Sunday morning streets. Aunt Fiona opened the door and hugged her without a word, then led her to Michael's room.

Other than a bruise on one cheek, his face bore no signs of damage, but his breathing was labored and his lips were pale to match his face. "Lilypad," he croaked. "What a pleasant... surprise."

"What in God's name, Michael." She sat in the chair next to his bed and gripped his hand gently.

"Ma, can you... give us a... minute?" Michael said with effort.

"Lillian, tell him he needs a *doctor*, for the love of Mary and Joseph!" said Fiona, but she left and closed the door behind her.

"So," said Lillian, "How was your Saturday night?" She managed a wry smile.

"Eh. I've had better." He shifted in the bed and winced.

"Where does it hurt?"

"Ah. Nurse Dolan... has arrived. It's my ribs."

Lillian lifted his shirt, damp with sweat, and saw a riot of bruising. She gasped involuntarily.

"You need some... work on your... bedside manner," said Michael.

She spied a bruise near his wrist and gently pushed his sleeves up to reveal more bruising on his arms. She brushed the tears from her eyes. "Michael, those ribs are cracked or broken."

"Is that your... medical opinion... Nurse?"

"No, that's the opinion of someone with eyes in their head. I think you should have the doctor come."

"If my nurse... says so... then OK." He squeezed her hand. "But stay with me... for a few minutes more."

Lillian went to tell Fiona to send for the doctor and then came back to Michael's bedside with the door shut firmly behind her. She grabbed his hand, careful not to move his forearm, and kissed his knuckles. "Are you going to tell me how this happened?"

"It was a boot…. Black. Size twelve…I believe."

Lillian squeezed her eyes shut. The bruises on his arms were defensive. She could see it in her mind's eye, Michael curled up on a filthy sidewalk trying to protect his chest, fists bunched under his chin, the boot finding its mark again and again, her cousin unable to do anything except absorb the blows and wait until it was over.

She resisted the urge to hold her head in her hands and start sobbing, and instead opened her eyes and took a deep breath. She pushed his hair off his forehead. At least he didn't feel feverish. "So someone kicked you. Repeatedly. That's all you have to say?"

"Lilypad," he said, his voice almost a whisper. "How much… do you really… want to know?"

Lillian blinked and a tiny tear scurried down the side of her nose. There had been a time when she would have been happier to know only what she would approve of, leaving her solid gold image of Michael intact. "I want to know it all," she said, a dam crumbling inside of her.

It took a while for Michael to tell her the whole story in three or four word phrases between shallow breaths. The first time he went down to the Bowery last year, he was sure it was a one-time occurrence. He had heard talk in the neighborhood of wild times and late nights down there, and one evening, after a particularly fearsome row with his father, he found himself on the Third Avenue El down to Houston Street. That first time, he just walked around, watching the people go in and out of various establishments, eavesdropping on their drunken banter, too nervous to enter anywhere. The second time he went, he went directly to a doorway he had identified on his previous trip, screwed up his courage and walked inside. After that, it wasn't difficult at all.

Not too long ago, he had received a recommendation from a man that frequented Abraham's shop. Lillian remembered Michael talking about this man and his companion. Mr. Davenport and Mr.

Sutherland came in regularly to "refresh their wardrobe", as Davenport liked to say. They were by far Abraham's best dressed customers, so much so that Michael often wondered why they didn't patronize a more upscale tailor. Despite their orders requiring the most expensive fabrics in the shop, Abraham's scowl always deepened when they arrived, according to Michael, the old man insisting he had pressing business in the back.

The establishment they recommended down on Bleecker Street was called The Slide, and Michael became a frequent patron. "It's a circus… every night. All types… of people." Michael was staring at Lillian intently.

The floorboards seemed to shift beneath her feet, but she asked, "And what type of people are the draw for you?" Although she knew. But she had to hear it.

"Other men. Like me. Men that like men." He gripped her hand in a way that, had she wanted to let go, she would not have been able.

Lillian thought for a long while, or what seemed like a long while. She wasn't sure how much time had passed before she said, "Josephine. Was she a test? To see how I would react?"

"Josephine… was a solution… to that drunken crone Oberman." He paused to gather some strength. "But you… accepted her. Made me think… I could tell you… about me."

"This still doesn't explain why you were beaten."

With labored breaths, Michael explained that he felt safe down on the Bowery. But a man he met last night wanted to take him home, and en route they ran into some fellows that didn't approve. Despite wanting to know everything, Lillian didn't press Michael as to what he was doing with his companion on the street to invite that disapproval.

"First it's… name calling. But then… not enough. 'Teach these… fairies a lesson.'" Lillian saw tears pooling in the corner of Michael's eyes. He swallowed hard.

"I'm so sorry you were hurt," said Lillian, swallowing the lump in her throat. "What happened to your… your friend?"

Michael chuckled, and then winced at the resulting pain in his ribcage. "Ran away. Not a scratch."

"Well," said Lillian, "I'd say he wasn't a keeper."

They smiled together as they heard the doctor in the front hall.

▒ Chapter 17 ▒

Uncle Martin went with Lillian out to Third Avenue to hail a hansom. "Thanks to you, my lass, that boy will at least see a doctor, so bless your heart." As they walked to the corner, he continued. "What the devil was he up to that he got himself into this mess?" Despite all the critical things Michael had said throughout the years about his father, Lillian could see Martin's concern.

"Just a drunken brawl, Uncle. Boys will be boys." Lillian figured her uncle would be able to accept a story about violence fueled by alcohol. "He just doesn't want to talk about it because he didn't get too many licks in."

"Ah, yes," said Martin, nodding. "He weren't much of a scrapper growing up. Now he's regrettin' it. Maybe this will put some hair on his chest."

As the cab pulled up, Lillian implored, "Will you send news of what the doctor says in the afternoon post?"

"That I will." Martin helped Lillian up into the cab and handed her the fare.

On the ride back home, Lillian's thoughts whirled and resisted being sorted into their proper compartments. Michael was... well, she would have called other men who did those things deviants, but she couldn't think of Michael that way. But what was the difference? Either Michael was deviant, or none of them were. But even though it seemed to change everything, it changed nothing, really. Michael was the same as he ever was, the keeper of her childhood secrets, the sharer of desserts, the one who gave her his life savings so she and Marie could move. She had initially been shocked at Josephine's inclinations. But after a while, when her mind would go there, it failed to shock her, the novelty gone. To think of Michael with another man was startling and yet in a way it was easy to believe. She thought of him and Uncle Martin clashing over the past few years, and now she could see that Uncle Martin had some sense that Michael wasn't the man he wanted him to be. She was sure Uncle Martin would never understand, would never accept, and that Michael was right to keep this from him. She realized how much Michael had trusted her today and it gave her a chill up her spine.

The hansom jerked to a stop in front of her building. Lillian didn't remember anything of the trip. She exited the cab in a daze, walking away without paying the fare until the driver angrily reminded her.

"How is he?" asked Josephine as soon as Lillian was in the door.

"It looks like a team of horses kicked him in the chest. The doctor is seeing him. His breathing is rough, but he's able to talk."

"And did he?"

"Talk? Yes, he did. Quite a bit." Lillian sat down without taking her coat off, lost in thought. After a moment, she said, "He told me that you and he had more in common than I thought."

"He wanted to tell you for a long time. But he was afraid you would think the lesser of him."

She started to say that she could never think poorly of Michael, but checked herself when she remembered the things she said to Josephine. The things she thought. So easy to think them of a stranger.

Lillian gazed out the kitchen window at the brick wall of the building next door. "When we were growing up, there was a man that lived in the building next door for a few years. Older, big silver mustache and muttonchops, carved rosewood cane. He lived with his nephew, the boy might have been twenty five. At least that's how he would introduce him— 'my nephew Tobias'. But people would talk. I didn't believe it. At the time, I didn't believe that there was anyone like that. But Michael did. He said there was the life that people presented to the world, and then there was the real life lurking beneath that. I got angry with him, wouldn't speak to him for days.

He couldn't understand why, and I couldn't tell him, because I didn't know. But I know now. It scared me. The thought of not being able to see anyone's true nature. Anyone could be anything." She realized she was trembling.

"But that's the appeal of the Bowery, don't you see. At The Slide and them other places, everyone is who they really are. It's a relief."

"Is he different there?" As she said it, she realized this was the thing, the nub of it all, the center of the swirl. If Michael had not been showing his true nature to Lillian for all these years, would she even recognize him fully revealed? Did she even know him?

"If you mean, is he still a prince of a man that would give you the shirt off his back, yeah, he's the same." She ran a finger across the scar on her face, barely touching it. Lillian had almost forgotten it was there. "He found me, ya know. Slumped in the alley, bleeding. I was seeing stars, I tell ya. And somehow he found the only sober doc down on the Bowery, sewed me up, doc even washed his hands before, according to Michael. Come to think of it, maybe that was Michael's idea. Of course he paid the doc. Checked on me while I was healing."

"Were you friends before that?"

"Not really. We knew each other, from the bars. He's a handsome fella, people notice him. And a lot of people knew me too."

"So that's how you came to be friends with him?"

"Are you surprised? That he would help me like that?"

Lillian shrugged. "Not really."

"After that bastard beat the daylights outta me and left me for dead, I was skittish around men for a while. Couldn't be alone with one. But Michael, well, I knew he wasn't interested in me like that, of course. He was easy to be with while I got my sea legs back."

Lillian felt the click of a puzzle piece pushed into place. She had often wondered why Josephine had taken this job. She could only imagine that what Lillian paid her paled in comparison to what she had earned selling herself. And there must have been a legitimate job in this city that would have paid better. But Josephine was indebted to Michael, and Lillian was the beneficiary.

"Can you really live on what I pay you?"

"I got some savings I can dip into." Josephine picked up a dishrag and folded it carefully. "Truth is, I told Michael I would do this job for a while, get you out of a tight spot, and while I figured out what the hell was next for me. But turns out I still don't know what's next, and that little scoundrel grew on me." She jerked her thumb toward Marie in the bedroom.

"Marie! I completely forgot about her. Is she up?"

"Up and braiding on the bedpost." Josephine and Lillian both collected twine and string to tie to the bedpost in sets of three, which would keep Marie happily braiding for quite a while. "I bet you don't know that I got me a new friend across the hallway."

"Mrs. Sweeney?" Lillian was incredulous.

"A week or two ago I heard a hell of a ruckus in the hall. The five year old screaming bloody murder, split open his chin from fallin' off who knows what, bleeding like Christ on the cross. Mrs. Sweeney had just started feeding the baby his mush, and he was screaming his head off at the interruption. I offered to take baby Cornelius and finish the feeding over here while she cleaned up the daredevil."

"Cornelius, huh."

"Quite the five-dollar name. Be a while 'til he grows into it. Anyway, now me and Sweeney are on regular terms. She dropped off a piece of apple cake the other day, and I give her the paper once I read it." Josephine looked pleased with herself. Lillian could only imagine the fits that Mrs. Sweeney would have if she knew more about Josephine.

Just then, the bells tolled at Sacred Heart of Jesus down the street, and Lillian remembered it was Sunday. "I shouldn't keep you on the weekend. You are already too kind to have come and stayed like you did."

"She was easy today. Only been up for a half hour. And her cough is almost gone."

After Josephine left, Lillian went in and sat on the floor next to Marie, who stopped braiding twine and lay her head in Lillian's lap. She smoothed Marie's hair from her temple and tucked it behind her ear. Marie purred a low hum in the back of her throat and closed her sightless eyes. Happy as a clam, thought Lillian. She won't be able to visit Michael for a while; Lillian could only imagine trying to block Marie from giving Michael's broken ribs a big bear hug. Michael, Lillian thought. Michael who was different. Michael who was the same.

Chapter 18

Since the arrival of Dr. Bauer, there had been an uptick in the number of surgeries. This, combined with a shortage of nursing staff, forced Lillian to assume some full-fledged nursing tasks. Just so that Lillian didn't get the wrong idea, Nurse Holt called her into her office on Monday. "You are still an assistant, make no mistake," she explained. "But you will take over whiskey rounds when nurses are called to surgery. You may have to help the patients dress if they feel well enough to eat in the dining hall." She pursed her lips as if considering whether to continue. "You've been with us over a month, a month with significant staffing changes, and you have been more reliable than I had expected, given your youth. This is why you are being given the honor of elevated responsibilities."

Lillian curbed her impulse to ask if elevated responsibilities came with an elevated salary. "I appreciate your faith in me." She stood but before leaving asked, "Have you had any luck hiring more nurses?"

Nurse Holt's nostrils flared slightly, signaling to Lillian that this was probably an impudent question. But after a breath Nurse Holt apparently changed her mind and said, "As it turns out, there is a new nurse starting tomorrow. We are still one short and the new nurse will have to be trained so relief is not imminent. I expect you to support the new girl and speed her training."

"Of course, ma'am." Lillian departed with a nod before she could say anything else that could be considered rude.

Her first whiskey round that day brought her to the bed of the amputation patient, Mrs. Sokolova. Sardonic eyes peered out from a pudgy face framed by rust-colored hair. "For your pain," Lillian said as she offered a cup.

Mrs. Sokolova took it with a firm grasp. "*Zazdarovje*," she said as she tilted the cup toward Lillian before downing it in one gulp. She placed the cup carefully back on the tray. "You have one more with my name?"

"If your pain is worsening I can have one of the nurses attend you."

"Not worth talking to those cows. But you have extra, cups nobody wanted, you come back."

Lillian smiled, but she knew the procedure. When cups were refused, the whiskey was poured back into the bottle, and she wouldn't risk her job just to give Mrs. Sokolova an extra shot.

"You are…" Lillian squinted her eyes, thinking. "Five days post-surgery, yes?" She reached for the chart hanging at the end of the bed. "Yes. You are beyond the worst risk of post-surgical infection. Now is when many patients start trying to get up."

"*Bah!* You find a leg to sew back onto me, then we talk."

"We have crutches. I can show you how to use them." Lillian had assisted Janey in training a woman with an amputated foot two weeks ago. It didn't look hard and she was sure the other nurses would be glad to delegate the task.

"You know where I live? Third floor. These fancy crutches gonna take me up those stairs?"

"Yes," she said, although that had not been part of the Janey's training. It had been all the patient could handle to cross the ward and back before she fell back in bed, sweating and exhausted. That had been the woman's first day out of bed, of course. Lillian was sure that Janey knew about crutches and stairs. Or if not, Lillian could practice with crutches herself and figure it out.

Mrs. Sokolova crossed her arms and turned her head. "Not interested."

"Are you interested in eventually getting a prosthetic?"

"What the hell is that thing," grumbled Mrs. Sokolova, still looking out the window. Lillian had the impression the woman knew what a prosthetic was.

"A false leg. Because if you are, the doctors only consider patients who have mastered crutches."

"Hmmph," muttered Mrs. Sokolova. "Not ready."

"All right." Lillian put the chart back on the hook. "Let one of the nurses know when you are ready."

"No. I let you know." She turned her head back to Lillian with a challenging set to her jaw. "Not the cows."

Lillian smiled as she continued her rounds. *A tough old bird, that one*, she thought to herself. If anyone on this ward was going to survive, Lillian would put her money on Mrs. Sokolova.

When the new nurse started the next day, Janey once again had been assigned to train her, but Janey had no problem asking Lillian to take over the training when she was called into surgery or was just tired of explaining everything she was doing. Between her new nurse-like responsibilities and showing the new nurse the ropes, Lillian felt bogged down. One evening she nearly fell asleep standing up on the El, jerking awake to realize she was a stop beyond where she should have gotten off.

On Thursday she was doing whiskey rounds with the new nurse when they came to the bed of a new patient, whose breathing was wheezy and shallow. Her eyelids were closed but underneath them her eyes moved from side to side. Lillian checked her name and diagnosis on her chart. "Mrs. Angelo," Lillian said gently as she shook her arm.

"What kind of cancer does she have?" asked Nurse Farrell. To Lillian, Nurse Farrell seemed slightly afraid of the patients, reluctant to get too close. Perhaps she was not entirely convinced that cancer was not contagious.

"The chart says they suspect the lungs." Lillian tried not to think about how Mrs. Angelo was feeling, or where her illness was going. Throughout her life, Lillian had occasional dreams where she couldn't breathe and woke up in a sweat. She and Michael had had long discussions years ago about the relative merits of dying in certain ways, Michael always rating fire as his least favorite and Lillian insisting on suffocation as the worst.

"Will they operate?" asked Nurse Farrell.

Lillian tried once again to wake Mrs. Angelo. She roused enough to take her whiskey and Lillian and Nurse Farrell moved on toward the next bed. "Whether they will operate or not is not relevant to how we care for them," Lillian said out of earshot of the patients. She thought this sounded a little pedantic, so she added, "They don't really encourage questions here. I'm fine with them, but you might as well try to get a sense of what is our business and what is not."

"All right," said Nurse Farrell softly. Lillian could tell she had other questions but accepted that they would not be answered. Lillian only wished that she herself could let things go that easily.

On Thursday night, Lillian stood in the rain outside of a brownstone and checked the address on the soggy slip of paper. She rang the bell with a quickening pulse and was relieved to see a servant answer. "He's in the study," the woman said, taking Lillian's coat and hat. "Ya need to take off those shoes before entering the study. Them Oriental carpets are valuable."

Lillian sat in an armchair outside the study and unlaced her old boots. There had been no extra money to replace her dilapidated footwear. She had resolved to wear these until they fell apart but was now embarrassed in front of the servant, although the woman seemed not to notice.

"Nurse Dolan, I trust you had no problem finding the place?" Dr. Bauer asked from the armchair by the fireplace. He did not rise in her presence, Lillian noted. She looked down at the carpets and saw they were indeed beautiful, although why someone would pay a lot of money for something to walk on was beyond her. She hoped Dr. Bauer would not see that her skirts were dripping rainwater onto his expensive rugs.

"No trouble, sir, although somehow I had thought we were meeting at a restaurant or some such place." Lillian immediately wanted to take these words back, fearing he would think she was angling for a free meal. Which, now that she thought of it, would have been nice as she was quite hungry.

"Restaurants—can't stand them. All the noise. I never have a meeting in a public place. Can't have a decent conversation." He picked up a cigar from a nearby ashtray and gestured toward the armchair opposite his. "Sit. Please."

Lillian sat on the edge of the chair, arranging her skirts to cover her stockinged feet. Thankfully, she had worn her better stockings today.

"How is our leg amputation doing?" said Dr. Bauer right before he pulled on his cigar and blew a perfect ring of smoke. The stink of it made Lillian feel a little ill.

"Mrs. Sokolova shows no signs of post-surgical infection at this point. But she refused to get up today. She does not want to learn how to use crutches."

"Some are lazier than others. She'll regret not learning once she's discharged."

"Sir, I don't think that she's lazy," Lillian said cautiously. "I think she's… despondent. She doesn't see how she can support herself. You see, she washes floors at —"

"And if I say she's lazy?" Dr. Bauer's icy eyes pierced through the cloud of cigar smoke in front of him.

"Well, certainly, then, she's lazy," said Lillian, confused.

"No, no, no!" grumbled Dr. Bauer, plunking his cigar back in the ashtray for emphasis. "I thought you understood this." He looked to the ceiling, as if to find support there. "Why do you think you are here?"

Lillian was greatly relieved that they would be discussing this question. "I would very much like to know that."

"I think you have an inkling, but let me save us some time." He got up and stood with his back to the blazing fireplace, gazing down at Lillian. "Do you know what a Devil's Advocate is?"

"No, sir."

Dr. Bauer picked up his cigar and began walking around the room. "Throughout history, the Roman Catholic Church would declare that certain dead people were saints, and thus they were saints, no questions asked. But in the sixteenth century, the Church created two positions, to be filled by lawyers: God's Advocate, and the Devil's Advocate. God's Advocate argued for the canonization of the nominated fellow, and the Devil's Advocate argued against. Why do you think they would create the Devil's Advocate, to argue *against* their own nomination?"

"To be certain." This concept appealed to Lillian greatly. "To argue all sides so that when it's all said and done, you can be sure you are right."

"Yes," said Dr. Bauer, stabbing the air with his cigar. Ashes fell to the carpet, but he seemed oblivious. He walked toward Lillian, grinding the ashes into the carpet with his slipper. "The stakes in canonizing a saint must have felt very high to the church. But what are the stakes in medicine? In surgery?"

"Why, they are life and death."

"Precisely. And yet no one challenges me." He walked to the window and watched the rain running down the glass. "At Presbyterian, they're all afraid. Sycophants. Trying to impress me but never contradicting me. At your little hospital, it's worse." He took another pull on his cigar. "But you have shown more gumption than most doctors I know. Perhaps it's because you will never be a doctor. But even among the nursing staff, you are more bold."

Lillian contemplated this. She supposed she was bold. Her decision to move to Hell's Kitchen, her pursuit of nursing despite all the obstacles. She liked this view of herself. She settled a little further back in the armchair.

"So," Dr. Bauer continued as he turned from the window to face her, "your role here is to challenge. To ask questions. With the respect that my position dictates, of course, but to articulate views that are contrary. Starting with this Mrs. Sokolova. Russian, is it?"

"I presume. She cleans the floors in a theater. She is despairing because she doesn't know how she will do this without her leg."

"So she will not try crutches."

"Can we offer her a prosthetic?"

"Can she afford a prosthetic?"

Lillian did not answer. She knit her hands together in her lap. She would bet next week's salary that Mrs. Sokolova could not afford to buy the prosthetic, whatever it cost.

Dr. Bauer strode from the window and sat down in his armchair. "You have the War to Preserve the Union to thank for decent prosthetics, by the way, specifically the kind your Mrs. Sokolova would need. The very first poor bastard to get his leg blown off in the war was a Rebel who was an engineer by vocation. Hanger was his name. Wasn't happy with the leg the government gave him so he crafted his own. Jointed at the knee and ankle. Made of barrel staves to reduce the weight. Now he has his own company manufacturing Hanger Limbs." The end of his cigar glowed like a furnace as he pulled on it. It made Lillian think of the crematorium, where Mrs. Sokolova's leg was incinerated.

"So the hospital will not pay for her to have a Hanger Limb." She tried not to show her annoyance. Why was he telling her this history of the prosthetic leg when one could not be procured for the patient?

"Your little hospital cannot *afford* to provide her with a Hanger Limb." He straightened his legs out toward the fire and crossed them at the ankles. "They are having some financial difficulties. It seems your benefactor Mr. Astor the Third was very specific about his donation. He was willing to fund the erection of buildings, but not to subsidize expenses, nor was anyone to solicit him or his family for expenses, ever. This is why the construction of the Men's Pavilion next door continues and yet in the Women's Pavilion you cannot afford Hanger Limbs."

Lillian thought of the construction site next to the hospital, which occasionally prompted complaints from Posh Row about the noise. When there *was* anyone on Posh Row. "But what is the point of constructing more wards if the ones we have cannot provide enough profit to completely help the patients?"

"What an excellent question. What should the board do?" Dr. Bauer looked bemused.

"Can they appeal to Mr. Astor to change his mind?"

"Mr. Astor passed on earlier this year, so I would say no."

Lillian pursed her lips as she thought. "What is the penalty for using construction funds against the expenses of the Women's Pavilion?"

"Legally? No penalty. But this restriction on Mr. Astor's very large donations was very specific and put down in writing."

In her mind, Lillian heard Mrs. Sokolova shouting to her that first day. *What job is good for woman without leg?* "They should use some of the construction funds for expenses."

"Interesting. Continue." Dr. Bauer nodded slowly.

"If the hospital creates more wards, more beds, their inability to afford their expenses will get worse. The construction will hasten the downfall of the hospital."

"Well reasoned mathematically, with nice dramatic flair at the end. But aren't you worried about what will happen when the Astor family finds out? When an ambitious newspaper man writes the exposé?"

"The newspaper story should consider what Mrs. Sokolova's life will be like without a leg."

"So the public hears both sides. Though I doubt the redirection of the Astor funds will encourage future donations."

Lillian hadn't thought of that. She rubbed her eyes; the cigar smoke was making them sting.

"Do you want to know what the board thinks the solution is?" When Lillian nodded, Dr. Bauer said, "Increase the number of high-paying patients on that upper floor."

"The nurses say that there aren't a lot of patients on Posh Row because doctors and surgeons treat them in their homes."

"Posh Row!" he exclaimed. "Why, that's a perfect name. And the nurses are correct. The campaign to convince wealthy women that they will be better off in a hospital will be a long and challenging one, I would wager. Perhaps your solution is the better one." He rose from the chair and stood in front of hers. He delicately placed his index finger under her chin. The fire lit one side of his face, leaving the other side in darkness. "My Devil's Advocate," he murmured.

Lillian tilted her face upward.

He looked at her and said, "Mrs. Donovan will see you out." He strode back to his desk with his cigar and ashtray. Lillian considered whether to thank him or say goodbye, but as soon as he sat at his desk he seemed to forget she was there, and so she left the study and laced up her ragged boots which were still soaked from the rain.

🏵 Chapter 19 🏵

Josephine had agreed to stay an extra hour on Monday so that Lillian could go visit Michael after work. It had pained her not to visit him on the weekend when she had free time, but she couldn't bear to navigate all that with Marie, who had been in a snit for days. She had refused to go out with Josephine to get the paper, dumped Lillian's sewing kit onto the bedroom floor, turned away from Lillian when they got into bed. On Saturday morning Lillian had put a spoon in Marie's hand so she could eat her oatmeal, and Marie threw the spoon across the room, which put a crack in the window pane. It had taken Lillian a while to figure out that despite Marie's childish mind, her moods were like that of other fourteen-year-old girls. This made some sense, given that Marie's body had been early to become womanly, her chest now well-developed, her hips no longer like a boy's. But the moods that came along with that were enough to keep Lillian from planning sisterly excursions this week.

When Monday finally came and she was done at the hospital, Lillian made her way to her aunt and uncle's apartment. Fiona wanted to give Lillian supper the moment she crossed the threshold, but she insisted she only had a few minutes. She quickly proceeded to Michael's room, walking past Martin snoring in his chair with an empty growler beside him, the smell of beer funking the air of the parlor.

She was pleased to find Michael dressed and reading in an armchair, looking almost as if nothing had happened. The bruise on his face had faded to a light yellow and he seemed to be breathing easily.

"Lilypad, there isn't a face I'd rather see," he said with genuine pleasure. "Forgive me if I don't get up, but I've probably had enough activity at Abraham's today." He stuck a bookmark in his book and tossed it on the floor.

"You went back to work already?" she asked as she sat on the edge of the bed.

"For most of the day. Moving slowly. Perhaps a tad ambitious. By three o'clock Abraham took pity on me and sent me home. But I think tomorrow I'll be right as rain."

"That's wonderful," she said with relief. She hadn't realized how anxious it had made her to see Michael debilitated. It had been so long since he had outgrown the fevers and colds of childhood that she had become used to him as the fortress in her life.

"On your way in here you must have passed my reason for returning to work so quickly," he mentioned casually, gesturing to the parlor.

"Have you two been at it?"

"I've tried to avoid him. We've both been doing that, until he gets the drink in him. Then he seeks me out. Like there's something unresolved for him about how I got hurt. Like it's not adding up in his mind, and the drink tells him, *figure out this puzzle, find the missing piece.* And take your son down a peg or two while you're at it."

"He was drinking less as of late, right?" Michael had mentioned this to her a few weeks ago.

"He was, but since I was hurt he's back on the growler."

"He's worried about you."

"How touching," Michael said with a grimace. "I'd rather he not."

Lillian leaned forward and grabbed his hands in hers. "When can you move out?" Her stomach tightened as she asked this question. She knew she was the reason he was still here, and the guilt wrapped around her gut like a corset pulled too tight. But Martin would never get the satisfaction he was looking for, and Michael would just continue to suffer under this roof.

"I'm a little set back from the doctor's bill. Martin insisted I pay him back for that, since it was all my fault. But I've put some away. Soon." He smiled and squeezed her hand.

Lillian always knew when Michael was lying but chose not to react. "I will help you move in. I will measure for curtains and sew them myself, and we will cook a big meal together and we will let Marie eat with her hands and we will stuff ourselves until we can't move and then we will eat dessert anyway."

"And we will *all* eat the dessert with our hands," he added. Tears filled Lillian's eyes. Michael ignored them, as she had trained him to do growing up. He knew that if he mentioned her tears they would spill over and then she would be angry that he had caused her to lose control, and so it was their unspoken agreement that her tears were always invisible.

He tucked a strand of hair behind her ear. "It has gotten me through this tough week to know I was honest with you, finally honest."

Lillian looked down into her lap. "Josephine said you had wanted to tell me for a long time. But you felt you couldn't."

"Every difference of opinion we had growing up was really about the same thing, at the bottom of it. You always thought there was a right and a wrong to a thing and never wanted to see that there could be a middle."

"That's not true. Well, at least not every argument."

"Regardless, I had many reasons to think you wouldn't accept me as I am."

"Michael, you could murder someone and I would not love you any less. That doesn't mean I think murder is right." Lillian hesitated. "Because you were honest with me, I am trying to be honest with you. I still don't think what you do is… natural."

Michael sat back in his chair gingerly. "What a man and a woman do, that is natural, yes?"

"Why, of course. It is how we have children."

"But that is not *why* most congress occurs. They do it not because it's right or natural, but because they want to. Because it feels good. Plain and simple."

"I suppose," agreed Lillian, blushing slightly.

"It feels natural because it feels good and they are driven to do the thing that feels good." Michael looked toward the parlor and lowered his voice. "But what if something else feels good to two adults? Can you not see that that would feel natural to those two?"

"It might feel that way, but that doesn't make it —"

"Right? What is right? Let's put aside the argument that the impossibility of conception shows us that God thinks it's wrong, because you've never once agreed that the Bible offers any proof of anything. Did you know that animals of the same gender have been seen having relations in the wild?"

"That can't be true!"

"Ah, but it is. And what could be more natural than what animals do in nature?"

"If nature wanted any two beings to come together in that way, then any two could create another being."

"Nature made one method productive, but why does that mean that there is a problem the other way? Do you see? For you, if one is right, the other is wrong. But what if one is just more common, or more productive than the other? Why does there have to be judgment when both parties are willing?"

Lillian stooped down to pick up Michael's book he had thrown on the floor and walked to his small chest of drawers. She placed it atop the chest in the very middle, nudging it slightly to center it perfectly. "It's a lot to think about," she said finally. She turned around to face Michael. "But I know you and Josephine are good people, and so I can say that whatever else I think, this… preference does not change that you are good people."

"Well," said Michael as he rose, wincing along the way, "I will take that, certainly. But I would urge you to think about whether every situation you encounter has only one right answer. Especially if that answer is one no one ever questions."

Lillian crossed her arms. "So you want me to be some sort of firebrand?"

"In all things that will change for the better, someone has to go first." He walked with her slowly to the door of his room. "And I can think of no better firebrand."

Michael insisted on hailing her cab despite needing to take the stairs very slowly, but once they made it to the front foyer of the building, he stopped her as she reached for the door. "I can't say this where my parents could hear, because I shouldn't know in the first place. They thought I was asleep the other night and their conversation got a little louder than they realized."

"Sounds familiar." When they were children, Michael had a knack for overhearing just what the adults did not want him to hear, and was always thrilled to share his newfound knowledge with Lillian. "Remember when you heard Fiona talking about her cousin who had the baby seven months after she married that —"

"Lilypad, it's about your mother. But it's good news."

Lillian took a step back in the tiny foyer as if to distance herself from any news, good or otherwise.

"Do you want to hear it?"

"Yes. No." Lillian bit her lip as she thought on it. "Yes."

Michael waited a heartbeat to see if she would change her mind again, and then proceeded. "She's come into a bit of money. Not a lot, but enough to clear her debts and stay above water, if she manages it correctly. Or so Martin believed during a sober moment."

"How?" said Lillian suspiciously.

"A friend of your father, repaying his debt."

"Well, that could be one of many. And I'd say he's a bit late, considering my father has been dead for years." Her father was well known as a soft touch for lending money, which led to frequent arguments between her parents.

"According to the word on the street, this friend spent some time in prison, stopped drinking, saw the light and God and all that. Got back on the straight and narrow, is trying to make amends."

"When did this happen?"

"I think recently. Fiona heard it from Mrs. Sweeney who heard it from who knows who. But that kind of news tends to travel fast. Of course it's all hushed, because our family is not supposed to be interested in Helen anymore."

Lillian frowned. Mrs. Sweeney had known Helen through Aunt Fiona, of course, but they weren't all that friendly. But above all, Mrs. Sweeney was an unrepentant gossip, so it made perfect sense that she would pass this tidbit along to anyone who was interested. "You know this doesn't change anything," she said.

"Of course not," Michael said kindly. "But I wasn't going to keep that from you."

She reached for his hand and squeezed it.

🎇 Chapter 20 🎇

As the week progressed, the drag of showing Nurse Farrell the ropes started to ease. Janey was sharing the burden more, and Nurse Farrell seemed quite content to roll bandages and organize supplies. Lillian noticed that physical contact with patients still seemed to make Nurse Farrell nervous, which didn't bode well for her longevity at the hospital. Lillian recalled Dr. Bauer's assessment of her as bold and felt a tingle of pride as she changed a pus-soaked dressing with dexterity and handed the bandage to Nurse Farrell, who placed it in the metal basin and then quietly stepped back, looking very pale.

At the end of her shift on Wednesday, Lillian picked her way carefully around the muddy ruts of 8th Avenue until she reached the 103rd Street El station. After a bit, a train arrived only half full, a rare bit of good fortune for her trip home. Just as the doors were about to close, a black man scooted in, one that Lillian happily recognized as Jupiter.

"Were you following me?" she asked in a mock serious voice.

"This one bothering you, miss?" A burly workman powdered with stone dust approached, lurching to one side as the train jolted forward.

"Oh, certainly not! He is a…. A work colleague." Lillian looked over at Jupiter whose gaze was directed down in the vicinity of the stonemason's knees. He said nothing. Lillian had never seen him look meek before.

"Work colleague? What kind of work could ya be doing that *he'd* be doin' too?" He laughed along with two men behind him that were similarly dusty.

"We work at a hospital," which Lillian hoped would put an end to this back and forth, but this information only seemed to engage the man more.

"Hospital! Wouldn't catch me near one of them death factories." He looked to his friends for confirmation which they readily gave.

"Actually, suh," said Jupiter just loud enough to be heard above the clatter of the wheels on the track but with his gaze still averted, "it's just an influenza clinic. They let us colored folk help out with the highly contagious."

After a heartbeat where no one said anything, Lillian added, "It's God's work."

Without another word, the workmen turned and quickly elbowed their way to the other end of the train.

Lillian and Jupiter moved in the opposite direction and found a place to stand where they could hold on to a bar to steady themselves. "You seem like you've used that line before," Lillian said, amused.

"I've had the need. Now that the weather's turnin', I take my chances on the El, hopin' nobody gonna bother the likes of me. Warmer weather, I walk."

"Fifty blocks."

"Fifty peaceful blocks." Jupiter smiled.

At the 72nd Street stop, two men stumbled into the car, laughing and bumping into other passengers. As the doors closed, they began singing "My Wild Irish Rose" but neither could remember the words after "the sweetest flower that grows", which caused them to break out into laughter again. When the hilarity died down, they looked around.

Jupiter turned away from the men and looked out the window. "I seen that look before," he said to Lillian quietly. "They lookin' for a victim."

"They're just drunk," said Lillian. "They probably can't see much of anything."

"You watch," whispered Jupiter.

Jupiter continued to look out the window, but Lillian moved a little to one side so she could see the scene through the other passengers. One of the men appeared to be scanning the crowd, squinting through bleary eyes. "Tommy," he said to his partner, "Lookit what we got over here."

He and Tommy staggered past a few people and stopped in front of a willowy boy who couldn't have been more than eighteen. He wore a wide brimmed cap which Tommy tilted back on the boy's head. "Looks like you ain't as white as you're tryin' to make these nice people think you are."

Lillian could see that the boy's skin was of a color that could have been that of a swarthy Italian, but his features were as African as Jupiter's. He looked frozen in place, his mouth slightly ajar.

"You one of them quadroons? Now, was it your momma that was the darkie or your papa?" said Tommy's partner. Tommy chuckled and moved a little closer.

The train slowed and pulled into 66th Street station. "This is where I'm gettin' out," said Jupiter.

"But this isn't our stop—we have one more to go."

"I ain't gonna wait 'til them two make their way down our end of the train. Good night, Miz Do—, I mean, Lillian," he said quietly.

"Wait, I'm coming with you." She pushed past some men in suits and joined Jupiter on the platform. As the train pulled out of the station, Jupiter looked through the train windows. Lillian followed his gaze and they could both see Tommy and the other man continuing to harass the boy. Jupiter shook his head. "That boy ain't figured out yet when he ought to cut bait."

They started down the stairs. "Maybe we should have helped him. Told him to get off."

"Would have made it worse. One skinny boy was threatenin' enough for them. Two black boys? Why, that's an uprisin' right there. That's sure to come to blows."

Lillian thought about what happened when they first got on the train. "Would the stonemasons have bothered you if I were not with you?"

"Hard to say," said Jupiter, but Lillian sensed his evasion.

"So just walking down the street with me now—does that put you in danger?" Lillian now noticed that Jupiter had pulled his cap down a little lower than when she had first seen him tonight.

"We keep walkin', long as I don't touch you, nobody gonna care."

As Lillian looked around, it seemed that what Jupiter was saying held true. An ocean of humanity flowed in both directions and everyone seemed to be in a hurry. The wind had picked up and people were ducking their heads against it, so all Lillian could see down the block were hats, bobbing like corks in the sea. Derbys, Hombergs and flat caps of drab colors mixed with women's bonnets and hats and the occasional fascinator. An ostrich feather bobbed above the fray. The tassel of a fez swung back and forth. No eyes were visible; all were hunched against the weather and focused on the three feet of sidewalk in front of them.

They walked on for several blocks while Lillian tried to reconcile the aggression of the men on the El with the apparent indifference of these pedestrians. Jupiter was evidently contemplating the same. "That don't normally happen, on the train. Winter time, I ride the El almost every day. Most weeks nothin' happens at all—it's as boring as a long sermon. Mostly this a good city for us, I think because it got so much color."

"Because there are so many Negros?" Lillian asked.

"I think it's because it got so many of all different colors. Think about it—if the only two colors here were black and white, well, that's just an us-against-them. That's a threat. That's Alabama. But you got all different types here, from every country, they speakin' languages and cookin' food and singin' songs that ain't familiar to no white man. Who his enemy? Hard to choose." Jupiter grinned.

"The men on the train didn't seem to have a problem choosing."

"Maybe they just had nothin' better to do while they waited for their stop. On the street, everybody rushin' off somewhere."

The crowd thinned as they neared Hell's Kitchen. Lillian could see her building down the block on the other side of the street. "The masons on the train. They weren't drunk. They didn't like me talking to you. I caused that."

"You didn't mean it."

"No, but in the future, if we find ourselves on the same train, perhaps we shouldn't speak?"

Jupiter's brow furrowed into the slightest frown, but he said, "All right."

"But we could get out at 66th Street and walk as we did today."

"Yes, we could at that." Jupiter's brow relaxed, and they arrived at her building. She gave Jupiter a little wave and ascended the stairs.

All the chatter at the hospital the next day was about Mrs. Banerjee, a woman who had been on the ward awaiting surgery. The day her surgery was scheduled, her condition took a downturn and her operation was canceled. It was assumed she would never make it to the operating theater and would instead live out her weeks on the ward. But weeks were only days for Mrs. Banerjee as she plummeted through her final descent more quickly than anyone anticipated.

She must have died early in the morning, because when Lillian first came into work she overheard Dr. Bauer grilling the junior doctors on possible reasons for Mrs. Banerjee's accelerated demise. The only thing Lillian remembered from the chart was that there was uncertainty about what type of cancer she had. A mass had been identified when palpating her abdomen, but only uterine cancer had been ruled out due to lack of bleeding. Nothing the junior doctors suggested—multiple cancers, a co-morbid condition yet undetected, a hidden infection—intrigued Dr. Bauer in the least. Later on, as Lillian brought breakfast trays back to the kitchen, she overheard from some nurses that Dr. Bauer had finally brought Mrs. Banerjee to the operating room, this time not to save her but to satisfy his own curiosity.

All of which was not particularly noteworthy—in Lillian's months at the hospital, she had heard of at least one other time where a deceased patient was sliced open for educational purposes, not to mention Mrs. Feinman's stomach cancer surgery which had not been intended to save her. But the reason Mrs. Banerjee became the subject of hospital chatter was that she was not a charity case with no next of kin, and evidently her next of kin had some religious objections to her post-mortem. Some very strong objections.

Late in the afternoon, Janey was telling two other nurses what she had heard as Lillian approached with a tray of empty whiskey cups. "He was demanding to see the doctor that operated. Nurse Holt was calm as water on a pond but this Banerjee fellow kept getting louder and louder. Religious objections, but you won't believe the specifics. These people actually believe that a soul comes back in another body, and that disturbing the body after death can interfere with the process!"

"Now you're pulling my leg, Janey." The nurse to Janey's right crossed her arms.

"Cross my heart. I heard it with my own two ears."

"So what did Nurse Holt do?"

"I suppose she tried not to laugh and waited him out. What could he do, after all? It's not like his wife was on Posh Row. Even if his reasons were not ridiculous, what power did he have to get Holt to summon Dr. Bauer?"

As she worked the remainder of her shift, Lillian thought about the Banerjees. She had never heard of a religion that believed in people's souls living on in another body. This seemed like the sort of thing that young children would believe, like St. Nicholas bringing Christmas presents. On the other hand, was this belief much more fantastic than meeting St. Peter at the pearly gates? Since Lillian didn't believe in that either, she supposed that the Banerjee's faith wasn't as crazy as Janey thought. Or maybe all religions were crazy.

As Lillian contemplated this, her hands rolling bandages without instruction from her brain, she thought about what she believed happened after death. It struck her as odd now that she had not thought about this once since she started at the hospital. After all, she was surrounded by death and dying every day. She remembered one summer day when she and Michael were young, it was so hot that Michael had stolen an egg from Fiona's kitchen (for which Martin later took a belt to him) so they could see if it would fry on the sidewalk. When the experiment ended with mixed results, their conversation turned to whether Hell would be hotter than the current weather. At the time they both agreed that people who did bad things would have a very unpleasant time after their death, with high temperatures and bad smells, and that good people would never be hungry and would have clement weather that would neither make them sweat nor force them to wear scratchy woolens. They spent much of the afternoon detailing the good aspects of Heaven and the bad aspects of Hell (she recalled that Hell had a no-desserts policy), and they spent no time at all, Lillian now realized, categorizing what would make a person good or bad.

With a jolt she looked up at the clock and realized that her shift ended fifteen minutes ago, and now she would have to rush to make it to Dr. Bauer's.

Though the hospital had many windows, Lillian had been so absorbed in work that she hadn't looked outside all afternoon, and she was dismayed to find even worse weather than her last trip to Dr. Bauer's. Not only was it raining, but the wind had picked up and the temperature had dropped since the morning. By the time she rang his bell, Lillian was shivering.

When she removed her dilapidated shoes outside of the study, she realized one reason why she was so cold. She must have stepped in a puddle or two in her haste to get here on time; she could see that both her cotton stockings were soaking wet up nearly to her ankles. She knew she needed new shoes, but a recent review of her finances showed that most weeks she was spending more than she earned. The little nest egg that Michael had given her was dwindling quickly, with much of her salary going to Josephine. And yet she knew Josephine was underpaid. But even if she could get more hours at the hospital, she would need more hours from Josephine. The circularity of her problem was maddening.

And then she thought about the embarrassment she was about to feel going in to see Dr. Bauer. She had not remembered to wear her best stockings, and the ones she pulled out of the drawer while she was rushing this morning had a hole in one foot and a big smudge of dirt on the top of the other. She pulled the stocking with the hole over the top of her foot and scrunched her big toe to hold it. Still shivering, she knocked and entered the study.

Dr. Bauer looked warm and cozy in his chair by the fire, a book in his lap. "Assistant Nurse Dolan, good to see you on such a stormy night!" He smiled. Like a cat with a saucer of cream, Lillian thought. It was unnerving to see him in such an affable mood.

She moved to the chair opposite him by the fire and let the blazing warmth wash over her. Dr. Bauer commenced some weather-related chit chat on which Lillian could barely focus. Between the exquisite heat of the fire and the peculiarity of Dr. Bauer's mood, it was all she could do to respond with nods and yeses at the appropriate junctures.

Finally, a pause in Dr. Bauer's stream of words allowed her to ask, "Can we speak of Mrs. Banerjee?"

"Of course, and I know precisely what you want to know."

"So were you aware —"

"It was pancreatic!" he exclaimed and snapped the book on his lap shut. The sound caused Lillian to jump in her seat. "The mass that I felt in her abdomen was a red herring, a benign—"

"Dr. Bauer, I was meaning to talk to you about her religion."

He frowned. "Religion?"

She realized that he likely didn't even know about Mr. Banerjee's visit to the hospital. She had heard Dr. Bauer was needed at Presbyterian in the afternoon and had left right after his surgical exploration. "Mrs. Banerjee's religion includes the idea that people come back to life as other people, and that your surgery disrupted that process."

"Hindus! Of course. But the idea of reincarnation is not limited to people. Mrs. Banerjee might come back as a giraffe on the plains of Africa. Or a tree frog in the Amazonian jungle." He looked amused, on the brink of coming up with more examples to entertain.

Lillian could not help but feel this was insulting to Mrs. Banerjee. "Regardless of how you feel about this reincarnation, it was her faith, and according to her husband who had a heated discussion with Nurse Holt today, she felt very strongly about it." She wasn't sure why she was defending this religion that believed in such a fairy tale, but she certainly didn't like Dr. Bauer ridiculing it. "And cutting her open was an affront to it."

"Well, even if I had been informed that she was of the Hindu persuasion, I was not aware that Hinduism precluded post-mortem surgical activity."

"But now we know."

"We?" Dr. Bauer raised an eyebrow.

"The hospital." She would not back down. "We should consider that belief in the future."

He got up and retrieved a cigar from his desk. As he lit it, Lillian could sense his good mood ebbing. "First of all, putting some policy in place for Hindus when we may not see another all year is preposterous. Secondly, are we to cater to every crackpot religion that walks through our doors? And must I learn of all the ins and outs of these religions? Should that have been part of my education at Columbia?" He walked back to his chair with his cigar leading the charge. "And thirdly, Mrs. Banerjee was on the ward. These charity cases are lucky that they can receive our excellent care."

"Mrs. Banerjee was a paying patient on the ward, not a charity case." Lillian remembered that from her chart.

"But unless she was Posh Row, as you call it, the hospital loses money even on the paying ward patients. So they are effectively charity cases."

Lillian let this sink in. "If you had known of her religious objections to the surgery, would you have performed it anyway?"

"Our mission is to cure cancer, both for our current and future patients. We could not cure Mrs. Banerjee, but she may have helped to cure a future patient. So, yes."

"What if she had been on Posh Row?"

Dr. Bauer laughed. "A Maharaja's wife, perhaps? I should live to see that day. But I will indulge you. I would likely not slice into the deceased wife of the Maharaja, or anyone on Posh Row. They have too many lawyers." He puffed on his cigar and regarded Lillian. "Oh, come now, don't pretend to be shocked. Come off your high horse. You are too intelligent to be blind to the way the world works. Within these walls," and here he held his hands up toward the high ceiling of the study, "we can be honest. No one will ever slice into me post-mortem, but you do not enjoy that protection. It's simply a matter of money."

Lillian found this so chilling that it chilled her physically, and she shivered despite the fire, which had not dried her out completely.

"Still feeling the effects of the storm?" said Dr. Bauer.

"It's mostly my feet, they're like blocks of ice."

"I have just the thing," he replied, his mood quickly restored. From the corner he brought out a footstool with an elaborate needlepoint cushion and placed it near the fire.

"Oh," said Lillian. Her feet had not dried because they were tucked underneath her skirts, hidden from the fire. How tempting it would be to prop her feet up on this stool. Why had she not worn other stockings? "I'm afraid my stockings are in poor repair. And as wet as if it were washday."

"Why, you must take them off and dry them. You can't take a risk with your health."

Lillian looked at Dr. Bauer's alert countenance and was confused. There was something too eager about his attitude. And until now, he had never shown any concern for her health or comfort, not even offering so much as a cup of tea. Curiosity dissolved her embarrassment, and she bent down to remove her stockings, keeping her legs hidden beneath her skirts. As she placed the stockings on the footstool, hole and smudge on full display, she looked back at Dr. Bauer, who was giving her stockings and hem his full attention. And while Lillian did not fully understand, she understood enough to know that Dr. Bauer was interested in more than just her intellectual sparring.

🌺 Chapter 21 🌺

All the way home, Lillian turned the evening over in her head. After she had set her stockings to dry, Dr. Bauer had talked of other things—the goldmine of information inside Mrs. Banerjee, the superior surgical instruments at the Presbyterian—but with an air of distraction. Lillian was glad when the evening concluded. As she picked up her dry stockings, she thought she saw an expectant look on Dr. Bauer's face, but what he could have been expecting at that moment she couldn't fathom. She donned her stockings outside the study and winced when she slipped her warm feet into her still-damp shoes.

With any conundrum she had ever faced, it was Michael she went to, but she knew his dubious view of these meetings would solidify into an insistence that she stop them. As she turned the knob of her apartment door, she heard laughter and thought: *Josephine! She will certainly know.*

Marie sat in the middle of the floor, and above her Josephine unfurled a bed sheet. As the sheet floated down, Marie bounced up and down with anticipation of when the sheet would gently make contact and drift down to cloak her body. As it touched her head, Marie erupted in peals of laughter, grabbing the sheet and rolling around on the floor, wrapping herself like a paper twist of rock candy.

"She loves this, sure enough," said Josephine, plunking herself down on a kitchen chair, copper curls bouncing. "Ya ever done it with her?"

"Never thought of it," said Lillian. Just when she had thought she had used every object in these two rooms to keep Marie occupied, Josephine seemed to come up with something new. "Listen, Josephine, I have a question for you, if you have a minute." They both looked down at Marie giggling and rolling around on the kitchen floor. "Let's try the other room," she suggested.

Josephine leaned against the windowsill in the bedroom and Lillian sat down on the edge of the bed. "I had a strange experience tonight. I... I'm hoping that Michael doesn't end up knowing about this."

"Since I don't know what it is, I can't rightly promise. He's a good friend and I ain't gonna do him wrong. But I'll try."

Lillian supposed that was fair. "Well, you know I meet with the doctor from the hospital on Thursdays, for discussions of medical issues and that sort of thing." She straightened her spine a bit. "It's quite educational, and he really has come to trust me with all sorts of information."

"Uh-huh," said Josephine, crossing her arms and looking thoroughly unimpressed.

Lillian blushed at what she now realized was her own puffery, but pushed on. "So my shoes were soaked through to my feet and he suggested I take off my stockings to dry them by the fire." She paused, unsure how to continue.

"And that was strange because that was nice and he's usually pretty much an arsehole?"

"No. Well, yes. But it was the way he...." She stood up and waved her hand in front of her face as if to shoo away flies. "Never mind, he did nothing and I am a fool. I must have—"

"Siddown," Josephine gently commanded from her windowsill. "Say what you were gonna say, even if it's crazy. Let's have a good laugh at you being a silly goose, if that makes it easier for ya."

"All right," she said as she sat back down on the bed, glad in a way to be forced to get this out. "I thought there was something strange about how he focused on my stockings. He seemed excited. Stimulated by my pair that has a hole and a soot mark. How ridiculous is that!" She forced a little laugh.

"I ain't laughin'," said Josephine. She came over to the bed. "Show me your feet." Lillian lifted her skirts to her ankles. "Mmm-hmm.

Tiny little ones ya got there."

"Marie's were bigger than mine since she was ten years old." Lillian remembered how her mother was dismayed to realize one day that Lillian could no longer pass down her outgrown shoes to her sister. "You don't think I'm imagining things?"

"Well, I wasn't there so I can't say what kinda man your Dr. Bauer is. But I will say a few things. First of all, there are men who think feet are better than tits."

"Surely not!" Lillian's voice came out in a whisper.

"Then you can tell that to the two clients I had like that. One of them washed my feet with that Yardley soap, all the way from London, England. My feet ain't never smelled so good, before or after."

Lillian tried to imagine a man kneeling before Josephine in some seedy Bowery room with a basin of soapy water. "You're not putting me on?"

"No I ain't, and I think you know it, because you knew what you saw in your doctor. I ain't yet met a woman who misread interest pourin' off a man. So the other thing I can tell you is that these types are usually pretty harmless. One of my fellas, he didn't need me to raise my skirts past my knees at all."

Lillian tried very hard not to visualize what Josephine was implying. "But that's down on the Bowery. This doctor is an educated man, respectable—"

"I'm gonna stop ya right there," said Josephine, irritation creeping into her voice. She pointed her index finger at Lillian. "You want to think there are different kinds of people. Respectable people, different from the people who spend their coin down on the Bowery. But that ain't how it works. We got all sorts down there. The foot man who *did* need me to raise my skirts past my knee? A judge. The one that beat the tar outta me? Some bigwig in shipping. I know, because the ones with *respectable* jobs, they always gotta tell ya what they do for a living, so you'll be impressed with them." Lillian saw the color had risen in Josephine's cheeks.

"I'm sorry, Josephine, I didn't know." She felt terrible, in part because she realized that she had also probably insulted Josephine, lumping her in with the nonrespectable. "Please forgive me."

"Yeah, all right," she said, somewhat mollified. "I just want you to know that a man's pedigree don't tell you much of anything about him."

Lillian took a deep breath. "All right, let's say I believe you that this... interest exists, and let's even say that this is what I saw tonight. What do I do?"

"You mean, how do you tell him you want to stop meeting with him?"

"Well..." Lillian looked down and ran her fingers over the seams between the quilt's cotton squares.

Half of Josephine's mouth turned up in a wry smile. "You're still gonna meet with him."

Lillian looked up. "How do I... manage him?"

"Manage him?" Josephine's ginger eyebrows rose.

"I am learning so much from him," Lillian insisted.

"But let's be honest," said Josephine, and she came over to sit next to Lillian. "You like that he talks to you about this stuff. On his level. It makes you feel smart."

"So what is wrong with that?"

"It's that he knows it."

"I just want things to go back to how they were before tonight."

"But they won't. He got a little something he wanted tonight, and now he's gonna want a little something more. He ain't yet satisfied."

"You said these men are harmless. If it's just about looking..." Lillian trailed off.

Josephine leaned back to better regard Lillian. "How were ya plannin' on finishin' that sentence? Are you sayin' yer gonna play his game? Give him what he wants?"

"Certainly not!" She wasn't thinking that. Was she?

"Good, because that would mean you're in the same business I used to be in."

Lillian let that sink in.

"Lillian, I gotta say these meetings got a stink about 'em."

"I can handle this. He can help me become a nurse."

"You don't even know what you're gonna have to pay to get that help. You pride yourself on bein' so smart—the smart move here is to wiggle out of these meetings. If you're good at this nursing thing, at some point you can go the route that the other nurses took. You just gotta be patient."

Marie trotted into the bedroom with the sheet and pressed it into Josephine's hands insistently. Josephine gave Lillian a meaningful glance and led Marie into the kitchen for one last game of Floating Sheet.

Lillian thought to herself: *But I'm tired of being patient.*

The next day, Lillian wondered if she would be flustered when she saw Dr. Bauer, but he did not come to the hospital. Lillian checked the schedule and saw that there were no surgeries scheduled for to-day, which seemed to explain his absence, especially when she over-heard some nurses reflecting that Dr. Metcalfe felt it was important to check on his own post-surgical patients while Dr. Bauer delegated this to the junior doctors.

When Lillian arrived home, it was Michael who greeted her at the door instead of Josephine. For a moment Lillian was worried that Michael had lost his job, but then she remembered it was Friday and Abraham closed his shop before sundown, which was quite early this time of year. As she hugged Michael, she looked over his shoulder and saw Marie sewing a new crimson button onto her button napkin.

"So you came to relieve the long-laboring Josephine?" Lillian asked as she unpinned her hat.

"Only for her last hour. I'm sure she was glad to get home to Madeline early."

"Oh, is that her sister?" They never talked about Josephine's home life.

"No, Lilypad, that's not her sister." Michael smiled at her.

"Oh, of course," Lillian said, flustered. "She hadn't mentioned Madeline."

Michael chatted with her about his day at the shop, how he felt almost 100% better, about a short-lived fight between Fiona and Martin over some financial matter—Lillian was only half listen-ing. She couldn't remember the last time she had kept something of significance from Michael, but her strange meeting with Dr. Bauer seemed too incendiary to broach. Still, her mind couldn't put it aside, especially after Josephine's contributions to Lillian's base of knowl-edge. The detail about Yardley soap kept returning to her mind like a mosquito undeterred by any amount of swatting.

Lillian forced herself back to the present and clasped Michael's hands over the kitchen table. "Are you really feeling back to normal?"

"Fit as a fiddle. Can't keep a good man down, they say." He grinned and squeezed her hands.

"Tell me this is not going to happen again. Please."

"It's interesting you brought that up, Lilypad." He looked out the cracked kitchen window. "I'm thinking about making some changes. Laboring to draw a breath for a few days as you lie in bed gives you a lot of time to think. Especially about how you may have brought all that pain upon yourself. I'm still working it out, but I'm trying to think of other people in my life. That maybe I shouldn't be acting so selfishly, and that maybe I should be thinking of the future."

Lillian wrinkled her brow. "I can't figure what you mean."

Michael chuckled. "Half-baked nonsense, right now. I'll let you know when I have it all straightened away. But I am trying to steer to the right course."

"I'm glad. And you know you can talk to me about it. When you're ready. We can work it out together if you want."

"Of course. With you I can be an open book."

Lillian thought of the openness of her book, but then decided not to think of it.

On Monday, Lillian braced herself for a conversation with Mrs. Sokolova that she had heard other nurses attempt in the past two weeks. Mrs. Sokolova had been steadfast in her refusal to get out of bed, and her wound was healing at a rate that would have her discharged in a week or two. She had a variety of proclamations: that she would attempt mobility when they attached a new leg, that she would concede to an attempt if they brought her a prosthesis, that she would never rise and end up dying in this very bed. The ward nurses had lost patience with her but as her discharge date drew closer, the problem did not go away. Lillian would try to make progress where the other nurses had failed.

"*Zdra..vstvuj..tye,*" Lillian said, slowly picking her way through the syllables as she stood in front of Mrs. Sokolova's bed with her whiskey tray. Mrs. Sokolova had been teaching her a few words of Russian during her dressing changes. It was hard for Lillian to believe that saying hello was so complicated, but Mrs. Sokolova assured her that everything Russian was complicated, and Lillian was inclined to believe her.

"Not bad, *Devushka*." She downed her cup and gave it back to Lillian. "You remember word for 'another'?"

Lillian thought for a moment, wishing she could remember. "*Dru...* dru-something?"

"Ach. Waste of time with you. You should go back to pen with other cows. They give you nice hay."

"Dru...." Lillian looked to the ceiling, drawing Mrs. Sokolova out.

"*Drugoy*." She pursed her lips, but Lillian knew she was pleased that someone cared to learn even a few words of her language. Certainly none of the other nurses had tried.

"So you would like... *drugoy*?" She tilted the cup.

Mrs. Sokolova swiveled her eyes to meet Lillian's. "You told me this is impossible."

"I told you it was against the rules." She took a step closer to the bed and lowered her voice. "I have something you want, and I want something from you."

"Ah, *Devushka*, you are more Russian than I thought." Mrs. Sokolova's eyes twinkled at the prospect of making a deal. "Maybe we come to agreement."

"First of all, I need to tell you that I spoke with your surgeon and the hospital is not going to provide you a prosthetic leg." Lillian had thought about this last night as she was planning this conversation. The idea of the false leg had not been motivating to Mrs. Sokolova weeks ago, but more importantly, Lillian suspected that Mrs. Sokolova would respect Lillian's honesty, even in delivering bad news. Maybe especially in delivering bad news.

Mrs. Sokolova nodded but didn't comment. Lillian took this as a sign that she had made the right call, and she pressed on. "But your discharge date is only a few weeks away, and you need to practice with crutches. And beyond that, as much as we rotate you, I know the night nurse told you that you have developed a bedsore on your backside, and this is because you have spent so much time in bed. Another place that is common for bedsores is the heel, and if you develop one on your one remaining heel, this will make walking very painful." Lillian took a breath.

"I don't hear deal," Mrs. Sokolova said evenly.

"Well, here it is. I double your whiskey, you walk. You walk once today, twice tomorrow, and so on until you have the skill. The full circle around the ward. No turning back."

Mrs. Sokolova rubbed her chin as she thought. "I do stairs with crutches, you give me triple."

"All right." Lillian did not know how she would arrange that, but at least she had figured out that Mrs. Angelo was unlikely to take her whiskey as she was slipping in and out of consciousness these days, so that cup could be diverted. Lillian took a full cup from the tray. "Ready to try?"

Mrs. Sokolova smiled and took the cup.

"Zazdarovje," said Lillian.

❧ Chapter 22 ❧

The whiskey-for-crutches deal was even more successful than Lillian had hoped.

At first, she was surprised at how an extra cup of whiskey was so motivating to Mrs. Sokolova, but in the days that followed, Lillian began to believe that the mere fact that they had made a secret pact was somehow energizing in and of itself. Although the other nurses made it clear in prior weeks that they wanted to provide this instruction, Mrs. Sokolova had crafted a new narrative. "Stupid cows didn't think I could do this," she proclaimed, panting, as she struggled around the ward. "Maybe they think, too fat. Lazy. Want me to stay, keep paying."

Lillian let her think whatever kept her going. "If you tighten your grip, it will hurt less under your arms." Mrs. Sokolova grunted but Lillian saw her hands squeeze the crutch crosspieces.

Lillian had braced herself for the blowback from the other nurses, but to her surprise, they seemed pleased at Lillian's success. "You'll get that old bag out of our hair yet," said Nurse Matheson with a little smile when Lillian passed by the central ward desk. "What's your secret?" asked Janey over lunch. Lillian shrugged modestly. "I learned a few Russian words. Maybe that was it."

"Well, at least she stopped plaguing us for more whiskey. Nurse

Holt caught wind of that and now she's started marking the bottles to monitor the levels. We must really be bleeding money."

Perspiration bloomed under Lillian's arms. Could the small extra amount she'd been giving Mrs. Sokolova be detected? Did they track if patients like Mrs. Angelo took her cup?

As soon as she had a free moment that afternoon, she stole into the medicine closet with a few ounces of water in a pitcher. As she held the pitcher up to the open bottle of whiskey, she paused to consider how all the other patients would have watered-down pain relief when they downed their cups. But then she thought of Nurse Matheson's approving smile, and she started pouring.

On Wednesday as she made her mid-day circuit with Mrs. Sokolova on her crutches, Lillian gazed out the tall windows of the ward. For weeks the weather had been dutifully following the calendar with its wet October winds and gunmetal November skies, but today the temperature dished up a day reminiscent of September. Lillian could see patches of sky the color of forget-me-nots as they passed by each window. She yearned to be outside, even just to be leaning against the warmed bricks of the building with the sunshine baking her closed eyelids.

She was brought out of her daydreaming by the abrupt halt of Mrs. Sokolova's progress. "Hey *Devushka*. Maybe you look at your patient instead of looking out window. There is some handsome boy out there in park?"

"I'm sorry," Lillian said, embarrassed to be caught out. "We don't get many days with this kind of weather in November. It's hard not to want to be outside."

"We go outside then." She moved forward on her crutches.

"I can't leave, and you can't be unsupervised," said Lillian.

Mrs. Sokolova grunted and continued on until they reached the door that lead out of the ward. "At least I need to get out of this crazy circle room. I need break from noise." Just that morning, one of the patients had taken a turn for the worse and started a soft but continuous moaning punctuated by pleas for water.

Lillian and Mrs. Sokolova made it to the common room where

Lillian improvised instructions on how to descend into an armchair and position the crutches where they could be easily retrieved. Sweat dampened Mrs. Sokolova's plump face, the extra walking distance clearly having taken a toll. The room had windows facing the front of the building, and from their chairs they could see two women being helped into a curbside carriage by nurses. "What about them?" asked Mrs. Sokolova, jerking her chin toward the window. "They get outside."

"They are from… upstairs." Lillian had been calling it Posh Row for so long she forgot what she was supposed to call it. But somehow Mrs. Sokolova needed no further explanation.

"Ah, high rent district. How much they pay up there?"

Lillian wasn't sure this was public information, but Mrs. Sokolova always seemed to sense when she was lying. "Twenty dollars a week."

"Twenty! *Pfffff.* You get carriage ride for twenty?"

Lillian nodded. "And champagne," she added.

"Champagne! And nobody moaning in ward. I like this high rent place. I give you twenty, you move me up there for a week, eh?"

"I don't think it works like that," said Lillian.

Mrs. Sokolova patted Lillian's knee. "Of course it doesn't." Her eyes followed the carriage as it pulled away from the curb. "How long I'm going to be listening to moaning?"

Lillian thought about what she knew about the moaner. Mrs. Hayes had been on the ward before Lillian had started at the hospital. She had had a radical double mastectomy and seemed to be recovering well if slowly. Until a week or two ago, she would take her meals in the dining room and use the toilet without assistance, but then she weakened and began spending more and more time in bed. Lillian had not heard any predictions from the nurses about the timing of Mrs. Hayes' demise, but even Lillian could tell that she would not improve. "At some point they will probably give her morphine. That will help her sleep."

"So, no hope for her."

"I'm afraid not. The cancer must have been spreading before her surgery."

"That gonna happen to me?"

Lillian covered her eyes with her hands. "I'm sorry. That was insensitive—"

Mrs. Sokolova pulled Lillian's hands away from her face. "Relax, *Devushka*. Maybe you need to work on sugar coat for other patients, but I like no sugar." She leaned back in her armchair and gazed out at Central Park. Lillian thought she looked worn out.

"I'm not a doctor or a nurse," said Lillian, "but I think you will be fine. The doctor was very aggressive in your surgery. Your recovery has been one of the quickest I've seen."

"Tough old Russian birds are hard to kill," she said. "But I don't want moaning."

"I'm not sure I can do anything about Mrs. Hayes."

"No, you don't understand." Mrs. Sokolova had a faraway look, as if she were trying to see clear across the park. "I don't want to be moaner. I go home and get sick again, I'm not coming back here. I sharpen kitchen knife…" She drew an index finger across her wrist without looking down. "No moaning."

Lillian automatically opened her mouth to protest but then stopped herself. What could this hospital offer her if her cancer returned? She had heard about a few people returning to the hospital with a recurrence; none of them left alive. She wondered how many charts marked "cured" were filed in this building for people who went out into the world and died of their cancer. She gently placed her hand on Mrs. Sokolova's wrist, on top of the imaginary knife cut. "May I call you by your first name?"

Mrs. Sokolova turned her head from the window with what seemed like great effort and looked at Lillian, too tired to keep up her guard. "You use first and middle together. Oksana Ivanova."

"Oksana Ivanova, you will not have to sharpen your knife." She knew she could not really make this promise, but Mrs. Sokolova had recovered so robustly and Lillian had such a strong feeling that it would not come to a bloody scene in a third-floor walkup, she felt no remorse in saying this.

"You're pretty sure for not-a-doctor, not-a-nurse." She tilted her head slightly.

"I will tell Dr. Snelling this afternoon that your progress on crutches has been excellent and I will see if he feels you can be discharged soon." She stood and handed Mrs. Sokolova her crutches. "Tomorrow, we will conquer stairs."

At the end of her shift, Lillian took a pair of crutches from the supply room and went down to the basement. At the bottom of the
stairs, she bent a knee and began ascending with the crutches. The
first thing she realized was that the crutches she took were too tall
for her, but she didn't want to waste time going back up to the supply
closet for the right size. Each stair she took had a moment where
she was suspended in the air while her only contact with the ground
was through the stub end of the crutches, and it gave her a whiff of
vertigo each time. She reasoned that even with the right size crutches, there would be an inflection point, a moment where you could
either lean forward slightly, keeping your balance and continuing
your intended progress, or lean the wrong way and... well, that was
unpleasant to contemplate. She made a mental note to talk with Mrs.
Sokolova about her balance before they started tomorrow.

By the time she returned the crutches to the closet and changed
out of her uniform, it was ten minutes beyond her shift, but she had
told Josephine that morning that she would stop on the way home at
the grocer open late on 53rd, so she had some time. As she exited the
hospital, she remembered this beautiful day, the one she had forgotten about in her zeal to be prepared for Mrs. Sokolova's stair lesson.
It was dark now and she lamented missing the sun's heat on her back,
but a gentle breeze brought fresh air coming off the park, carrying
away the smell of horse manure that had been heating on the streets
all day, and Lillian was determined to enjoy this night.

She walked up the stairs to the El platform and as she wove
through the crowd she spied Jupiter leaning against the railing, looking her way. Her hand reflexively rose to wave but then she remembered their plan to avoid attention. She put her hand down and nodded instead, a nod that was returned by Jupiter. Lillian felt the thrill
of something clandestine.

They exited at 66th Street through different doors of the train.
"Were you waiting for me?" asked Lillian as they descended the stairs.

"If there ever was a day in November that was made for walkin',
this here is it," said Jupiter, which Lillian interpreted as a yes.

"It was positively painful to be indoors today. Every window was
taunting me. It was almost warm enough to open them, although the

patients feel the cold more so it wasn't really an option."

"Least you got windows. Down with the ovens, weather's always the same: hot and dry. And dark."

Lillian remembered that there were no windows in the crematorium. "How awful. It doesn't bother you?"

"Hard to miss something you don't know is happening." Jupiter took in a deep breath. "But this is nice, I ain't gonna deny it."

They chatted about the hospital as they walked, the clement weather adding a patina of amusement to everything they discussed. Jupiter reported on Nurse Farrell's timidity when Janey had shown her the crematorium, and Lillian recounted the drama that ensued when a set of ward sheets was accidentally put on a Posh Row bed to the horror of its sensitive occupant. As they neared 53rd Street, she slowed down without thinking.

"Seems like you draggin' your feet a touch," observed Jupiter.

Lillian sighed. "I'm supposed to go to the grocer." She stuck her lower lip out a little bit.

"And that ain't gonna be all that fun?"

She laughed. "No, it's not. It feels like I'd be wasting this evening."

Jupiter looked down and toed the curb. "If you go all the way to 10th Avenue on this street, there's a place where they don't care what color drinks with what. It's respectable—I know the owner."

Lillian was equal parts excited and nervous. "Is it safe?" She remembered what Mrs. Sweeney told her about parts west of 9th Avenue.

"If you stay with me you ain't gonna have no problem. But if you don't like the feel of the place, I'll take you straight home. Or to the grocer."

"Not the grocer!" Lillian smiled. "Lead the way, please."

As they walked, she thought of how the likes of Mrs. Sweeney would be horrified by where they were going, but that sort of opinion mattered less and less to her.

"So Sonny, he owns this black-and-tan we goin' to," said Jupiter as they paused at the corner to allow a few horse-drawn vehicles to go by. "My brother helped him out of a fix a few months back."

"You have a brother here?"

"Well, he in Brooklyn, if you count that as here." The last cart rolled by and they crossed the street. "He the pride of the family.

Real book smart. Don't rightly know how he's related to the rest of us. I stayed in school 'til I was fourteen and that was more than most in our town, but Solomon went all the way to Howard University School of Law. Now he got his own law practice over there in Brooklyn."

"How did he come to help out a barkeep in Hell's Kitchen?"

"I dunno, but ain't a lot of Negro lawyers around, so people just know people." Jupiter pointed to a doorway up ahead. "Sonny got him a white common-law wife, and he about as big as Goliath so don't nobody mess with him. Anybody start fightin', he throw them out. Solomon say he saw Sonny toss two men out on the sidewalk at the same time, grippin' one with each hand."

They stopped outside of the doorway, which was flanked by two grimy windows through which they could only see the glow of lamps. No sign gave a clue as to the name of the establishment, if there was one. Jupiter cocked his head. "You OK with this? We ain't far from your place and I don't mind—"

She yanked open the door. "After you," said Lillian.

A gargantuan man greeted Jupiter from behind the bar with a booming voice. "Jupiter Scott! How you doin', son?" Lillian looked back at Jupiter who was several inches shorter than Lillian and saw that there was more than a foot's difference in height between the two men. Sonny's chest seemed a yard across, clad in a pristine white shirt that stood out like a beacon in the dimly lit bar. Lillian marveled at how much fabric it must have taken to make that shirt, and how clean it was in this gritty place.

"Good to see you, Sonny. This here is Lillian."

"Nice to meet you, Lillian. Jupiter, how's Solomon doin'? I ain't heard from him in a while."

"He doin' fine. Lotta people know him in Brooklyn, he ain't hurtin' for work."

Sonny set up two glasses on the bar. "He find hisself a nice lady-friend? His business doin' that good, time for him to settle down."

"Not that he told me about."

"He-he-he." Sonny had a surprisingly high-pitched laugh that didn't match his baritone voice. "You want two short?"

"Sure thing."

"Y'all take any table and Loretta bring them right over. And you tell that brother of yours I said hey!"

They took a table and Lillian looked around surreptitiously. At first all Lillian spied was Negro men in ones and twos, and she began to doubt Jupiter's characterization of this place, but when her eyes adjusted to the dim gas-lamp light, she saw a white woman chatting amiably with a young black man at a table in the back.

"This OK?" asked Jupiter.

"Stop asking me that," said Lillian, and then realized it came out more harshly than she intended. "What I meant to say is, thank you for your concern, but let's agree that if I feel uncomfortable, I will bring it up right away, so you don't need to ask me." After she took off her gloves and laid them in her lap, she added, "I'm sorry, I suppose I am a little on edge actually. This sort of thing is new to me."

"You don't say. I thought you do this all the time." She looked up to see Jupiter grinning at her, and she laughed and felt the tension ease.

Loretta appeared with their beers. "How ya doin', Jupiter?" she asked as she set them down. "Your brother all right?"

"Sure is, Miz Loretta." He held out some coins and she shook her head.

"I told you a hundred times, you call me Loretta, and Sonny told me you first round is on the house."

Just then the sound of a disagreement crescendoed two tables away. "I paid you back when we was at that bar on 8th!" one man shouted. "Y'all were just too drunk to remember!" As the other man insisted at an even louder volume that this was not true, Sonny approached their table, and their protests died on their lips. Sonny silently picked up each glass to wipe the table down with a little smile on his face and then sauntered back to the bar. Once he was behind the bar, the men continued their argument in hushed tones.

"Ya see that?" said Loretta with evident pride. "He don't even have to say a word," she said before giving Jupiter's shoulder a friendly squeeze and walking back to the bar.

Lillian turned to Jupiter. "And no one bothers Sonny? About his business that allows... mixing?"

"Well, to bother Sonny you got to be at least as big as him, and there ain't a lot that is. And the police, Sonny knows who to pay. He pay a little extra, but that's the only way he stay in business."

"Does everyone pay?" Lillian thought of how many saloons were in the city. She could not remember ever walking a city block without seeing more than one.

"I don't know about much outside of Hell's Kitchen, but I bet you a silver dollar every saloon in the Kitchen is payin' graft."

Lillian picked up her beer and took a polite sip. She had never liked the taste of beer, and the smell reminded her of the worst rows she witnessed between Michael and her inebriated Uncle Martin. But this beer was icy cold, and she realized she was thirsty from the warm evening. She took a longer sip and realized that she could like beer. At least this beer right now.

She told Jupiter about her progress with Mrs. Sokolova, omitting the whiskey-for-crutches agreement, and they talked about what her life would be like after her discharge. Before Lillian knew it, Loretta was by her side asking if she wanted another short beer, and Lillian realized both their glasses were empty.

"I would love to," Lillian replied to both Loretta and Jupiter, "but I have to get home to my sister." Loretta bid them goodbye and went to another table. "Jupiter, I had wanted to ask you about what brought you to New York and now we have no more time."

"I'm happy to tell you, but truth is, I don't like talkin' about it at the hospital."

"Well, we have this place, right?"

"Yeah, I suppose we do got this place." Jupiter looked around with an expression of satisfaction. "That we do."

🦚 Chapter 23 🦚

Between her efforts with Mrs. Sokolova and her experience with Jupiter at Sonny's, Lillian had been distracted from thinking about Dr. Bauer, but by Thursday their previous meeting preoccupied her thoughts. After her talk with Josephine last week, Lillian figured she would have days and days to figure out the best way to control the situation, but she hadn't ended up thinking about it much. Now that she was to meet him in a handful of hours, her mind froze whenever she remembered the way he had looked toward the hem of her skirts, as if a treasure chest had opened and provided a glimpse of gems. No one had ever looked at Lillian that way before. Alert. Hungry. But it was not her face or even her décolletage that inspired such interest. She was mildly repulsed and thoroughly confused.

At lunchtime she walked in on a spirited conversation. Nurse Farrell was bright pink and tittering. "Oh, it's not like that," she protested with a grin as Lillian sat down at the table.

"Well, it sure sounds like it!" said Janey. "Chocolates? And he wrote you a poem? Although if it was me, I'd press for more chocolates."

"But I've only known him for seven weeks and two days," Nurse Farrell demurred.

"But who's counting?" asked Nurse Matheson. "Sounds like by springtime you'll be long gone." She took the last bite of an apple and deftly tossed the core in the corner bucket.

"And to think of all the training I've put into you," grumbled Janey, although she didn't really look angry.

"But that's how it goes, eh?" said Nurse Matheson. "Love enters the room like a lightning bolt." She gazed upward with a dreamy look. Lillian had a hard time reconciling this romantic version of Nurse Matheson with the one that gave the patients sponge baths with military vigor.

"Oh, fiddlesticks," interjected Janey. "Her whirlwind romance wasn't born fully-formed in a flash of light. Romances build over time. It takes time to get to know a man you'll spend the rest of your life with, and have to be scrubbing his drawers every week."

Nurse Farrell raised an index finger. "Well actually, the day I met—"

"If you're talking about boring romances, I suppose they need time," said Nurse Matheson said to Janey. "And it is precisely because you will be scrubbing those undergarments that you need to have a fierce love, the kind that blinds you. So you can go the distance."

Nurse Farrell tried to interject again but was overridden by Janey. "Who do you know who's got a fierce love after years of scrubbing?"

"I'll tell you who," countered Nurse Matheson. "My grandparents. My mother used to say my grandfather would bring my grandmother a nosegay every Sunday, and they held hands walking in the street."

"If you didn't see it yourself, it doesn't count." Janey was not giving in that easily.

"OK, I'll tell you who else. There's an old man that comes in here every few months, was here a few weeks ago, looking for his wife. Senile she was, and unwell to boot. One morning he woke up and she was gone. Wandered away. He makes the rounds at all the hospitals looking for her. Dresses in his best suit, says he'll never stop looking. Knew each other since they were ten years old."

There was a pause where no one spoke. Lillian thought of this man putting his suit on in the morning, looking in a dusty mirror as he put on his bowler, maybe leaving the door unlocked as he headed out in case she comes back.

"Sounds fierce," Lillian said quietly, almost to herself.

"What do you think, Lillian?" Nurse Matheson swiveled in her chair. "Love at first sight, or the kind that builds over time?"

Lillian could not decide if she were more surprised that Nurse Matheson was asking her opinion or that she used—or even knew—Lillian's first name. Quickly she considered the question. "I believe the lightning bolt variety exists," she began, and noted the expression of satisfaction on Nurse Matheson's face. "But that it's rare. And that it's not a guarantee that it will last."

"So then which is better?" pressed Janey.

Lillian had not spent any time mooning over her romantic future, but in the back of her mind she always hoped someday she would have one. "I guess whichever you are lucky enough to get."

This answer seemed to satisfy no one in the room, but before anyone could respond, Nurse Collins appeared in the doorway, looking more irritated than usual. "There's been a request for assistance in the 2pm surgery." She squeezed her lips together until they were bloodless.

Nurse Matheson stood up. "I can have Janey do the inventory while—"

"It's a specific request," said Nurse Collins, and the nurses followed her gaze until everyone was staring at Lillian.

Though it was clear that Nurse Collins did not want to answer any questions as she escorted Lillian to the operating theater, Lillian could not stop herself. "What is it that I am to do?" she probed politely. She remembered her one and only venture into the theater to retrieve Mrs. Sokolova's leg. But this seemed different—today she was not being summoned in the middle of a surgery. She now remembered that she had planned to tackle the stairs with Mrs. Sokolova this afternoon and wondered if she would have time. Well, there was always tomorrow.

Nurse Collins picked up the pace, her starchy skirts keeping time as they plowed down the center of the long hall. "I suppose you could ask Dr. Bauer," she remarked, staring straight ahead.

When they were in front of the doors to the operating theater, Nurse Collins stopped and crossed her arms, no expression on her face. Before Lillian could come up with an appropriate fare-well—"*Thank you for the escort?*", even though Lillian had known how to get here—Nurse Collins whisked away.

Staring at the richly stained wooden doors in front of her, Lillian struggled to get her anger under control. Things had been going so well. The other nurses were starting to include her, she was no longer the newest staff member, and the attentions that Dr. Bauer paid her were well away from the hospital. She had all the benefits of being Dr. Bauer's—pet? protege?—while appearing the humble assistant within these walls. Until this. He was dismantling what she had built. She clenched her fists at her side.

But when she pushed through the doors, her anger dissolved into the sea of white before her.

When she had been in this room before, she had walked in to an active surgery, and she only saw the staff hunching over Mrs. Sokolo-va. If Lillian were being honest, her gaze was mostly directed at Dr. Bauer, whom she imagined had requested her. And then the sight of all those clamps on Mrs. Sokolova's stump and her leg cradled in sawdust blotted out everything else. But now, there was no pa-tient here yet, no doctor. One nurse milled around with her back to Lillian, humming to herself, straightening instruments on the tray, topping off a bowl of carbolic acid on a side table. Everything was white: white cloth draped over painted white metal, their white uni-forms, all made whiter by the round skylight drawing light from the white overcast sky. Lillian had to squint until her eyes adjusted. She couldn't remember being anywhere so clean, so orderly. Her spine straightened in an effort to be worthy of this place.

The nurse turned around and Lillian saw with relief that it was Nurse Larson. She stood out among the nurses by her pale skin and blond hair so fair it was hard to distinguish from her cap, but Lillian remembered her more for being one of the few that had not engaged in the smirks and tittering during Lillian's early weeks at the hospital. "Can I help you?" she asked Lillian.

"I... I've been told...." Lillian desperately did not want to start off on the wrong foot with Nurse Larson, but it was hard to know what to say. "I've been told that Dr. Bauer would like me here. For the surgery."

Nurse Larson raised her eyebrows and said, "That's quite a compli-ment for a nursing assistant."

"Certainly. I'm honored." Nothing in Nurse Larson's reaction warned her off, so Lillian took the plunge. "But I don't know what I'm doing. I don't even know why he asked me. I don't know what to do." She stopped herself there, recognizing that she had made her point about being ignorant.

"Well, I don't know why he asked you either, but we'll figure it out together. There are plenty of tasks that don't require a lot of medical knowledge. I'm happy to hand them down to you." When Nurse Larson punctuated her sentence with a smile, Lillian's relief brought a tiny tear to the corner of each eye, which she quickly blinked away.

Nurse Larson showed Lillian how to wash her hands with the foul-smelling chunk of yellow soap, and then dip her wet hands in the bowl of carbolic acid, drying them with a cotton towel. "You're ready to operate!" proclaimed Nurse Larson, her eyes twinkling. "But let's get down to brass tacks. The best thing you can do once it all starts is to listen. Listen to Dr. Bauer, listen to the junior surgeon—I think it's Dr. Snelling today—listen to me. If no one asks you to do anything, you stand nearby, listening. If two people tell you contradictory things, you do what the higher-ranking person has said. If someone asks you to do something and you don't understand, look my way or say my name quietly and I will put it in a way you can understand." Nurse Larson mopped up some splashes of carbolic acid near the bowl with Lillian's hand towel and then threw it in a bin. "Dr. Bauer likes to talk during surgery." Lillian waited for her to go on but she didn't.

"About what?" asked Lillian.

"About anything." Lillian found this easy to believe given her experiences with him. Nurse Larson continued. "It's easy to think that you should respond, like a normal conversation. But it isn't a conversation. So don't respond. He's not looking for input."

Lillian thought about their evenings in his study and how different they were. He was actively looking for her input there. Wasn't he?

"So today it's a hysterectomy. Twenty-five, got married late and now uterine cancer before she's had any children. Although best that there are no children if she doesn't survive it." Nurse Larson sighed. "As they say, the only kind of nurse that sees happy endings is a wet nurse."

"And you don't need a nursing degree for that," added Lillian.

"Evidently, *you* don't need one either," said Nurse Larson, but not unkindly. "You really don't know why Dr. Bauer has you here?" she asked, cocking her head slightly to one side.

Lillian could feel herself starting to blush. She did have an inkling, of course. But before she could embarrass herself stammering out a reply, Nurse Patterson wheeled the patient into the room, and both nurses sprang into action preparing her for the surgery. As she watched, Lillian wondered why they were shaving her abdomen when she was not particularly hairy, and marveled at Nurse Patterson's application of iodine in just the right quantity so that it did not dribble down to the gurney sheet. Periodically, Nurse Larson would speak kind words to the patient before resuming her work with Nurse Patterson. Lillian recognized the patient from the wards: Mrs. Griffin, admitted two days ago. Stone-faced then as now, the set of her jaw like a rock as if she were preparing for battle. Lillian wanted to tell Mrs. Griffin that she would be able to relax after the surgery, that this was one that she had seen have a successful discharge a number of times. Unlike the breast cancer surgeries, women with hysterectomies were not deformed when they left here, and this was the most straightforward of abdominal surgeries, according to what she'd overheard from the nurses, because the organ could be removed entirely, unlike a liver or a stomach. But she dared not risk stepping beyond the boundaries, as unclear as they were. She resisted her impulse to reach for Mrs. Griffin's hand.

Once the nurses were done, they stood with hands clasped in front of them, the ticking of the clock on the wall strangely loud, though Lillian had not heard it at all before. She assumed the same pose and wondered how long they would all be standing there. She glanced down at Mrs. Griffin who was still staring straight up through the skylight at the colorless sky, not even a bird flying by to mar that perfect white circle.

Just as Lillian was checking the clock again—ten past the hour—the doors burst open to admit Dr. Bauer with cleansed hands held high and chin aloft. Dr. Snelling scurried in behind with hands at half-mast, as if his position as junior surgeon required a more modest elevation.

Once everyone was standing around the patient, Dr. Bauer barked, "Dr. Snelling!" which triggered from him a droning patient history. Dr. Bauer stared intently at Mrs. Griffin's abdomen as Dr. Snelling went on and on (from memory, Lillian noted, impressed) and did not seem to notice anyone in the room. Lillian had anticipated that Dr. Bauer would not recognize her presence and thus his snub hardly stung at all.

Dr. Snelling placed the gauze-lined paper cone over Mrs. Griffin's face and held an eyedropper above it. The sweet smell of ether drifted around the room, a smell that Lillian recognized from the post-surgical patients whose bodies continued to emit this smell for a day or two after surgery. Mrs. Griffin started to struggle. "Hold her arms," said Dr. Bauer calmly to the nurses. "Pick up the pace a bit, Snelling," he said peevishly. "It's never the ones you think will be excitable that end up fighting it. Curious." Bit by bit, Mrs. Griffin gave up the fight, and Lillian could see the nurses relax.

As Nurse Larson passed Dr. Bauer the scalpel of his choice, he paused to feel its weight. "German made. There's nothing like these. Perfectly balanced. When I insisted we get rid of old Metcalfe's knives with the mother-of-pearl inlay—a perfect nest for germs!— they tried to push back on the extra expense, but I had to put my foot down. Well worth it." He looked at the scalpel with affection. Lillian wondered what it had cost the hospital, and if it were more or less than a Hanger Limb.

Dr. Bauer leaned over Mrs. Griffin and brought the knife to her skin. Lillian took a tiny step forward, careful not to make contact with the others but intent on seeing everything. As soon as she had a clear line of sight, the people standing around the gurney faded away and it was as if she shared the room with only the knife and the abdomen. The knife pressed down into the skin, and it seemed for the briefest of moments that the skin would not yield, but then the knife sunk in as neatly as if tucking into a birthday cake.

From the point of entry, the knife slid down the abdomen, the line just left of the navel, and as it made its journey, a perfect rope of crimson followed in its wake. Time stopped for Lillian to appreciate the elegance of the rope, standing at attention with tidy cohesion.

She only realized she was holding her breath when she let it out as the scalpel was removed.

The doctors and nurses snapped back into view as they applied retractors to wrench open the incision and little clamps to stem the flow of blood. Nurse Patterson applied squares of gauzy cotton and Nurse Larson handed Dr. Bauer the instruments he demanded.

Lillian peered into the abyss of Mrs. Griffin's belly and was shocked to find such a variety of color in there. She had assumed it would be a landscape of organs bathed in red, but as Nurse Patterson blotted the terrain, Lillian could see blue veins and yellow clumps of fat and bulges of white and lavender, hills and valleys and rivers.

Nurse Larson removed some saturated pads out of Mrs. Griffin's belly and handed them to Lillian. "Put them in that bowl. You'll have to count them later to make sure we got them all out." The pads made a wet smack as they hit the bowl, and the coppery smell of blood mingling with the sweetness of the ether.

"Color is ruddy," remarked Dr. Snelling, still standing by Mrs. Griffin's head.

Dr. Bauer ignored him, absorbed in his snipping and prodding. "It is still remarkable to me," he said, "that there are those so dubious of a man's ability to wash his own hands that they would resort to rubberized gloves. Down at Hopkins it's all the talk. And for their nurses, I suppose that's fine, their skin is more delicate and their dexterity is of little consequence." Lillian looked at the nurses to see what they thought of this comment, but they hardly seemed to be listening. "But surgeons! Touch is everything. Why, you might as well try signing your name wearing mittens!" He went on in this vein for a while, Nurse Patterson occasionally handing Lillian a cotton square or two to put in the bowl, until Dr. Bauer slowly pulled out what looked to Lillian like a blood-saturated rag but what had to be Mrs. Griffin's uterus. As Nurse Patterson swung a bowl under the organ, Dr. Snelling said, "Dr. Bauer. Her color." The urgency in his voice caused all in the room to look to the head of the gurney.

Mrs. Griffin was a grayish shade of violet. Dr. Snelling took the paper cone from her face and leaned down to place his ear near her mouth. "I don't believe she's breathing!"

"Damn it, Snelling!" Dr. Bauer slapped the uterus unceremoniously in Nurse Patterson's bowl. "Nurse Larson, intravenous whiskey!" Nurse Larson grabbed the pre-filled syringe from the tray and went to work on Mrs. Griffin's arm. Lillian stepped back with her heart racing and was torn between wishing she could help and hoping no one would ask her to do anything.

All the activity of the next few minutes was unlike any she had seen at the hospital. To say it was chaotic would be untrue since commands were given and obeyed with all due speed. But desperation lay heavy in the air like a humidity that made it hard to breathe, and the orderliness of the room degenerated as clamps became dislodged and fell to the floor, and the bowl with the uterus was knocked off the table.

When everything stopped, the silence was crushing.

No one moved until Dr. Bauer untied his smock, now streaked with scarlet stains, and threw it on the floor. "This is one of our simplest surgeries," he said with quiet venom, and he left the room.

Dr. Snelling waited a beat and then left the room as well. Nurse Patterson crossed herself and Nurse Larson retrieved her cap from the floor where it had fallen. Lillian picked up the bowl with the saturated cotton squares: her contribution to what had transpired in this room.

"You won't need to count them," said Nurse Larson wearily.

🦃 Chapter 24 🦃

Lillian took her time cleaning up in the operating theater. Before she left, Nurse Patterson had removed all the clamps and retractors hanging from Mrs. Griffin and placed a clean drape over the incision. Nurse Larson instructed Lillian on what to rinse and gather and wash, and told her someone would be by for the body later. Not a no-next-of-kin case for Jupiter—the husband would come for "collection" as Nurse Larson put it. Lillian had felt sympathy for those who went to the crematorium but now realized that this was worse—Mrs. Griffin's suffering was over but Mr. Griffin's was just beginning.

After she had put everything to rights, with the instruments soaking and the bloody linens in a bin to go to the laundry, she paused by the gurney. She remembered Mrs. Griffin's jaw set like stone. Had she known what was coming? Now her jaw was slack. It wasn't true what people said, Lillian decided, that the dead look like they're sleeping. This stillness was unmistakable.

She had time before the hospital's dinner hour to help Mrs. Sokolova with her crutches on stairs, but she had no appetite for it. She was overwhelmed by the fact that no one was leaving that operating theater with what they wanted, despite the years of academic study, the cleanliness and preparation, the desire for a good outcome.

Death on the ward was a train you could hear coming from a long distance, but today the time from when Dr. Bauer waxed on about surgical gloves to the time he threw his smock on the floor was only minutes.

Later, after an afternoon of volunteering for the most menial and solitary tasks and avoiding the wards altogether, Lillian made her way to Dr. Bauer's brownstone. She feared his mood but since he had sent no word that their meeting was cancelled, she proceeded ahead.

When Mrs. Donovan answered the door, she told Lillian that Dr. Bauer was not at home.

The only good thing to come of the surgical debacle was that the other nurses didn't seem to hold it against her that she had been requested to participate. Whether that was because it was something no one wanted to witness or because they were glad they could not be blamed for what happened, Lillian wasn't sure.

The next day, she was even able to ask Janey the question she had hoped Dr. Bauer would answer. "No one knows," said Janey. "Some patients have a respiratory reaction to ether. If there is a history of respiratory problems, they'll use chloroform, but I checked Mrs. Griffin's chart—there was nothing."

"Then why don't they use chloroform all the time?"

"Because with chloroform, the difference between the right dose and a fatal dose is very small."

Lillian shivered, though the room was warm.

When the weekend came, it was the first time since starting her job at the hospital that she was grateful to get away from it for a few days. She let Marie do whatever she wanted, and she did whatever Marie requested. She let Marie braid her hair, she played Josephine's Floating Sheet game, she let Marie eat lunch with her hands. She thought about how Marie almost died of her bout with scarlet fever, how Lillian's life and their mother's life would have been so, so different.

On most weekends, Lillian would strive to take Marie outside at least once, but it didn't always end up happening. Marie had endless energy for fighting off Lillian's attempts to get her dressed, even though she was always happy once they were outside. This weekend, Lillian decided to not even try. Which was why Lillian had to laugh when on Sunday morning, Marie came out of the bedroom dressed for an outing, or at least dressed as best she could manage. Her blouse was inside out and her skirt was on backwards, but she looked so proud that Lillian said, "A fine job!" and grabbed their coats.

Given Marie's level of enthusiasm, Lillian had them walk east and in less than ten blocks they were strolling through the Grand Circle to Merchant's Gate. She always felt a tinge of sadness in Central Park when she was with Marie. For Lillian, the park was a feast for the eyes, with its arches and pavilions and fountains, so many things Marie couldn't appreciate. But Marie loved the park. Was it the smell? The sounds? One time, Lillian had sat on a bench with Marie and closed her eyes, gripping Marie's wrist to make sure she didn't wander off. She wanted to know what it was like for Marie to be here. The ever-present smell of horse manure was more faint than on the streets, but beyond that, her nose didn't really know the difference. But sound was... softer. More muffled. She imagined the grass and the trees soaking up the sharp edges of children's laughter and feet moving along the path, sound that would bounce off the hard buildings if it were outside the confines of the park.

Today it was too chilly and windy for Lillian to want to sit on a bench. They made their way west, weaving through the curvy paths. Helen would always point out the names of all the pathways in the southern part of the park, and though Lillian couldn't remember which was which, the names floated back to her: Spur Rock and Dip Way and Green Gap and Grey Shot. She recited all the names she could remember to Marie and had a crazy thought that maybe Marie would tell Lillian one she had forgotten, but Marie just kept walking.

Eventually they arrived at the Menagerie, and when the smell of the animals hit them, Marie pulled ahead, dragging Lillian behind her. They walked along the rows of cages, Lillian reading each sign. In this weather, most of the animals had retreated to their inside lairs, but she figured Marie might not know that. "This is a Syrian gazelle," she said, as they walked past empty outdoor cages. "Here is the trumpet crane." There was no rhyme or reason to the sequence of animals, although Lillian assumed they had taken care not to place predator and prey side by side. Or learned not to do that the hard way.

At the end of the row there was a larger cage. Near the back there was a log that had been shredded nearly to pieces. Lillian saw the deep wide scratches and imagined the claws that had gouged them. She looked at the sign. "This is the Bengal tiger," she said to Marie. "He's a big one. King of the jungle." Or was that the lion?

From the opening at the back of the cage, the tiger emerged, zig zagging slowly to the front of the cage with a liquid gait. His shoulder blades rose and fell under the striped fur of his back as he placed one enormous paw in front of the other. He came to a stop right in front of Marie and stared her down. Involuntarily, Lillian pulled Marie back a step but was mesmerized by the tiger's gaze. They could hear the huff of his breathing, smell his meaty breath. Marie stared right back into his face as if she could see.

The tiger roared with no warning, so loudly that Lillian could feel it through the thin soles of her shoes.

Marie gripped Lillian and buried her face in Lillian's shoulder, muffling her sobs. Lillian pulled her away from the cage and hugged her, uttering what comfort she could, until she realized that Marie was actually laughing. She pulled away and laughed so hard she doubled over with tears streaming and Lillian had to catch her before she lost her balance and fell to the ground.

All the way back through the park, Marie would walk a few steps and then growl like the tiger, eliciting more than a few odd looks from passers-by. *Let them stare*, Lillian thought, and she growled along until Marie burst out laughing again.

They were still growling and laughing when they got back to the apartment to find Fiona sitting at their kitchen table. "The landlady, she let me in, took pity on a poor soul stamping her feet to keep warm on the stoop," she said as Lillian took Marie's coat off and hung it on the nail.

"What are you doing here, Aunt Fiona?" Then Lillian checked herself. "I mean, of course you're always welcome—"

"Can Marie play in the other room?" Fiona asked. Looking at Fiona's knitted brow, Lillian could see this visit was not to deliver any happy news.

Once she had set Marie up with her bedpost braiding, she sat with Fiona at the table. "Has something happened? Is it Uncle Martin?"

"Oh my lass, it's Michael." Tears gathered in the rims of her eyes.

"What happened?" Lillian's heart began to hammer in her chest.

"I don't know. He didn't come home. He's never done that before."

Lillian felt a tide of relief. "Good God, Aunt Fiona, I thought he was dead!"

"Don't you take the Lord's name in vain, and for all I know he is dead," Fiona sniffed.

"If he and Uncle Martin had another row before he went out last night, he might be staying away on purpose."

"But that's just it," Fiona said and scooted her chair closer. "Things were good. They were getting along. Mostly because of Bridget."

"Who is Bridget?"

"Why, I thought for sure he'd have told you. You remember Bridget, from… before. Last spring, dinner at our house."

Lillian thought back on their dinners and did remember one with a guest. "Yes! Pretty, freckles, that one tooth slightly turned. Not overly bright." One of Fiona's attempts at finding a girl for Michael.

"If there were ever a lass that judged people more than you, I've not met her. Can't you be civil?"

"I am civil! But it's true. She was quite nice, just not very sharp." She and Michael had several laughs at poor Bridget's expense after that dinner, but Lillian refrained from mentioning this to Aunt Fiona.

Fiona frowned but continued. "Well, evidently Michael didn't share your opinion because they have been courting these past weeks."

Lillian started to laugh but turned it into a cough. What nonsense was this? "Michael is interested in Bridget? Romantically?"

"Absolutely. He's treated her like a queen, and it has been a blessing for our family. I haven't seen your uncle this happy in years." She took a handkerchief from her sleeve and started twisting it. "But he went out last night, we assumed with Bridget but looking back now it wasn't entirely clear, and he didn't come back. Bridget came 'round today and said she hadn't seen him since Friday. And now it's been almost a full day and we've heard neither hide nor hair, and Lillian, I don't care if you think me off my head but I know something is wrong. A mother knows."

Lillian looked out the kitchen window and saw that the sun had almost set. A trickle of fear ran down her spine. What if something *had* happened to Michael? She thought of those bruises on his chest, the rattle of his breath after he was beaten.

"What can I do?" she asked.

"You know that before Bridget, Michael would go out at night. He wouldn't tell us where, but it must have been somewhere... rough. Do you have any idea where he would go?"

Lillian considered how to respond. Michael had often told her that his parents were perfectly comfortable living in denial of whatever they didn't want to face, so she was sure that this was not the time to be specific about Michael's outside interests. But she had to do something. "I'm not sure," she said, "but I know a friend of his that might be able to help."

🀐 Chapter 25 🀐

A t first, Lillian thought her offer to help would go nowhere because she could not find Josephine's address. When Josephine had written it down for her months ago, Lillian had only glanced at it before stuffing it in a drawer, and now she couldn't even remember what drawer. But fortunately there were not too many drawers in their tiny apartment, and eventually she found it.

Fiona told Lillian she would stay with Marie for as long as it took. Lillian bundled up and wondered how much money she should take with her. They would have to take the El down to the Bowery, but she didn't want to have a lot of extra cash on her person. Peering into her father's old shaving mug where she stored her savings, kept on a high shelf in the kitchen cupboard, she realized that there actually wasn't a choice to bring more than a few coins.

Only when she started walking down 9th Avenue did she start to think about the trip to Josephine's. Her plan as conceived sitting in front of Aunt Fiona was to let Josephine know the problem and follow along with whatever Josephine thought they should do. But first she had to make it a half dozen blocks south and then over to 11th, the latter part of the journey bringing her into territory that even now was making her heart beat faster. And what would she do if she got to Josephine's, in the middle of the rankest part of Hell's Kitchen and no one opened the door? *No, no, no,* she said to herself as she quickened her pace. *I'm doing this, and Josephine will be there, and if she isn't I will figure out what to do then.* The muscles in her face ached where she was clenching her jaw, and she thought of Mrs. Griffin with her set jaw, facing down a surgery that she ultimately did not survive. *If Mrs. Griffin could face the knife and not fall apart, surely I can find a woman who lives six blocks down and two blocks over.*

Perhaps it was her fierce demeanor, but for whatever reason no one bothered Lillian a whit on the street as she plowed toward Josephine's address. As she rapped on Josephine's door, she heard nothing from within but she refused to believe that there was no one home. She knocked again and told herself she would wait here for as long as necessary, and just as she was deciding which part of the top step was the least dirty patch she could sit on, the door opened.

A tall woman with an aquiline nose dressed in a satin robe opened the door. "Can I help you?"

Lillian looked down at the address on the slip of paper. Could she be at the wrong door? "I'm looking for Josephine?"

"Friend of hers?" said the woman snidely, crossing her arms.

"Oh don't be such a bitch, Maddie," Lillian heard from behind the woman, who was shoved out of the way to reveal tiny Josephine. "Lillian! Is Marie OK?"

"Yes, she's fine, but I need your help. It's Michael."

Josephine ushered Lillian in to their small parlor. Lillian remembered Michael mentioning Madeline, the woman that Josephine lived with, and turned toward the woman in the robe. "I'm Lillian. Josephine cares for my sister." She held her hand out.

Madeline looked down at the hand and then up at Josephine. "I'm going to finish getting dinner together," she said and sauntered off into the kitchen.

"Please forgive her," said Josephine as they sat down, "She's on the rag and she's jealous of everything in a skirt for the whole week."

Lillian just smiled because she could not think of an appropriate reply to that.

"So what's this about Michael?" Josephine asked.

Lillian relayed what Fiona had told her, including the part about Bridget though Lillian wasn't sure if that were relevant. "Bridget?" said Josephine. "Not that stupid one with the freckles? Michael used to tell me all about the gals his mother forced on him. We'd always have a drink and toast to them, poor things."

"So he didn't tell you he was courting her?"

"No, but he's considered it before. Mostly just as a shield, to get his father off his back."

"Well, it worked. My aunt says things are right as rain in that house now. But the important thing is we have to find Michael."

"Hmm." Josephine thought about this. "I can't say I know where he is right now, but I'd bet my boots he was at the Fairy Ball last night."

Lillian had a fleeting image of the little sprites from The Water Babies, a book with illustrations at Aunt Fiona's house that she used to flip through as a child. A moment later she realized what Josephine must be talking about. She remembered Michael repeating what his attackers had said: *Teach these fairies a lesson.* "You weren't there?"

"I wanted to go, but Maddie woulda scratched the eyes out of the first pretty thing that wanted to buy me a drink, the mood she's in. Michael told me last week he wasn't going, but I could see that he wanted to."

"Well, someone must have seen him there if he was there. Right?"

"You gotta realize that this is a big event. Hundreds of people go, and lots are wearing masks."

"Masks?"

"It's a masquerade ball."

Lillian rubbed her eyes and took a deep breath. "Are you saying that we have no way to find him?"

"Hell no!" said Josephine and got up from the settee. "I can find someone who saw something. The hardest part of this night is going to be explaining to Maddie why dinner's going to have to be late." She smiled, and while Lillian realized this was probably an overly-optimistic plan, she was happy to accept it.

After a tumultuous scene in the kitchen that Lillian pretended not to hear where a pot was thrown, she and Josephine left the apartment and made their way to the 6th Avenue El station for a trip that would dump them out further south in Manhattan than Lillian had ever been. As the city grew, the rich kept moving farther north and the poor readily filled the gaps in the south like water rushing in. Lillian had assumed that the establishments down there supported only the local residents, but Josephine had been quick to disabuse her of that notion. Still, Lillian was puzzled, and as they found a seat on the train, she figured this was a good time to get a clearer picture of where they were headed.

"So," she said to Josephine, "this ball you think Michael was at last night. Are we going there first?"

"Nah. Walhalla Hall is just the place it's held—nobody there now. They need a really big place. I went last year, this was before I met Maddie, and it was quite the wild ride. The costumes! Ya never seen so many sequins in one room. Feather boas! Things you can't even imagine. Everyone still talks about how Princess Toto wore a bird-cage on her head with a pair of live canaries inside. That was a helluva mess."

"Is she a real princess?" asked Lillian.

"She's not even a she," said Josephine. She shifted in her seat to face Lillian a little more. "So I see I should give you a bit of a primer here. People like me and Michael, we like our own kind. But we are who we are. I'm a woman, he's a man, we're happy that way. But not everyone is like that."

Lillian started to ask a question but then decided she should just hear what Josephine had to say.

"There's men that act like women, and a lot of them dress like women. Down the Bowery, they can do that. And people come from all around to see it. Some just want to look, but others, they want to sample the wares." She stopped to let that sink in.

Lillian frowned. "But if men can be with men in these places, why do they need to dress like women to be with men? And aren't the, uh, visitors angry when they find out they've been fooled into think-ing they were striking something up with a woman?"

"You're thinking about this all wrong. The men sampling the wares, they know. That's what they want. And the men dressing as women, they just do it because it suits them."

"That makes no sense."

"You have to stop trying to fit it into what you know about men and women. It's not going to make sense that way. Hell, I know a man that dresses like a woman so that he can have a tumble with other women."

"But…" Lillian stopped and just thought about that, too confused to blush.

"Think of it this way," advised Josephine. "Down there, anyone can be whatever they want and do whatever they want with anyone who's willing. Simple!" Lillian could see that Josephine was having a little fun with this, but it was making Lillian's brain feel swimmy. She looked out the window as they arrived at the 8th Street station, watching the people getting on and off the train, snugging up their scarves against the cold, pulling their hats down lower. "Bleeker is next, that's our stop," said Josephine, but Lillian barely heard her.

Their train car began to swerve and screech as they zigzagged on the tracks. Wherever Lillian took the El, it went in a straight line, but apparently everything was different in the southern tip of the island. Even the orderliness of the numbered streets and avenues, an order that gave Lillian comfort and confidence when navigating around New York, was gone here. The street for which the area was named didn't even conform; Michael had corrected her when she referred to it as Bowery Street. "It's just The Bowery," he had told her. Looking out the window, fear crept into her chest, fear of a world that was lawless and unpredictable, this universe that had such a strong pull on Michael.

She thought about Michael, somewhere down here, a needle they needed to find in a messy haystack, dancing last night among the feathers and the sequins, and maybe a birdcage. She asked Josephine, "You say Michael is happy being a man, that he's a man here as he is at home. But is he looking for… a man in a dress? Is that why he comes down here? Why he went to the ball?"

"No. Michael's just looking for his Maddie. Maybe one that's less moody." She squeezed Lillian's arm. "I guess that's one of the reasons he and I get along so good. We enjoy the spectacle, but at the end of the night we're just looking for love with someone just like ourselves. No costume change required."

When they exited the Bleeker Street station, Lillian stuck close to Josephine as they made their way through the muck of the unpaved streets. "Calm tonight," commented Josephine, but Lillian assumed she was kidding. For an early Sunday evening, there were plenty of folks out in the street, the whole place humming with energy, a powder keg near an open flame. Despite the chill, people were not hunched against the cold just trying to get to their destination. Conversations buzzed all around her, one blossoming into fisticuffs right in front of them between two men barely older than Lillian. Josephine grasped Lillian's arm and nimbly steered them around the scuffle without comment. They came across a pair of women with low cut dresses that defied the November evening. One approached them. "Care for a third?" the woman asked, smiling lecherously through painted lips. She boosted her breasts up a little higher with her hands. "I can handle both of ya at the same time."

"It's just the two of us tonight," said Josephine and they walked on. A few steps later it dawned on Lillian all that Josephine had implied to that woman, but that thought was quickly banished by the steady stream of characters and scenes that unfolded as they walked.

They stopped in front of a dirty doorway with no sign. "We'll ask here first, the Black Rabbit. There are rooms in the back, maybe Michael slept there." A man staggered over to a barrel next to the door, and Josephine propelled Lillian inside before he could decide whether to vomit or not.

"Jo!" said the barkeep when they neared the counter. His elaborately waxed mustache rose at the tips as he smiled. "Where the fuck have you been? All these nancy boys are boring me to tears, for fuck's sake." He whipped a dirty rag over his shoulder and reached for a glass with each hand. "Shot of firewater to start you two off?" He held the two shot glasses in midair, awaiting instructions. He looked over at Lillian. "That your new piece? Kicked Maddie to the curb?"

"Nothing to drink for us, and she ain't my piece. She's Michael's cousin."

"Ah, your delicious friend Michael, with his glossy black mane and those cheekbones that go on and on." He glanced at Lillian. "Frankly, I don't see the resemblance."

"Don't be a bitch, Stan. We're looking for Michael. He didn't come home last night. Did he stay in the back?"

"No, and come to think of it, I haven't seen him in quite a while. Almost as long as you've been off doing who the fuck knows what. What's with you two, ya found Jesus or something?"

"Hardly. Maybe he's just going to a better grade of shithole than this place."

"No such thing. This is the best shithole on the Bowery."

"If you say so. But if you see Michael, tell him we're looking for him?"

"Anything for you, Jo. And you tell him to come back to the Rabbit. A face like his is good for business."

They went to two other saloons, all indistinguishable to Lillian with their weak gas lighting, sooty windows and sticky floors. Those barkeeps didn't seem to know Josephine or Michael by name, but when she described him, they confirmed that no one of his description spent the night in their back rooms.

As they were leaving the last place, a patron at the bar buttonholed Josephine. "I think I have some information for you." Based on the high, lilting voice, Lillian at first thought this was a woman but as she got a better look, she could see the shadow of facial hair and an Adam's apple.

"You know where Michael is?" asked Josephine.

He looked longingly at his empty glass on the bar. Josephine gestured to the barkeep to fill it and put some coins on the counter.

"Your boy had quite the time last night at the ball." He crossed his legs and sipped his drink daintily, making it last. "I've had my eye on him for quite a while, though I hadn't seen him in weeks. Rumor has it he took a drubbing from some Neanderthal a while back but I was so relieved to see they hadn't damaged that pretty face of his. Not that he has ever given me the time of day, but hope springs eternal and all that."

"You said you saw him at the ball," Josephine reminded him.

"Mmm, that I did. But honestly, I wasn't that tempted because that little honey was as drunk as a skunk. Now, others don't mind but personally I like mine conscious." He took another tiny sip. "I've got standards."

Lillian could feel the impatience radiating from Josephine, who said through gritted teeth, "We think he's still down the Bowery, never made it home. Any ideas where?"

"Well, as I said, there's many that would have been happy to take him home, especially the slummers which was always what he was looking for anyway. But by now if he didn't turn up, he might be drinking at The Slide. Most of the fairies go there the night after the ball to relive the high points and gossip about who left with who."

"That was our next stop anyway. Thanks." Josephine pulled Lillian toward the door.

"If you see him," the man called out, "tell him Georgie was asking after him and we could have fun together sometime!"

When they were out on the street and proceeding forward, Lillian asked, "What's a slummer?"

"Yeah, so remember when I told you about how the high-falutin' will come down here to scratch their itch, leaving their respectable lives back on the Upper East Side? They're slumming when they come down here."

"And that's what Michael was looking for? That's what Georgie said."

"I suppose. In Michael's dreams he'd meet a guy he could live with, so he could move out of his father's place. But the best these slummers would likely do is keep him as a plaything on the side, get together for a poke when they could get away from the wife and kids. Michael wasn't looking for that. He wanted an equal. Trouble is, Michael's a peach and most of these bastards don't deserve to shine his shoes." She looked over at Lillian. "If he liked girls, with those looks, he could find a great girl. They'd line up around the block. But this is much harder. Not really fair."

They stopped in front of a storefront that looked empty. "This can't be the place?" said Lillian.

Just then the door opened, revealing a narrow staircase twisting down beneath the building. From the depths Lillian could hear faint singing in falsetto, and then a burst of applause.

"I think you're almost ready for this," Josephine said, and they descended.

Chapter 26

The first thing Lillian noticed when they cleared the last step was a tall singer in a flowing pink dress standing next to a piano where a Negro played an elaborate glissando. Patrons sat at tiny tables surrounding the piano, hooting and whistling. "Petunia," Josephine said, which Lillian took to mean that was the singer's name. They stopped to hear the song begin.

I was strolling through the park one daaaaaaay...
In the merry merry month of Maaaaaaay.....

Though the voice was pitched high, Lillian could harbor no illusions that the singer was female. The padding needed to fill out that dress was something Lillian turned over in her mind. Was it sewn into the dress? Was that a bustle underneath the skirts?

The sound of breaking glass directed their attention to the bar, where to Lillian's surprise she saw Michael arguing with the barkeep. Their mission had seemed so daunting to her—how to find one person in a city of this size—that it seemed a great stroke of luck to find him, although Josephine had made this anything but a random search. She rushed over to the bar, comfortable for the first time tonight stepping away from Josephine's side.

"Michael! You're all right!" she said as she grabbed both his arms, but when she looked into his face she was not so sure. His hair hung down in strings and his eyes were bloodshot and red-rimmed. Still, he was overjoyed to see her.

"Lilypad! My cousin, my sweet! A sight for sore eyes. Sit with me and we shall toast your arrival." He pushed her gently onto the barstool next to him while struggling to stay perched on his own.

"Michael, look who else is here too." She gestured to Josephine who had walked over.

Michael swiveled his head in her direction and squinted. "JoJo! Why, this is fantastic! Let's order a bottle."

The barkeep put both hands on the bar, leaning over with elbows bent. "Not a drop more for you. I ain't changin' my mind."

"Lilypad," said Michael, over-enunciating. "Can you please explain to this gentleman that this is a special occasion where my *cousin* and my *friend*—"

"Hey, there's a table over there where we can all sit!" said Josephine as she pulled Michael off his stool. "Much more comfortable, and we can really talk there."

"Yes, that's it, we really should talk, talk about things, so many things…" Michael allowed the two of them to guide him to a table in the corner.

To Lillian's relief, Michael seemed to forget about the drinks once they sat down. She laid a hand on his arm. "Your mother is so worried. Why didn't you come home?"

"My mother?" He looked as if the concept were new to him. "Fiona? Oh, Jesus, Fiona…" He rubbed his eyes.

"So, just one question," said Josephine. "What the hell has gotten into you?"

He sighed. "JoJo, I might have gone a little overboard last night."

"And today. This wasn't one drink too many on a Saturday night. You're still stewed."

Michael closed his eyes and ran his hands through his greasy hair. "Well, this seems as good a time as any to tell you two." He opened his eyes to half-mast. "I'm getting married."

Lillian went numb with shock.

Josephine said, "No you are not."

"Ah, but I am." Michael suddenly seemed almost sober. "I have already asked dear Bridget, and we are going to tell our parents this week."

"That's…" Lillian paused. "Great." Isn't that what one says when someone announces their marriage?

"The fuck it is," seethed Josephine, and her chair clattered to the floor as she left the table and ran up the stairs.

Somehow Lillian got Michael to go with her to catch up to Josephine, who wouldn't stop walking at an angry clip even when Lillian grabbed her elbow. "Please," Lillian pleaded with her, "can we talk about this, the three of us?"

"What is it you want to talk about? Roses or lilies for Bridget's bouquet? I would say, hmm, I don't give a shit."

"Please." She tugged hard on Josephine's arm to make her stop walking, and grabbed Michael's. "This is important."

They all looked at each other without speaking. Finally Lillian said, "But I'm begging both of you, it's freezing out here. Can we talk on the El?"

The train car was warm and almost empty, but once they were seated no one seemed to want to talk. Josephine fumed and stared out the window and Michael's head bobbed as he struggled to stay awake. Lillian was exhausted, and it was tempting to just sit here as they were transported away from the chaos of the Bowery, to let the heat slowly thaw her feet, to close her eyes and just wait for the conductor to announce they were at the 50th Street station. Michael would get married, her aunt and uncle would be so happy, Josephine would get used to it. Maybe Michael would be a father. She would have a niece or nephew! And Michael would never be beaten again, would never have to be retrieved from the Slide.

Or would he?

Try as she might, she could not ignore a different set of thoughts, ones with sharp elbows. Just because Michael gets married, would that mean he would never visit the Bowery again? What about those men from the Upper East Side leaving their families to go slumming? What kind of marriage would that be?

"Hey," she said to Michael and slapped his face gently. "Why are you doing this? Why do you want to get married?"

Michael tried to focus his eyes. "Isn't that every man's dream?" He smiled a sloppy smile.

"You're not every man and don't be smart with me," she admonished. "Why?" She sensed Josephine was listening even though she continued to look out the window.

"The truth is," he said softly, "it's hard. It's just too hard." He took a deep breath. "The fighting with my father, dodging the girls my mother offers up, sneaking out to the Bowery, slinking back home, the guilt. God, the guilt." He looked up at the ceiling of the train car and Lillian could see tears welling in the corners of his eyes. "It's so heavy. Sooooo heavy to carry. I'm tired. I'm going respectable, Lilypad. Everyone will be happier that way."

Josephine turned on him like a viper. "*Really*. Everyone happier. Tell me, are ya gonna tell Bridget about the past you're renouncing?"

"Are you off your nut? Of course not."

"Look at me, you idiot. Are you telling me that you will never be with another man again? Never take a southbound El? It's all over now, your big carousal, got that outta your system, the next forty years you're straight as an arrow?"

Michael said nothing.

"You can't even pretend that will be true. How do you think Bridget is going to feel when you start disappearing late at night?"

"What the hell do you care about Bridget? You called her a freckled dodo bird!"

"All right, I don't care about Bridget. But you, I somehow still care about. If you don't like the guilt of sneaking out of your parents' house to go to the Bowery, how the hell are you going to feel slipping out of your marital bed?"

Lillian watched as the tears crested and ran down Michael's fine cheekbones.

Fiona chose to overlook Michael's bedraggled appearance and boozy odor, at first just relieved to see him and then irate that he had made her worry so. After they left the apartment, Lillian could still hear Fiona admonishing him as they were walking down the stairs.

As she helped Marie get ready for bed, Lillian thought about Michael's intention to marry. She had not been sure of her opinion, but Josephine had no such problem, certain that Michael could not renounce his desires. It was easy for Josephine to prescribe a follow-your-heart path for him; she clearly didn't give a fig about convention. And she had Madeline as a companion. Even with Madeline's histrionics, Lillian understood the value there.

She recalled what Josephine had said on the train. *Michael's just looking for his Maddie.* She imagined Michael finding a man who could be his companion. Would that be enough for him to give up his surreptitious trips to the Bowery? If her cousin and some kind man could live together like Josephine and Maddie, would that be better for Michael than a conventional life with Bridget? Uncle Martin could never accept it. But if that's what Michael really wanted, how could she advocate for a life of deceit?

Despite her active mind, her body soon dragged her down toward sleep, and as she descended she wondered: what would she do if she could only love someone that would make her an outcast?

The next morning as she ran a wet rag under her arms in the hallway toilet, she thought of Mrs. Sokolova. No nurse, including Lillian, could complete a sponge bath for Mrs. Sokolova without hearing a litany of complaints. *Too cold! So rough!* But Lillian smiled at the thought. She knew that Mrs. Sokolova needed a certain number of things to complain about or her day was not complete. And today would be no exception since Lillian would be teaching her crutches-on-stairs. And yet, Lillian looked forward to their session. She knew that Mrs. Sokolova would be proud of her achievement, and that the choicest criticisms would be lobbed at the other nurses, something that gave Lillian covert pleasure.

She thought about if there was any way to sweeten the pot for today's lesson. Wasn't there some bakery treat Mrs. Sokolova was talking about last week? Vat-something. Some sort of cheese Danish thing. She imagined Mrs. Sokolova's pudgy face light up as she pulled the pastry out of a paper bag. Lillian would say, *Not so fast, you have a flight of stairs waiting for you!* Mrs. Sokolova would grumble, make a face, try to negotiate. Lillian couldn't wait.

There was a Jewish bakery a few blocks up on 9th Avenue that seemed to have baked goods from all sorts of countries. She could stop there on the way to work. She picked up the pace of her morning routine and was out the door before Josephine could even take off her coat.

She was five minutes late as she crossed the threshold of the hospital but felt victorious nonetheless. Not only had the wizened man at the bakery known what Russian pastry started with "vat", he had a fresh batch of *vatrushka* in a rack behind him. Now, avoiding the glare of a few nurses who knew she should have already been on the wards, she scooted quickly to the changing room and donned her uniform, slipping the bakery bag into the pocket of her apron.

As she picked up her tray of whiskey cups, she was so engrossed in her thoughts that she was taken up short when she reached Mrs. Sokolova's bed.

Nurse Larson was blotting a trickle of drool that ran down the side of Mrs. Sokolova's chin. "Stroke on Saturday," she murmured to Lillian.

Lillian wobbled. Several cups on her tray tipped over, the whiskey pooling in the corner of the tray. Nurse Larson grabbed the tray to steady it. "I know you worked with her," she said, and she traded the tray for the towel she had been using to blot the drool.

Lillian approached the head of the bed. Half of Mrs. Sokolova's face was as Lillian had remembered it, but the other half sagged as if gravity had a greater pull on that side. Her eyes stared straight ahead, immobile until one of them blinked. "Oksana Ivanova," Lillian said softly as she leaned in, and Mrs. Sokolova's turned her head to meet Lillian's gaze.

"Dev....uzh....ka." Mrs. Sokolova struggled to pronounce the syllables as the saliva ran.

Lillian was flooded with relief that Mrs. Sokolova recognized her but was still horrified at this turn of events. She turned to Nurse Larson. "How did this happen? Why did this happen?"

"It might have been related to the surgery. But she's stout, was short of breath often. She might not have told us everything about troubles with her heart. We can't really know. Best to think of it as just being her time."

"Her time for what?" Lillian shot back. "Her time to have an amputation and then a stroke, but not to..." She caught herself before she said 'die'.

Nurse Larson knitted her brow. "I understand this is a shock to you," she said in steely tones, "but that is no excuse to forget your place around here. I can be understanding but not all the nurses would be so kind. Remember that this is part of the job. I'll leave you two alone for a few moments, but then report back to the desk and pick up your tray." She went off to refill the spilled cups.

Lillian looked back to Mrs. Sokolova, who was still staring in a way that seemed to lock the two of them together. She reached for one of Mrs. Sokolova's hands but it was unresponsive, like grabbing something the butcher handed to you. She reached for the other hand and felt a squeeze returned. "There, now," Lillian murmured. Between the stare and the squeeze, Lillian was sure that all of Mrs. Sokolova's mind was in there, and this seemed most tragic of all.

"Can I get you anything?" A stupid thing to say, but Lillian could not think anything better.

"Whissss....key," Mrs. Sokolova said. The non-sagging half of her face attempted a smile.

"I'm not sure if you can swallow. I will ask the nurses."

"Cowwwwws," Mrs. Sokolova managed.

"Yes, I will ask the cows when they are done eating their hay," said Lillian as she squeezed Mrs. Sokolova's one good hand, and felt her heart break a little.

Lillian found Nurse Larson refilling the cups in the supply closet and peppered her with questions while trying to remain sufficiently subservient. She learned that Mrs. Sokolova had been able to swallow since the stroke but with difficulty, and that if her ability deteriorated they might attempt a feeding tube, although that generally didn't go well. Lillian declined to press Nurse Larson on exactly what 'not going well' meant. She heard the rest in a daze—the need for liquid food, the possibility of aspirating food or drink, the increased risk of pneumonia—but she snapped to attention when Nurse Larson said that Mrs. Sokolova would be transferred to an institution as soon as they could find a bed for her.

"She's cured of the cancer, you see," said Nurse Larson, the sadness in her voice revealing that the irony was not lost on her. "Our job is done."

Lillian stayed behind after Nurse Larson left the supply closet, thinking about the people attending Mrs. Sokolova at her next destination, no doubt a place for charitable cases where the care could not be expected to be good. How they would never know Mrs. Sokolova's personality, her sense of humor. Just a piece of meat to feed, to clean, to rotate. Lillian's breath started coming in short puffs as her anger rose. She pushed her clenched fists into her apron and felt the bakery bag there. The pastry Mrs. Sokolova could not chew or swallow. She yanked the bag out of her apron and threw it down, and stomped it over and over again, first with one foot and then the other when the first was tired, until the *vatrushka* was a flattened mess on the floor.

🦚 Chapter 27 🦚

L illian sat in the dark on a park bench just inside Merchant's Gate, the first place she could find to sit in Central Park. She had asked Janey to cover for her leaving almost an hour early, feigning pain with her monthly courses, after a day where all of her energy had gone into pretending she wasn't a cauldron of emotion. Nurse Larson had seen to it that Lillian was allowed to feed Mrs. Sokolova her meals, marrow broth begrudgingly created by the cook. The process of spooning in the silty soup was painstakingly slow; Nurse Larson had warned Lillian that impatience on her part could cause the broth to "go down the wrong pipe". Lillian feared making this mistake but didn't trust anyone else to do it better. She felt like a pocket watch wound too tightly but she labored to present a calm exterior, for both her patient and the nurses.

Now her feet under the park bench were completely numb with cold, and her fingers were tingling even though her hands were tucked under her arms. She was vaguely aware of the wet wind blowing across the park and threatening to unseat her hat. She stared straight ahead at the constellation of gas light halos, stars of different sizes depending on their distance. Two men walking on the path approached her bench. One said something to her, but Lillian could barely hear him; he sounded as if he were far away. Soon they tired of her lack of response and walked away. She forgot them as soon as they were out of her line of sight.

All day her brain had been frantically thinking and information gathering. She had pored over Mrs. Sokolova's chart when the nurses weren't looking. Widowed, no children, she knew that. A box was checked for "Non-Christian". Jewish? Atheist? Was any of that helpful? She tried to talk to Mrs. Sokolova but could not get a word out of her. Mrs. Sokolova's breathing was labored and it seemed to exhaust her. After the effort of eating both her morning and afternoon broth, she immediately nodded off. Lillian grabbed her good hand but could not get a return squeeze before sleep took her.

As she had stepped outside the hospital at the end of her shift, the cold air hit her like a slap and it turned her brain off. When she got off the El near her building, she had turned in the other direction and walked to the park as if in a trance, not a thought in her head. Now she was starting to feel the cold surface of the bench through her skirts. She had no feeling in her nose and her cheeks stung. But it was preferable to all that thinking at the hospital today that got her exactly nowhere.

When she got home, Josephine had to rush off, something about an anniversary with Maddie, and she hadn't noticed anything amiss with Lillian, but Marie gave her a long hug. This was not the first time that Marie had sensed her mood when others did not, and it loosened something in Lillian. That night as they climbed into bed, Marie hugged her around the neck and wove her fingers in Lillian's hair, nuzzling her nose in Lillian's ear, and Lillian finally broke down in guttural sobs. This did not distress Marie at all, and they lay there intertwined until the wave of sadness ran its course.

The next day she was tired but resolved. The fact of the matter was, she could do nothing. She was a nursing assistant who befriended a patient who had a run of very bad luck. The doctors could do nothing, the nurses could do nothing. What made her think that she could do something? She was as powerless as the cook, more so in fact, because at least the cook could make the marrow broth.

She trudged to work, bracing herself for another day of hospital tasks. 'Helping people', as she had always thought of those tasks. When she was rolling bandages, changing linens, emptying bed pans, in her mind she always attached the job to the surgical patient who would be wrapped in those bandages, the newly-admitted patient who would rest on her well-made bed, the incapacitated patient who could not walk to the toilet. But today she could not make those connections. What was the point of it all? Was there any amount of suffering that she had ever relieved? Even the whiskey seemed like putting a gauze square on a severed artery: too little to help, and nothing curative about it.

She arranged with the other nurses to do jobs that would allow her to avoid the wards all morning. She took extra time cleaning a Posh Row room, not because she really cared how it turned out, but because it allowed her to be alone and talk to no one. Finally it was lunchtime and she gritted her teeth retrieving Mrs. Sokolova's broth. She would expect nothing, perhaps a decline in function. Maybe Mrs. Sokolova had had another stroke, or even passed away. Lillian was ready for anything, a shield of low expectations guarding her bruised heart.

Mrs. Sokolova was sitting up in her bed. "*Devushka*," she said slowly, her words a little slurry but understandable, "You get lost... on way to ward... this morning?" One half of her face pulled up into a smile and the other half tried to follow.

Lillian rushed over to the bed, slopping the broth over the side of the bowl and saturating the napkin on the tray. "You're... better!"

Mrs. Sokolova took a labored breath before speaking. "You call this better?"

"You can speak. You're stronger than yesterday, not sleeping." Lillian blinked away nascent tears. She couldn't fall apart in front of Mrs. Sokolova.

"Maybe that soup... that tastes like dead mouse... will help." Mrs. Sokolova gestured with her good hand at the tray that Lillian forgot she was holding.

"Yes, of course!" Lillian hurriedly arranged the tray to start the feeding. "This will give you more strength," she said as she began, sitting on the side of the bed.

The eyebrow on Mrs. Sokolova's good side scrunched down, casting doubt on Lillian's claim, but she opened her mouth to receive the broth. Lillian was dismayed to find that feeding Mrs. Sokolova was as time-consuming and messy as yesterday; any gains Mrs. Sokolova had made did not translate into easier eating. Still, Lillian was hopeful for the first time since she had seen Mrs. Sokolova in her stroke-induced state.

When they were done, Lillian looked around the ward and could see the other nurses were absorbed in their duties. "I can sit a while if you like, I think."

Mrs. Sokolova reached out her good hand to Lillian. "Yes," she said, "we need to talk."

"How can I help you?" Lillian was already thinking about how she could get more whiskey. She had already watered down the bottles here more than she probably should have. Could she bring in a small bottle from the outside?

"Come close," said Mrs. Sokolova. Lillian leaned in. She could smell the broth that she had spilled on Mrs. Sokolova's pillow. "I need... relief," Mrs. Sokolova whispered.

"Yes. I will get it for you. As much as you want." Lillian glanced at the beds on either side of them. One was empty and the other had a sleeping occupant. No one could hear their conversation.

"Just make sure... is enough."

"You don't have to worry. I will buy a bottle just for you. I will keep your cup full." Lillian wasn't sure how she would get Mrs. Sokolova all this whiskey but surely the nurses couldn't deny this poor woman alcohol that Lillian herself had purchased?

Mrs. Sokolova's eyebrow contracted in confusion. "*Devushka*. You are not... understand." She closed her eyes as she inhaled and then opened them. "You need to get morphine." She paused long enough for this to sink in. "And you need... to finish me. For good."

Lillian jerked backward and knocked the soup bowl to the floor, breaking it into pieces. A nurse quickly walked over in their direction but Lillian called out, "I've got it, I'll take care of it," and the nurse seemed content to go back to the nurses' station.

Lillian left the shards of the bowl on the floor and stared at Mrs. Sokolova, who held up an index finger to stop Lillian from saying anything. "You don't say those things," she instructed Lillian. "'*I can't!*' '*Against rules!*' '*Must save life at all cost!*' Pffff!" She was sweating visibly from the effort of talking and saliva had begun to travel down her chin, but she pressed on. "Friday they move me. Bed found. Will be like prison. You are good girl. You will not let me go to prison."

Lillian put her hands to her face but Mrs. Sokolova's good hand pulled them down. "No pretend."

Lillian blushed, because once again, Mrs. Sokolova had seen through her. She had been momentarily pretending that this was not happening. That she was not involved in this impossible situation, where there was no good choice, no favorable outcome.

"*Devushka*," said Mrs. Sokolova as her plump hand encircled Lillian's wrist and pulled Lillian ever so slightly toward her. "I would do this for you."

This, Lillian believed.

By the end of the next day, Lillian was exhausted. She had fallen asleep the night before as soon as her head hit the pillow but awakened in the middle of the night with her mind spinning, playing out the pros and cons of any action she would take on behalf of Mrs. Sokolova. Lillian tossed and turned until dawn slowly lit the room. She was so wide awake for those hours that she half-hoped Marie would wake up and distract her from her own thoughts, but Marie blissfully slept on beside her no matter how Lillian agitated their bed.

Janey commented on the dark circles underneath Lillian's eyes and assumed they were related to her female complaints of yesterday. Lillian did not try to dissuade her. She asked Janey to take Mrs. Sokolova's feedings and found ways to avoid the ward for most of the day. When she did need to venture into the ward, she gave Mrs. Sokolova's bed a wide berth. Mrs. Sokolova, for her part, did not try to flag Lillian down. She sensed that Mrs. Sokolova understood that Lillian needed time to contemplate everything. She could feel Mrs. Sokolova's patience radiating from across the room like heat from a hearth.

She was in a stupor coming home from work on the El until someone gently bumped into her as the train approached the 66th Street stop. "Pardon me, Miss," said a familiar Southern accent, and she happily followed Jupiter out onto the platform when the doors opened.

"I could not catch your attention before the train came, for love or money," said Jupiter as they headed for the stairs.

"Well, almost knocking me over certainly did the trick," she answered. She didn't realize how much she missed Jupiter until she saw him. Why hadn't she maneuvered to go to the crematorium yesterday or today, if only for distraction? "How have you been?"

"Looks like maybe better than you." He looked at her face more closely as they walked. "Them's is some dark circles you sportin'. You all right?"

"Didn't sleep well. I'm fine." In fact, right now was the best she had felt since she had found out about Mrs. Sokolova's stroke. She took a deep breath, catching a whiff of perfume as a woman passed them on the sidewalk. "Jupiter, can we go to Sonny's?"

"What about the woman that take care of Miss Marie? Ain't she expecting you home?"

Lillian thought about Josephine and how indeed she was expecting Lillian very soon, but Lillian's desire to continue on in Jupiter's soothing presence was overwhelming. "It's fine. Let's go."

Sonny's was more crowded than the last time they were there, but they still managed to find a small table in the back. Jupiter went to the bar to get a pair of short beers from Sonny, and everyone in the saloon could hear how happy Sonny was to see Jupiter again. As the two of them chatted, Lillian realized that she was totally comfortable sitting at a table by herself, surrounded by Negro men, only some of whom had female companions. Between Sonny and Jupiter, she knew no harm would come to her here.

When Jupiter arrived with the beers, Lillian took a long pull before Jupiter even sat down. The cold bitterness swept across her tongue like little sparks and cut a cleansing path straight down to her stomach. She felt scrubbed clean, like stepping out of her weekly bath. She took two more gulps. How did she not realize on the walk here that she was so thirsty?

"So I'm takin' it that you like that beer?" said Jupiter with eyebrows raised.

"It's magical." Lillian closed her eyes in pleasure.

"There's many a man that think that."

She took another sip and announced, "Jupiter, I think it's high time that I finally hear the story of why you are here. I mean, at the hospital."

He scratched the back of his neck. "It's ain't the prettiest story, I gotta be honest."

Lillian thought briefly of the story she could tell Jupiter, the one she was now avoiding thinking about, but the buzzy feeling that was starting in her brain blurred the edges. "I'm no stranger to an ugly story."

"All right then," he said. He took a sip of his beer and then stared into the glass. "I come here lookin' for a man." He swirled the beer around in his glass, and Lillian thought that might be all he would say, which would not be much of a story at all, but just as she was about to point this out to him, he continued. "I was lookin' for revenge."

"This man did something to you?"

"Not to me. To my auntie." He shifted in his chair. "You sure that—"

"Continue."

So Jupiter talked, and Lillian drank, a second beer arriving for her at some point without her remembering how it got there.

Back in Alabama, Jupiter lived with his parents and siblings plus his aunt and her son. He was the youngest of all of them and had a happy childhood with all his older siblings and cousin, but there was always a cloud hanging over his Auntie A. He knew that something bad had happened to his aunt but he didn't know exactly what. Some days Auntie A wouldn't get out of bed, and Jupiter's mother Lavinia would have to take care of all the children, but she never complained. Since they had all been slaves before Jupiter was born—Jupiter was the only one in the family born after the Emancipation Proclamation of '63—he always assumed it was something that happened during the War Between the States, which seemed like a time when a lot of bad things happened.

One night, a mosquito bit Jupiter over and over again as he slept, and Jupiter woke up scratching and couldn't get back to sleep. He heard voices from the next room, his mother and his Auntie A, and when he peeked through the partially-opened door, he could see them sitting at the kitchen table, a jug of corn whiskey between them.

"And I decided I would spy on them," Jupiter told Lillian. "My momma and my Auntie A. *Eavesdroppin'*, they call it. See what they would say whilst they tucked into that white lightning. If I had just got back into bed, I couldn't a heard all them details, but I stood by the door and I could hear everything. That's why I'm here talkin' to you, ya see. Because I stood by the *door*." He tapped the table with his index finger to emphasize that last word.

Lillian's second beer wasn't helping her to make sense of this, but she propped her elbows on the table and continued to listen.

At first the conversation he overheard was just his mother trying to convince Auntie A to talk about "what happened" so that she could "move past it," a phrase that didn't sit well with Auntie A.

"You don't know what you talkin' 'bout if you think this is somethin' you can move *past*, sister," said Auntie A.

"Well, you not talkin' 'bout it ain't workin' out all that good, so maybe you got to try something different," countered Lavinia. "You talked some in the past, it seemed to ease your mind."

They dispensed more from the jug and circled around these opposing positions for a while.

"You already know all about it, anyway," insisted Auntie A. "Why you draggin' all this up from the bottom of the swamp?"

"It ain't for me, you stubborn mule, it's for you."

After a while, Jupiter considered going back to bed. This seemed like an argument they must have had before and both sides seemed dug in. Both women were silent now as they sipped their whiskey, and he figured it was over. But as he turned back toward the bed, he heard his aunt say softly, "You just don't forget the pain."

Jupiter froze, and then turned back to the door. His mother said nothing, just sipped her whiskey and nodded.

"And he was always working from behind. He couldn't see my face. My tears. And he didn't seem like he heard my screams neither."

"Mmm-hmm," said his mother, like a congregant answering the call of the preacher.

Once his aunt started talking, she went on and on, and Jupiter pieced the story together. His aunt had been 17 when she had Jupiter's cousin Moses, and she didn't heal correctly. Her master had no patience for her continuing health problems and so jumped at the chance when a doctor came around and made an offer to fix her. At first the situation seemed too good to be true, because the doctor would not even charge her or her master. What she didn't understand until later was that this doctor had not quite perfected the curative method. Not, as it turned out, by a long shot.

She kept track. Thirty operations. Thirty, and not one with anesthesia.

Jupiter knew that anesthesia was a relatively recent invention, and so at first he assumed this occurred before they knew about those drugs. But Auntie A set the record straight on that.

"He said that the Negro don't feel pain like white people, so it would be a waste of good ether." She closed her eyes and covered her mouth with one hand.

And that was when Jupiter became angry.

He burst into the room and demanded to know the name of this doctor. His mother was livid. "Don't you tell him, Anarcha. You gonna start a fire you can't put out."

But she told him.

Lillian was literally on the edge of her seat when Jupiter stopped talking. "Who was he?" she demanded.

He looked straight into her eyes. "That man was one of the founders of the New York Cancer Hospital. Dr. J. Marion Sims."

"What? Really?" Lillian struggled to put this together in her mind. Had she heard that name before at the hospital? Had she perhaps passed him in the hallway one day?

"So I came here to find him."

"And do what to him?" She thought for a moment. "Did you do something to him?" Her eyes widened.

He paused. "I ain't exactly sure what I was plannin'." He drew a five-pointed star on the table with the condensation from his glass. "I was burnin' up to talk to him. To, you know, confront him. Let him know my auntie felt that pain, felt it so bad it messed up the rest of her life. Maybe that man should feel some pain, too."

"Jupiter, what did you do?" said Lillian breathlessly.

"I didn't do nothin'." He stared at the watery star on the table.

Lillian brought her voice down to a whisper and leaned in unsteadily, gripping the table for purchase. "You can tell me!"

"No, I mean I really didn't do nothin'. The man was dead before I got here. Heart attack, didn't even have no long, painful death." Jupiter looked disappointed.

They sat for a while, surrounded by the din of the crowd, laughing and arguing and clinking glasses. Lillian looked around the room and it seemed to swirl slightly, and she couldn't feel the tip of her nose. But through the fuzziness of her thoughts, she knew there was a piece of Jupiter's story that was missing, a piece that darted away from her when she tried to grab it. She rubbed her eyes.

"You know," said Jupiter, "it ain't my place to tell you what to do, but it might be a good time to get you home."

Home. That sounded nice. Quieter than here. "Yes, take me home, please."

They were about to cross the street when Lillian grabbed his arm, finally remembering why the story seemed unfinished. "Your job. You came to the hospital to find that awful man, but he had died. Then you took a job at the hospital. Why would you do that?"

He steadied her before he answered. "I sure have spent a lot of time thinkin' about that very thing. I took the job first—I couldn't find out much about him before that. Seems people don't like to offer up information to a Negro askin' around about some white doctor. But once I was in the hospital, that's when I found out what happened to him."

"But you stayed."

"Yeah, I stayed. I had alla this anger and it had no place to go. Maybe I thought I'd find some other evil doctor I could take it out on. Maybe I'd find other doctors doin' other terrible stuff."

An image of Dr. Bauer appeared in Lillian's mind, surprising her. Did she think him evil?

"But that was stupid," continued Jupiter. "I guess the truth is, I got stuck. I had a purpose, and then when I didn't have that purpose no more, I just got stuck."

Lillian teetered on the curb as she thought about Jupiter, stuck shoveling bodies and limbs into an oven in a dark room, all alone, speckled with ash from human remains by the end of the day. "Oh, Jupiter," she said, and she started to cry.

"Lordy, we got to get you home now," he said and he hastened them down the street.

At Lillian's building, after a furtive glance to the left and right revealing no witnesses, Jupiter helped her into the building and up the stairs. Josephine opened the door before he could reach for the doorknob, and Lillian saw her angry look turn to one of surprise as she took in the scene. Once they were inside, Josephine said, "I don't know if I'm more surprised to see you drunk or bringing your dark friend up here."

Lillian put a hand on Jupiter's shoulder. "He came to New York to kill a man that was already dead," she slurred.

"There are worse reasons to come to New York," Josephine said.

🌁 Chapter 28 🌁

The headache that woke Lillian the next morning had her immediately worrying that she was coming down with something before she remembered her evening at Sonny's. She wished she had some willow bark tea, the kind her mother had always kept in the cupboard, but she had nothing stronger than the plain tea that she had every morning, which would have to do. After she steeped the leaves, she positioned her face above the mug and inhaled the steam, which gave her some relief.

Josephine arrived with a cat-that-ate-the-canary look on her face. "So, that Jupiter seems like a lovely feller," she said breezily as she hung up her coat. "Quite the gentleman to fish ya outta some groggery where you were throwin' back whiskey."

"It was beer, I'll have you know." Talking sparked her headache, but she pressed on. "I may have miscalculated how much is a... healthy amount."

"Looks that way!" she said cheerfully right before Marie came charging out of the bedroom to give her a bear hug greeting. She tousled Marie's hair. "Ah yes, today is hair brushing day," she commented, and Marie ran back into the bedroom and shut the door, the slam reverberating in Lillian's head. Josephine laughed.

Lillian consoled herself with the thought that at least she wouldn't have to brush out Marie's hair.

The El arrived just as she ascended to the platform, so she decided she had time to get off a stop early and walk the extra blocks. The day was clear and dry, the kind that had people reversing their opinions on November weather in New York, with cool breezes whipping through the streets ruffling the feathers on women's hats, and by the time she arrived at the hospital, she felt nearly back to normal. But looking up at the building with its fat round turrets, she remembered Mrs. Sokolova and it hit her like a punch.

Avoiding the situation was not fixing anything, she could see that. If anything, it was driving her to sleepless nights and too many glasses of beer. But tomorrow was Friday, the day Mrs. Sokolova would be carried out of the hospital, and no amount of hiding from this was slowing down time.

When she arrived at Mrs. Sokolova's bedside with her broth, Mrs. Sokolova looked as if she had been expecting her, and not just to feed her breakfast. Without a word, Mrs. Sokolova patted the bed next to her with her good hand. Lillian put the tray on the table and sat.

"You did some thinking," Mrs. Sokolova stated, straining to pronounce the words with a drooping lip, "and you also did not-thinking."

Lillian nodded. This was an excellent description of the last few days.

"I have story," she said.

Lillian got the sense that Mrs. Sokolova had been saving up her energy all morning to tell her this story. She reached for a small towel that a nurse had left by the pillow and blotted Mrs. Sokolova's chin. "Tell me your story," she said.

"Everyone on boat was sick like dogs. My papa, mama, older sister, all the others. But not me. I found way to sneak on deck, fresh air, no sound of retching. One day I see boy, same age as me, eighteen. Also not sick. Also sneak on deck. Handsome! A chin like cut with chisel." She closed her eyes and Lillian saw her eyelashes tremble before she opened them again. "But shy. So I unbraid my hair. Was long, red, was secret weapon. Wind blowing it behind me like flag. Worked like charm. He couldn't resist!" Here Mrs. Sokolova stopped to take a few shallow breaths. Lillian blotted beads of perspiration from her brow before she continued. "Maxim. My Maxim. Married six months later. Other girls, they tell me about husbands. *He drinks. He slaps. He looks through me like I'm window.* After while, I realize what I have. Not everyone feels thrill when they hear key in door. Not everyone want two bodies melt like candle wax and make one."

Lillian blushed but Mrs. Sokolova was staring far away. She waited while Mrs. Sokolova gathered her strength.

"First year, I lost baby. Then another. And another. Maxim, he holds me. Tells me I am everything. Baby is extra, icing on cake. I am cake. I fill him up. Never he will be hungry."

Lillian looked at Mrs. Sokolova's dry eyes and resolved that hers must be too. She clenched her teeth with the effort. Mrs. Sokolova continued. "He was almost forty when he died. Influenza. I ask God to take me too. God not listening."

Lillian made fists with both hands and gripped so tightly that she could feel her fingernails cutting into her palms.

"Seven years Maxim is waiting for me. Waiting for his cake. Hungry. Every night I talk to him. Tell him I'm coming someday. He says he's on boat, waiting. Then God gives me cancer. Then stroke. Now I'm done with God. I only want Maxim." She ripped her gaze away from the distance and peered into Lillian's eyes, invading her. "Don't keep me from my Maxim any longer."

Lillian rose from the bed with ramrod posture and left the ward without a word. She nodded politely to a pair of nurses on her way to the washroom. Once she had locked the door behind her, she sat on the toilet and sobbed.

That day passed as if Lillian were in a dream. Her mind was like a big empty room with a locked closet off to the side. Inside the closet was a decision that had been made, red and pulsing. She steered clear of the closet and just went about her business in the big room where things were flat and gray and had no consequence.

She went through the motions of her job. The bed making, the bandage rolling, the sponge bathing. She talked as little as possible, to patients and nurses. She attended to Mrs. Sokolova in silence. Mrs. Sokolova did not try to engage her. She made a mental note of where the morphine and syringes were kept, the safe dosage Nurse Matheson administered to a post-operative patient.

Mostly, Lillian felt alone. Only now did she realize how lucky she was to have people in her life she could turn to: Michael, Josephine, Jupiter. But they were good people. Every time she thought of bringing her troubles to their doorstep, it felt as if she were dragging them into the mud. And it wouldn't change anything.

At the end of her shift she left the hospital just as a sleeting rain began in earnest, as if the crisp and dry morning had never happened. She trudged along the street, looking at women trying to protect their hats, men ducking into doorways and considering whether to wait it out. Lillian put one foot in front of the other, feeling her skirts get heavier and heavier as they soaked up water, until she was standing in front of Dr. Bauer's door.

Her footstool was waiting for her by the fire, and she wasted no time using it to warm her feet despite her ragged stockings. Dr. Bauer looked pleased but surprised at her bold display as he took the wing chair across from her. She gazed at him, more directly than she had ever done before.

"Good evening, Nurse Dolan."

"I'd like to talk about Dr. J. Marion Sims," she stated, surprising herself. It just popped out of her mouth, unbidden.

He arched his eyebrows in surprise. "Sims, you say?" He paused. "Well, I never had the pleasure of meeting him before his untimely demise, but women everywhere benefit from his talent and foresight. As you must know, he founded your little hospital when other hospitals would not take cancer patients."

"But he is also known for a type of operation, is that right?"

"Why yes. I see you've been doing your homework. Vesicovaginal fistula repair. You see, the breakthrough was using silver sutures—"

"He perfected this operation in Alabama?"

Dr. Bauer tilted his head slightly and looked at her curiously. "I believe so. It was in the South, I know that."

"And he used slaves to practice. Without anesthesia."

"How do you know this?"

"Am I wrong?"

"I'm not sure I like your tone, Nurse Dolan."

"My apologies," Lillian said as she rose from her chair and walked toward the study door, reaching for her shoes.

"Yes," said Dr. Bauer, and she stopped. "I had heard there was no anesthesia."

She returned to her chair.

"Do you know what a fistula is?" he asked.

She shook her head.

"A fistula, well, the type Sims repaired, is a lack of integrity between the vagina and the bladder. The bladder dumps urine into the vagina which discharges continuously. There are also fistulas that involve the rectum. So you can imagine how awful these are for afflicted women. And for the past thirty years, we have a surgical solution to this terrible problem. Hundreds of women have had their lives and normal functions restored. If a few women had to suffer a bit—women who, by the way, had their fistula repaired free of charge—was that not a fair price to pay? Even the Negro women's lives were better after the discomfort was all over."

"But they didn't have to suffer. That is the whole point. Ether was already being used in surgeries."

"Ah, well," said Dr. Bauer, reaching for a cigar and cigar cutter from his desk. "Who knows. Financial considerations, perhaps. Lack of availability in Alabama—quite a backwater, after all. Could be anything." He clipped off the end of the cigar and tossed it in the fireplace.

Lillian turned this over in her mind as she fanned out her wet skirt hem to better expose it to the fire. She supposed there was no circumstance in which a doctor would criticize another doctor in front of the likes of her.

"Penny for your thoughts," Dr. Bauer said as he lit the clipped end of his cigar, his cheeks puffing in and out comically.

What were her thoughts, she wondered, trying to push away the headache that was forming. She had not planned to ask Dr. Bauer about Dr. Sims. Yet there was nothing to be done about Auntie A's situation, given that Sims was dead, and Lillian had a far more pressing issue on her mind. What connected them?

"My thoughts," she said, "are of suffering."

"All that we do to relieve it?" He contemplated the smoke rising from the end of his cigar.

"All that we do not relieve."

"I see your glass is half empty today." His eyes wandered down to her footstool. "Are you drying out sufficiently?"

"Is it worth preserving life at any cost? I mean the cost to the patient."

Without looking back up at her, he murmured, "Not in the mood for frivolous topics, I see."

"You did not ask me here for frivolity." At least she thought that was true. That was certainly not why *she* was here. "How do you know, as a doctor, when it is worth preserving a life?" She tucked her feet further under her skirts, causing him to look up as if a spell were broken.

He straightened in his chair. "Our job is to preserve life without judging its worthiness."

"But you do judge. You judged the worth of Mrs. Feinman, the stomach cancer patient a month or two ago. You said the information we could gain was worth the last few days of her life. Especially because she was suffering. If she were feeling fit as a fiddle, would you have operated?"

"Well, I've yet to see an incurable cancer that doesn't cause suffering in the end, but hypothetically, no, I would not have performed that surgery."

"So suffering is a factor in judging whether a life is worth living." Lillian could feel her heart beating in her chest.

"Yes, your reasoning is sound." He looked amused, as if she were a lap dog that had performed a trick.

"What about suffering that isn't physical pain? Is that a factor too?"

"Such as?" He tapped his cigar into the ashtray.

She did not want to mention Mrs. Sokolova, but there must be other examples of patients losing abilities, leaving them distraught. She thought for a moment. "The War Between the States," she said. "So many lost limbs, you told me. Some of those men must have been... their minds must have been..."

"Devastated? Without a doubt. Men left their hometowns in the prime of their lives, supporting their families, and some came back forever dependent. Unable to walk, to bathe themselves. To perform their husbandly duties." He looked at her, Lillian thought, as if to see if she would look away, but she would not give him the satisfaction.

"Did any of them ask you to end their lives?" Her breath was shallow. She hoped Dr. Bauer did not notice.

"That, Nurse Dolan, is quite a weighty subject. Perhaps one for another day." He rested his cigar in the tray and rose to prod the fire with a poker.

No, Lillian thought. *Another day will not do. I don't have another day.* Lillian had a vertiginous feeling, one that she had had before in situations where it wasn't clear whether she had gotten in over her head. But she couldn't seem to stop herself. She knew this was a dangerous subject, but after all, didn't this fit with the pattern of their meetings, this ethical sparring that was so stimulating to him? She stared at him, not moving, her insides like a tightly-wound watch.

"All right," Dr. Bauer said after a moment, and he took a deep breath. "It was at the end of the war that this soldier, Capstone was his name, he took extensive injuries on the battlefield. I treated him several years later, when I was fresh out of medical school. He had been in and out of hospitals with various reconstructive efforts and infections, tin mask for the cheekbone that was blown away, missing an arm, et cetera. Quite a mess. But according to the doctors that had treated him, he had remained remarkably chipper. However, soon after I met him, his demeanor changed entirely. He seemed to be in agony, despondent, no will to live. I asked him about his pain but my interview with him seemed to be going nowhere, until he revealed to me that his wife had recently left him and taken his twin boys to parts unknown. She could not tolerate his level of dependence, or so he explained to me. And he didn't blame her. He told me he wasn't a man anymore, just a mangled pile of bones and muscle. A heart that continued to beat for no reason."

"And he asked you to end his life."

"Yes. At first he refused treatment and food, but that wasn't getting the job done fast enough. They were going to send him home soon, to be cared for by a parent who was not in good health, if I remember correctly."

Everything seemed sharply in focus in the room: Dr. Bauer's fingers knitted together in front of him, the arms of his wing chair, the smoke rising from the cigar in a lazy ribbon. "What did you do?"

"I moved to another department before his discharge day."

"But what would you have done if you hadn't moved?"

"Why is this so important to you?"

Lillian felt a trickle of fear run across her scalp. "I am a curious person." Perspiration dampened the back of her neck, but she forced a little smile, hoping to distract him. "It's what you like about me, isn't it?"

Slowly he stood and walked over to her footstool. "It *is* what I like about you," he said, barely audible. Gently, he lifted her feet from the stool and sat down on it, holding her ankles. "The truth is that I would not have done it." He gripped one ankle very gently with his index finger and thumb. "So slender," he said quietly.

"So it is wrong? It is a wrong thing to do?" The situation was careening out of control, putting her in multiple types of danger, and yet she needed to know.

"In this case, yes. What if his wife returned to him? The cause of his despondency was not etched in stone." Dr. Bauer closed his eyes as he cupped her heels in his hands. "Had he been a late-stage cancer patient..." He trailed off, breathing deeply.

Lillian knew she had pushed this subject too far and only Dr. Bauer's distraction was blinding him to her inordinate interest. Now she had to focus on extricating herself from this situation. She prayed for an interruption of any sort—a knock at the study door, a clap of thunder—but none came. She wanted to bolt from the room but feared the consequences. Finally, when she felt her feet being pulled toward Dr. Bauer's lap, she just started speaking.

"Sir, I am flattered that you have always shown an interest in me," she began, and she pulled one leg back and placed her foot on the floor, gingerly, as if backing away from a snarling dog. "And I am intrigued at how our acquaintance has grown." She gently extricated her other leg, keeping his face in view to gauge his reaction. "I wonder where it may go in the future. Can we speak again next week?" She cringed inwardly at this last part, since he already expected her to come every week, and her whole monologue implied an interest that she had no intention of ever pretending, but she couldn't think of any more to say. She forced herself to remain seated and hoped her trembling was not visible.

For a heartbeat he just stared at her, and then with a sly smile he said, "I look forward to it."

❧ Chapter 29 ❧

B ack at home, Lillian knew that sleep would not come easily after such a day. She would have sat in a chair all night had there been one more comfortable than the wooden kitchen chairs. So she lay in bed, letting her gaze wander around the room, taking inventory of the ambient sounds: Marie's breathing, a distant argument on the street, the clip-clop of hooves from a hansom cab splashing in puddles from the earlier rain. Something clumsily rooting around in the trash cans below.

When enough hours had passed, she stared at the window to catch the first hint of dawn, but just as the black of night began to turn to indigo, she nodded off and was awoken by Josephine pounding on the door.

"Another late night with your knight in shinin' armor?" teased Josephine, but she stopped when she caught a good look at Lillian. "Say, you look like something the cat drug in. You feeling up to snuff?"

"I'm fine, fine. Just overslept." Lillian ran her fingers through her hair. Her eyes felt gritty.

"If you tell the hospital you're sick, I can take the little monkey out for a while, let you get some rest."

Much as this idea had enormous appeal, today was certainly a day that Lillian could not stay home. "I have to go in," she mumbled, heading back to the bedroom to get dressed.

"Oh yes, lives to save and all that Florence Nightingale stuff," said Josephine merrily as she put the kettle on to make herself a cup of tea. The comment felt like a knife twist in Lillian's gut but she didn't break stride as she left the kitchen.

It was more than a half hour past the beginning of her shift when she walked into the hospital. Perhaps she would be reprimanded, sent home, banished from the wards. Anything to take today's decision out of her hands. But Janey let her know that today was her lucky day. "Nurse Holt is out with a fever, and Collins is cooking up a migraine so she's 'doing paperwork' in Holt's office, meaning she's lying down. Not to be disturbed, and to that I say, not to worry!" Janey's mischievous look faded. "But not everyone is as lucky as you, I'm afraid. Your Russian friend had another stroke, looks like."

"What?" Lillian felt dizzy and had to lean up against a wall. "Is she dead?" *Please, please let her have died*, she thought and was too tired to contemplate whether this was a monstrous thing for someone in nursing to wish.

"No, just a little one. The doctors said this could happen. She just can't talk at all anymore." Janey took a more careful look at Lillian. "You're not looking well. Larson told me you're thick as thieves with the Russian. Let's sit down." They moved from the hallway to the sitting room and sat side by side on the settee. "I probably should have seen this coming, and I know Collins put me in charge of you, but frankly, I took my eye off the ball with you because you've really done a great job picking everything up. But we should talk about getting involved with patients."

Lillian had to suppress the giggle of a madwoman when she thought of how bad Janey's timing was. Exhaustion seemed to be nibbling at the edges of Lillian's sanity.

"We're drawn to this work because we're compassionate. But that very part of us makes us prone to get pulled in too far. It's easy to keep your distance from some cranky witch on Posh Row, or any of them that are rude, or silent, or that sleep a lot. But with the nice ones, it's hard. Though frankly, I didn't peg your Russian for a nice one. But she must have had some charms hidden in there somewhere if you liked her."

Had Janey asked, Lillian would not have been able to explain what was nice about Mrs. Sokolova. Lillian only knew that it was too late to not care, like getting back a penny that you dropped in the harbor.

"The point is," said Janey, "when they leave here, you need to forget about them. And so your relationship with them here needs to be professional but forgettable."

Lillian could not imagine a time in the future where she would forget Mrs. Sokolova.

A part of Lillian's mind was convinced that circumstances would prevent her from following through with Mrs. Sokolova's request. After all, nurses were everywhere in the hospital for all sorts of reasons, including oversight of the junior staff. But today, in addition to Nurse Holt being out and Nurse Collins lying prostrate in a darkened office, Lillian heard that Nurse Farrell had become engaged to her beau, and the sizable diamond he gave her had set the nursing staff abuzz. "Hard to tuck a sheet with that piece of ice on your hand!" Lillian overheard but she was too weary to turn her head to see who had made this comment. Discussions ranged from romantic ponderings to jealous snipes, and it all seemed outrageously stupid to Lillian. She thought of Maxim. She doubted that Maxim could have offered Mrs. Sokolova much in the way of a ring. But of course, what Mrs. Sokolova had valued in that marriage wasn't something you put on your hand.

Lightheaded, she stumbled to the slop sink room to catch her breath but no one was around to notice. That is when she realized that the nurses were not out in force as they usually were. The wards were half empty today, and the combination of fewer patients, the absence of senior nurses and the distraction of Nurse Farrell's engagement produced a near ghost town. It was the perfect time, she realized with horror, for her to act.

She walked swiftly down the hallway, passing the room where the medicines were stored and turned into the linens room. She sat and began rolling bandages mechanically, staring ahead without seeing. Of all the jobs at the hospital, she had found this one to be the most soothing, and the one that required the least attention. She rocked back and forth a bit in her chair as her mind careened.

She tried to organize her thoughts with facts. Today was Friday. Patient transfers happened at the end of the day. It was approximately 10am. Lunch rounds would not be for another hour and a half. Some nurses took tea in the lunch room mid-morning. All life ended at some point.

She grabbed another strip of linen to roll.

The rigid wall of facts in her mind began to crumble, revealing a woman in an iron hospital bed. A woman who would never walk again, would never feed herself again, would never sit on a toilet again. Who could not even tell her new nurses that the cloth beneath her was soaked with urine. How often would they check to see if her bedding was dry? What if she was thirsty? What if her cancer came back, a throbbing menace spreading through what was left of her body—how could she tell anyone? And even if she could, what could they do about it?

Lillian threw the linen strip on the floor and walked to the medicine room.

Mrs. Sokolova's gaze followed Lillian as she entered the ward and approached the bed. She looked around. One nurse was just starting a sponge bath with a patient on the far side of the ward, but there were no other nurses in the room. She sat down on the edge of the bed. "Hello, Oksana Ivanova."

Mrs. Sokolova's face was still, but Lillian could see hope in her eyes.

They sat for a while. The pendulum clock at the nursing station in the center of the room counted the seconds in pedantic rhythm. The nurse giving the sponge bath talked to her patient, soothing tones but too low to make out any words from across the room. Sunlight streamed in through the tall windows, revealing dust motes dancing to their own music.

"It's a beautiful day," said Lillian. Mrs. Sokolova managed the slightest of nods. Lillian's eyes filled with hot tears.

Mrs. Sokolova made a small motion with her good hand. Lillian grabbed it and gave a squeeze, but Mrs. Sokolova pulled it away and made the same motion again. After a moment, Lillian realized what she meant and rummaged around in her apron for her pencil stub and hand-made notebook. She flipped to a blank page, glancing at her most recent notes: "Why so many patients have post-op diarrhea" and "How often to rotate to avoid pressure ulcers." She couldn't remember writing those questions.

Lillian positioned the pencil in Mrs. Sokolova's hand and the notebook under her wrist. After some readjustment, Mrs. Sokolova was able to mark the paper although she could not turn her head to see what she was writing. When she stopped, Lillian went to take the pencil and paper but Mrs. Sokolova had an iron grip. "All right, you're not done. Take your time," Lillian said, although she desperately wanted to see what was on that paper.

A very long minute later, Mrs. Sokolova dropped the pencil on the bed, and Lillian grabbed the notebook. All the letters were upper case, and most of the lines overlapped or did not connect, but Lillian could read:

MAXIM
BOAT

Lillian leaned forward, her tears dropping onto Mrs. Sokolova's blanket. "He's waiting for you," she whispered. "On the boat. Right?"

Mrs. Sokolova nodded.

Lillian reached around the back of Mrs. Sokolova's neck and unpinned her hair, spreading the russet locks across her shoulders. Without even looking around the ward, she reached into her apron and brought out the syringe. She strained to remember how Nurse Larson pushed the needle of whiskey into Mrs. Griffen's arm during that awful surgery. With the heel of her hand she pushed the tears from her eyes, clearing her view.

Though Lillian was unskilled with the syringe, Mrs. Sokolova did not flinch. As her eyes slowly dimmed and closed, Lillian held Mrs. Sokolova's good hand, and just before her breathing stopped, she gave Lillian's hand a tiny squeeze. Lillian closed her own eyes and saw two young lovers on a ship plowing through the Atlantic, one with red hair streaming behind her like a flag.

🎴 Chapter 30 🎴

T he next thing Lillian knew, she was making a bed on Posh Row when Nurse Larson grabbed a pillowcase and began to help. "I wanted to be the one to tell you that Mrs. Sokolova passed this morning." She slipped the pillow into the case and then looked up at Lillian. "You shouldn't be so surprised. We discussed the heightened risk of another stroke."

But Lillian's look of shock was caused by her inability to recall what had happened since she sat by Mrs. Sokolova's bedside. "What time is it?" she said. She dropped the flat sheet onto the bed and stared at the crumpled pile of cotton.

"It's just after 11. You will need to do bedpan rounds before lunch. I will arrange for someone else to take the patient downstairs."

She means to Jupiter, Lillian realized as a sort of side note, while she determined that she had lost at least a half hour of her memory. The last thing she remembered was closing her eyes and envisioning Mrs. Sokolova reunited with Maxim. Then she was here on Posh Row. What had she done in the interim? Had anyone seen her crying? Did she clean up the injection site, which she recalled had bled slightly? Where was the syringe? She put both hands in her apron pocket and pricked her finger on the needle. At least she had not left it lying on the bed. She began to sweat.

"You need to steel yourself and move on." Nurse Larson squinted slightly. "Unless you are actually unwell."

"No, ma'am, I slept poorly is all. I will steep my tea for an extra few minutes at lunch and get to bed early tonight." Just thinking about how she slept for only an hour or two last night was like a sodden blanket dropped on her shoulders, pulling her down. She looked longingly at the bed in front of her, eyes lowering to half-mast. The pillow looked so soft… With a start, she remembered her circumstances. She straightened her shoulders. "Nurse Larson, I would like to take Mrs. Sokolova downstairs. I am capable of keeping my emotions in check and performing my duties."

"Well," Nurse Larson said, looking relieved, "I will take your word for that. It is difficult enough today to get the nurses away from Nurse Farrell's ring just to do their regular jobs on time. I've half a mind to rouse Nurse Collins from her migraine."

"Yes, ma'am." Lillian picked up the sheet. "I'll be down as soon as I put this bed right."

After retrieving the paperwork for Jupiter, Lillian assisted with the transfer of the body onto the gurney. Once on the gurney, Lillian saw that Mrs. Sokolova's long sleeves were pulled down so the injection site was not visible. And though she could not bring herself to look at Mrs. Sokolova's face, she saw all that red hair had been tucked back in place. Had Lillian done that?

Before she began to push the gurney, she took one look back at the bedside and saw her notebook splayed on the side table. Who had seen that lying there for the past hour? Quickly she grabbed it and shoved it in her apron pocket.

When Jupiter opened the crematory door, Lillian realized that she had never even mentioned Mrs. Sokolova to him. As he wheeled the gurney in, he noticed the sheet draping asymmetrically and peeked underneath. "Amputation here? Was this the leg you brought to me a while back?"

Lillian nodded.

"All that recoverin' from surgery and then she don't make it. Bless her soul." He shook his head.

"She had a stroke. More than one. And they were going to move her to some other place. Because the cancer, you see, she's cured. She's cured!" Lillian giggled and found she couldn't stop. The more she tried, the more impossible it was to suppress. Even the look of alarm on Jupiter's face did not deter the laughter that was determined to keep coming.

When she doubled over, Jupiter brought a chair. Eventually, her outburst was spent. She used her apron to wipe the snot and tears from her face, and tried to tuck a few strands of hair back into her cap. She felt she should say something to Jupiter, some sort of explanation for her hysteria. But what could she say?

He brought a chair for himself and sat down next to her. "Lillian," he said, and he reached to put a hand on her knee, but pulled it back and settled it in his lap. "What is wrong?" He looked at her imploringly, worry written across his brow.

She had the urge to tell him everything. Spots danced around the edges of her vision. She thought she heard the tinkle of carousel music in the distance, though that seemed impossible down here in the crematory.

She ran out of the room.

Only her need to make everything look like a typical day forced her to work through the rest of her shift. In a brief moment of clarity she managed to nestle the syringe from her apron pocket in with the other used syringes. As she turned to go back into the hallway, she looked over at the shelf with its brown bottles standing at attention. She briefly thought of taking a cup of whiskey herself—after all, what was a little more water added to the bottle?—but was afraid another nurse would smell it on her breath.

As the day wore on, it felt like the whiskey would have been unnecessary; Lillian was numb with exhaustion. The possibility of someone asking her questions about the circumstances surrounding today's death didn't even bother her. If a case of bubonic plague was detected in the hospital, it wouldn't have bothered her. All she cared about was making it to the end of her shift.

On the El home, she repeated in her mind what she needed to

tell Josephine: "I will double your wages for today if you stay until Marie's bedtime." She had just enough money to do that. Of course, when the food ran out tomorrow she would have nothing to pay the grocer. That didn't seem important.

When Lillian trudged into the apartment and made her offer to Josephine, she didn't stop walking toward the bedroom. She heard Josephine say something about how it was Friday and it wasn't the best evening to stay late, but after Lillian shut the bedroom door she couldn't hear Josephine any more. She crawled into bed with her clothes on and fell into a dreamless sleep.

🏵 Chapter 31 🏵

After almost a week, Lillian had stopped imagining that every nurse that approached her would question her about Mrs. Sokolova's death. In fact, no one seemed to even remember Mrs. Sokolova, which, though it worked tremendously in Lillian's favor, she found somewhat offensive. But she thought of all the deaths that had occurred at the hospital since she began here, and realized that her memory didn't linger on those women. Even Mrs. Griffin's bloody demise on the operating table had stopped being a part of her daily thoughts.

Since last week, she had been waking up in the middle of the night with her heart racing and her thoughts keeping pace. In the pitch black, her criminal act loomed large, threatening her livelihood, tainting her, damning her soul. To calm herself, she imagined Mrs. Sokolova and Maxim on the boat, how they had both shed their earthly shells to be together again, how the alternate fate of Mrs. Sokolova would have been a horror show without a shred of dignity or hope for improvement. Each night it took a little less time to fall back asleep.

But today was Thursday, and she took a meandering route on her way to Dr. Bauer's home. Thinking back on how she left things last week, she cringed. All she had cared about in their last meeting was stringing together scraps of information and opinion to help her wrestle with her predicament, but now she could see that she had arrived at a place to which she hadn't intended on ever going. It was as if she had had a fever and wasn't in her right mind. But regardless, the doctor's preferences were tacitly acknowledged between the two of them, and she had forfeited her ability to be shocked.

With dread, she entered Dr. Bauer's study. She had seen him in passing several times at the hospital this week and he had all but ignored her. Now, however, he looked as pleased as punch. For the first time, a caddy with tea had been set up on the table between the two wing chairs, the steam rising from the pot. Lillian did not consider this a good turn of events. Her footstool was in position.

Dr. Bauer poured tea for her without asking. "To warm up on such a night," he said, though it was not particularly cold. He dispensed a cup for himself and sat back, nearly purring with satisfaction. "Darjeeling. They didn't always grow tea there in that dark corner of India. Seeds brought from China fifty years ago, and by whom? A doctor. I would bet that contribution to the world tops anything he did in the field of medicine." He took a dainty sip.

Perhaps we will just talk of tea, thought Lillian. She sipped from her cup and tried to remain hopeful.

"I've been thinking about our meeting last week. You seemed very keen."

Lillian blushed. "Sir, I fear I may have given you the impression that—"

"You seemed keen on the subject of mental anguish. This stuck with me, somehow. Do you have a patient who is anguished?"

"No," she said honestly. *Not anymore*, her mind silently added. Her pulse quickened.

"Because if you did," said Dr. Bauer as he stood up, "or if you do in the future," he continued as he took a few steps and gently sat on her footstool, "that would put you in a difficult position, would it not?"

"Very difficult, sir." Did he know something? Suspect something? She swallowed but it felt like something was stuck in her throat. "I would report it to the senior nursing staff." She hoped this was the right response.

"Or to any senior staff. Could even be a doctor."

The idea of going over the heads of the senior nurses to report something directly to a doctor was ludicrous, but she said nothing. She focused on the fact that he was not touching her and that he had not accused her of anything. That nothing irreversible had happened yet.

"And yet, I find you breaking the rules," Dr. Bauer said, tilting his head slightly to one side.

Lillian froze. Her mouth was bone dry.

He reached a hand under the hem of her skirt and carefully brought out her foot. "You have not taken your shoes off before entering my study." A smile emanated from under his thin mustache.

She knew an apology was the conversational expectation, but she could not animate herself. This didn't seem to bother Dr. Bauer at all. Lillian watched as he balanced her heel on his knee and tugged at the ends of her shoelaces, two tiny tugs as if testing the tightness of the knot. Then he pulled delicately in a continuous motion until the bow helplessly fell apart. The situation was unspooling in agonizing slow motion and yet was also moving way too quickly for Lillian to react.

It wasn't until he removed her stocking and she felt his smooth hands on the tender arch of her foot that she could move, and it was only because the sensation was so startling that she spilled her tea. She had not even realized she was still holding the cup, but the tea was still hot enough to burn her wrist where it splashed. She sprang from the chair and took two steps toward the door before she realized that she was only wearing one shoe. As she spun and reached back to grab the shoe from the floor, Dr. Bauer grabbed her wrist, painfully—intentionally?—in the same place the hot tea had landed.

"Lillian, I hope you are all right," he said quietly.

She could not meet his eyes. "I've got to go. I've made a mistake. I'm sorry." Her voice trembled.

"There's no mistake." He uncoiled his fingers one by one from around her wrist. "And I'll see you next week."

By the time she was about to put her key in the door to her apartment, she felt more desperate than when running down Dr. Bauer's street with one shoe in her hand. She started the day thinking that her worries at the hospital were receding, and that she could somehow rectify her reckless actions in Dr. Bauer's study last week. Instead, the twin horrors in her life intersected in the span of a few minutes and she was more panicked about them than ever. She ran their conversation over and over in her mind. Was he saying that he knew something about Mrs. Sokolova? Or just that he would be checking up on her patients from now on? Or just fishing around based on her strange insistence last week that they discuss ending a patient's life? She thought she might be sick and grabbed the door-frame but the feeling passed after a few deep breaths.

Josephine was as chipper as ever. Josephine, who had advised her against continuing on with Dr. Bauer. Lillian could barely look her in the eye.

"Well," said Josephine, "we found a new use for them old news-papers today. Hope ya don't mind that we took your dress from the mending pile and stuffed it full of crumpled up balls of the stuff. The old girl's propped up in the bedroom, might scare the water outta ya but Marie's still in there havin' a ball... hey, what's goin' on?"

"Josephine, I am so... I am so stupid." She cradled her face in her hands.

They sat at the kitchen table in silence for a moment until Lillian could talk. "You told me that I shouldn't play games with Dr. Bauer. Not to believe I could control the situation. And you were right."

"That prick. Could you be up the pole in a month?"

It took a few seconds for Lillian to translate Josephine's slang. "No, no, nothing like that."

"OK, well that's somethin'. You want to tell me what happened?"

"He... he..." Every way she could think to phrase it sounded ridiculous, but she pressed on. "He took off my shoe. He held my foot." She laughed so harshly it hurt the back of her throat. "I can't explain. Forget it."

"Can you forget it?"

"No," Lillian whispered.

"Listen to me," said Josephine, and she pulled her chair a little closer to Lillian's. "I seen a man drop his pants in front of me and not felt the least bit threatened, and I had a man kiss my hand as soft as you please and I feared for my life. It ain't just about what they do."

Lillian leaned over and wrapped her arms around Josephine, and she let the tears soak into Josephine's collar as she sobbed.

When the wave of sadness ebbed, Josephine handed her a dishrag for her face. "If you go back there, to his home, you know what's gonna happen. So you can't go back there. Tell him at the hospital. Give whatever reason you want, even if it don't make sense. The worst that can happen is you lose your job. But it'll keep his paws offa you."

But that's not the worst thing that could happen to me, she thought. How could she explain this? That she took a life but it seemed like the right thing to do? That she committed a crime and felt justice would be served if she got away with it? That it was unclear whether Dr. Bauer knew anything about it, but if he did, it was completely her fault by broaching the subject with him?

Lillian looked over at Josephine. Josephine's eyes peered out below her mop of curls. She looked as if the sordid business of her former life had left no mark on her, and Lillian felt a pang of envy. "I'm afraid," she told Josephine.

"Every path from here has got some afraid in it. Choose the one that's gonna let you sleep better."

She couldn't imagine any of them would let her get much rest.

🦚 Chapter 32 🦚

The next day, Lillian checked the schedule and saw that Dr. Bauer had a morning surgery, which would mean he would be in his office afterward writing up his surgical notes. She tried to stick close to the wards to see when the patient was wheeled back in, but hours later no one had arrived. As she was assisting with a dressing change on a double mastectomy, Lillian asked the nurse, "Wasn't a surgical patient supposed to return to the wards?"

The nurse looked at her and shook her head before resuming wrapping bandages around the carved and ravaged torso.

Lillian made a beeline for Dr. Bauer's office as soon as the dressing was done, but she stopped in the stairwell to gather her thoughts before she reached his floor. Her knees shook as she thought of her last encounter with Dr. Bauer, and her thoughts tried to turn her around and walk her back down the stairs. *He's a doctor. You're not even a nurse. You encouraged him. He will fire you. You need this job. It's not that bad at his residence. Nothing improper has even happened.* She turned and started to descend.

But then she thought of Josephine. Josephine understood the underbelly of the world. When she had advised Lillian last night to make a break of it with Dr. Bauer, Lillian would have agreed without hesitation if it were not for her other fear: that Dr. Bauer suspected something about Mrs. Sokolova. But after Josephine left last night, Lillian decided this was unlikely. Maybe impossible. He took no interest in anything the nurses did at the hospital. Because his primary hospital was still Presbyterian, he acted as if he were merely bestowing surgeries upon their patients as acts of charity. The worst he could do, as Josephine said, was fire her for some trumped-up charge, and that seemed preferable to what might evolve in their weekly congregation.

Lillian turned and headed up the last few stairs, keeping the image of Josephine and her bobbing curls in the forefront of her mind.

Once she had knocked and entered, she was taken aback by the energy emanating from the pacing figure of Dr. Bauer. His brow was knitted, a forelock of hair sprung from the confines of his shiny pomade. One hand wrapped around the other fist.

"You are," he said evenly, "perhaps the last person I wish to see right now."

Lillian turned to go, recognizing that her timing was poor. She knew that the surgical patient's death this morning must be the cause of his anguish, but she doubted it had anything to do with sympathy for the woman now cooling on a gurney. Likely it was that he may have made a mistake that irked him so. But as she put her hand on the doorknob, she thought again of Josephine, and turned to face him.

"Sir, I am sorry for what happened."

"As if you could understand what it is to lose a patient. No one dies from an ill-changed bedpan," he sneered.

She pressed on past this insult, guessing that despite all he had said, he wanted to talk about it. "A challenging surgery?"

"It was not projected to be so! A quick, total hysterectomy, I should have been back at Presbyterian by lunchtime. But there was previously undiagnosed and pervasive endometriosis..." He went on for a few minutes as he paced, citing a vascular anomaly, a lack of good light in the operating theater, and a complaint about the sharpness of the scalpels at this hospital. It seemed that there were any number of reasons why this woman's death was not Dr. Bauer's fault.

Finally he was done with his tirade and sat down at his desk with a deep intake and exhalation of breath. "And I shall have to write up all of this," he said with irritation, but the energy had largely dissipated from him.

"I appreciate the work that lies ahead of you today, so I will be brief about my purpose in coming here." She pressed her knees together underneath her skirts to steady herself. "You have been kind to offer your wisdom to me on Thursday evenings but I'm afraid I can't continue." She held her breath and watched for his reaction.

"And why is that?" he asked. His face revealed nothing.

"I fear the other nurses may suspect I meet with you."

"Have you not been discreet?"

"I have tried my best but I fear it has not been good enough."

He leaned forward, planting his elbows on his desk, his mustache resting on his knitted fingers. He stared at her without blinking. "The hell with them. You are smarter than the lot."

Despite it all, she felt herself blush with pride to hear him say that. Yet another part of her knew this was what he wanted her to feel. "That is kind, but even if it were true, they have great power over me. And if one were to know, all would know within the day—they chatter constantly."

A long pause ensued, during which Lillian could hear all that was unsaid in this conversation. A memory surfaced unbidden of Helen making shadow puppets on the wall for her and Marie. Her mother's nimble hands in front of an oil lamp forming dogs and ducks and butterflies. This conversation with Dr. Bauer seemed like that shadow play, simple on the surface but far more complicated if one chose to look away from the wall to the contorted hands at the root of the illusion.

Dr. Bauer broke the silence. "I thought you were a risk-taker, Assistant Dolan. A girl with aspirations of putting her talents to use. But it seems I was mistaken. It seems the high opinion of the other nurses is more important to you."

She clenched her teeth, longing for this conversation to be over. "Sir, I think a while back I gave you the wrong impression. That I was more bold that I truly am. Perhaps it is how I wanted to be seen. But you can't oppose your true nature for long." She turned to go rather than wait to be dismissed. Anything to end this before it took a bad turn.

As she gripped the doorknob and turned it, she heard him say behind her, "Quite so. In the end, the truth will out."

A shiver ran down her spine.

Her relief was immense. She rushed down the stairs, turning her ankle on the landing in her hurry, but she ignored the stab of pain and proceeded on pace. Her corset, however, felt like it was squeezing the air out of her and so she ducked into the slop sink room to catch her breath. It would not do to show up on the wards huffing and puffing. The stink of urine was strong; she saw that someone had not adequately rinsed the sink. She turned on the faucet and swiveled it back and forth, watching the waste and water spiral down the drain.

He did not threaten to fire me, she said to herself, tingling with relief. *He was not overly angry. He went along with my pretext about the other nurses.* She turned off the faucet. *Was it too easy?* She immediately berated herself for seeing bad in what was undoubtedly a good outcome. But it really had gone so much better than she had a right to expect. And what did his last comment mean, "The truth will out"?

Janey breezed into the small room holding a pan aloft. "Vomitus, please make way," she sang as Lillian scooted to the side. "Mrs. Pratchett can't keep a thing down," she said as she rinsed the pan. She wrinkled her nose. "Have you been finding that someone isn't rinsing this sink properly?"

"As a matter of fact, yes," said Lillian.

"Two bits says it's Nurse Fiske. A corner-cutter, that one!" Janey declared as she rested the pan on a rack to dry. "I could use some help with Mrs. Pratchett's sheets—she sweat right through them like a racehorse at Pimlico. Are you with me?"

"I am," said Lillian, and she walked out of the slop sink room with Janey, leaving the smell of waste and any lingering worries behind.

✦ Chapter 33 ✦

As tumultuous as the first months at the hospital were, the next few were far less eventful. Deaths continued, in the wards and occasionally in the surgical theater. But Lillian was not invited to attend any more surgeries, and most of the deaths in the ward happened at night when she was not working. "Died in her sleep," the nurses told the families to soothe them, although Lillian often heard at the lunch table that dying during the night did not always mean going peacefully.

Dr. Bauer ignored her in the hospital now as effectively as he had always ignored her, thought it felt different to Lillian. Before, his snubs had felt like a secret shared, whereas now they were just snubs. At first she had felt a bit deflated; there was no one now who believed she was especially smart or promising. But she got used to the fact that that had all been a lie anyway, and those false feelings of her own importance were not worth acquiescing to Dr. Bauer's perversions.

At first she had wondered often about how easily he had let her go, but she soon came to think that she had overestimated his desire for her. She realized a man in his position could have any number of other women who would not resist him, at Presbyterian or in his life outside of work. She was just a minor trinket he wanted in his collection but was happy to pass up when the cost was more than he expected.

Thanksgiving and Christmas came and went, both spent with Michael and his family and Bridget. Aunt Fiona was over the moon about Michael's announcement that he and Bridget would wed. Her only disappointment was that the wedding was not to be until the late spring, a delay that Michael would not explain. His father, second only to Fiona in his joy, was unperturbed. "Marriage is forever, what's a few months of waiting?" he proclaimed, beer in one hand as he clapped Michael on the shoulder with the other. Only Lillian who was studying Michael's face saw that he flinched at that clap before quickly recovering with an affirmation and a smile.

Josephine had not mentioned Michael to Lillian for a while, and after Christmas dinner featuring Fiona's famous turkey with oyster sauce, Michael admitted to Lillian that he and Josephine had fallen out. "She's being so pig-headed," Michael groused as they washed dishes while the rest of the family and Bridget digested the heavy meal in the front parlor. "I know she doesn't agree with my decision, but that's no reason to cut me off completely."

Lillian had not pushed Michael on the subject of his marriage plans since their trip back from the Bowery, but it was more because of the events in her own life occupying her mind rather than any generosity in respecting his choice. Embarrassed by her lack of involvement, she pressed on with vigor now. "It's not right that Josephine won't speak to you, but it's born of worry, and I am equally worried about you. More so, in fact."

"Really, Lilypad. Because you've been strangely silent on the matter these past months." Michael continued to scrub the roasting pan without looking up.

Lillian blushed. "I've been... caught up in myself. There were things that happened. At the hospital. It's all worked out now, but it wasn't clear if I was in trouble. My job, if my job was in trouble." She cleared her throat. "But it's all worked out now."

Now Michael stopped scrubbing the pan and looked up, frowning. "And all this happened, and you mentioned nothing to me."

"Well, I knew you had so much on your mind, I didn't want to burden you with..." This was a lie, and she didn't bother to finish a sentence that Michael was not going to believe.

"Didn't we agree that we don't keep things from each other? Or was that another cousin of mine?" He rinsed off the pan, banging it around in the sink in irritation.

"You don't understand, I couldn't involve you. I wanted to tell you, I wanted your help but it was too…" She stopped herself before she revealed too much. This was all in the past and the last thing she wanted to do was stir it up again.

Michael turned to her, the wet pan in his hands. He squinted a bit in confusion, his irritation dissolving. "Too what, Lilypad? What happened? Why couldn't you involve me?"

She took the pan from his hands and put it back in the sink, then hugged him. "It's nothing. It's over. Please, I want to talk about you."

He kissed Lillian on the forehead. "Well, I'm fine. Bridget is growing on me. She's nicely chatty, not too chatty. An excellent seamstress. We will have curtains that will be the envy of the block."

"Can she cook?" asked Lillian.

"Oh, she's a dreadful cook. We will be a regular fixture back here for Sunday dinner."

Lillian imagined Michael and Bridget at Fiona's table every Sunday afternoon, how happy everyone would be, how excited his parents would be the day they announced that they were with child. At least, she assumed that day would come. "Michael, will you be able… will you have children? Is that possible?"

He laughed. "I believe I can muddle through," he said with a grin.

"That's wonderful! I mean, about the children. You will be such a good father."

"Yes, it's all mapped out for me now, isn't it?" His smile remained but the happiness had leaked out of it.

Lillian lowered her voice, although no one was close enough to hear them. "You can still change your mind. Be true with me, no making jokes. Is this the right path for you?"

He gripped her shoulders and gently brought his forehead to hers. "This path is very clear. This path makes so many people happy, and I like her. The alternative, there is no path. I don't know what that looks like. I'm not sure what I would be choosing."

Lillian thought of their neighbor from long ago with his "nephew" Tobias. He had found some sort of path, hadn't he? But she said nothing. If Michael could make his peace with his decision, who was she to steer him toward a life of difficulty?

🦎 Chapter 34 🦎

The frigid winds of January rattled the tall windows in the wards. Designed to admit sunshine and fresh air in balmy months, the windows provided mostly noise and draft in the winter. Nurses who had been around for several years knew to jam rolled up blankets along the sills, much to Nurse Holt's disapproval after reviewing the budget for supplies. But she didn't remove them, given that some patients were still complaining of the cold.

New admissions fell off a bit in the colder months. Janey theorized that the frail ones would rather suffer at home than brave the elements and a trip up 8th Avenue. The unpaved street, rutted in the muddy late fall, had frozen with its peaks and valleys, made worse by snow pushed here and there by carriage wheels. Walking from the El station, Lillian made better time than the vehicles on the street.

One Monday as Lillian began her shift, Nurse Larson told her about the new admission over the weekend. "Haven't had one like this in a while. Police brought her in, wandering in the park, no coat, old as the hills. Can't tell us her name but she's aware of her cancer. Palpable mass in her abdomen. Dehydrated when she arrived but she's coming around. Make sure her water glass stays full. No whiskey for this one until the doctor says she's hydrated enough. See if you can get any information about her identity." They walked to the patient's bedside. "Meet Jane Doe," said Nurse Larson before she made her way back to the central desk.

To Lillian's eye, Jane Doe looked impossibly old and improbably happy. A halo of curly white hair surrounded a wizened face with eyes like little sapphires. Her smile revealed more teeth missing than present. "Hello, my dear," she said, her enunciation clear as a bell despite her dentition.

"And you are....?" Lillian asked, hoping for a moment of clarity.

Mrs. Doe looked momentarily confused. "It will come to me, I'm sure. Your name, on the other hand, interests me greatly."

"I am Assistant Nurse Dolan. You must keep drinking water." She brought the water glass from the table and placed it in Mrs. Doe's hand.

"Now I'm sure your mother didn't name you Assistant. What is your given name, child?"

"Lillian. Lillian Dolan."

"Lillian! Why that's lovely. Like that beautiful Lillian Russell on Broadway." She smiled, unashamed or unaware of her teeth, and then sipped from her water glass daintily.

Talking with Jane Doe felt both comforting and dangerous. All these many months since she had helped Mrs. Sokolova, she had taken pains to distance herself from patients. Occasionally this meant being somewhat brusque, even cold. But she was resolved to take Janey's advice and not become drawn in to the personalities of the patients. In this case, however, Nurse Larson had asked her to see if she could find out more about Mrs. Doe's identity, and how could she do that without establishing some rapport?

Lillian sat down on the side of the bed, glad to use her assigned task of probing this woman's memory as an excuse to rest her feet. She looked at the woman's hands. No wedding ring, but the dehydration made her fingers as thin as pencils—perhaps it slipped off. Or was stolen. "Are you married, ma'am?"

"Certainly! Oh, if you could only have seen my bouquet as I walked down the aisle. White lilies as perfect as if they grew in God's Kingdom. And the scent! To make you swoon!" She closed her eyes and inhaled deeply as she floated in the memory, with no seeming perception that the air on the ward carried the essence of unemptied bedpans.

"So your husband's name is...?" Lillian let the sentence linger unfinished.

Jane Doe opened her eyes and her smile began to droop. "It's…
He's…." She reached for Lillian's hand and her good mood revived.
"He's very tall. And handsome!"

"Where is your husband now?"

"Oh, he's not with me anymore." The woman looked out the ward
window to some faraway place. Lillian didn't move, hoping Jane Doe
was reaching for some information deep in her mind that would help
place her. But after a breath or two, she turned to Lillian and said,
"How about you? Do you have a beau?"

After several more attempts that yielded nothing, Lillian excused
herself and walked back to the nurses station, where Nurse Larson
was filling out paperwork. "Anything?" she asked Lillian.

"Her husband was tall and handsome, but he's not with her anymore."

"You're a regular Scotland Yard detective!" She smiled as she
stuffed forms into a folder. "Well, that's more than we got out of her.
You know, the admitting doctor thought she might be as old as 75!"

"Really." Lillian tried to think if she had ever met anyone that
old. The oldest person she could remember being admitted to the
hospital was just over 60.

"Look on the bright side," said Nurse Larson. "She can't even remember her husband leaving her, or dying or whatever happened to
him."

Lillian nodded but thought of all the good things Jane Doe
couldn't remember about her tall, handsome husband.

For the rest of the week, Lillian took it on as her personal mission
to find out more information about their Jane Doe. It was a relief
not to have to fabricate a wall of indifference, because she was often
intrigued by the patients' personal stories. The Posh Row residents
didn't interest her much; they often treated their time there like a
stay in a hotel that wasn't up to snuff. But the women on the wards
were often as stoic as they come. Many of them had been suffering
for a long time, working at their jobs through their pain, refraining
from mentioning it to their family, hoping it would go away. Lillian
wondered what she would do if she ever discovered a lump on her

body. Would she go straight to a nurse or a doctor? Or just quietly hope for the best? She had seen what happens when women come to the hospital only when life becomes unbearable, and those stories never had a happy ending. Almost no one came at the first sign of trouble. But if they did, could the doctors really cure them? There was no way to know. Even if a dozen early-stage patients walked through the door tomorrow, the hospital wouldn't know their fate after they were treated and left.

She assumed Nurse Larson had told the other nurses that Lillian was helping with Jane Doe's identity, because none of them came by to criticize her when she spent more and more time sitting beside Jane Doe's bed. Since the wards were only half full, work was light anyway. On the whole, their time together was unremarkable, with one exception. One day, as Jane Doe was telling Lillian about how much she enjoyed seeing H.M.S. Pinafore with her husband, whose name she still could not recall, she stopped and looked over Lillian's shoulder. "That one," she whispered and pointed to Nurse Fiske, who was passing by with a patient's lunch tray.

"You mean Nurse Fiske?" asked Lillian.

"Yes, she's been stealing from me."

Lillian started to laugh before she caught herself. Jane Doe had nothing to steal, not even a wedding ring. But Lillian could see from the expression on Jane Doe's face that this was not said in jest. It was hard to know how to respond. After a moment, Lillian said, "What is it that you think Nurse Fiske stole from you?"

"Oh, this is no one-time occurrence. She's been doing this for months. All my jewelry, piece by piece. She thinks I don't notice. But I'm on to her."

Given that Jane Doe came to the hospital less than a week ago and was admitted with no possessions, Lillian knew this was not so. She squirmed in her seat. "I can assure you—-"

"I want to make a formal complaint. That nurse should be dismissed."

"Perhaps you should have some water." Lillian picked up the water glass from the table. The woman couldn't still be dehydrated after so many days in the hospital, but it couldn't hurt as Lillian stalled for time to think. "Here."

Jane Doe knocked it away. "You're not listening!" Now she was soaked from shoulder to shoulder, though she seemed not to notice. "I want to register a complaint!"

Lillian saw Nurse Fiske approaching to help. "I will get you dry clothing," she said quickly and intercepted Nurse Fiske. "Just a water spill. She's agitated, I'd stay away if I were you. I'll take care of it." Nurse Fiske looked all too happy to turn on her heel and avoid the situation.

As Lillian dug around for a new patient gown, irritated that some-one had mixed linens in with the gowns, she thought about how she would report this to Nurse Larson, this disconnection with re-ality, this paranoia. Should the woman be transferred to the lunatic asylum? She seemed so normal otherwise, aside from her gaps in memory.

By the time Lillian returned to the bedside, Jane Doe was beam-ing. "And you are, my dear?"

"I'm Lillian," she said, as she had said many times before.

"So pleased to meet you. I'm Rose."

Lillian's eyebrows shot up but she kept her voice neutral. "Hello Rose. And your last name?"

She looked down at her chest. "I seemed to be soaked through. Can you help me before I catch my death?"

Lillian quickly changed her gown and left Rose happy as a clam while she beetled over to the nurses' station, though Nurse Larson was not there. She found her upstairs on Posh Row and waited for the patient there to finish a long list of complaints against the hos-pital. When she was finally able to proudly tell Nurse Larson in the hallway that Rose had a name, Lillian had forgotten all about Rose's bout of paranoia.

The next evening, Lillian was trudging home from her El stop, wea-ry from an especially busy day where her only moments sitting down were in the lavatory, when she spied a woman descending the steps of her building. She was bundled against the cold in a coat Lillian did not recognize, but the hat was all too familiar. Even without the hat, Lillian would have had no trouble identifying her own mother.

"Hey!" Lillian called out, but the wind swept her words away.

"*Hey!*" The woman hurried down the street, and Lillian started after her, but then stopped. Did she really want to talk to her mother? And more importantly, what had she been doing here? Lillian looked up at the window to her apartment and felt a red hot anger bubbling up inside of her.

She burst into the apartment, startling Josephine. "Hell's bells and little fishes!" Josephine exclaimed. "You scared the p—"

"What was she doing here?" demanded Lillian.

Josephine waited a beat as she considered her answer. "She was checking up on her daughter."

Lillian unpinned her hat and threw it on the floor, just so she could have something to throw. "And who said she could do that?"

"And who said she couldn't? Not like you left instructions on the matter. 'If my Ma shows up, turn her out on the street like a dog.' Now that woulda been clear."

Lillian paced in the small kitchen. Of course, Josephine was right. She hadn't mentioned her mother. But her anger could find no other target. "She is never to come in this apartment again. One time is one time too many." She saw Josephine look away briefly and understood. "This is not the first time. How long has she been coming here?" She concentrated on not strangling Josephine before she had a chance to answer.

"Listen, I will tell you everything but you gotta sit down and calm down. You want some tea?"

Lillian sat down at the table with Josephine and took a deep breath. "I will sit and I will be calm but we are not having a tea party and I need to know everything about my mother. And you can start with how she even knew where we live."

"Well, she did tell me that. Turns out my pal Mrs. Sweeney across the way heard about your swarthy friend walking you home a few weeks back when you were in your cups. Not sure why it took so long for her to hear, but lickety split she got word to your Ma."

"*What?*" Even for a busybody like Mrs. Sweeney, this seemed outrageous. She only knew Helen through Aunt Fiona and had probably only talked with her a handful of times.

"Yep. Seems she felt an obligation to let yer Ma know that you were fraternizing with an 'African', I believe was the phrase. Or maybe yer Ma cleaned that up for me. Interesting that the fact you were three sheets to the wind that night weren't important."

"So my mother came here to criticize my choices when she is the last person who should—"

"I gotta stop you right there," interrupted Josephine. "Yer Ma didn't give a good goddamn about Jupiter. She pretended to with Mrs. Sweeney to get your address. She just wanted to see you and Marie."

"She gave up that right! She should have thought of that before!" Lillian paused. "Did she tell you what she did? Why we left?"

"No, and I didn't ask. She said there was a misunderstanding."

Lillian snorted. "A misunderstanding. What whitewash." She clenched her fists. "How many times has she come here?"

"Just twice. Today was the second time. She begged me not to tell you, that she wanted to tell you herself, soon. I told her it wasn't right and I was gonna tell you today."

"And I'm supposed to believe that?" Lillian shot back.

Josephine cocked her head as she looked at Lillian, and then she stood up. "I've had about enough of this conversation. You know, one of the things yer Ma asked me about was how I felt about this job. Something you ain't been that interested in askin' me. And I told her true, that money was gettin' tight and I didn't know how much longer this was gonna work out."

"Of course! So that she can push you out and then she is the only option I have to take care of Marie? Over my dead body!"

Josephine pinned on her trilby and looked at Lillian with disappointment. "If you want to see it that way, that's your choice. But pretty soon you are going to have to find someone else for Marie."

As Josephine closed the door behind her, Lillian trembled with equal parts rage and fear. The small corner of her brain that was not lit up with hot emotion realized that she had handled that badly. Josephine was not her enemy. Far from it; in fact, without Josephine she was... well, she was in trouble. And her mother would be back at some point for a conversation that Lillian was not prepared to have. She walked away from the past to erase it, but now it was seeking her out. She planted her elbows on the table and covered her face with her hands.

❧ Chapter 35 ❧

"Assistant Dolan!" The clerk at the front desk flagged her down the next morning before she could even clear the lobby. Lillian wished that whatever it was, it could have happened on a day where she wasn't running late. To Lillian's great relief, Josephine had shown up at her usual time, and while she had not been very chatty, neither did she give her notice. But Marie had thrown herself down on the bed this morning to roll around just where Lillian had laid out her blouse for the day, and Marie's sticky mouth from her honey bread breakfast made landfall in all the wrong places. By the time Lillian could iron another blouse, tapping her toe while the iron heated on the stove, all her plans to arrive at work with plenty of time had fallen to pieces.

"Yes," she said as she approached the desk. "Can this wait until I have my cap and uniform? I can come straight away—"

"You are to report to Nurse Holt's office. Directly." The clerk had the satisfied look of someone imparting bad news.

Lillian held her head high as she walked, refusing to succumb to apprehension. This could be anything, she told herself. There had been no mishaps recently. A few late arrivals, but no reprimands, and she had finished last week with the victory of procuring part of Rose's identity, which no one else had managed to do. She had nothing to fear.

When she arrived, Nurse Holt told her to wait on the bench outside. As the minutes ticked away, she remembered sitting on this very bench as she waited for her interview. She recalled how Nurse Holt had warned her about punctuality. Perhaps that was what this was about. She wished she had not been late today, of all days, but compared to things she had faced before in this building, this couldn't be much to worry about.

She heard the unmistakable clicks of a doctor's footsteps coming from the long hallway around the corner. Lillian had long ago tuned her ear to the energetic rustle of nurses' skirts and the long, noisy strides of the doctors. Janey had claimed she could identify each doctor solely by the sound of their footsteps on the long tiled hallways, and Lillian tried to do this now. Definitely not Dr. Snelling, who had a more timid gait, and not Dr. Featherstone who was too short for these strides. In fact, it sounded most like…

Dr. Bauer rounded the corner and stopped in front of Nurse Holt's door. He looked at her pointedly with eyes glinting. "Shall we?" he asked.

Lillian's mouth went dry as she frantically tried to imagine why he would be here. She found she could not rise from the bench, nor could she look away from his stare.

"Don't make this worse," he said softly, and held out his hand.

The only thing she was sure of at that moment is that she would not touch him if she could avoid it. She rose unsteadily on her own steam and went through the door he politely held open for her.

Nurse Holt always had a perpetually grim look about her, but it was now apparent that there were further levels of displeasure possible. After a respectful head nod to Dr. Bauer who had lowered himself primly into a chair, she focused her unhappy gaze on Lillian. "You have been spending considerable time in conversation with patient Rose Travers, is that correct?"

Lillian blinked. "Travers? Is that her last name?" Despite the circumstances, she felt a thrill of pride at the thought that she had cracked the case of Rose's identity. When Nurse Holt didn't answer, Lillian digested the other part of the question. "Yes, I spoke extensively to Rose—Mrs. Travers—at the request of Nurse Larson who—"

"Nurse Larson says that she simply told you to see if you could ascertain her identity."

"Yes, of course, which I did through my conversations with her. It was how I figured out her first name." Perhaps Nurse Holt hadn't known that Lillian had been so helpful in this effort.

"There has been an accusation," stated Nurse Holt. The clock ticked twice in the silence that ensued. "There is no easy way to phrase this. Mrs. Travers says that you offered to end her life. Recommended it, in fact. And that she feared you would do this regardless of whether she consented."

Her mind struggled to process the nightmare that had bloomed before her. She was dimly aware of Dr. Bauer peering at her expectantly, as if he were gauging her reaction. Her fate seemed to hang on what happened next, what she said or did not say. To delay would make it appear that she was thinking too much about her reaction. "I never spoke with her about ending her life. In any way."

But though Lillian spoke the truth, she *was* thinking about her reaction, thinking very intensely. She couldn't let her experience with Mrs. Sokolova influence this situation with Rose in any way. Did she look guilty? What did guilty look like?

And then she remembered that Rose had a different accusation last week. "Nurse Fiske!" she blurted out, louder than she had intended. "Mrs. Travers accused Nurse Fiske of stealing her jewelry. Jewelry she did not have! And she said it had been happening for months, but she hasn't been here for months! Clearly she's off in the head. She might say anything."

"Did you tell anyone about this accusation of theft?"

"Of course." But then she remembered. "Well, I went to go tell Nurse Larson but after I told her about finding out Mrs. Travers' first name... I... forgot."

"You forgot." More ticks of the clock filled the room. "So this is something only *you* know about." When Lillian didn't respond, Nurse Holt continued. "Nurse Larson has found Mrs. Travers to be generally credible. There is much the woman can't remember, but no one has witnessed her stating fiction as fact."

As Lillian's whole life seemed to crumble around her, she looked over at Dr. Bauer. *What was he doing here?* He had not said a word so far. Was he here to support her or sentence her?

Nurse Holt began to speak again, but Dr. Bauer cut her off. "I'd like to speak to Assistant Dolan alone, if I might. I'm a tad confused about a few things on which I feel confident she can set me straight."

From the look on Nurse Holt's face, this was not how she had expected him to participate, but even the head nurse would not question a plan of action put forth by a doctor. "As you wish," she said. "I will be down the hall in the office when you need me."

As bad as this meeting had been so far, Lillian dreaded this next phase more. As Nurse Holt reached for the doorknob, Lillian had to restrain herself from grabbing her sleeve and begging her to stay.

After Nurse Holt's departure, Dr. Bauer got up and sat in her chair. He took some time to casually rearrange the things on the desk, though the surface was tidy enough. With a long index finger he pushed the ink well closer to the oil lamp, and his pinky aligned a pencil perpendicular to the blotter. When he was done, he looked up with an incongruous smile. "Lillian," he said warmly, and the familiarity sent a quake through her.

She forced her voice to be steady. "With respect, sir, why are you here? What is your involvement?" Though she feared the answer, she sensed Dr. Bauer might talk of pleasantries for a while just to dangle her on a string, which she could not bear.

"Ah, I've missed that. Your direct approach. Not one for chit-chat. Right to the heart of the matter." He ran his thumb over one side of his mustache, smoothing it down over and over. "It seems you are in a bit of a pickle."

"What Mrs. Travers said was completely false."

"So you say. Although her husband is fit to be tied. I think it's safe to say he is not inclined to believe you."

"Her husband?"

"Yes, he's been searching for her for a while. Evidently she wandered off some time ago and he has been bereft."

Lillian remembered Janey and Nurse Matheson talking about a man who would come in periodically to look for his wife. Was this the husband? Nurse Matheson's example of enduring love?

Dr. Bauer continued. "But back to your question. When I heard that this crone registered this... complaint against you, it triggered something in my memory. A bee in my bonnet, if you will. Something that had never sat quite right. About our last congress." He looked as though he were savoring that last word on his lips, a sweet taste lingering.

Oh no, please no, thought Lillian.

"You were quite adamant about discussing this very subject. I would even say, agitated. Insistent. It has a name, you know. Euthanasia. From the Greek, meaning 'easy death.' Not a new concept at all." He leaned back a bit, forcing a groan from Nurse Holt's chair. "Now, at the time I had chalked up your agitation to the, let's say, evolution of our relationship. Its unconventional aspects. And your fixation on this subject hadn't entered my mind since. But when I heard about dear Mrs. Travers' claim, I went back to my journal." He paused. "Did you know I kept a journal? No? Ever since my university days, I've jotted down my musings on the day's occurrences before bed each night. Wonderful exercise." He leaned forward a bit. "And I'll answer the question forming in your head: *Yes*, you are in there."

Lillian felt queasy. She gripped the seat of her chair tightly.

"So once I had the date of your distress, it was hardly any effort at all to look at the hospital records around that time. To see if anyone had unexpectedly shuffled off this mortal coil. And what do you think I found?"

Lillian tasted acid in the back of her throat.

"Some Russki woman who couldn't even talk took an unfortunate turn the *very next morning*! On the day of her transfer to a real hellhole. Quite a coincidence! I wonder what her children thought about that."

"She couldn't have children," Lillian said bitterly before she could stop herself. Too late she saw the satisfaction on Dr. Bauer's face. A heartbeat later she figured out that he was goading her into admitting her closeness with the patient. Oh, how stupid she was.

"Now my first thought was to call a few nurses into my office and ask about whether you were particularly close with this patient, or conversely, if you had any animosity toward her." He rose from his chair and headed toward her side of the desk. "But then I had another thought." As he passed by the door to the hallway, he lazily twisted the skeleton key in the lock, quick as a cat. It was so fast Lillian almost didn't see it, but the sound of the lock sliding into place was unmistakable. He positioned the chair next to hers so that it faced her directly and then sat in it. "I thought maybe I would just talk to *you* first."

She braced for what was coming. Could she convincingly deny she had anything to do with Mrs. Sokolova's death? She would have to try.

"So Lillian," Dr. Bauer said in low and patient tones, "did you have any discussions about intentional death with Mrs. Travers?"

Travers? Mrs. Travers? Wasn't he just talking about Mrs. Sokolova? "I'm not... I'm sorry, what..."

"Rose Travers. Did you threaten to kill Mrs. Travers?"

"No!" she said in a rush, anxious to answer honestly. "She's out of her head, I never even came close to talking to her about any such thing! I don't even know if her cancer is a hopeless case! She doesn't know what she's saying! She's mad as a hatter!" Tears burned in her eyes.

"All right then, I believe you. I can go out there and tell Nurse Holt that you said nothing of the sort, that the crone is senile and no harm was done. By the time I tell her husband that her abdominal mass is operable, everyone will move on. That was rather simple, wouldn't you say?"

Lillian could only allow herself a moment of exquisite relief before she recognized the fact that this was far from over.

She knew he would reach for her hands before he even moved to do so. When he gently gripped them, his hands rested in her lap, and she could feel the heat of them on her thighs, even through her skirt and petticoat. His voice was softer now. "But this other issue, your Mrs. Sokolova—am I pronouncing that correctly?—that's not so simple, is it? I think that subject will merit a much longer conversation, in a more comfortable place."

She managed to hold on through the statement of his terms, and when he unlocked the door, she bolted down the stairs and made it out the main doors before she vomited into the box hedge.

🦚 Chapter 36 🦚

Standing in front of Abraham's shop, Lillian reached for the door handle but then hesitated. All the way over here, on the southbound El and then walking to the East Side where Michael worked, she debated with herself. She knew what Michael's reaction would be: convinced she was doing the right thing involving him now, angry that she had not involved him earlier, devoted to helping her. But to go through that door and admit all of her decisions, all of her mistakes, all of her shame… she didn't want to see herself reflected in his eyes.

But it was too late for the luxury of that choice.

Once she passed through the door, Michael took only an instant to size up the magnitude of the problem. "Lilypad," he said as he came around from the counter.

"Is Abraham here?" she said hoarsely, looking around.

"He went down to Mendel Goldberg's to buy fabric. Just left."

"Can we sit in the back?"

"Sure, as long as I can see if anyone comes in."

As he guided her to the back room and hooked back the curtain that separated the two rooms, he said nothing. But as they perched on two stools amid the threads and fabric scraps, he took his hands in hers, in a manner so similar to Dr. Bauer's recent actions that she flinched and pulled her hands away.

"Lilypad?" Michael ventured, looking confused.

And then it all came tumbling out of her, words in a landslide of pebbles and boulders crazily spilling down a mountain, with little regard to sequence or severity. She could hear herself babbling and how her bouts of sobbing made some phrases incomprehensible, but she could not stop this unorganized confession.

When she was done and practically panting from the effort, she looked up at Michael, who was staring at her blankly. She gripped him by the shoulders. "Say something! Please! Tell me I'm not a monster! Tell me how to fix this! Tell me... tell me that you still love me!"

He placed a palm on each of her temples and kissed her forehead. "Of course I still love you."

"Michael," she whispered as fresh tears ran down her wet face, "I do not know what to do."

He got up from his chair and walked around the room, pushing scraps of fabric out of his way with his boot. He stared at the path he was clearing as he spoke. "So he suspects your... involvement in the death of this Russian woman, but does he have any proof?"

"I told you, I was going on and on with him asking him if it were ever the right thing to do to put someone out of their misery, at their request."

"But that's not proof. In fact, it's only his word against yours that you even had that conversation."

"But he is a doctor. Who would believe me?"

"Never mind that for now. Is there any proof beyond that conversation?"

"Well, her body went to the crematorium, so there could be no further examination of her body."

"All right. So you need to fight this. You need to be resolute in your denial."

She rose from her stool and intercepted his pacing. "But I did... help her. I told you. I did the very thing he suspects me of."

"Lillian, I understand that you performed a merciful act at the request of this woman. But it is a crime to end a life. You're going to need to deny it."

"What if I could come to an understanding with Dr. Bauer?"

He looked at her incredulously. "What are you suggesting?" But when she began to respond, he cut her off. "I can't even hear what you are about to say. This sort of thinking was what got you into this fix with him in the first place! But just in case you are tempted, consider this: Once he has his satisfaction from you, there is nothing stopping him from going to the authorities at that point. And then you will have lost your virtue *and* your freedom."

Lillian said nothing, letting the logic of what Michael said sink in.

"So I think we need to seek the advice of a lawyer."

"Michael, I have no money for that."

"Well, I have a bit of savings—"

She held up her hand. "Stop. You will not spend another penny on me. I have already set your life back more than I care to think about."

"We are talking about whether you walk free or sit behind bars. Think of Marie! You need a lawyer."

"I know." She got up from her stool, straightening her spine. "And I know how I will get one."

"You do?" Michael's eyebrows arched.

"Yes, I do."

As she approached the entrance to the hospital, she realized she was not clear on her status there. She had left her meeting with Dr. Bauer in a rush, and once her stomach calmed she had rushed to Abraham's shop, only thinking of her need to speak with Michael. But now, once she entered the building, would she be berated for the hours she missed? Or was she suspended from work? Or fired? Did Dr. Bauer make good on his word to clear her name concerning Rose Travers? She had not waited around to hear.

She stood on the entrance steps and looked to her left at her own vomit in the box hedge, now frozen. She formed a plan and then pulled the door open.

She managed to get to the crematorium without running into any who questioned her, despite the fact that she was not in uniform.

"Lillian," Jupiter said warmly. It looked like Jupiter had been cleaning some tools. He wiped his hands on his apron and invited her in. "You ain't got no gurney or no paperwork, so I hope nurses up there ain't wondering where that Lillian got to."

"I can't stay long, but I need a favor. I need some legal advice and would like to talk to your brother."

"You got some problem with yo landlord? Solomon helped out one of my neighbors on that kinda thing."

Lillian thought about how wonderful it would be if her problems were about her tenement building. "No, it's not about where I live. It's that... I may be accused of doing something wrong at the hospital." Her stomach knotted as the words came out of her mouth.

"That serious like it sounds?"

"Yes, I'm afraid it is."

Jupiter scratched at the back of his neck. "I'm happy to help you any way I can, my brother and everything, but I ain't sure what you need is his specialty. He mostly about property and such."

"I have no other choice, at least that I can think of. And I don't have much money. Really, I don't have any money." She hung her head. She knew she was abusing her friendship with Jupiter. But dragging Michael into this would be even worse.

"Well," said Jupiter with a little smile, "at least Solomon ain't no stranger to helpin' people that ain't got no money."

"Oh, thank you!" She bounded toward him and hugged him, and felt his arms and back stiffen. "I'm sorry, I didn't mean to..."

"Naw, it's all right. Just surprised is all." He looked down at his boots for a moment before he looked up again. "So when you want to talk to Solomon?"

"As soon as possible. I don't know quite how I would get out to Brooklyn but I can figure it out."

"You know, Solomon been meaning to come see Sonny, maybe I can get him over to the Kitchen. Not to mention he ain't been to see his little brother in a while."

"That would be wonderful. I don't know how to thank you!" She curbed her impulse to hug him again.

"You don't gotta thank me, at least until we see if Solomon can help you out."

"Well, I'm grateful no matter what." She turned to go but then thought of something else. "You haven't asked me what I've done. Or what I've been accused of."

"Don't matter to me. You need help, that's what I heard."

She closed her eyes and thought about whether she deserved this generosity.

Buoyed by accomplishing the first part of her plan, Lillian proceeded to Nurse Holt's office for the second. Whether she was suspended, fired, or welcomed back, she couldn't hide from her fate.

Of all the outcomes Lillian considered, the one that transpired was not one of them. She was sure that at a minimum, there would be some consequence for her leaving the premises this morning, but Nurse Holt seemed to be pretending that nothing had happened. "Assistant Dolan," she said to Lillian while jotting something down on a form, "they require you on the wards." Lillian waited for further commentary but none came. When Nurse Holt doggedly refused to look up from her desk, Lillian thanked her and left, closing the door softly behind her.

Janey intercepted Lillian after she donned her uniform and was checking that her cupcake was securely fastened. "It's all the talk," Janey said as they walked down the hallway. "That crazy old bat told anyone who could listen that you were a murderess with a heart as cold as a welldigger's rump. But then Dr. Bauer gave her the once-over and declared her senile, and dressed down old Holt for not calling him in sooner before they accused you! Best part is, all this ruckus pushed that chatter about Nurse Farrell's engagement to the back burner. She's been pouting all morning. Serves her right, waving that gaudy ring around in the lunch room."

Lillian murmured agreement and split off from Janey when they entered the ward, which brought her to Rose Travers' bed as if drawn by a magnet. "Hello, Mrs. Travers."

"Why, hello dear," she said amiably, crow's feet radiating from her twinkling eyes. "Tell me, what's your name?"

🦚 Chapter 37 🦚

The wind blew down 10th Avenue like a locomotive. Lillian and Jupiter gave up trying to have a conversation as they walked and just concentrated on making their hunched progress toward Sonny's. Once they scooted inside and shut the door, Lillian's cheeks burned as they warmed to the stuffy, smoky air in the saloon.

They stood together, scanning the room once their eyes started adjusting to the gaslight. Jupiter spotted Solomon at the bar talking with Sonny and trotted over to him, but Lillian was rooted in place. Even through the haze she could see Jupiter's brother clearly, more clearly, it seemed, than she could see others near him.

To say that he was handsome would be a statement of truth, but Lillian had seen other handsome men. There was also something familiar about him, though she could see it was just that he looked a lot like a taller version of Jupiter. It was as if Jupiter's features had made tiny migrations all in pleasing directions: Jupiter's close-set eyes were widened, his ears flattened, his lashes thickened. And yet all of that would not have moved Lillian if it hadn't been for the confidence that seemed to radiate from Solomon's every movement. Both Sonny and Jupiter were grinning at him and slapping his back as if he had hung the moon, and though he looked down with a grin and shook his head gently at whatever they were saying, he was clearly a man that was comfortable in his own skin.

She might have stayed there indefinitely, staring in fascination, but Jupiter came over and gently pulled her arm. "He's over here," Jupiter said, as if Lillian had not noticed.

Jupiter placed his hand on his brother's shoulder and, with a note of pride, said, "This is Solomon."

"A pleasure to meet you," said Solomon with a polite nod of his head. She took in the closer view and decided that she had not been generous enough in her assessment.

"Lillian, you all right?" said Jupiter with a frown of concern.

"Yes, of course, I'm perfectly...." She trailed off and then realized she ought to end that sentence. "Fine." She was vaguely aware that she should at least glance around at Jupiter and especially Sonny, whom she had not even greeted, but her eyes wanted to stay where they were.

Solomon, for his part, seemed in no way uncomfortable with her gaze. If anything, he seemed amused.

Sonny came around from the back of the bar. "Y'all can take my office, it's loud as hell in here." Sonny motioned them to follow him. Lillian looked back at Jupiter as she walked and saw him give a little wave of encouragement as he settled himself on a barstool.

Sonny's office had only one chair, which Solomon offered to Lillian as he perched on a crate of gin bottles, which clanked softly in their wooden box when he sat. Now that they were alone in this small room, her pulse quickened and it occurred to her that she had a problem. This man was the only one she knew who could save her from being arrested, maybe jailed, and her emotions were flitting about as if they had just met at a dance. She closed her eyes and told herself that she was here to answer his questions about all the terrible things that had happened. She forced herself to think about the needle going into Mrs. Sokolova's arm, the sound of the lock sliding home in Nurse Holt's door, the revolting heat of Dr. Bauer's hands in her lap. She took a deep breath.

"Lillian, are you all right?" Solomon asked.

Lillian opened her eyes and nodded. "Let me tell you what happened."

In contrast to her chaotic confession to Michael, Lillian's

chronicle for Solomon was fairly organized. It was as if she were telling a story about someone else's actions. It helped her to not look at Solomon directly. He stopped her several times to ask clarifying questions, but mostly he let her speak, until she got to the part about the Dr. Bauer's threats.

"Wait," Solomon said, "go back to the part about the newspaper."

"He said that newspapers love sensational stories, and that there was one just last year about a female surgeon who killed a bunch of patients. In Brooklyn, actually. Did you hear about it? Is it true?" Lillian clung to a hope that Dr. Bauer had made that up to scare her.

Solomon hopped off the gin crate and started pacing slowly in the small room. "Heard about it? You couldn't not hear about it. Dr. Mary Dixon Jones. Every newsie was calling out the highlights from the courtroom." Solomon tapped his index finger against his upper lip, deep in thought. "It all started in the Brooklyn Eagle. I actually know the editor there. He said they had a big increase in sales running the exposé."

"All from one story?"

"That's not the way this kind of thing goes. When they have a story with, well, drama to it, let's say, they dole it out in pieces. *Serialize* is the word. Dixon's exposé ran for weeks. The interest builds over time, more and more readers catching on. And they were fascinated by this story. All the people who never trusted the medical profession felt this proved their point."

Lillian's heart sank. "So Dr. Bauer is right? I will be infamous?" Her palms began to sweat.

He leaned against Sonny's desk. "I'll be honest with you. It's not good news that this doctor is already thinking about the newspaper angle. These stories whip up public opinion before the real legal action starts, and it makes it more challenging to get a fair shake. But his hands aren't entirely clean in all this."

She looked into his eyes, so much like Jupiter's, and then realized something. "You don't speak like your brother at all."

"No, I don't. I did, back in Alabama." He walked over and plunked down on the gin crate again. "In law school, at least my law school, that was part of your education. Your transformation. Every Howard professor has a version of a speech that goes something like, 'You can go back to speaking like your mama any time you want, but to be taken seriously in the white man's world, you need to speak his language. You need to be bilingual.' If they called on you and you said 'he ain't' or 'she don't', they would ignore you and call on someone else, even if you had the right answer."

"So how do you speak with Jupiter? Or with your mother when you see her?"

He looked at her for a heartbeat. "We really need to talk about your legal situation."

"Yes, yes, I'm sorry," she said, flustered. What must he think of her, that she could chat about his family when she was facing such a serious situation?

"Where were they planning on taking Mrs. Sokolova?"

"Blackwell's Island." She had overheard this from a pair of nurses the day before Mrs. Sokolova's scheduled transfer.

Solomon frowned. "I didn't know there was a medical institution there."

"Well, if you call the lunatic asylum a medical institution, there is."

"Are you saying that they were transporting a paralyzed woman to a *mental* institution?"

Lillian nodded. "She didn't have cancer anymore, and she didn't have money to hire a nurse to care for her at home."

"Is that standard practice?"

"I don't know." She thought about it. During her tenure at the hospital, every patient who left either walked out 'cured' of their cancer or had died.

Solomon rubbed his eyes. "This city. It can eat you up." He took a deep breath. "When has Dr. Bauer asked you to come to his residence?"

Lillian blushed at the thought of this. "Thursday. Always Thursdays." She felt ill thinking about his study.

"All right. I have some ideas, and Thursday gives us some time to work something out. Keep thinking of any other details you may have forgotten that could help us."

She turned the word "us" over in her mind and it made her feel warm all over. But it seemed too good to be true. "Solomon, Jupiter did tell you that I can't pay you, at least right way, didn't he?"

"He did." He hopped off the gin crate, bottles clanking, and brushed the dust from his pants.

"I'm so grateful, but I'm curious as to why you would do this. For me." She feared this might cause him to reconsider, but she had to know.

"Well, I could say it's because you are a friend of Jupiter's, and that would be partially true, but your hospital… it has some history. Having to do with our family."

"Jupiter told me about your aunt."

Solomon looked relieved that he did not have to explain. "Yes. That's how I ended up here. I followed him up here to make sure that he didn't do anything crazy. I stayed in Brooklyn with friends of my family, and one thing led to another. There is a lot of legal need there in the Negro community." He gently ran a slim index finger along the edge of the desk. "But I understood Jupiter's rage. That's not my way, but I loved my Auntie too. And you have to understand that this doctor, Sims, he did fix her. Her life was a misery before, and the fix stuck. It's just that he could have done it without any pain, and he chose not to. Which does make him a monster."

"But you know Sims is dead."

"Exactly. And now there is another doctor at that hospital who is using his position to do something wrong, and he thinks he can get away with it because he's a doctor. But maybe this one won't."

Lillian thought about this, a sort of sideways justice. She could understand it.

Solomon picked up his coat and hat. "But I must tell you, because I always try to be honest with my clients. I am not a criminal lawyer. I mostly help with property disputes. I cannot guarantee that I can help you."

She looked him full in the face, something she had been avoiding, and her whole body warmed. "I am better off with you than without you."

Chapter 38

They had arranged to meet at Sonny's again on Wednesday after work, but Josephine had a bout with bad oysters the night before and sent an urchin with a note that said she could not come. Lillian sent a note in the morning mail to work saying she was sick and one to Solomon requesting that he come to her apartment. Michael usually came to visit on Wednesday evenings and she welcomed his presence for this meeting. She needed all the support she could get, and if Marie decided to act up, Michael could help out.

She was just explaining to Michael that the lawyer she had secured was coming over when they heard a knock at the door. When Solomon walked in, Lillian experienced that same relaxation she had felt in Sonny's office. There was just something about Solomon that made her feel hopeful.

As she introduced Solomon to Michael, who shook hands with a look of mild wonder on his face, Lillian realized she had forgotten to tell Michael that Solomon was Negro.

"He's Jupiter's brother. You know, who runs the crematorium."

"You and your brother went in somewhat different job directions," said Michael as they all sat down at the kitchen table. Lillian was thankful she remembered to borrow a chair from Mrs. Sweeney so they could all sit.

"We did indeed," said Solomon. "Although I'd like to think that Jupiter is bound for bigger and better things."

"So," said Lillian, "I don't mean to rush things along but while Marie is content in the other room, we should talk." Lillian had told Solomon about Marie at Sonny's while they were arranging their next meeting, but she knew the length of frilly lace Michael had brought Marie tonight would only entertain her for so long.

"I wish I had better news," said Solomon. "I did a little research into the hospital's practice of transferring patients to Blackwell's. They have done it several times before. It's not common practice for other hospitals, maybe because they have more of an obligation to treat all medical conditions. Even then, for patients who cannot pay, I would guess that there are ways they send these patients off somewhere. But as for your hospital, I'm not sure how we can use this information to help you. It doesn't appear that the hospital broke any laws."

Michael turned to Solomon. "You are obviously an educated man, so forgive me this question, but you cannot really represent my cousin in a courtroom, can you? I mean, this isn't Brooklyn. If you take my meaning."

"If your meaning is that I am a Negro, the fact is that I *could* legally represent Lillian. But it would be a mistake. Putting aside the fact that I am not a criminal lawyer, your case would become sensational for the color of my skin, and you would be unlikely to have an impartial judge. I wouldn't do it even if you asked me. It could put both Lillian and me in some danger."

They all let that sink in before Michael said, "So given that tomorrow is Thursday, and this monster is expecting Lillian to waltz into his study, what do you recommend she do?"

"If it were my cousin or sister, I would advise her not to go. It's possible Dr. Bauer will not follow through on his threat."

"That's an awfully big gamble to take," said Lillian.

"The bigger gamble is to show up at his doorstep," said Solomon. He looked discouraged. "The problem is that you have no leverage."

Lillian stood up and walked the length of the small kitchen and then turned around. "But I think we actually may have leverage." An idea was sprouting in her mind, and when she sat down at the table, Solomon and Michael leaned in as she began to talk.

They talked for another half hour, although for a while Michael went to occupy Marie as Lillian and Solomon kept working out the details. Finally they could think of nothing more to add.

"So you realize you cannot continue to work at the hospital after this."

Lillian was tempted to challenge this assertion, but resisted the urge. She needed to do whatever would make it most likely they would succeed. "I understand."

"And that if this doesn't work, you may be charged, and I can't represent you. A lawyer will be assigned to you but you won't have a choice in the matter."

"Then it will just have to work, won't it?" She raised her chin in defiance of failure.

"She's braver than the both of us," Michael murmured to Solomon, who nodded his head.

When Solomon left, Michael leaned up against the door and stared at Lillian, one side of his mouth tilted upward in a smile that was familiar to Lillian from their childhood.

"What," she said. "I know that look. You have something to say, so let's hear it."

"Perhaps it's you that has something to say."

"Michael, I don't have time for games. I'm in a lot of trouble here, if you haven't noticed."

"Oh, I've noticed. Which is why it is so curious that I felt such interesting... currents in your kitchen tonight. Practically an undertow, I would say."

She stood up and busied herself at the sink with the dishes that had piled up today. "Silly goose. Stop imagining things." She clanked the dishes together noisily.

"I'm not good at everything, but one thing I am good at is picking up on attraction. I can size up the people in a saloon before I even reach the bar, but it's even easier when everyone is sober. So don't waste your breath trying to deny it."

"Fine," she said, and turned around, wiping her wet hands on the rag by the sink. "He is handsome and I may be a bit... distracted by him. Temporarily. I'm sure it's because he is my knight in shining armor, saving me."

"And yet, it looked like you saving yourself. Who came up with the plan, after all?"

She sat down at the table, too tired to pretend, and Michael sat next to her. "All right," she admitted. "I confess. Though I don't even know him, I have feelings for him. I have no experience with this. My heart has chosen the worst possible time, with the most inappropriate man I could choose, one that will soon be out of my life whether our plan succeeds or fails, one that looks at me as a friend of his brother's and an interesting legal case."

Michael laughed and tilted his chair back. "Really. He's interested in your 'legal case.' To build his burgeoning criminal lawyer career. Or because it's so convenient to come here from Brooklyn." He brought his chair down and got up to reach for his coat and hat. "All right, if that's what you think. So I'll be here tomorrow night to see how it all went, let's say around-"

"Michael." She stared him down. "Finish your thought."

"He likes you, Lilypad. He's pretty good at hiding it. He's a Negro who's helping you in a professional matter, so he has every reason to keep it hidden. But he's no match for my superior detection abilities." He touched his index finger to the side of his nose.

"It would be cruel if you were teasing me."

"It would, but I am not. And if he were at all on the fence, the fact that you came up with this plan, well.... I saw it in his eyes. Admiration. He wishes he had thought of it. And it's a rare man who has a woman best him and it only makes him more interested."

🦋 Chapter 39 🦋

The look on Mrs. Donovan's face when she answered Dr. Bauer's door told Lillian and Solomon several unsurprising things: first, that two were not expected, and second, that the appearance of a Negro on this doorstep was not a welcome sight, at least to Mrs. Donovan.

Lillian stepped over the threshold but when Solomon went to follow behind her, Mrs. Donovan held up her hand. "I'll be askin' the good doctor if the likes of you is invited in. And keep yer hat on down low so yer not lettin' all the neighbors see ya. This here's a respectable neighborhood."

As she went to close the door, Solomon forced it open and produced a calling card. "Solomon Scott, Attorney. From the firm Scott and Knickerbocker, Fifth Avenue." She squinted to see the fine print. Lillian knew that Solomon was counting on the fact that this woman couldn't read very well, since Solomon's card listed only him at his Brooklyn address.

Lillian cleared her throat. "I believe the good doctor is waiting for me. Please see us in." She was relieved to hear that her voice did not betray the fear she felt.

With a scowl, Mrs. Donovan lead them to the study.

As they had discussed, Lillian entered first and was pleased to see Dr. Bauer's look of smug satisfaction turn to confusion when he spied Solomon behind her. "Lillian, my invitation did not extend beyond yourself," he said from his wing chair by the fire.

"Your invitation wasn't so much of an invitation as a demand. But I take your point." Lillian stood to one side of the fire as Solomon approached Dr. Bauer. "Solomon Scott, Attorney," he said and sat down in the opposite chair that was clearly intended for Lillian. She looked down at the footstool and felt queasy but forced herself to direct her gaze to Dr. Bauer, who was clearly struggling to gain the upper hand.

He looked up at her. "If you think that some darky lawyer can help you, you are more naive than I had ever thought."

"Dr. Bauer," Solomon began in his most sonorous voice, and Lillian was satisfied to see that Dr. Bauer could not help but turn his eyes to Solomon. "I'm sure my presence in your study is unwelcome, so it will be in everyone's best interest if I say my piece so we can be on our way."

"Well, at least so *you* can be on your way."

Solomon pressed on. "I am here not only as an attorney but also as a very good friend of a Mr. McKelway, the editor of the Brooklyn Daily Eagle. I'm told you are familiar with the exposés that the Eagle likes to run, most recently the extremely popular series of pieces last year on Mary Dixon Jones."

"I wouldn't expect you to know," Dr. Bauer said, "but for your medical edification, Dr. Jones was the first ever to perform a total hysterectomy just a few years ago, saving some poor woman from a uterine myoma. And yet the Eagle dug up a few families of her patients who were probably too far gone to save, and made a mint scaring people away from surgery."

"Perhaps. But at least we can agree on the power of the press."

Dr. Bauer settled back in his chair and made a steeple of his fingers. "Why yes, I suppose we can agree upon that. I hope our dear Lillian mentioned why I had brought up that example to her as a cautionary tale. It's clear that the papers love a good juicy story about wrongful death at the hands of a medical professional."

Lillian's breath quickened at the thought of this, but she looked at Solomon who seemed unperturbed. "Indeed. But there are other juicy hospital stories out there." Solomon picked a bit of fluff off the arm of the wing chair and let it float to the floor. Lillian counted two beats of her pounding heart before Solomon resumed. "Let me be specific. I think Mr. McKelway—St. Clair to his friends—would be interested in a story about what your hospital does with patients who are cured of their cancer but can't go home. I think a lot of readers would pay a nickel to read about stroke victims being sent to the lunatic asylum on Blackwell's."

"Ah, but the woman in question never got a chance to make that journey, did she? Thanks to someone playing God," he said snidely, glancing at Lillian.

"Mrs. Sokolova did not," agreed Solomon, "but two other women in the past five years did manage the trip."

The smile dropped from Dr. Bauer's face. "That was before my involvement with this hospital."

"True, but this series of stories isn't about you. It's about the New York Cancer Hospital. St. Clair told me how these stories go. First, it's all the talk in Brooklyn. But if it's about something with broad appeal, and especially if it's about something in Manhattan, the story spreads to the papers there. Mr. Pulitzer at the *New York World* would almost certainly have interest."

"I can easily disassociate myself from this hospital. These stories will give me the perfect excuse to go back full time to Presbyterian. They are no threat to me."

As if Dr. Bauer had not spoken, Solomon continued. "Then, with interest in the New York Cancer Hospital peaking, the second series of stories will begin. The stories about a doctor there who had a certain... preference. A peculiar preference. And a habit of forcing this preference on young women, like poor 16-year-old Lillian Dolan."

Dr. Bauer looked up at Lillian. "I've read your file, you are eighteen."

"It's a shame when the papers get the little details wrong," said Solomon.

"The word of a ladder-climbing slut from nowhere will not be believed over a Columbia-trained surgeon. If this is the best you've got—"

"Of course, if it were just one girl, many readers would be skeptical. That's just the first story. But the second one will be about a girl from Presbyterian."

Lillian held her breath. She glanced at Solomon; his posture was relaxed but she could see a faint sheen of perspiration at his temple gleaming in the firelight. She hoped that Dr. Bauer could not see it, and could not hear her heart thumping against her breastbone.

Time seemed to stand still. The three of them were frozen in their poses, the only movement in the room the mantel clock insistent on counting the seconds in a relentless tempo. Lillian and Solomon had talked about this moment, how once they made their risky move they needed to let it sink in no matter how uncomfortable the silence was, but part of her had not believed it would come. From nowhere, she remembered practicing with outsized crutches on the stairs at the hospital, the vertiginous feeling in the moment when you aren't sure if you will go forward as you want or tumble backwards down the stairwell and break your neck.

Finally, Dr. Bauer asked, "What exactly do you want?"

"You will forget your accusations against Lillian, which are without any evidence anyway. Lillian will leave the hospital with a good recommendation from the head nurse, which you will do nothing to jeopardize. That's it."

Dr. Bauer got up slowly and stood on the other side of the fireplace opposite Lillian. He leaned an elbow on the mantel. "You've been awfully quiet."

"My lawyer represents me," she said.

"He's rather clever," he said, as if Solomon were not in the room. "Especially for a Negro. But actually, I see your hand in this."

"I don't see how."

"Oh, come now. Why did I take a shine to you in the first place? Your *mind*, Lillian. You are more clever than you know. I believe it was you that cooked up this strategy. I'm impressed."

When they had first met, Lillian had not seen it. Later on, she glimpsed it, but now she could view it plainly. She remembered what Josephine had told her, about how some men know how to tell a homely girl that she's pretty in a way that makes her loyal as a hound. She could see Dr. Bauer manipulating her now, seeing it as if she were a separate person standing nearby. It seemed instinctive to him, like a lion chasing a gazelle without knowing why. She saw herself as she was when she started at the hospital, so eager to be seen as clever, as worthy. Now his words seemed a cheap trick, like three-card

Monte on the boardwalk.

She moved from the fireplace and positioned herself behind Solomon's wing chair. "Do you agree to our terms?"

After several moments of silent tension that Lillian felt she could not bear, Dr. Bauer said, "Pfff," waving a hand as he went over to his desk and sat down. "Your terms are fine with me. As if I had time to testify against a lowly staff member. Your threats of slander in the papers have nothing to do with it."

"Thank you, Doctor," said Solomon. He and Lillian walked to the door. "And by the way," he added, "for your legal edification, it's libel, not slander."

Lillian hid her grin until they were clear of the study.

Chapter 40

Two days later, Lillian struggled up the stairs with a burlap bag of groceries and Marie in tow. She had been able to convince Marie to carry a small sack of potatoes by pretending it was a hat Marie could wear. But midway up the first flight, Marie tired of her hat and threw the sack down on the landing. Lillian tried not to think about how bruised the potatoes would be and made a mental note to go pick them up after she got the other groceries into the kitchen.

Now that she wasn't working, she had plenty of time for things like going to the grocer, which was good because now that she had to take Marie with her everywhere, everything took twice as long. Even so, there were long stretches of time with Marie in the apartment where Lillian learned the true nature of boredom. She had plenty of time to reflect on the brinkmanship between Solomon and Dr. Bauer, how many things could have gone wrong that didn't, the giddy aftermath. She recalled how they relayed the whole experience to Michael, blow by blow, after they had made their way back from Dr. Bauer's that night.

"So when you said, 'the girl at Presbyterian,' what *exactly* happened?," asked Michael.

"My heart stopped," said Solomon.

"You looked as relaxed as a summer's day," said Lillian.

"All right," said Michael, "Let's allow that Solomon was masterful, but what did Bauer do?"

"It took a few moments, but he folded, asked us what we wanted him to do. Lillian, you couldn't have been more right," said Solomon.

"I told you that I couldn't have been the only girl. He was too smooth. He'd done that sort of thing before."

"Still," said Michael, "if you had been the first and only, or even if there was another girl but not at Presbyterian, all the rest of it added up wouldn't have been enough."

"But it was enough," said Solomon. He smiled at Lillian, and her pulse quickened.

Thinking about that smile now as she put away sacks of beans and cornmeal, she made a plan to send him a note. But what would she say? Yet another "thank you"? She would have to think of something more clever than that.

Just then, she heard a knock at the front door. *Maybe he had come to check up on her!* She threw the door open to see her mother with the sack of potatoes in her hands.

"I think you dropped these," she said softly, holding them out to Lillian.

They stood there for a while, Lillian in shock that her mother was here, that there was no time to prepare her anger, her arguments. In all the tumult of the past few days, she had forgotten that this was inevitable now that her mother knew where they lived.

Finally, Helen placed the potatoes in Lillian's arms and walked past her, sitting down gingerly on a kitchen chair, her hat and coat still on. Before Lillian could gather her thoughts, Marie came charging out of the bedroom, and the happy reunion was more than Lillian could bear. She tossed the potatoes on the counter, went into the bedroom and closed the door. She stood by the window, looking at the brick wall of the next building, fuming. She could feel a flush creeping up her neck, igniting her.

After a minute or so, Marie burst into the bedroom and plunked herself on the bed with a set of beads and string Lillian had not seen before. When she sat down across from Helen in the kitchen, the bedroom door firmly closed, Helen said, "A little gift to distract. I knew you would want to be alone when we talked."

"Why would you think I would want to talk to you? How dare you come here!"

"We never talked. You just left. You never heard my side of it."

"There is no other side!"

"There is always another side."

Lillian saw with satisfaction that Helen looked older than she did months ago. Her hair, the same shade of brown as Lillian's, now had a few more gray strands. There were shadows beneath her eyes that Lillian didn't remember. But the rest was the same: her voice with its faint trace of a French accent, her wide jaw, her unblinking gaze.

"The worst part of you being here," said Lillian, "is that you are making me remember it all over again."

She had done a good job of forgetting that night when she thought Marie was eating Lillian's peppermints. Marie always gobbled up her Friday night treats as fast as she could, but Lillian often saved some for another night. Helen had brought home a small bag of broken peppermints; she was friendly with the penny candy owner and he dug to the bottom of the bin for the broken bits to sell her at a discount. Lillian had eaten exactly half of hers and hidden the other half under her pillow.

After Helen had dragged out the tin tub to the center of their bedroom and heated the water on the stove, she managed to get Marie settled in her bath. Helen and Lillian began the week's mending in the parlor when Lillian thought the splashing she heard sounded like Marie getting out of her bath. *To steal my peppermints!*, Lillian thought, and she tossed aside her mending, aware of her pettiness but unmotivated to curb her childish attitude. As she reached for the doorknob—why was the door closed, anyway?—she felt her mother's grip on her wrist.

"She's taking my peppermints!" Lillian said.

"Leave her alone now," said Helen.

"You always take her side—you let her get away with murder!" Lillian wrenched herself free from Helen and barged into the room.

Contrary to what Lillian's imagination told her, Marie had not left the bathtub, nor was she eating peppermints. But what Lillian could see all too clearly was that the window shade was open, and a man gazed down intently from the building next door with unobstructed view of her sister in the bath.

"That man is looking at her!" cried Lillian, and she moved to pull the shade. But Helen grabbed her and pulled her out of the room, to Lillian's shock and, moments later, horror. Because she could see that Helen knew. It even looked like she had arranged it.

Now, looking at her mother sitting across from her, Lillian felt that revulsion and anger come rushing back to her. "I want you to leave."

"You don't have any curiosity? Why I would do such a thing?"

Lillian hesitated. The problem was, beneath all the rage, she did have curiosity, if it could be called that. Because as much as she hated to admit it right now, Helen had been a good mother up until that point. Which is why that night was so devastating.

"Fine. If it will get you to leave, say whatever you want." Lillian crossed her arms, feigning impatience for Helen's departure, but in truth now she tingled with dread and anticipation in equal measure for what would be said next in this room.

Helen unpinned her hat and lay it carefully in her lap before she began. "The landlord, he manages both buildings. We were behind on rent. Not a little. Many months. Finally he tells me we have to go. But we have nowhere to go. A week before we need to leave, he is in the apartment across from us, a floor higher. It is vacant and he is fixing something there. I'm putting Marie in the bath and I look up and see him looking at us. I pull the shade. Disgusting, the look on his face. The next day, he makes me an offer. A disgusting offer. But I take it. He thinks this will go on and on, every week, but I count out how many times until I can save enough that we can leave, and not for the poorhouse."

Lillian has so many questions that she doesn't know which to ask first, but strangely what came out of her mouth was, "How could you have gotten so far behind on the rent?"

Helen looked down at the hat in her lap. "It was Dr. Pratt. When you were sick, after Marie had been so sick… I thought I was going to lose you. Someone told me that Dr. Pratt was the best. Very expensive. But I needed the best for you. You have to understand, I could not lose you, there was no price I would not pay. I have no regrets about Dr. Pratt. You lived, you recovered with perfect health. But paying off that debt and the rent and everything else, it was too much."

"But your own daughter! She is innocent!" Tears burning the corners of Lillian's eyes.

"She is still innocent," said Helen, as her own tears pooled. "She never knew. I would never do anything to hurt her. She never knew."

All these months, Lillian had an unchanging response in her mind whenever it veered toward that night. She turned away from what she had witnessed, labeled Helen a terrible person, and an iron door slammed shut to lock away that part of the past. She had been steadfast in her refusal to think about it. But now Helen had pried that door open, and Lillian found that she could not look at what was inside in exactly the same way. She had always been sure that she would never have done what Helen did to Marie. But Lillian could not push away the facts of her life since then. That she had ended another person's life. And concocted a charade to get away with it. That she had, even momentarily, contemplated going along with a man's perversions to save herself from facing justice. The moral ground on which she stood to judge her mother did not seem as solid as it once did.

"It was a terrible thing," Lillian stated, as if for the record.

"It was a terrible thing," Helen agreed.

Neither elaborated on their statement. Lillian went to fill the kettle with water.

❖ Chapter 41 ❖

Spring came early to New York that year, not the false warmth of early March only to be yanked back to coal-dusted snowbanks and frozen horse water troughs, but a warming that started early and stuck around. Lillian and Marie sat on their front stoop with the sun shining down on them, Marie sewing the first button on a new napkin.

Michael rounded the corner and approached the stoop with roses in his cheeks. "A cornucopia of cousins!" he called out. Marie threw down her napkin and ran to Michael, nearly knocking him over with her hug.

Lillian picked up the napkin and shook the dirt off of it. "Two is not a cornucopia," she commented.

Michael peeled Marie off of him and they sat down together next to Lillian. "But two is all I need."

"You're chipper today."

"I am, because I just gave some of my hard-earned cash to a gnome-like man with terrible breath who is now my landlord!"

"Oh Michael! You got it!"

"I did. There may not have been much competition for this particular place, what with the mouse droppings and the warped window that doesn't shut all the way, but it's all mine."

"How did your parents take it?"

"Like you'd think. Ma was sad, why do you have to leave and all that. Martin said nothing. Kate, of course, is thrilled. More room for her."

Lillian squeezed his arm. "I'm thrilled too."

"Well, it wouldn't be happening if it weren't for you and Solomon."

In the months since their confrontation with Dr. Bauer, Solomon had not faded from Lillian's life as she had once feared. Before Lillian could send him a note, he had sent one to her, and for a while they had gotten to know each other through letters. They talked about the difficulty of being together, even being seen together, in a city that could be unpredictable in its tolerance. Every few weeks Solomon came to see Jupiter and the three of them would meet at Sonny's, which is where Lillian learned that Jupiter was leaving his job at the hospital.

"Solomon found me a job at a printing press over in Brooklyn," Jupiter said as Loretta set down their drinks. "I think I'm 'bout ready to be quit o' that hospital."

"Without Lillian there, not much reason to stay, I would say," said Solomon, grinning.

"It ain't nearly as good without Lillian, surely. But mostly I'm just ready to move on."

"I'm so glad for you," said Lillian. "And you'll be much nearer to your brother."

"Maybe we'll see you out there sometime?" asked Jupiter.

Lillian smiled and sipped her short beer.

She hadn't yet been out to see Solomon. He told her that it was easier to be white in a black area than vice versa, but she was nervous. She had never been interested in or been courted by anyone before, so to have to navigate the extra confusion and even danger of her interest in a Negro man was too much for her sometimes. And yet, she read each of his letters over and over. For his part, Solomon seemed equally cautious, and equally devoted.

A week later, when Lillian and Marie had gone to their aunt and uncle's house for dinner, the meal was particularly somber. Lillian tried to lighten the mood with stories about her new job, caring for a woman in the next building who could no longer walk or hear and begrudgingly let Lillian bring Marie. But the fog refused to lift from the dinner table, and Michael told her why as he walked them out.

"I broke it off with Bridget. Of course I didn't tell them why. But in a sense, it's all your fault."

"Mine? But I never said—"

Michael kissed her forehead as they paused on the landing. "It's not what you've said. It's what you've done. What you're doing with Solomon—"

"I'm not *doing* anything with him, if that's what you're implying, you beast."

"Well, thank you for that update on your intimate life, but that's not what I meant. It's not easy to have a romance outside of your color. It takes a certain amount of brave," said Michael. "And I thought, she doesn't have to be the only brave one in the family."

"But what about all that you said about taking the easier path, and not feeling guilty? I don't want to be the one who made you choose the wrong thing."

"I'm choosing, Lilypad. You just gave me the courage to make my own choice."

Now, on the sunny stoop, Lillian realized that she had not seen Michael this relaxed in a long while. She was relieved. For weeks after Michael told her he wasn't marrying Bridget, Lillian felt the burden of responsibility for that, despite how he had reassured her. To make matters worse, Michael had had a tremendous fight with his father when Michael announced he was moving out and now the two were no longer speaking to each other. Michael's theory was that Martin could not abide Michael having the freedom to live the life that Martin could not even acknowledge. Fiona refused to get in the middle, which further upset Michael. But even given the rift with his family, the proof of the pudding is in the eating, and it would be hard to see Michael as anything but content now.

"So," he said, "there will be a celebratory party this Saturday at my new home, and you and Marie and Solomon must of course come. Jupiter too, if you want."

"Will Josephine be there?"

"With bells on. And Maddie. They're bringing some sort of pudding, Maddie's specialty. Brace yourself." Michael stretched his legs out over the steps, his heels nearly reaching the sidewalk. "I'm not inviting my parents. Not like Martin would come anyway. But I did wonder how you would feel about inviting your mother."

Lillian pursed her lips. Despite their long talk over tea where they tried to mend fences, Lillian could not totally let go of her animosity. She fluctuated between nearly understanding the choice her mother was forced to make and feeling that, had they walked away to an uncertain future, even the poorhouse, it would have been the better thing to do. Lillian had grudgingly agreed that Helen could visit Marie in the apartment once a week, only with Lillian there, although the last time Lillian had ducked out for a walk around the block in the sunshine. Still, she wasn't ready to socialize with her, or introduce her to Solomon. "Please no. Not yet."

"Fine by me. Moving on to other subjects: so what's the future with your Brooklyn prince?"

"Well, I'm not contemplating any changes my life at the moment. But did you know that Brooklyn Hospital has a nurse training program?"

"But don't you have to live at the hospital? What about Marie?"

"I don't know." She took Michael's hand. "I haven't figured it all out yet. You have to be twenty years old for the training program. And I have a job now that's paying for my rent and food, now that I'm not paying Josephine." When she told Josephine that she'd left her job at the hospital, she thought Josephine would be—relieved? Happy? It has been hard to tell what Josephine thought in that moment. But thinking about all that Josephine had taught her, all the advice and support, Lillian had burst into tears at the thought of all she would be missing now. Josephine said she would be sorry to not see them every day, and they hugged long and hard before she left. Lillian couldn't wait to see her at Michael's party.

"Does a nursing program fit in with a future with Solomon?" he asked.

"Who knows?" She thought about it. "Or maybe it's better to ask your question the other way around. I'm going to find a way to be a nurse, and we'll see how everything else fits. If I have to be patient for one or the other, then that's what I'll do."

"No longer seeking the short path to your career?"

"That didn't work out so well, did it?" She rested her head on his shoulder.

"Do you ever think about the Russian woman?" he said quietly.

"Only every day." She took a deep breath. "Some days I'm angry with her. For putting me in that position. For making me carry her around in my head every day now, still. It wasn't really right what I did, but it wasn't wrong either. I'm not sure I'll ever make sense of it. But I don't think I would do it differently, even if I could see what was coming."

She closed her eyes and felt the sunshine on her lids, and tried to imagine what was coming in her future. Everything was hazy. But she could live with that.

New York Cancer Hospital, 1893:

455 Central Park West Condominiums, today:

✺ Afterword ✺

When I read historical fiction, the first thing I do after finishing the last chapter is to turn the page to see if there is an Afterword where the author reveals what was fact and what was fiction.

And so, without further ado, here it is.

The New York Cancer Hospital was a real hospital. It was the first cancer hospital in the United States and the second in the world (the first was London's Royal Marsden in 1851). J. Marion Sims was one of the founders of the New York Cancer Hospital, and he did perfect his fistula surgery on slaves with no anesthesia despite its availability. One of those slaves, 17-year-old Anarcha Westcott, endured 30 painful operations over four years before Sims perfected his technique. So while Anarcha was a real person, the characters of her nephews Jupiter and Solomon Scott and their mother are fictional.

When I set out to write a book about medical ethics in general and the New York Cancer Hospital in specific, I did not know about Sims and his legacy. But when I discovered he was a founder of the hospital, I knew I had to find a way to bring his ethically-dubious history into the story. Dr. Sims has long been lauded as "The Father of Modern Gynecology" and only in recent years has his fistula work come under scrutiny, especially given that once he had perfected the surgery, he performed it on many white women—all with anesthesia.

All other characters are of my creation. Dr. Bauer is very loosely based on Dr. William Halsted, the brilliant surgeon of that era who championed aseptic surgical practices and pioneered the radical mastectomy for breast cancer. He did not, to my knowledge, manipulate women over whom he had authority as Dr. Bauer did, but like Dr. Bauer he was an arrogant egotist and always pushed for excising more and more tissue during cancer surgeries. To be fair, there were no other tools in the 1890 cancer toolbox beyond the scalpel – chemotherapy was unheard of and radiation therapy was years away. And since people came to hospitals as a last-ditch attempt to stay alive, cancer surgeries were generally performed on advanced disease. But post-surgical functionality was apparently not of great concern to Dr. Halsted, nor was quality of life, and informed consent was not something with which doctors needed to be bothered.

The New York Cancer Hospital was built in pieces: first the women's wing, then the connecting chapel, then the men's wing. It is unclear whether the men's wing ever opened. The hospital had financial difficulties from the very start, in large part because benefactor John Jacob Astor III specified that the money he gave for the hospital was not to be used for ongoing expenses, as is discussed by Lillian and Dr. Bauer. At the time, all nurses in hospitals were required to live on the premises; this may have been in part to ensure they were living a morally exemplary life, an ideal influenced by Florence Nightingale. I used these facts to create the position of Nursing Assistant, which to my knowledge didn't exist. But it made sense that a financially-strapped institution that needed more nursing care might hire someone that they did not have to feed and house.

The design of the hospital building was considered cutting edge due to its circular wards, where there were no corners to harbor dirt and germs, and the wards' central air shafts that provided good air circulation. But despite these progressive ideas, care was still mostly palliative since late-stage surgeries were rarely curative. They did offer champagne and carriage rides in Central Park to the wealthy patients, who paid more and, I assume, were housed far away from the poorer patients (though the nickname "Posh Row" was my invention). And yes, they did inject patients on the operating table with whiskey! I would not have believed this if I had not read it in the surgical notes from the hospital's archives.

In 1955, the hospital relocated to the Upper East Side where it eventually became Memorial Sloan-Kettering Cancer Center. The old building became a nursing home for the next twenty years and was eventually shuttered due to horrendous conditions. It stood vacant for decades, was nearly demolished, and was recently turned into 16 luxury apartments.

Much of my research for this book had to do with nursing and cancer, but I also spent a fair amount of time learning about the gay scene in turn-of-the-century Manhattan. The Bowery was evidently the place to be, and The Slide was an actual gay bar there, one of many but more famous than most. I was surprised to learn that having male homosexual encounters was seen by many as not especially identity-defining; having occasional sex with a man did not automatically brand you as gay. However, I had to assume that not everyone was comfortable with a pair of romantically-involved men, hence Michael's injuries from being beaten. On the other end of the spectrum, there were a fair number of gay men who dressed as women, known as "fairies." The balls that were thrown down on the Bowery were enormous and legendary, and one did include a wig with an embedded birdcage containing live birds, as is mentioned in the book.

For more reading on William Halstead, I recommend the book *Genius on the Edge: The Bizarre Double Life of Dr. William Stewart Halsted*. And for a fictionalized version, watch the Cinemax series *The Knick*.

For more reading on the history of homosexuality in New York City, I recommend *Gay New York: Gender, Urban Culture, and the Making of the Gay Male World*, 1890-1940.

About the Author

Connie Hertzberg Mayo is the author of *The Island of Worthy Boys*, which won a gold medal for Regional Fiction at the 2016 Independent Publisher Book Awards. She has a literature degree from Tufts University and lives in Massachusetts.

Book Club Questions

- Did Lillian make the right choice to end Mrs. Sokolova's life? Why or why not?

- Should Lillian have faced more consequences for ending Mrs. Sokolova's life?

- Was Lillian justified in taking Marie away from Helen? Was Marie violated by what Helen did?

- Why do you think Jupiter stayed at his crematorium job after he discovers that Dr. Sims is dead?

- Why do you think the author chose to have Dr. Bauer have a foot fetish?

- How many medical ethics issues can you identify in this story?

- How many "victimless crimes" can you identify in this story?

- Did you find Lillian's evolving view of Dr. Bauer credible?

- How did the experiences in this story change Lillian?

- Could the events involving Lillian, Dr. Bauer, and Mrs. Sokolova have happened in current day? Why or why not?

- Have you had experiences in your own life that are similar to what Lillian faced?